THE CRACK IN THE HALO

By Racer Lynch

Strategic Book Publishing and Rights Co.

Strategic Book Publishing and Rights Co., LLC
USA | Singapore

For information about special discounts for bulk purchases, please contact Strategic Book Publishing and Rights Co. Special Sales, at bookorder@sbpra.net.

ISBN: 978-1-948260-61-9

Book Design: Suzanne Kelly

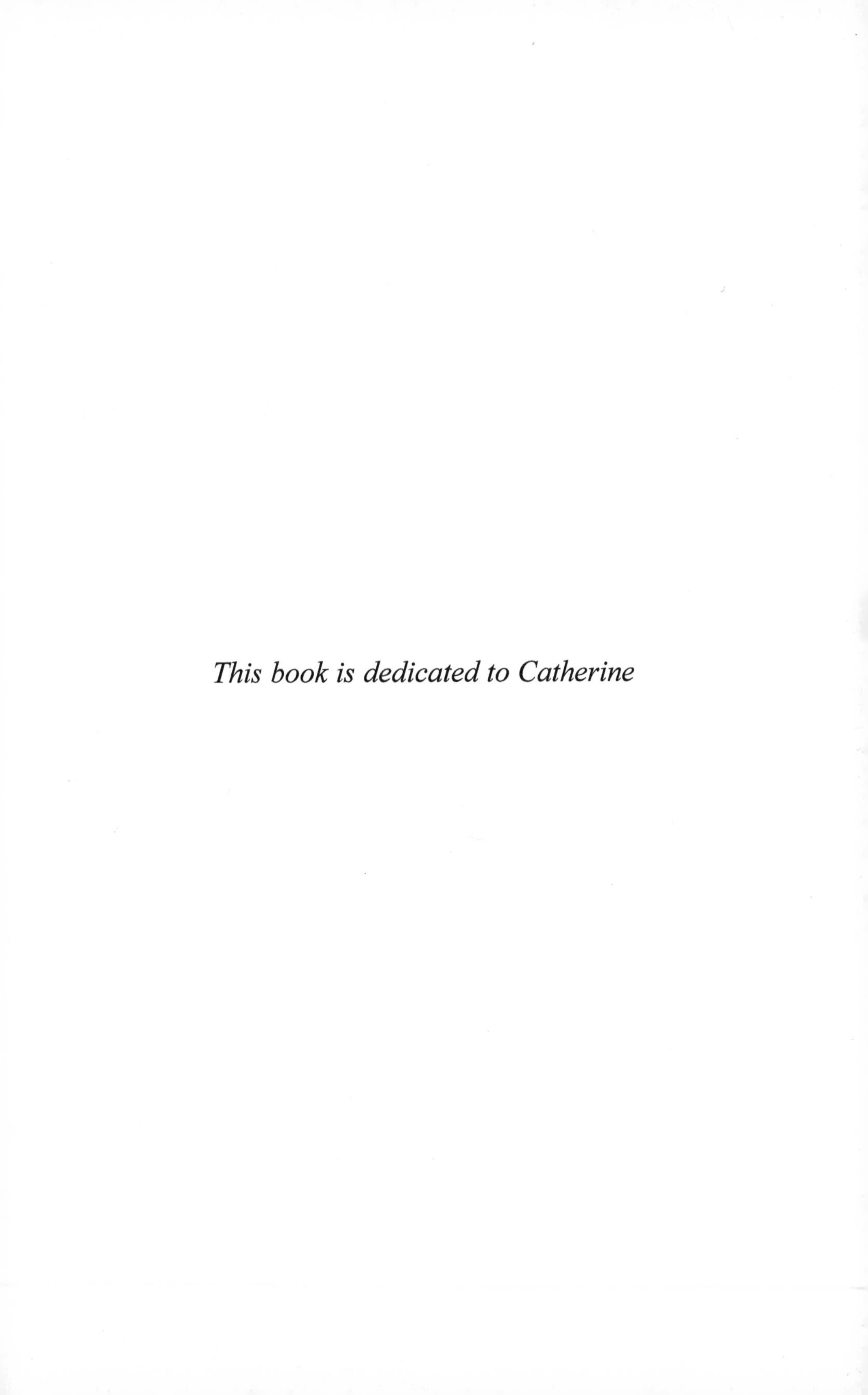

This book is dedicated to Catherine

TABLE OF CONTENTS

CHAPTER ONE

AFTER ALL THESE YEARS

July 16, 2011—11:48 a.m.

The sun was shining fully as I took a left at Faulkner Hospital onto Allendale Road in Jamaica Plain near Boston. My heart raced in my chest, and every breath was an effort to control. The excitement felt unbearable. I was on my way to meet a man I had not seen in forty years, a man I had loved all those years ago when I was in Syracuse teaching in our convent school. A chance phone call when I had recently returned to Syracuse for a friend's funeral put me in touch with Jim again. At sixty-two years old now, things had certainly changed from my arrival in the United States in August 1968. Talking to Jim again after decades of separation made all the years disappear in an instant. It was as if all the layers of life and living, all the challenges and accomplishments were gone in a flash as soon as I heard his voice. Of course, I cried when I heard him tell me again that I had broken his heart. He said these words lightheartedly, but I felt the pinch of truth. I had broken his heart and, in the process, had left part of mine with him. As soon as I heard his voice, I wanted to see him. It had only been ten days since that phone call. I would be with him within the hour.

It was a strange coincidence that tonight I would be meeting with one of the administrators of the religious order to sign the final papers to release me canonically from the vows I had taken over forty years ago in Fairview Convent in Ireland. At sixty-two years old, I found myself still in the whip and cruelty of abusive religious superiors. I was weighted by their rules and regulations and unreasonable demands. It was time to free myself from the shackles that had tried to hold me bound for forty-five years. My plan was to return to Ireland and settle there. I had already purchased a plane ticket for my departure, which was scheduled for August 14, 2011.

The Allendale Farm Stand boasted a host of greenhouse fruits and vegetables, all aglow with color. I pulled onto the gravel and heard my tires crunch as I tried to find a parking space. I needed to breathe. I grasped the door handle, opened the door, and let the humid air splash on my face. I had to take some deep breaths. A young woman next to my car was carting boxes full of pansies and petunias. She stopped and smiled at me, and I smiled back.

"I am going to be busy," she shouted with a smile that broadened as she picked up the boxes of the most beautiful flowers that seemed to dance inside their containment.

"They are beautiful," I responded.

"I want to put them in an old tin sink my husband was going to throw out," the young woman shouted as she opened the trunk of her car. "I repainted it and put it at the end of the garden. I am going to tilt the sink and these will fit in there nicely." She looked at the flowers with obvious pleasure and closed the trunk.

"What a great idea," I remarked. "That is very creative."

Her smile broadened. "I had better get going," the young woman retorted.

She waved goodbye, and I sat in my car, aware that I had a smile on my face. It was a refreshing encounter. I turned on the ignition again and slid out of the parking lot very slowly. I took a right, aware that I was leaving the bustle of a bewilderingly colorful scene. I had recovered my sense of calm and felt a surge of delight.

Within twenty minutes, I raced along Centre Street in Newton to meet Jim at a hotel. By the time I got close to my destination, I felt I was on fire with a sense of longing and excitement. I pulled into the Marriot Hotel and drove straight past the entrance. For some reason, I expected Jim to be standing there ready to wave as he caught sight of me . . . or at least waiting. Instead, I saw scores of young men and women in army uniforms clustered all over the place. He wasn't there. My heart was in my throat, and for a second, I uttered, "Oh God, I am an utter fool Maybe he had cold feet." My foot pushed into the accelerator, and the car sped to the end of the parking lot. I took a right turn. I was already looking for the exit sign.

The rows of cars were long and full. I glanced down each row as I slowly pulled into the heart of the parking grid. The parking lot was brimming with cars. There was a convention of some sort here today involving military personnel. That fact at least was clear.

I slowed down as I passed each row of perfectly lined-up cars. I was beginning to despair. I stopped for a moment to process what I was doing. At this point, I was just looking forward to seeing Jim. Over the years, we had kept in touch. First, there were the letters I had received a few times a week. There were numerous phone calls. Thirty years later, and there still continued to be a birthday card and a sporadic phone call. Jim was never quite gone. I thought of him often when I had the chance to be alone, which was mostly at night when a feeling of emptiness took hold. I told myself over the years that the feeling of emptiness was just part of the vow of celibacy. Sometimes in my wise moments, I realized it was partly the fact that I was pouring myself into my work, but it never seemed to satisfy my deepest core. There always remained that deep longing for physical intimacy.

I jolted as a young man accidentally bumped into my car. He was not looking where he was going. He was obviously intent on finding someone in the distance, among the milling crowd of young army men and women, while texting on his phone. He smiled an apologetic smile. I took another deep breath, which sounded more like a sigh, and slowly started off again, somewhat distracted by the young men and women who continued to spill out of cars and buses and head for the entrance of the hotel.

Finally, at the end of one of the rows of cars, I saw a tall man leaning against a black Lincoln, gazing at the sky. I felt the leak in my heart stop. It felt full again.

CHAPTER TWO

My Lost Love

July 16, 2011—1:20 p.m.

Jim's long, lean frame was unchanged from all those years ago. His hair was a little overgrown by his former standards, and a lot of gray had taken over his once black-wavy mane.

I stopped my car close to his and took him in for a few seconds. He wore a green polo shirt, which hung over his beige shorts. His legs were tanned. There was no doubt he had recently spent his free time on the golf course. He wore no socks—I remembered he could not bear to have socks on in the summer. He absentmindedly kicked his leather shoes into the tarmac. Sunglasses hid his sky-blue eyes. Whatever he was looking at in the sky certainly held his attention. My heart throbbed in my neck.

I unstrapped my seat belt, and as if on cue, he saw me, punched the air a few times, and raced over to the driver's side. The window was already open, and before I could say a word, he leaned in and invaded my lips with his. I felt warmth jolt through my entire body. The kiss sent a deep desire to all my senses. I wanted to taste him, to smell him, and to touch every part of him.

"It has been too long, Ann," he said finally. "It has been far too long. Don't get out. I want to get in there beside you."

He was soon beside me and immediately folded me tightly into his arms. His lips were pressed on mine again. Our tongues searched for each other and delighted in their every move. I longed for him.

Thirty-five years ago, Jim and I had been so much in love and had furtively met on many Saturday afternoons at his apartment in Syracuse, where we completely wrapped ourselves in each other, loving the physical rapture, hour after hour, before I returned to the convent.

"Yes, Jim," I whispered finally, "it has been much too long." I felt I had found home again. I felt I belonged in his arms. The depth of that kiss filled me, and I wanted more.

"Let's go," he said finally. "We have to make up for lost time, right?"

He looked at me expectantly. He had driven six hours to be with me. I was definitely going to be with him. I was not going to disappoint him. It had been too long, and the old feelings stirred into life very easily. I could feel the flame rise to lick my every sense with the deepest of heat.

"We have room six-oh-four," he said as he pushed the button on the elevator.

He clutched at my hand tightly, as two young army privates rushed to catch their ride at the last minute. I hardly saw them, as I was so full of urgency. I felt a gush of delight in my groin, and when the door to the hotel room opened, I fell into his arms again. We both were ready, good and aroused, as any two in their early sixties could possibly be.

It was July 16, 2011, and Jim had turned sixty years old that day. He had told me over and over these past few weeks, that all he wanted for his birthday was to be with me.

I had struggled with that invitation and finally told him, with some apprehension, to come to Boston. We would talk at least. Here, in that hotel room, there was no need to talk. My strong feelings for him, which had been shelved for so long, suddenly erupted, and I melted against him, feeling his hardness and strength against me.

We stripped in seconds. His shorts were bulging, and when they fell to the floor, his long penis sprung full, cocked and ready. And so was I. He was huge, and I remembered that first time when I thought he would never get it inside me.

He put his arms around me. I felt the hair on his chest rub against me. His penis touched me, and I could feel his ooze drip onto my stomach. With that, I gushed with desire. We held each other as tightly as we could. Thoughts flooded through my mind. This was the man I had left behind all those years ago. I squeezed him. I wanted to make up for all those years we had been separated.

It was not long before he was astride me on the bed. He very gently took his penis in his hand and rubbed it against me. He was taking it slowly. He rubbed me with his fingers. He looked longingly and lovingly at me, and then put his mouth into my wetness so I could feel his tongue flip rapidly into me. He inserted his fingers into the opening in my vagina, and I gasped with sheer bliss. I could feel that pleasure in my groin building into frenzy. I was already moving up and down, until I erupted in his mouth, and the sound of my groaning filled the room. The feeling in my groin exploded, and I relished a moan of sheer, shuddering delight. I was already pulsating and had cleared the way for him to come inside me.

He straddled me again. He was urgent now, and I as anxious for him to be inside. He pulled my legs further apart as he leaned over and slid easily inside. There was no space between us. I felt his penis, hard, moving up and down as we rocked in perfect rhythm. We quickly got comfortable as he continued moving inside, sending prickles of bliss through me. He rose up to my mount and kissed me tenderly, as he continued to thump his hardness in definite thrusts. It was the greatest feeling I had ever allowed myself to feel.

He lowered his body onto mine, and my legs wrapped around his back. He held himself steady. I felt another rush of wetness take over as he again spread my legs further to accommodate himself. He quickly put his hand under my shoulder and continued to push and push fully. I totally surrendered to him, grasping him and not wanting him to stop. I eagerly embraced the rhythm he set and shuddered with delight. I wanted to suck him in like a vacuum. I wanted every part of him.

He put his arms on each side of me and whispered, “It has been too long.”

I tried to say something, but this great feeling was pulling me into its vortex. I was hardly able to control the longing, as he began to fill me up, coming in slowly, and then beginning to thrust gently at first, while emitting a soft groan. I could not believe the intensity of the delight that flooded every inch of me. He pushed into me over and over, and my delight was throbbing, as he began to find his comfort zone. I felt his veins pulse. He drew me into his rhythm, and I was lost in the need to be totally satisfied. He pushed into me, and the groans in me lengthened, as I savored the pleasure he brought to every sense. I was lost to everything except the knowledge of him deep and throbbing inside me. The pleasure continued unabated, and I was lost in him. I did not want this to end. I gave myself to this man, and he groaned until he sent an explosion through every part of my body. His persistent thrust sent a voltage of pleasure that invaded me. He began to pulsate in short, fast, consistent spurts, moaning deeply, enjoying that we had come together.

I felt full and enjoyed the moan in my own throat. I could not stop, as each thrust sent me frantically into a propulsive response. He pushed hard into me, and I was caressed in his groin. He expelled a shout of delight. I was in heaven with his every movement. I began to spasm with a propulsive urgency as I felt him flood into me. At the same time, I felt him pitch me with quickness and certainty. Pleasure surrounded me. He savored his orgasm. It was deep and long, and he expelled such a deep groan that I could feel the saturation and satisfaction of his pleasure. His thrust finally subsided, and he fell on top of me, utterly satisfied. I was steeped in the rush of his emitted delight. He rolled on his side, breathing heavily. I felt his breath on mine. We put time into silence, as we continued to feel each other. I felt his arms, his hip bone, every inch of him as he did with me. We kissed deeply, pausing to look into each other's eyes. Shortly after, he felt my wetness and rubbed that place gently, until I felt another flame lick me. I put my hand on his stomach. It was firm. He read my mind.

"Oh God," he whispered. "I have so looked forward to being with you again."

He put his mouth to my ear and then kissed my face. I still had my hand on his stomach and felt the sweat pouring out of his body. I could feel his smile. I did not say anything. We held each other for a long time until we fell asleep.

I awoke again to his hardness, and we began to kiss again. My heart began to race in my ears, resounding and throbbing intensely, as I moved with him for his urgency to be inside me again. Every pulse roared with pleasure. His lips met mine again, and I was drawn into the warmth of his breath and the moisture of his tongue. My hand reached down to touch him. I explored his bulging flesh and felt the ooze on the tip of his long, hard penis as he shuddered and groaned at my touch. We lay together enraptured in each other's arms for a long time. I felt spent, and it was urgent that I hold onto him. After a long while in his arms, I felt his hand gently rub at me until I felt another jolt ecstasy. He pushed his hand hard against me. I vibrated in his hand. Every part of me was hooked into that depth of insatiable desire.

"It has been far too long," he whispered in my ear.

We lay together, devoured in kissing each other. He held me tightly.

"I can't let you go again. You know you broke my heart."

He inserted his fingers and moved them in a circular motion. Shortly after, I felt his tongue flicking furiously once again, and soon the boom of pleasure delighted my every sense. Jim smiled, and creases formed on both sides of his bright blue eyes. I pulled my fingers through his hair. He was soaked. We lay together, enjoying the sensation of being close with each other again. It felt good and it felt right.

We snuggled into each other, feeling comfortable and full. Feeling good felt new to me. *How did I ever leave him?* I thought to myself. I drifted somewhere between light and darkness and groaned again as he began kissing me. I felt his tongue and responded. I felt him hard against me. I spread to let him in, and he entered with ease, filling me with a thousand splinters of pleasure that pierced delightfully into every part of my body. He moved over me, moaning, in a delicious rhythm that sent the depth of my pleasure into a dimension I did not ever want to leave. The spasms reached an unbearable intensity as we coursed in a river of pleasure that abated only after complete ecstasy. He wrapped his arms around me after flooding me with a stream of delight. I was soaked with him. I was saturated in him, and my every sense was heightened with this unbearable charge of pleasure. We both shuddered as we continued to hold each other tightly, afraid of letting go, not wanting this to end.

In the course of the afternoon, we were entangled with each other, not wanting a moment of separation. Over and over again, we were full with each other, needing each other as a desert needs rain. His thrusts brought life into me and set me ablaze with a deep longing that he not stop, not let me go. He plunged into me again and again, satisfying himself. I burned with him into the early evening. After quite some time had passed, I was finally wrapped tightly in his arms. I slept a most pleasurable sleep, better than I had in a long time.

When I woke up, held within his embrace, I wished I could stay like this forever. I looked at the clock beside the table. Jim was asleep, and I did not want to wake him. It was 8:30 in the evening. We must have slept for at least an hour, though bliss is a timeless thing, and I wanted to remain where I was, wrapped in Jim's arms and feeling that the moment should never end. I waited until he stirred. When he did eventually awake, I had dozed off. I was aroused out of my slumber. I felt Jim's hardness as he kissed me tenderly. He turned over and climbed on top of me, and I spread my legs so he could enter.

The feeling of deep pleasure came spreading into my body. I was aflame again with Jim's energy and thickness. I was completely his, and he pushed inside me with renewed intensity, his swift breathing caressed by a moan when he came. He pulled me into his arms again and began kissing me. I could feel his tongue, hot, pushing, and exploring into my groin.

The pleasure was intense. I lay there as his tongue rubbed hard against me. He kissed and sucked, sending me into a thrilled frenzy. I felt his tongue on my pubic hair, and when he found his way to my nipples, he sucked with much urgency and hunger, as if desperate to find some source of sustenance. I wanted to cry with the pleasure that the sucking produced.

His mouth found one breast, and then the other, flicking his tongue now and again over the hardness. He engulfed each of my breasts with his mouth, which became fully engaged. His teeth felt hard as he softly caressed my breasts and gently explored my nipples. Soon he heaved himself inside me again, and I enjoyed the satisfaction that pulsed through every thread of my body. I could see flashes of light in the room. I was wet with him. I did not want this to end. We exploded together again. He wrapped me tightly in his arms. I felt alive. I felt vibrant. I felt normal.

Finally, I whispered to him that I had to go home. I realized that I needed to rouse myself from the deep connection that I felt with this man. He sighed and put his arms around me. I did not want to get out of bed. I wanted to snuggle in close to him, so that I could feel the pulse in his neck.

###

I had received a phone call the night before from one of the nuns in the administrative office, telling me that she was coming to my apartment so I could execute the final documents to leave the religious order, which I had been a part of for over forty-five years. She said she would be staying with me for the night. She planned to arrive in my apartment just before midnight. I raced back to ensure that I would be there when Sister Theresa arrived.

After she arrived and had settled, she asked me to sign the documents she had brought with her. My signature was strong and definite. I felt no emotion. I had poured my life into a religious order that, for decades, had held me under a heavy yoke of abusive superiors, who exercised too much control, smothering many of us who had suffered constantly under the weight of their authority. If I stayed in the United States, I would eventually be confined to nursing facilities, where I would be left to fend for myself. Many elderly nuns already found themselves in this situation. After a lifetime of devotion and dedication, they were warehoused in second-rate facilities until they died. That future, which was not that far away from me, made me realize the futility of remaining in this religious congregation. Months ago, I had requested permission to retire and work part-time in Ireland. The terse letter I received from the woman in charge of the congregation in Rome ended in the words, *going to Ireland to work and retire is not an option for you.* That was the final blow after a life lived in total dedication to the work I had invested in so much.

After I signed the documents, there was no further conversation with Sister Theresa. I offered her something to eat, but she shrugged and said she did not need anything. As soon as we finished an almost silent breakfast in the morning, I went back to the hotel and Jim. I told him what happened that morning. I explained my plans about retirement.

"Please rethink your plans. We have just found each other again, and I feel I am truly at home with you after all this time. We belong together."

Jim and I took a shower together. We kissed and held each other for a long while, but it was time to check out of the hotel. I pushed the elevator button, and we exited the hotel together amid cheers and merriment of the young army group. When I got into my car, I relished the reality that Jim was back in my life. He returned the following week and stayed with me for ten days. I realized that, no matter what my decision was, he would never quite be gone.

CHAPTER THREE

DERRY, NORTHERN IRELAND

November 28, 1948—2:15 p.m.

I was born in the bosom of an ancient city in Northern Ireland on November 28, 1948. Doire, the City of the Oak, spread itself comfortably, overlooking the winding River Foyle. Often called the Maiden City, or often by its English title, Londonderry, it was the second biggest city in Northern Ireland, humbled to that state by the city of Belfast about ninety miles up the road and over the Glenshane Pass. Depending on which side of the River Foyle you lived, the pronouncement of the city's name pretty much heralded your religion and political affiliation.

Growing up, above the bank of the river that separated alliances, I enjoyed a childhood that knew no political or religious discord, precisely because we all were Roman Catholics, and presumably, our political loyalties reflected that reality. My family marched along the same track as our neighbors. Most of us who lived on that side of the river were baptized in the same church, went to the same schools, made our first communions and confirmations, all under the shadow of the same ancient spires. There was not much discord because there was no great diversity among us on our side of the river.

Until the end of the fifties, we did not even have to venture to the other side of the river except for serious medical care. In the 1960s, Altnagalvin Area Hospital, the new healthcare facility, beckoned us to the other side of the river. If it were not for that hospital, I wonder if any of us would have made it over there to the other bank. Most people in the world just could not understand that.

The division of the city was not really important in my life growing up. Generally, however, and very gradually, I learned that Derry City was a divided one, most seriously divided by religious affiliations. The Protestants generally lived on one side of the River Foyle, and the Catholics on the other. Children of the different religions were segregated into different schools. There were schools that educated only Protestants and schools that educated only Catholics. In the early 1950s, growing up in a housing estate that overlooked the city, it did not seem to be an important issue to its hundreds of inhabitants. Later we learned about gerrymandering and the concomitant abridgement of civil rights that Catholics had to endure. Those issues and inevitable results would explode in the late sixties. For that moment, however, our entire world in the fifties centered in that housing estate.

Our playmates and childhood friends were pooled from the huge number of neighbors who hurtled into the street after school each day and pushed into the pulse of life every weekend. Boys crafted carts from discarded scraps of wood and were constantly on the lookout for small wheels to attach to the carts, which became a great source of mobility. Some of the carts were even painted with all sorts of emblems. You definitely were someone to be reckoned with if you had a cart on wheels and the ability to drive down hills and lanes. It was a constant source of excitement. For a long time, the scores of playmates were the only ones important to my siblings and me. They were our world, and we argued and fought and reconciled in that world on Kylemore Pass.

It was in that street and the surrounding streets that we kneaded our way into making every single second matter before we were transported into the chore and challenge of adulthood. Life was good growing up there. Our house stood at the edge of a housing development that was a stone's throw from the pull of the countryside. Just beyond us, about a fifteen-minute walk up some winding paths, we could enter the magical spaces of country lanes and lush green fields.

These were our playgrounds, and together with our play companions, who were sturdier than the Derry Walls that surrounded the city, we jumped and ran and sang our rhymes, engulfed and primed by weather that drenched us with its energy. Going out to play was an all-day affair. We slammed and banged into every child's game that was ever created, and we created many of our own. We made up games with balls and bats and skipping ropes and changed the rules and boundaries invariably the next day. The pod of each moment was full and flexed and saturated, and every day it burst open with life.

Kylemore Pass was a very special place. It was a street in the housing development built in the early 1950s on the west bank of our river, and I lived there with my family. Kylemore Pass was situated at the top of the housing development, and a short walk brought us into lush countryside with trees to climb and opportunities to play in meadows stretching to the bottom of the Derry hills. When we went to school every day in the early morning atop the estate, we had a bird's-eye view of a river, whose waters had been rich in traffic in the late nineteenth century until that flow stopped in the sixties. The river had, at one point, been a key salmon-fishing haven for both licensed fisherman and poachers, who found their prey in ways that were more furtive.

Fishing was hard work, back-breaking work, and men toiled all hours of the night and day on the river to make some kind of a living. Most of the fish are gone now, and the nets have been folded and put aside for good.

Our housing estate eventually boasted of a large church that was perfectly situated on top of the hill from which the estate emerged. St. Peter's Church was like a fortress; its green roof could be seen for miles, and you could get a great view of it, especially from the other side of the river. City Cemetery was close to the church and hosted the bulk of the deceased on our side of the river. The panoramic view from the cemetery was stunning. It overlooked the river, and the dead could see for miles.

The railway station on the left side of the river ran up to Coleraine and Belfast. The road beyond the bridge, that stretched to the right, went all the way to Dublin. The development was an answer to overcrowding that had every house in the adjacent areas of Rosemount, Lone Moore Road, Stanley's Walk, Lecky Road, the Bog, and the Wells that bulged with young families. The name of the new road that was built was called the New Road and was carved out of the hill overlooking this valley. It led to the huge housing complex that would eventually include a number of schools overlooking the areas that garnered and harvested the new inhabitants.

It was a great place to live. We were never short of children to play with. Neighbors generally had huge numbers of offspring and providing for them was demanding for their parents every day of the week. We were a family of seven children. Many families in the street had well over twelve kids to take care of. There were fourteen houses on our street. The cumulative number of children produced by this number of houses was well over eighty. Each house had a front and back garden.

Generally, the front gardens were full of bright colored flowers in the spring and summer. The back garden was the place where long clotheslines sagged with the chore of the daily wash. It was great to see all the washing blowing high and swinging into the air on a bright, blustery, Derry day. Those were the days before washing machines, when the only way to wash clothes was in the deep kitchen sink, known as the job box.

We had a way of keeping things simple and descriptive in those days. The job box was a huge sink that resembled a box and was usually in the back wall of the kitchen where all the important jobs were done. Back then, the only way to extract the excess water out of the clothes was by a special, manual, twisting and strangulation of the garment. Everything was labor-intensive, from cooking all food from scratch to washing clothes that were stored daily in huge baskets in the small scullery adjacent to the kitchen. Drying them between the constant rain showers and ironing them was a continual challenge.

CHAPTER FOUR

The Mangle

June 25, 1958

I was just a little over nine years old at the time, on a particularly hot summer's day. The street was full of children, and the air was heavy. Around the middle of the day, when the best of our energies was about to be spent, a horse and cart trundled around the corner. I recognized the horse. It was Dolly, my uncle Sam's horse, and she was pulling her cart behind her. Dolly was a gentle animal. She was content to go out into all kinds of weather, pulling a heavy cart full of vegetables and fruits and flowers. My uncle Sam, together with my father and their two other brothers, ran a small grocery business out of a front room in the brothers' home in the Rosemount area. They had two horses and two carts in their backyard, and six days a week, the horses ploughed through streets and alleys and lanes and trudged over hills in Derry. The two carts, laden with their wares, were delivered to various neighborhoods from early morning to late afternoon in every season

Today, Dolly had nothing much on the cart, only what seemed to be a small piece of white machinery. She neighed and snorted as she stopped outside our garden gate. Soon, she was comforted and rewarded with a bag of special corn that was placed around her mane and hung under her mouth. She began chomping readily and became oblivious of all around her.

Ronan McVeigh, a small, red-headed, and freckle-faced youngster from up the street, shouted, "Mister, is that a cannon or something?"

My father smiled at him. "No, son. It is a machine that is going to help the wife with the clothes." With that, Ronan ran up the street most unimpressed, kicking the life out of his football.

With the help of a neighbor, who had run down the street out of neighborly curiosity to see about all the commotion, my father struggled with the machine, and with great effort, they dragged the mangle into the back kitchen and displayed it triumphantly before my mother.

"What do you think of it, Lily?" my father asked my mother, who was standing over the kitchen sink.

"Well, you are just in time to demonstrate its capabilities," my mother said. Smiling, she pointed to the sink and the clothes that had just been rinsed and were ready to be wrung. She went to the back door and down the steps to retrieve a metal bucket sitting in the grass under the clothesline. She poured out the water that had collected in it, brought it into the kitchen, and placed it neatly under the rollers of the mangle to catch the water.

My father pulled the wringer next to the sink. He rolled up his sleeves and gave the sheets in the sink a tug. He put the edge of a sheet between the rollers, grunting as the rollers caught the sheet in their grasp, while, at the same time, he awkwardly pushed forward on the handle controlling the rollers.

That mangle was introduced to us some time in the early fifties. It was the latest thing on the market, and we thought we had brought something unique to our street. The mangle looked a bit like an artist's easel, but was made of a sturdy, white material and was the newest appliance on the market to wring excess water out of dripping-wet clothes. Many of the neighbors called it the *mangle*, maybe because it strangled the clothes without mercy as it pushed them through the rollers. No matter its name, it proved to be helpful for saving intense physical energy, which left most women exhausted by the early part of the day.

This was long before plastic came on the market, so the mangle was strong and durable and able to ingest the huge amount of washing poured into it like a libation every single day of the week. The mangle had a mammoth appetite, which every house on the street was more than able to satiate. It was not generally used on Sundays. Generally, most heavy labor stopped on the Lord's Day.

The mangle stood neck-high to my mother, who was generally the only one who continued to pour herself out in the kitchen at all hours of the day and night. The mangle was a simple construction designed to torture clothes. It had two heavy, rubber rollers that were set right on top of each other near the middle of the appliance. These rollers were pushed into motion by leveraging a handle on its side. Every day, maybe several times a day, depending on the weather, the soaking-wet garments were placed almost like bait into the space between the rollers, and once the rollers started moving, easily snapped them into its jowls and squeezed the water out of them, only to spit the washing out on the other side of the rollers. Drier clothes came at a price. It took dexterity and an expenditure of energy to constantly crank the handle and retrieve the clothes before they fell into the bucket of water below.

The work was tedious, but deemed less so, compared to the alternative of standing over a sink, pouring with sweat over the steamy vapors, fragranced by Sunlight Soap, a brand that everyone on the street smelled like. Given the weather in Derry, sometimes it was a futile effort, oftentimes fraught by the meteorological reality that rain seemed to pour from the heavens once it saw those clothes blowing high on clotheslines in the back gardens. Often, no sooner were the clothes pegged securely on the clothesline than the rain began to drench them into a soggy, heavy droop. Oftentimes, the line sagged so much that it snapped under the load. Hanging clothes in the backyards in Creggan all those years ago, was as much about being able to read the skies as it was to wrangle with the mangle.

In the weeks following, almost every neighbor had a mangle. Equality on the street remained an important part of growing up. Once I was in a nearby home when the evening tea was being served. The tea was distributed to the children in glass jars, which had long since been emptied of their contents. Those were the days when a sandwich could be made of sugar, ketchup, or simply jam. There were many empty glass jars in every household, and they were often put to the most creative of uses, including drinking milk and orange juice and any other beverage out of them.

When I went home that day, I begged my mother to give me my tea in an empty jam jar. My mother was not happy about the request, but she indulged me this one time. That particular fad did not last in our house for more than the one incident. My mother insisted that we drink our beverages from cups.

CHAPTER FIVE

THE FIELD ON OUR STREET

Timeless

We lived in a street that was full and lively and noisy. Our house number was twenty-four. We were the third house from the top of the street. The street had twelve adjoining houses, all with the same architectural plan. There were three bedrooms upstairs in each home. The main floor included a sitting room, a bathroom, and a kitchen. In the fifties, the floors were usually spread with linoleum. It was not until the sixties that carpet was laid in the homes. The trick was to learn to read the sky. And that is just what we all instinctively did there on Kylemore Pass. A wire fence was the boundary line for each house, so there was never any privacy.

On the street where I grew up, there were three lampposts. One was outside Murphy's house, another was outside O'Connor's house, and the third was at the bottom of the street near the Wilson's house. The lampposts grudgingly gave us light during the dark. The lampposts were strung with long lines of rope of various thicknesses. These ropes more than adequately provided at least three swings for the children to enjoy on the street. The ropes were considered the property of the street, and it was a question of first come first served as to who got to swing. The lampposts were the places that provided the experience and appropriate training for all the children to vault to a higher performance level in the nearest playground several miles away. Brooke Park, which was located about three miles away in the Rosemount area, was the epitome of childhood pleasure where slides and roundabouts sent us reel-ing into dizzy pleasure during the summer months. Even when it rained in the summer, we still managed to swing and slide and use up our childish energy going nowhere with great gusto and feverishness.

In front of the houses on our street, a big green field spread itself out like a huge invitation. When it was not saturated with water, it was invaded by kids conjuring up every kind of game known to humankind. The field had stood the test of time and torture—on a recent nostalgic walk to the old street, the field is still a lush green.

I recall riding my father's bicycle around the perimeter of the field as we competed with other kids in the street. That last bend, just before we reached the bottom of the field, was at an almost ninety-degree angle and a great challenge to the most courageous of us. Many kids sustained bruises and fractures as we hurtled into the bushes of Mrs. O'Reilly's garden. However, the field never looked any worse for the wear and tear to which we subjected it. It hosted the yearly bonfire night on August 15 for the Feast of the Assumption. The field was an old companion. There we played cricket and camogie and football and hurling. At the edges of the field, the younger kids played house and school. They would venture into the center of the field much later.

The field accepted the children's first efforts to walk, as much as it did the heavy tread of the most competent of cricket players. The field endured being battered, tramped upon, danced on, and skewered by sticks as the boys fenced in their medieval finery of tin hats and long coats borrowed from their older brothers or fathers. The field heralded all of these fights, victories, disenchantments, sulks, wails, and every other emotion that could be tossed, hammered, slammed, and flung at it at any hour of the day. And yet, it always recovered and remained lush and green in every emotional season.

There were multiple adventures happening simultaneously in the field in front of the house. Eventually, as dusk grew into darkness, we still played under the lamplight and often by the light of the moon. It was hard to get us out of that field. She was like an old friend who welcomed us at any time of day or night. She never wearied of us. She accepted us with all our moods and whims and childish mischief. She was our best friend. She held our deepest secrets. She heard our arguments and our frustrations. She was there when night yawned into day. She waved us off to school, saluted wakes and funerals, and absorbed weddings and births. She was our most cherished companion.

The field was available to us in all kinds of weather. We enjoyed her daisies in the spring of the year to make necklaces for our friends. We learned to hunker around the daisy pile and chattered and spoke of our teachers and the homework we were loaded with each night. We danced among the buttercups that cluttered the field in the summer. We threw snowballs in the winter and crunched into the autumn leaves when the field lay open wide to receiving them from the trees lining the neighborhood streets. The field had a welcome all its own. It never faded. It made no distinction about who we were, how old we were, or how sophisticated we had become. Yes, the field was our common friend. She was always there for us. She still sits there outside our houses on our street where we grew up and still contains the memories of every tread of every inhabitant. The grass may have changed, but it still holds the chatter, the delight, and the voices of those inhabitants who are now flung to the four winds, which are held in the embrace of every corner of the world. The field still holds us all somewhere deep below. We were rooted in her rich soil and, in some fashion, continue to be deeply connected with one another because of that rooting. No matter where we go, we bring that field with us somewhere in our common memory. It held us together as playmates. It still does.

On that recent visit to my street, the field was deserted. Video games and the latest technology had taken the children indoors. The field is greener and much lusher now, but she seems to brood in her deep green color, and I felt her longing for the laughter of bright faces and the tumble of young feet at play.

It lay wide open, its invitation still vibrant and as important as when my school friends and I ran and skipped and hopped our way through our childhood. In my mind's eye, I was young again and happy to play in a space opposite our house on Kylemore Pass. The bustle of youth was gone and replaced by another time. It is now a time when children play in a completely different way. The field is still young. It is still full and fertile and ready to embrace whatever is flung at it. I can sense its hopeful expectation in its vast, empty space. It is strange how silence and quiet speak to us and pull us to a place of longing, a place where we can never recover, recapture, or replicate. However, I left that field feeling a little younger, lighter, and happier for having spent a different kind of time with my gentle, old friend, who gave up everything for all who entered her embrace. I was again enriched by its embrace for just having been there.

CHAPTER SIX

THE FAMILY

Forever

My family unit was one of the smallest on the street with seven children—five girls and two boys. My sister, Eleanor, died as a baby. I often have to check myself when asked how many brothers and sisters I have. I often leave her out, only because I did not know her. She was born when I was about eighteen months old. She is buried in City Cemetery in a special place for stillborn children. All those years ago, these children were disposed of quietly and without a ceremony of any kind. My father probably just handed the baby to the undertaker who, in turn, placed her in an unmarked grave in that quiet place. We never really talked about her as we hurtled through our days in Creggan.

My eldest sister, Margaret, helped with her younger siblings. She could be found on the weekends with four of her youngest siblings in tow, taking them for long walks to the local parks. My brothers, Dan and Christopher, charged through their days with a pack of boys of similar age, playing games that took them well into the night. The three youngest—Louise, Rose, and Theresa—spent their time after school on the street with a multitude of friends, skipping rope, playing hopscotch, and creating races and rules for playing games they made up as the day sighed into night.

Most of our neighbors had more than ten children. Babies abounded in that housing estate, and neighborliness was a way of life. Mothers and fathers up and down the street instinctively were able to give advice to all of us, correct us if we did anything wrong, steer us home if we got too rambunctious, instructed us spontaneously in the rules of our games if they just happened to be passing by, coached us in the art of sportsmanship when someone got the better of us, and generally looked out for our welfare. The woman next door often stood at her front gate at certain times of the day with a comb in her hair, and if she saw that any of us needed our hair combed, she would stop us, take the comb out of her hair, and groom us. Most of us, who knew of this intrusion into our sacred space, hastened our steps as we approached her territory or skipped to the other side of the street before she snatched up some wandering child who was not aware of her ways. It was just something she felt called to do. She stood at her gate like a sentinel, ensuring that no child was left behind with matted hair. God help you if you had curls. We accepted that that was how it was on Kylemore Pass all those years ago.

We had a house that was big enough for the nine of us. The boys shared a bedroom, and the girls shared the large front room that had a fireplace. Often, in the winter months, my father would light the fire, and we would go to bed hugged with its heat. Downstairs, a large living room was the center of most activity in the home. A standard heating-range was stirred into life each morning by my father, providing life for embers by his breath. His breath, blown in steady pulses, put a furious, fiery flame into that hearth. I used to think that my father was a magician. Later, I realized that the fire in the hearth of the range never quite went out. It was just a matter of my father's breath reigniting the flame.

The range served to heat the house, keep the water hot, and cook our meals. It was all-encompassing in its abilities. It dried our clothes and gathered us together for its warmth. It served us in all kinds of ways. It was a place to hear ghost stories on a dreary, winter night. It was where the neighbors sat and whispered into the night, as they discussed some major developments in the world or exchanged the local gossip and affairs of the community. It was the center of the home.

Every morning during the week, the kitchen and living room were a hive of activity. My father made a huge pot of oatmeal, and rain or shine, we went to school warmed with the contents of a thick bowl of oats, hurriedly eaten as we rushed through the door for the nine o'clock school bell. We all attended the local schools when we were younger, and as we got older, moved to the next level of education, where we hurtled out much earlier, laden with more books than we could carry, and were happy to get to the school buses that heaved with the burden of all of us as we bustled with the excitement of getting educated. Those days were not without challenges, because we were taught by nuns, most of whom were strict and stiff and tried to bend us into their narrow ways. Each school had its own uniform, and as we gathered in the town after school, we could identify our religious groups by the uniforms we wore. We never mixed with the students of the Protestant schools nor they with us.

CHAPTER SEVEN

ENTERING THE CONVENT

Kilfennan, Ireland

September 8, 1966—3:05 p.m.

The date rolled around all too quickly. It was a dull September 8 in 1966, and I slipped out of my family home in Derry, Northern Ireland, by 7:00 a.m. I was upset at the thought of leaving home to travel two hundred miles to the other side of Ireland to enter the convent. My stomach churned as I slid into the back seat of my cousin Pat's car. I shivered in the lack of welcome in the car. My cousin was not at all interested that I should be throwing my life away by entering the convent. The four-hour journey there kept him tied to this position. He did not utter a word the whole time. My mother, who was in the front seat, turned to look back at me from time to time to ask if I was all right. I was uneasy and apprehensive; she did not have to ask me. My mother knew instinctively how hard this was for me. I wonder, did she see the rough road ahead for me as she sat in that cold car on that cold day in September 1966 as we slowly eased our way from Kylemore Pass and flew over the Craigavon Bridge before the inhabitants of Derry shuddered into life. We had left the house while everyone was asleep. My father, four sisters, and two brothers would all wake up and find me gone.

I was seventeen years old and had made the decision to enter a religious congregation just months ago. It really was a very quick decision. I had met someone in the neighborhood who had left a religious institution, and that simple conversation propelled me on a path that has so many twists and turns that I am at a loss to put pen to paper to unravel the journey. This is a story of how a heart's journey met resistance at every bend in the road, how a soul's desire to soar was brought back to earth with a sore landing on a daily basis, how hopes were pulverized by the snap of a finger, and dreams shattered by the stroke of a pen.

Pat's car rolled down the street at the top of the housing estate where I lived. I closed the door behind me. I did not look back. That house had been my haven for the past seventeen years. I had opened the door of the car when it arrived outside the house and shivered. My mother looked behind me, "Are you sure about this, Ann?" I felt a lump in my throat and swallowed a sea of tears. I nodded my head. I could not find my voice and was afraid to speak because I knew the tears would spill and tumble down my coat. I had to be in control.

"Would you turn the heat on, Pat, please?" I muttered. He turned on the engine, and we made our way to the end of the street. There was a stiff wind that shook the trees at the side of the road. Just ahead of us, on the main road, the Ulster bus trundled to a stop as a sole passenger got on. We stopped behind it and watched as the bus sputtered into life on its way to the next stop around the corner on Dunsfort Drive. There was barely a stir from any household, and only here and there did lights spill from houses. Most people were still fast asleep.

We turned left onto Central Drive. The cluster of shops along Central Drive were just beginning to bustle with the smallest stirrings of life. There were lights on in the bakery and Boyle's shop as we sped along the deserted road. We eventually passed my old school, Saint Mark's, on our right, and St. Peter's Church, the strong, religious fortress that overlooked the city and its sprawl of a river in the distance, was soon in the rearview mirror. When the church disappeared, I felt I was well and truly on my way to a whole new path. I could not look back. I did *not* look back. It would have been too much to say a final goodbye to the place where I had lived, gone to school, laughed with my friends, and enjoyed seventeen years of sitting around the hearth with the most important people in my life.

The River Foyle ran dark and deep as we crossed over the Craigavon Bridge, which had spanned the river for more than one hundred years. It still was lit by the semblance of a Victorian gas light. It was a charmed bridge, one that had always ignited my childish imagination. When I was much younger, I used to imagine men in caps and long dark coats and women in long frocks and large, decorated hats crossing over the bridge. I envisioned horses and carriages from a time long past. Such was the magic of the bridge. In my mind's eye, the bridge still carried with it the ability to go back in history and enjoy a time where the fast pace of the horse was the most preferred means of transport.

I looked over the river as we took a right at the end of the bridge. City Cemetery stretched from the top of the hill almost to the river. I wondered when I would see Derry again. I had a feeling that I was leaving my heart somewhere beyond the cemetery, on a street that would spill over with children by late afternoon.

Minutes rolled into hours. We passed a thousand fields every hour. Each field painted its own portrait. Some fields were heavy with huge haystacks, their heads held high to the sky, enjoying the gentle breeze and a bit of sunshine. Soon, the hay would be baled and stored in barns for the animals' oncoming winter feed. Sheep enjoyed the slopes and abundant rich, green grass. The fields looked so green, so rich in this color, that, coupled with the bright blue sky, the world was embraced in splendor.

I was leaving this all behind me and felt a pain somewhere in my heart, a feeling of being so forlorn that I pictured myself asking my cousin to turn the car around and head back to Derry, but that did not happen, and the miles rolled on. Just before noon, we approached the convent. I felt lonely the minute the car passed through the black, ominous-looking, wrought-iron gates that led to a winding driveway about a quarter of a mile long. To the left appeared a large lake, its gray water chopping with the wind, which had obviously picked up since we left in the early morning. It felt like I was in another world far from everyone. There was no one in sight. All seemed quiet, except for the wind whistling through the trees in a forest that was on the right side of the driveway.

A huge, gray house stood regally overlooking the lake. Its windows glinted in the dull sunlight, and I wondered what they saw beyond themselves. I wondered what they contained. The car stopped with a creaking sound beside a wooden fence opposite the front door. The wood of the fence was weather-beaten and cracked in numerous places. There was no welcome about the place.

When we got out of the car, my mother shivered. It was so cold that I began to shake. Very soon, I was longing for the heat I always felt when I entered our living room at home. My cousin wanted to take a photograph. I stood with my mother as Pat snapped a photograph of the two of us. I still have that photo. In the background are tall trees frozen in time. It shows a piece of the large driveway leading to the convent. Our backs faced the driveway.

While the photograph captured the magnificent foliage behind us, full and bulging with life, it was a black-and-white print. There, standing beside my mother, I remember feeling that I did not want her to go home. My heart had a sinking feeling, and all those years ago, from here to there, I still wonder what would have happened if I had retreated back into that car. I can now tap into that feeling.

The photograph Pat took was the last one, before I said goodbye to my mother. My heart was heavy the day I entered the convent, and I can only imagine how my mother's heart felt. I had never ever spent a day away from my home. Our family was intact every night. This was a major change for me and for my family. Both would eventually adjust. Life would never be the same without them, and I would forever carry a huge stone of emptiness inside that would never be filled again. I look at that photograph every day. As I look at my mother's face, I have a feeling of missing her all over again.

The main door of Fairview Convent looked to be made of heavy, black oak. It was set beyond two white pillars that were ornate on top, decorated with scalloped shells. While Pat was taking my suitcase out of the car, I felt my mother's arm link mine as we approached the door. I felt her warmth in the chill of the day. I rang the doorbell and heard it resound with a boom in some hollow space inside. We stood at the front door of the convent in a chill that pierced our very bones. The chill that had found us came from the dark river embracing the edge of the property. The flow beyond its banks was fast and furious. The water looked black and ominous in that flow. At some point, we heard the crack of footsteps, and the door quickly opened with a creak. A long, slender woman stood in front of us, caught in a sea of darkness behind her, which seemed to swallow her whole being.

"Good day," she said without a smile. I could feel my mother's discomfort and saw her smart for a second. "Who are you and where did you come from?" The impersonal greeting was a little too much for my mother to tolerate.

"We have come from Derry, and this is my daughter Ann. My name is Elizabeth."

The woman, who was probably a little older than my mother was, flinched and stared at her for what seemed a very long time. My mother prevailed in the staring.

"Well, I suppose you had better come on in from the cold," the woman, clothed entirely in black, uttered with a shiver. There was a roughness about her manner that I was not used to. She seemed curt and her movements quick and robotic.

Years later, I would come to realize that people from the north of Ireland were barely tolerated, even in the rank and file of this cavernous place. There were a few northerners among us in the group of young girls who made up the members of the 1966 postulant class. We would be definitely singled out for extra, spiteful heaps of bitterness from the nuns who were to be in charge of us. From the moment of that first cold stare, which tried to rivet my mother into some kind of servitude, the reality of a completely new landscape was gradually emerging as I stood and observed this interaction. The woman in black was swollen with misery. There was more than a hint of unwelcome. The taming had begun.

The woman in black told me to unlock my suitcase and bring it to a room that looked more like a big closet. Other suitcases were stacked in a row there. We were then guided into a parlor on the right side of the corridor. The room had heavy curtains that trapped the brightness of the sun in them. The room was drab and dull. It was painted dark green, which did not help lighten the load that I was suddenly aware was sitting on my shoulders. It was hard enough leaving home hundreds of miles away, but this lack of hospitality and welcome stood in great contrast to the wide embrace of family I had lived with and the neighbors whose friendship and familiarity I had been entwined in on a daily basis. I felt I was entering an entirely different world.

The burden I felt that first hour in this house never quite went away, and over the years, would be reinforced by abusive superiors, who simply wanted us so encased in the concrete of dependence and servitude that it was almost impossible, as a young nun, to chip away that burdensome reality. Before we sat at the table, my mother poignantly asked the nun if we were going to eat in the dark. My mother's voice was light and good humored. The light switch was snapped on quickly, and the nun uttered something under her breath.

"There is your tea and sandwiches," she spat out quickly. "I will be back in a half hour, and you two will have to leave at that time." Pat was taken to some back kitchen to eat, since he was not permitted to eat with us. My mother and I sat at the table that was set for tea. In the middle of the table were several large plates stacked with ham and cheese sandwiches. Two small pitchers of milk and a large sugar bowl were placed beside one another at one end of the table. The tablecloth was made of green plastic. It certainly complemented the color of the paint on the wall, but made the room seem even duller in the dimly lit room. A huge metal pot of tea was dressed up in a brightly colored, knit tea cozy. It was the only bright color in the room. The reality of our last moments together dawned.

"I hope you are doing the right thing, Ann," my mother said to me as she began to pour the tea. "Now remember, if you do not like this place you do not have to stay."

I nodded, feeling quite nauseated by the lack of connection I felt with this place already. Apprehension was creeping into my bones. I felt totally unprepared for this most unwelcome space. Visions of getting my suitcase from the storeroom across the hall flashed before me.

My mother squeezed my arm. "If this is not the right thing for you, you can home any time, so do not forget that."

This gave me the reassurance to smile. It was a forced smile, and my mother knew it. An hour later, the nun who continued to remain nameless, came into the room and told my mother she had to leave. A feeling of panic sat in my throat. This was the moment when the realization of what I was doing really hit me like a lightning bolt. In all my years, I had never been separated from my family. I could see the same realization in her face.

I shivered as a blade of deep longing engulfed me. I turned away from the darkness and hugged my mother on the threshold of the blackness that was pulling me back inside the door.

She whispered, "You can come home any time. You can change your mind right now."

Behind her, a field of bright wildflowers spread their color into the distance. My mother stood in stark contrast to the tall nun whose face was taut, a face that had forgotten how to smile, a face that was used to dark oak panels and the smell of septic polish, a face consumed by the demands of structure and timetables, a face devoid of sentiment, a face that had lost the ability to understand the lingering taking place in front of her, a face completely oblivious to the ripping of hearts that had never been separated before. My heart felt robbed of its strong beat, as I hugged my mother goodbye, and then stepped into the dark. This emotionless woman tugged at me, as I stood at the threshold of a big, heavy slab of darkness that was to envelop me in its tomb.

In the time we had together in the parlor, my mother had given me some firm instructions. I was to put a small dot over the stroke of the letter "A" if I was feeling distressed and needed her to come and get me. I heard the car start and felt alone and empty and swallowed up in this cave of an entrance.

Just inside the door, my eyes adjusted to this new space, and I saw several stately, carved chairs standing vigil against dark green walls. I squinted into the veil of blackness and noticed that even the stained-glass windows were reluctant to send their light into the entranceway. Silence was everywhere.

"Hurry up," commanded the nameless nun without a word of welcome. "One of our nuns died yesterday and is being waked in the chapel, so you can make a visit there before you get changed out of those secular clothes."

"What happened to the nun who died?" I asked. I had felt quite sad when my mother stepped back out into the world of color, and this news compounded the sadness I felt.

"You are not allowed to speak until supper," spat the nun, whose face had forgotten how to smile.

I followed the nun to the chapel. The nun's shoes clattered heavily on the wooden floor. My heart was heavy with loss. The gravitational pull of that feeling made me aware that I could hardly walk. The nun genuflected as she entered the chapel and splashed some holy water on her face. The chapel was laden with the air of candles and the fragrance of incense. The smell was pungent, and I felt I was going to be sick. I concentrated on the scene before me.

The chapel held row after row of polished pews. The open, wooden coffin had been placed up near the sanctuary, and two tall, waxed-candles stood vigil on either side of it. I did not want to approach the coffin. I had no desire to peer into a gaping box to view a corpse. There were no tears in that chapel. There was no sense that this woman was being grieved in spite of the fact that there were many nuns in that chapel. Here and there, I heard a sigh blow through the air, but it would get trapped in the high, ornate ceiling. The nuns were stilled and chilled like icicles in the depth of winter. They were all immobile. There was no emotion. There was no movement anywhere except for the flicker of the two candles that sentried the coffin. Everything stood still in that chapel on the day that I entered the convent.

I felt a pull on the sleeve of my cardigan and was ushered from the cavernous chapel and led toward a steep stairway. I suddenly felt tired. I leaned into the climb of the stairs and suddenly felt swamped in the climb. My legs were strong, but the stairs seemed endless. I was worn out by the drabness and dullness of the place, which seemed to have the power to drain oxygen from the air. I had already counted twenty-four steps and stopped to take a breath.

"Keep moving," the nun ordered as we turned yet again to face another flight of stairs.

No one had ever spoken to me in such a harsh tone before. I felt a tinge of fear. The nun stopped at the fourth flight of stairs, and in a stiff voice, ordered me to "go in there with the rest of the new girls." She left me abruptly. I followed her request and entered a large room full of beds organized into two rows. I counted quickly. There were nine other young girls in various stages of donning the heavy, black-gabardine, floor-length dresses and black veils. Not a word was spoken in that room. I gasped at the silence. I had not imagined that my entrance into the convent could be so cuttingly quiet. Another nun suddenly appeared and brought me to one of the beds. Laid out on the bed for me was a black dress and black veil. A dark-green tunic rested on the pillow, and black stockings were rolled up and placed on the nightstand. A pair of black shoes were placed on the floor. I noted they were not any of the three pairs I had been instructed to bring with me. These shoes looked scuffed and appeared to be a larger size than what I wore.

I looked around me. Everything was crisp and starched and too utterly white. There was no color in this huge, gaping dormitory. The nun snapped her fingers and told me to get into these clothes. She handed me a brown bag and hissed to me that my clothes were to be put into the brown bag.

"Your mother can collect this bag with your clothes when she comes in the spring," the nameless nun uttered curtly. She sniffed the air and quickly added, "Of course, you might not last that long. Hurry up and get ready, you are the last one to arrive."

I pulled a curtain for privacy and took off my cardigan. On impulse, I folded it and put it under the mattress. No one would notice. The others were too busy organizing themselves. I put on the ugly, dark-green tunic. It felt stiff and cold. It took a while for me to figure out how to put on the heavy, black dress. It felt like a ton weight when it slipped over my shoulders. It fell to the floor and covered my ankles. I felt trapped. I hurriedly put on the black stockings and slipped into the black shoes. The shoes were much too large, and they clattered as I made my way around the bed. A whiff of moth balls arose from the black dress. I put my own dress and other items into the brown bag. I noticed my name had been written on the bag already. Everything was so organized. I pulled back the curtains around my bed and saw a breeze engulf the trees beyond the narrow windows. The sun was folding in the early evening sky. I felt a stab of loneliness. I longed for the comfort and color of my home. I wanted to smell the fire in the hearth and hear the chatter of my brothers and sisters. I suddenly thought of my cardigan tucked underneath the mattress and felt some comfort.

CHAPTER EIGHT

MUTED VOICES

September 8, 1966—5:30 p.m.

I was finally fully frocked in a long, black dress, black veil, black stockings, and scuffed black shoes. I felt I could walk out of those shoes at every step. I felt uncomfortable in these new clothes. The nun who answered the door had finally confiscated my clothes. I had exchanged the silk petticoat that my mother gave me for a long, dark-green, starched tunic. I missed the softness of my petticoat, which had been replaced by this rough garment. I did not realize the feeling of having no color around me. The feeling of starch was uncomfortable, and the lack of noise unsettling. I had no idea that silence was so heavy.

A slap landed like a lightning bolt on the dormitory door, giving us all a bit of a jolt. It was followed by a woman of middle height, thick at the waist, and without a trace of a smile. She came out of the same mold as the nuns we had already encountered. She clapped her hands to draw attention to herself, and we all looked in her direction. The nun slipped one of her hands into the pocket hidden on the side of her back habit. She produced a folded piece of paper.

"Everyone come here to the center of the dormitory," she commanded in a high-pitched tone.

We all moved in unison in her direction and waited for her to speak again. I looked to the person standing beside me. She had a grin on her face. I was a bit surprised, since I felt nothing in this vault of a space deserved a grin. The nun coughed.

"My name is Sister Dolores, and I will be in charge of you for the next year. You will now be ranked in order of age. Put up your hands when your name is called out. Una Murphy, 1992; Nancy McCarthy, 1993; Mary Ita Ahern, 1994; Nuala O'Reilly, 1995; Julia Higgins, 1996; Margaret Logue, 1997; Mary O' Brien, 1998; Annie Boyle, 1999; Ann Ferry, 2000, and Jean O'Doherty, 2001." The nun stopped and looked sternly at me as she sniffed the heavy air. "So, you have the pleasure of being number two thousand. What county are you from, madam?"

I was glad to have an opportunity to speak. It would take me a long time to get used to this quiet. "I come from Derry," I answered quite enthusiastically and nervously. My northern accent echoed around the room. As soon as I had blurted out my birthplace, I detected a shadow on the woman's face. On the other side of me, the girl with the smile smiled even brighter. The nun totally ignored my response.

"Hands up any of you who come from my county. County Kerry," she demanded." Three hands shot up. The three—Una Murphy, Julia Higgins, and Jean O'Doherty—received a hint of a smile. Something told me that they would be treated a bit differently than the rest of us.

CHAPTER NINE

The Refectory

September 8, 1966—6:00 p.m.

The large refectory had brightness about it, because of its natural light, which mainly entered through a skylight in the ceiling. Though, by this time, the day's glow was in its first stages of waning, there still was plenty of daylight left to beam its way through the glass. The brightness was more than a little buttressed by four huge lamps standing in the four corners of the vast dining room. The space was filled with multiple, large, rectangular tables. In spite of their geometrical shapes, they were placed in such a way as to give an appearance of a circle, with two tables at the one end of the room, four slanting on each side of the room, and two more at the other end of the room. I estimated at first glance that about six nuns sat at each table.

The top tier faced the bottom tier and the side tables, chevron shaped, held more nuns who all looked alike. A few tables were teeming with novices in white veils. The nuns with black veils were the bulk of the group. No one spoke. They all looked grim. Just after the ten newcomers entered the refectory, someone at one of the top tables rang a bell, and everyone snapped expectantly to attention.

"We will be allowed to speak during supper to welcome the ten new postulants," the grim nun in a black veil pronounced from that top table. I had not really given any thought about what my official status as a beginner in the convent was called.

Our hesitant postulant group was ushered toward the bottom of the room. Five of us were assigned to one table and five to another. I approached the table and was about to sit in my chair, when Sister Dolores came quickly to my side, grabbed my chair, and placed it against the wall of the dining room. It was obvious that I was not allowed to sit, and I could not understand the harshness that was my welcome on that very first evening in Fairview Convent. The rush of humiliation rose to my face. The sisters were making so much noise that they did not seem to notice that I was standing. They seemed so glad to break into the silence and make noise.

Numbers 1992 to 2001 noticed. They cringed in their seats, and even in this opportunity to greet each other, could not overlook the fact that the one from County Derry in the north of Ireland had been made into a spectacle. I felt awkward and embarrassed. I felt a tickle rise in my throat, and a cough began to take shape. I started coughing. Very quickly, number 1999 lifted a pitcher of water from the table and quickly poured some into a tin cup in front of me. She gave it to me quickly, and I sipped it, very much aware that I needed to tame this nervous cough. The cough subsided.

A nun with large spectacles appeared in an arched doorway, pushing a two-tiered cart of food. She made her way to our tables at the bottom and placed a small plate of bacon and eggs and toast in front of each of us. I felt hungry all of a sudden. I lifted a small earthenware canister, presuming it was salt, and poured the contents over the bacon and eggs. The flow from the canister seemed rather fast. I placed it back on the table. I had a great vantage point standing there at the bottom table. I looked around me. Some were engaged in conversation. Others simply looked at their food. It was the first time I had heard the nuns speak, and the noise they made seemed to thunder and spill through the skylight. I smiled at myself, temporarily enjoying the fact that I had the best view in the room.

One older nun sitting at the end of one of the top tables caught my glance. She smiled and nodded her head kindly toward me. I smiled back. *Had I made some connection?* I wondered. I reached to my plate and grabbed a fork. I put the food in my mouth and quickly realized that I had saturated the bacon and eggs with sugar. I wanted to laugh, but put the brakes on the smile that normally would have consumed my face. I finished my meal rather awkwardly. When I had finished, Sister Dolores conspicuously got up from her table and limped towards me. She told me quite abruptly to get the chair and sit down.

"That will teach you to have a decent tone when you speak to me again," Sister Dolores spat her command. She was being watched carefully by the nun who smiled at me. With a feeling of exhaustion, I turned to the wall, picked up the chair, and placed it between Annie Boyle and Jean O'Doherty.

Annie Boyle, who was sitting to my right, appeared relieved that I finally got my chair and took my rightful place at the table.

"I would have died if that happened to me," she pronounced, hesitating a little as she spoke. There was a hint of delay between her words. I thought I detected a familiar accent that could only hail from Northern Ireland, despite the din in the room. "Where are you from, Ann? I heard you say something in the dormitory when Sister Dolores asked you, but I was so nervous about everything I wasn't paying attention."

"I'm from Derry City," I quickly responded, quite delighted that I was finally having a conversation with someone. I began to relax a little, though I noticed some tension in my back.

"I'm from near Derry, too," Annie responded. "So, here we are at the end of the marching season. The Apprentice Boys must be tired by now. I am from Strabane, County Tyrone."

I was quite thrilled that I was sitting beside someone who had a similar accent and who came from a unique place in Ireland where Catholics were treated like second-class citizens. Her accent made me feel, in a strange way, that there was a hint of home around me, and I was very pleased to hear it.

Annie Boyle had flaring, red hair and a face full of freckles. She appeared friendly, with a kind disposition. Annie, just like me, had a tendency, like most people in the north of Ireland, to talk with some buoyancy in her voice. Words tumbled out of our mouths quickly. I made a note in my head that I would have to try and slow the cadence of my speech so that people could understand me. Later on, I realized that I need not have bothered making that mental note, because there would be so few opportunities to speak in the days and weeks and months ahead.

I certainly knew what Annie Boyle was referring to when she mentioned the Apprentice Boys. I knew that the marching season was the celebration of Protestant triumphalism and political dominance. It was a sobering time for Catholics in the north of Ireland, and they generally kept their distance.

My family usually watched the parade and marveled as these men marched to the War Memorial within Derry Walls with all their pomp and color. As children, we danced to the sounds of their drums and flutes and enjoyed this annual scene, with no real understanding of what all the pageantry meant. Other Catholic families stayed home. My father had a great friend who played the biggest drum we ever saw. We went to the Derry march to wave to my father's friend, Mr. Anderson, as he, in turn, heard our shouts of delight, and beat his drum louder when he passed us. When he saw us, Mr. Anderson showed us a smile as big and as wide as the four gates protecting the Derry Walls.

###

Jean O'Doherty was on my left side at the end of the table. She was from County Kerry. I already knew that, though younger in rank than me, she was held in higher regard by Sister Dolores. I already felt a distance from her. Jean leaned over me to address Annie Boyle with some sharpness in her voice.

"I do not know what you were talking about. I did not understand a word you said. You people from the north of Ireland should stay where you are and not come over the border to us."

I had been poised for a good conversation, but this one seemed to have a razor blade scrolling through her. Annie Boyle ignored the comment. It was as if she was used to such comments, and she expertly changed the topic of conversation.

"My mother gave me a bar of milk chocolate, and I put it in my pocket. I just realized I transferred it to the pocket of this long tunic when I changed. Would you two like a wee piece of chocolate?"

Annie took the bar of chocolate from her tunic pocket before we had a chance to respond. There was something about this act of generosity that felt ominous. Annie quickly produced the block of chocolate. The fragrance of the chocolate seeped through the silver wrapper. Annie tore at the paper and broke off a piece for Jean and me, and then handed us the sweet treat. No sooner did the piece of the broken chocolate bar get into Jean O'Doherty's hands than Sister Dolores, in an instant, was in front of us at the table. She snatched the pieces of chocolate from us and erupted in a volcanic steam.

"How dare you bring anything into the refectory!" she screamed at the top of her voice. There was a slow hush among the postulants.

The other nine postulants seemed stricken with shock and apprehension. The other nuns in the room barely looked in our direction. Only one nun at the top of the table on the other side of the room was paying attention.

Annie Boyle was shaking.

Sister Dolores heaved in shallow breaths above the section of the table where Annie Boyle was sitting. The nun's face grew red, and it soon took on a purple hue. I noticed that she fisted her hands, which frightened me a little. In that moment, I felt that Sister Dolores had the capacity and lack of control to actually strike Annie Boyle. I discarded the thought, but felt sweat pour through me. The refectory seemed to be getting hotter by the second. Slowly, a hush spread and consumed the room and all who were sitting in it. Sister Dolores was, at this point, shaking with rage.

She bellowed, "Sister Mildred, fetch the jar of mustard!" A nun sitting near the top of the room got to her feet slowly and headed toward the food cart. We postulants were sitting frozen in our chairs, looking at this nun convulsing with anger. There was utter silence when Sister Mildred handed Sister Dolores the jar of dark mustard. I heard a groan come from Annie Boyle. She held her hands tightly on her lap, and I could see her knuckles had whitened with distress. I had a foreboding that something terrible was going to happen, to the point that I thought of fleeing from the table.

Sister Dolores put her hand on the lid of the jar that held the mustard. She twisted it in a clockwise motion. The lid did not budge, so Sister Dolores leaned on the lid of the jar with a greater degree of concentration and grunted as the lid responded to her weight and effort. Sister Dolores snapped a tablespoon from an empty dish on the table and deftly scooped out an enormous portion of mustard. The spoon overflowed, and some of the mustard landed on the table. The smell from the jar was pungent.

Sister Dolores approached Annie Boyle and spewed out, "Open your mouth, madam."

Annie stiffened, and without a thought of disobeying this command, opened her mouth. She quickly felt the sting of the mustard engulf her tongue and fill her mouth as Sister Dolores shoveled this mixture in.

"Do not spit that out, madam," Sister Dolores whispered right into her face.

Annie Boyle, from Strabane, County Tyrone in the north of Ireland, was frozen in fear, and the more she tried to breathe, the more her mouth was on fire.

Not one person in that refectory spoke. Not one person moved. Everyone sat and watched as Annie Boyle was stripped of her dignity. After what seemed to be an eternity, Sister Dolores spat out the words, "Now swallow it."

I sat transfixed beside Annie Boyle. I felt a knot in my back, and my hands went numb. Everyone who sat in that huge dining area remained silent. Not one nun came to Annie's defense. Not one person addressed the glaring incident of abuse that had unfolded. No one spoke the day Annie Boyle endured the fire of humiliation and was forced to swallow more than mustard. That first day of her entrance into the convent, Annie Boyle swallowed her tears. She swallowed her words. She swallowed her spontaneity. She swallowed her free spirit. She swallowed her confidence. The nun at the end of the table at the top of the room, who had smiled at me, now wiped her eyes. This nun, whose name I would later come to know as Sister Kate O'Flaherty, would go to her room later, record these events in her journal, and at a future time, write an accounting, slip it into the post office in the local town, and send her observations off to headquarters in Rome. The congregation's major superior, Mother Benedicta, and her team of councilors resided there and monitored the mission and development of the congregation's affairs. The congregation had provinces all over the world, and it was not unusual to hear from Mother Benedicta when she was in New Guinea, Australia, Egypt, Canada, Ireland, the United States, or Africa.

Sister Kate O'Flaherty wanted to ensure that the major superiors were informed about the blatant abuses that were rampantly occurring in this convent. She hoped that these disgraceful abuses would somehow be addressed and prohibited. Little did she realize that Mother Benedicta, the nun in charge of the whole religious institute, removed from everyone in the eternal city, cared little about what was happening in Ireland. The young woman who entered needed some challenges to build character. Being abused had been a way of life for her when she was a young nun. Character building should be perpetuated.

CHAPTER TEN

A RUDE AWAKENING

Daybreak September 9, 1966—5:15 a.m.

The night crept crisply into the light of daybreak after a fitful sleep. For the first time in my life, I felt utterly alone. I knew there were four other bodies in surrounding beds not too far from me, and five others on the other side of the dormitory, but the feeling of loneliness hugged me so closely I felt lost in its grasp. All these people were total strangers to me. I had never slept in a room with complete strangers before. Silence crashed quietly out of everything in this first moment of entering the waking world that crushed me on September 9, 1966. The moment felt like splintered glass, and its mirror was all around me. It was everywhere. It brought a sense of transparency and a feeling of sterility in its reflection of everything in its sight. *Oh God, where am I?* I thought desperately, as I looked at the bright, white curtains sentineled around me, separating and disconnecting me from everything in that deep, cavernous space. I was lost in whiteness. I was wrapped in whiteness, shrouded, and I was appalled by the lack of color. I was cold.

I stretched to look out the window behind me. It was laced with spider webs. An evergreen stood strong just beyond the window. It, too, was stalwart, encased in silence. I took a deep breath and watched as it sputtered out of me like fog or smoke or steam or a puff of air. I had the most profound desire to unwrap myself and be propelled to my kitchen at home many miles away. I imagined my father blowing breath into the embers in the fireplace as he rekindled the flame that just never seemed to go out. My father, the keeper of that flame, always made sure we woke to warmth and the noise of the crackle and pop of a boisterous fire in the hearth.

While I was lying there between those cold white sheets that first morning, I felt a stark contrast to my home experience, and was overcome by a feeling that this was a place where the windows were rarely opened and the rooms rarely infused with fresh air. I was going to live in a box of ice for the next two years. The place was devoid of noise. Quiet invaded everything and trapped everything in its strong hold. It seems, not only could there be no movement, but also there was a sense that things were being strangled in this room. There was barely a breath of air.

What air there was, was lifeless. There were no stirrings of life. I shifted in the bed and the curtain rail shook. It seemed I was the only one awake. I did not hear a sound, not even breathing. At least if someone coughed, it would create some semblance of life, but there was only stillness. I could only think of home, and I felt the emptiness within the miles that separated me from my life and the liveliness so far away. This was a shock to my senses, and I could feel a headache begin to seep into the front of my head. I had endured a restless sleep, and upon waking, did not like the utter strangeness that was around me. I felt the sheets; they were thick and coarse. They also had a different kind of smell, which probably was linked to the carbolic soap we had found on our nightstand the night before. There was a chipped enamel basin on each nightstand and a small glass that held a toothbrush and toothpaste. Everything was sterile. All color had disappeared.

Everything I owned now was contained within these curtains. My long, black frock was folded on the chair beside my bed. All other garments were folded neatly in the small stand beside my bed. It was comprised of two small shelves inside a deep brown door. There was no dresser. There was no wardrobe. I did not need anything other than that little box-like stand. I had been totally stripped of everything I owned. I missed the color and felt wrung out in this black-and-white space. At least the sky would be blue now and again, and the grass was always green. Even they seemed so far away. I felt I had woken up on another planet, or in another dimension, utterly foreign to anything I had ever experienced.

I began to sense anxiety, as an uncomfortable feeling took hold. I tossed in the bed. I could not shake this feeling. I wanted to get up and leave it behind me, but we had been told before we bedded down for the night that we were not to get up before the morning bell was rung outside the dormitory in the morning.

Eventually, I fell asleep again.

CHAPTER ELEVEN

LOST

September 9, 1966—6:15 a.m.

I felt the coldness of the air as soon as I opened my eyes. I felt a sudden pang in my stomach. My heart ached for home as I looked at the white curtains hanging in folds around me. The sheets were cold. I pulled with my feet to find my cardigan and felt its warmth make my feet come to life. I knew that I would have to be very vigilant about keeping my cardigan hidden. It was my greatest treasure. After a while, I pulled it from around my feet and legs and silently eased out of bed. I folded the cardigan beneath the sheets and then slipped it under the mattress. I felt the cold breeze snatch at my legs.

I quickly got into bed again. My cardigan was my direct connection to my mother. I would guard it with my life. This was the only item in this shroud of white fog that was really and truly mine. I felt stripped of everything as I watched the curtains shift here and there, as someone moved in her bed. All the curtains were attached. I had never been in a place stripped of color before. I did not realize that I would be ever color-blind here. I thought about the wildflowers swaying in the fold of the hills beyond the convent door. I was determined to find color in places that no one noticed. I would find color in deep crevices if I had to. I heard breathing all around me and wondered if anyone else was awake.

At that very moment, I heard the clang of a bell that sounded like the echo of a can in a bucket. Three loud knocks poured through the dormitory door. "Let us bless the Lord," a voice proclaimed as a thick hand thumped on the door. The bell and the voice galvanized the occupants of the dormitory into activity. I heard thuds and tumbles. I coughed and yawned as sighs began to fill the space. I kept my eyes closed for one more minute as I got used to the bustle.

I sat upright as the frigid air embraced me and sent prickles of ice through every part of me. I felt like ice as I bolted onto the floor. I automatically felt around for my slippers, but realized I had none. By the sounds emanating from beyond the curtain, I knew the others were thumping around in their bare feet. The bare feet produced a slapping sound on the hard floor of the dormitory. There was no way I was going to do that. I reached for my black stockings and struggled to put them on.

The flurry of activity beyond the white curtains was becoming convulsive. I reached for the wash cloth and soaked it in the water of the basin on my nightstand. The cold cloth hit me hard on the face and sent a tingling cold around my neck and head. Speed was the key here, and I realized that if I hurried sufficiently, I might not feel the cold. Speed would gird me from the harshness of the steel freeze that was to become part of the awakening. I learned to wash and dress lightning fast. I decided that if I hurried, I might not have to deal with the anxiety, dread, and fear that I had been feeling intermittently after I woke. Those feelings seemed to stick with me and sent shudders of disquiet to lodge deep inside me. All the emotions of that first terrible day in the convent might drown in this cold basin if I scrubbed and cleansed them from my skin. I did not know that clean could feel so cold.

I grabbed the black frock that I had cast on the chair beside my bed the night before. I shivered as I tried to find the long black sleeves. It felt heavy this morning, more like a suit of armor than a large mass of material. Little did I know that first morning that I would need armor to meet and greet every day upon awaking in that cold cave of a space. Within fifteen minutes, I was ready to stand in line with nine other postulants. I checked on my cardigan under the mattress and pushed it further into the middle.

Rank already had been established, and I knew exactly where to fall in line. I heard the click of Sister Dolores's shoes in the distance and automatically stood upright. No one spoke as we held ourselves beside our beds, consumed in the Grand Silence, while listening to the steps getting closer and closer. I thought of home. Everyone would be snug in bed still. I thought for a moment of my sisters and brothers. They would wake up to warmth and be sent off with my father's blessing. I muffled a moan that stuck in my heart, and I felt the need to escape. I wanted to cry. Thinking of the glow of the morning fire in my own kitchen felt so very far away. I wanted to return home in that instant.

There was high tension as the clatter of shoes echoed just outside the dormitory and finally stopped. My heart was beating loudly in my chest, and I had a feeling of dread this first morning in the convent. The feeling of positive anticipation that I had had at some point the day before was replaced by a feeling that I had never had before, and I wished it would go away. The other postulants quickly emerged from their small, white, coffin-like cubicles. Each of us was standing straight and stiff as boards, as if poised to endure a pummeling. I looked straight ahead at the person in front of me. She was a little taller than I was, making me partially hidden from the view of Sister Dolores. A sense of tightness gripped the little group. Sister Dolores walked darkly over the threshold. The announcer of the "Let us bless the Lord" salutation presented earlier had brought one dim light to life after she thumped on the door three times.

In that dimness, Sister Dolores brooded over us. She limped her way noisily past each of us as we stood in trepidation. I looked at her and saw her eyes dart from one end of the line to the other. There was no sign of brightness from her, no sign of humanity lurking anywhere in her face. Her nose was pointed. Creases were deeply carved on both sides of her mouth, and she held herself as tall as she could to make up for the tilt she walked in as a result of her limp. Her countenance appeared to be stiff and controlled, as if cemented by a life of rigidity and emptiness. There was no softness, no twinkle in her eyes, and no gesture of kindness. When we were ready and stood in rank before her, she eventually spoke hoarsely.

"We will be having a funeral Mass this morning. One of the sisters died in our convent in Roscommon, and she will be buried in our cemetery."

That description was the sum total of this dead nun's life. She was without a name, without an age, and her passing had little impact on Sister Dolores. She finally snapped her fingers and motioned for our little group to follow her. She limped forward. We obeyed in silence. There was barely any light as we made our procession down the numerous flights of stairs. The statutes that hugged each corner of the landings and stood silent and stern in the evening light greeted us with that same grim look in the glimmer of the morning light. They were stark and bulky and lifeless. They were right at home here in this convent. They were lost in the canyon of dimness that forever hugged those landings.

CHAPTER TWELVE

A RED TIE AT A FUNERAL

September 9, 1966—7:00 a.m.

On that cold morning on September 9, 1949, our group of postulants, on cue from Sister Dolores, took our assigned seats in the convent chapel. In front of us were four rows of nuns in white veils. These were novices who were at the beginning of their second year of training in institutional religious life. These white-veiled novices had, by now, endured one year in Fairview Convent. I counted at least twenty of them. Beyond them were about thirty women donned in black veils extending from their heads to their waists. All had bowed their heads. I later learned that the nuns in black veils had been in Fairview Convent for at least four years and most of them a lot longer than that. I was to glean later that these nuns were assigned specific duties and responsibilities so that the convent would run smoothly.

Sister Maureen, a short, portly woman with a ruddy complexion, was in charge of the laundry. She ensured that soap and washing powder were renewed on a regular basis and that the equipment there was in proper working order.

Sister Theresa, known as the porter, answered the doors. There was a different ring to each door, so she was frequently seen rushing from one end of the place to the other. Only she could open the doors.

Sister Rose was in charge of the sacristy and had to handle the sacred linens and vessels that were used for masses and other liturgical events.

Sister Clare was in charge of feeding the poor who came to the side door on occasion. Sister Agnes supervised the garden at the rear of the house where vegetables and fruits grew and were harvested. Sister Margaret's duties seemed to be centered in an office. She did the typing and sorted the incoming and outgoing mail. Sister Edward was responsible for ensuring that the farm animals, consisting of six cows and a donkey, were properly supervised and cared for by the young farm hand, Jimmy McGinty, who lived at the gate lodge at the end of the property.

Other nuns were responsible for the upkeep of the house. Sister Leo cleaned the chapel and kept the fire in the main parlor lit during the winter. In late autumn, it was generally the work of the novices to stack the chopped logs that Jimmy McGinty had stacked against the shed for the long, dreary winter. The only thing exuding any life was the occasional small explosion from the sparks of the logs that broke into the dark silence there.

Everyone had her part to play in the proper running of the huge residence. No one could be idle at any time. The older members of the religious group took their places in front of the chapel. They mostly spent their days in prayer or reading spiritual books in the convent library. They shuffled through their days in silence and prayer. I noticed two sisters in black veils who sat on the side aisle and seemed to be separate from the rest of the group. I gave no special thought to that. Everyone sat in that stone-cold chapel wrapped in silence.

My focus was soon on the lit candles that surrounded the coffin of the nun who had died. The dead nun continued to remain nameless. I wondered who the nun from Roscommon was. I wondered how old she was. What had she done with her life? I wondered if she had traveled to mission lands and taught or nursed.

I felt stifled for lack of noise. I looked at the red lamp in the sanctuary, pulsating with movement close to the altar. The candle inside the long, glass container flickered its life onto the wall beside it. Sometimes the flames on the wall danced happily, and at other times, the light did not move. The lamp was cushioned in a large, long, brass stand. The brass gleamed golden from the light of the candle.

The altar was adorned with a blanched-white cloth decorated along the edges in bright red embroidery. I imagined that someone put a serious amount of work into that. I had learned a great deal of such stitchery from my mother and was adept with a needle and thread. I appreciated the detail of the work displayed before me.

A cream-colored beeswax candle kept vigil on both sides of the altar. In a niche carved into the right side of the wall stood a marble statue of the Blessed Virgin. The wall opposite contained a marble statue of Saint Joseph. Everything was symmetrical. Bright purple and yellow flowers adorned each ledge where the statues of the Blessed Virgin and St. Joseph stood. A stained-glass window above each statue provided a small burst of light now and again when the clouds reorganized themselves in the sky as they were buffeted by the strong winds whipped up from the lake. The colors that spewed into the sanctuary of the chapel were mostly purple and yellow hued so that the mantle that hung there was heavy with darkness, recovering now and again with little points of brightness where the yellow pierced through.

"The first Mass in the convent has to be a funeral Mass," I almost whispered, feeling a sense of foreboding. For some reason, I really felt annoyed by this. I hated funeral Masses. They contained a weight that hung over you for days and weeks—even years. They are not easy to shrug off. Funerals sit on your shoulders as much as the load of a dead corpse sits on the pallbearers' shoulders. Funerals ooze through your pores. I remembered that, a few months before, my mother had received a letter from America informing her that an elderly aunt had "passed away" in New York. I heard my mother's voice. "Maybe in America you pass away when you die, here in Ireland you simply die." There had been a genuine jolt of sadness in my mother's voice when she remembered her aunt Margaret. Mother had left us sitting in the kitchen and gone to her room. We knew there were certain times when we should not disturb my mother, and that was one of them.

I glanced to my left. Annie Boyle had her eyes closed, and a sense of sadness had taken hold of her face. To my right, I could see that Mary Ita Ahern looked poised and disinterested in what was going on around her. I noticed, however, that Mary Ita shifted from one knee to the other quite often, and her knuckles were tight and white.

I was taken out of my reverie and entered reality when the priest boomed into the sanctuary, stood at the bottom of the altar steps, and bowed before ascending the steps and kissing the altar. I had seen this a thousand times at the multitude of Masses I had attended at home over the years. He began to recite the once familiar Latin at the top of his lungs. This was quite different from what we had become used to since Pope John had convened the Second Vatican Council a few years before. Now priests usually said Mass in the vernacular. The priest was a slight man, vested in black garments over his white alb. A short, black cloth was draped over his right arm.

I breathed in deeply with a heavy sigh. The hum of the Mass responses put me in a hypnotic trance. I could barely keep awake. Incense filled the sanctuary and filtered into the main chapel, imbuing the aisles and pews with a white, fragranced fog. I felt a cough lurking deep in my throat as the foggy fragrance engulfed me. I had begun to feel as if I was going to sleep, but sputtered into life when I realized where I was.

I invested every ounce of effort and concentration into suppressing the tickle that feathered my throat, but I exploded in a splutter in an effort to catch my breath. I sensed the eyes of Sister Dolores rolling to the chapel ceiling as I caught myself gasping for air. I needed to gulp air as tears rolled down my cheeks. I began to shake and felt myself gasp loudly. My companions on either side of me sat frozen in their seats. I told myself not to panic, to take little shallow breaths. I assured myself that I would breathe deeper once I established regularly paced, shorter breaths.

Eventually, I was able to control the cough and wiped my wet face with the back of my hands. In order to remain calm, I concentrated on the colored threads of light penetrating the stained-glass windows in the sanctuary where the priest continued to drone in his efforts to save this dead nun's soul and send it off to heaven. I finally left the shallow breaths behind and felt much stronger and determined to go in for deeper air. I had controlled this coughing spell. I would learn to control dozens more in the days and weeks and months to come. I gleaned trouble lurking in Sister Dolores's flinches, which were no doubt pulsating through her body every time I seized.

Ultimately, the Mass concluded, and the coffin pallbearers, provided by the local undertaker, lifted the coffin, and with the nuns following, made their way to the back of Fairview Convent where the cemetery overlooked the caress of Lake Fennan. A short sermon after the Gospel reading during Mass had revealed that the dead nun was Sister Mark. The damp earth, sodden and heavy, mounded around the gaping grave. With a piercing wind chilling the already cold, forsaken morning, the muted crowd gazed at the slim coffin that was slid skillfully into the ground. One of the nuns began to sing "Regina Coeli," and most of the others in the group joined in. I watched as a man stood at the edge of this black, bundled group. He wore a bright red tie. I later learned that the man with the bright red tie was Sister Mark's brother. It was very strange to see a man wearing a red tie to a funeral. Generally, men who attended wakes and funerals wore a black tie out of respect.

Sister Mark's brother, Michael, had driven from Galway for the funeral. His red tie was a stark symbol of his repulsion for this religious group. He bade a wordless goodbye to his sister by leaning forward and throwing a bunch of white roses onto the sleek pine wood. "Goodbye, my dear Nellie," he uttered in a clear voice as he let the flowers go. He turned quickly and disappeared into the background, leaving the little group without waiting for the final burial prayers. The roses were soon covered in mud as the sides of the mound of earth shed onto the coffin. I felt an ache pierce deeply into me, and it stayed lodged somewhere deep inside for the next few days. A sob lay frantic in my throat and stayed trapped there. I felt the gravitational pull of grief and knew it was not for this dead nun. It was for my mother and father and all I had left behind. It was for the heat of the fireplace. It was for the security of my family that seemed at this point so very distant. Grief froze there on the side of Sister Mark's grave that ninth day of September 1966.

Sister Kate O'Flaherty was at my side as we began the slow walk to the dining room. "You'll be all right, dear," she whispered to me.

She squeezed my arm and smiled. I felt that at least there was some kindness hidden in this cold, concrete house. With the flush of hot tea and toast quickly consumed, I, and my ranked companions, at the direction of Sister Dolores, were ushered out of the dining room into a large room on the second floor.

CHAPTER THIRTEEN

THE CLASSROOM

September 9, 1966—10:00 a.m.

After breakfast and the mandatory refectory cleanup on September 9, 1966, we, the new crop of postulants, was taken by Sister Dolores to a large, narrow room on the second floor. It was set up as a classroom. The large room had pale-green paint on its walls, much of it peeling, leaving the walls pockmarked. The room was dominated by a well-worn blackboard in the front of the room. Ten shoddy, dark desks were lined together in two rows. Ranked again in the classroom, I found myself in the last desk beside a window, sitting behind Mary Ita Ahern, who was at least five feet ten inches tall. I felt a sense of immense relief at having been assigned a seat by the window. I was actually overjoyed at this good fortune. The window instantly became my link to the outside world. As long as I could glance at the trees and the sky and have a view of the hills in the distance and see the spread of the wildflowers coloring the hill, my heart could remain fixed and steady. This spot could anchor me. I knew instinctively that I would do nothing to jeopardize this coveted spot. I would be attentive to all that was going on in the classroom and never draw any kind of negative attention to myself. I had no sooner thought about this great reality, then the sharp knife of drama began to unfold before me.

Sister Dolores perched herself awkwardly on a raised desk and peered over her classes at the ten of us sitting stiffly before her. She began listing the rules and regulations that were to shackle us for the next year. We would get up every morning at 6:00 a.m. We were instructed to wash quickly, assemble in rank in the dormitory so that we could move together into the chapel for the recitation of morning prayers, which began promptly at 6:30 a.m. On Sundays and special days, we would be allowed to stay in bed an extra half hour, as prayers began at 7:00 a.m. On weekdays and Saturdays, meditation would begin at 6:45 a.m., and this lasted for forty-five minutes. At 7:30 a.m., Mass would begin, and by 8:40 a.m., we would be expected in the refectory for breakfast. On Sunday, the daily prayers and services were again delayed by a half hour.

Sister Dolores continued with the expectations for each day. There was no variation. Every act and deed that we were to perform was so scheduled that very soon we would become robotic about how we coursed through the days. She droned on, explaining that on weekdays we postulants would leave the refectory after breakfast and go straight to the dormitory to make beds. We would have to clean the dormitory and the bathrooms. Those chores generally took an hour to complete. Everything in the dormitory, including the inside windows, were expected to be cleaned to perfection. From 9:30 a.m. to 10:30 a.m., there would be a class in this very room on the holy rules and regulations of this religious institute. This rule laid out the mandates for daily prayers, monthly retreat days, and behavior that was expected from postulants, novices, and the professed nuns, both inside and outside the convent. The holy rule was the straightjacket that kept everyone trapped in structure and rigidity. From 10:30 a.m. to 10:45 a.m., tea would be served from a cart outside the kitchen. We soon learned that the tea contained in a huge, steel teapot was pre-milked and pre-sugared. The tea was strong and served in enamel mugs.

After this hasty repast, we were expected to go to the barn behind the chapel area to peel vegetables for the following day. All vegetables were to be scraped and cut and sliced in silence. This task took up to one and a half hours. No matter the day or temperature, we would be hauled into this freezing winter barn or stifling summer barn every day for the next year. On Saturday, we spent twice the usual time in the barn at this menial task so that we would not have to engage in chopping and slicing and cutting on Sunday. Our fingers were a perpetual orange color because we cut so many carrots. At all times, we were supervised by Sister Dolores.

Dinner was served at 12:30 p.m. After dinner, we had refectory and kitchen cleanup. We would be assigned in pairs to rotate these duties. From 1:30 p.m. to 3:30 p.m., we would work in the garden, cleaning pathways, weeding the vegetable patches, and planting and picking whatever fruit or vegetables were in season. The garden was full of fruit that had been planted and harvested by generations of postulants and novices who went before us. Working in the garden was a unique way to keep connected to those former generations. As I knelt there on an almost daily basis over the next year, that connection seemed to grow, as we dug our bare hands into the damp clay, backs aching, every afternoon. It began to feel like slave labor early on.

The garden was full of gooseberries, strawberries, raspberries, cabbage, carrots, parsnips, potatoes, turnips, and a plethora of other delights. Tomatoes and grapes were grown in both greenhouses in the corner of the garden. All our meals came from this garden as much as possible.

At 3:30 p.m., we would clean the barn and carry the urns of vegetables to the kitchen. There we would wash our hands and be told to consume one of the enamel cups of tea sitting outside the entrance to the kitchen. Seeing the hot steam coming from those cups was a welcome sight, especially in the winter. From 4:00 p.m. until 5:00 p.m., we would assemble together at the barn door and walk for almost an hour around the convent grounds and up to the main gate. We would walk with one other companion. The late afternoon stroll was the one time in the day that provided the postulants an opportunity to not walk in rank. This rule was devised to ensure that, right there at the beginning of the entrance into religious life, we did not get too friendly with one particular person. Sister Dolores continued to march us through our day in her Kerry accent.

Before the first walk we took, Sister Dolores warned us about the dangers of "particular friendships." She made it very clear that friendship was frowned upon. "It is wrong and against the Holy Rule to single out one person to be friendly with," she spat out on that first day before the walk. "It is the way of the devil."

We listened attentively, but most did not have any idea to what she was alluding. Mary O' Brien caught my eye and raised her eyes to the sky. We could talk to that companion, who accompanied us, as we promenaded around the perimeter of the property. We could not, obviously, walk with the same companion every day. A rotation system was developed, which was the only way we would get to know each other, although, as time marched on, the postulants from the north of Ireland began to walk in silence with the Kerry girls. They were not interested in any of us.

The effort of trying to deal with the demons of loneliness and anxiety gripped us more deeply as the days seeped into weeks. It was a happy relief for me when Mary O'Brien, Nuala O'Reilly, and Annie Boyle were my companions on the daily trail. Sister Dolores looked quite satisfied and smug as she delivered the content of the text she had in front of her. She was not finished, however, much to our great dismay.

It was on September 9, 1966, that the ten of us who came from the far-flung corners of Ireland would be burdened with the reality that we could not talk about our families while in Fairview Convent. There would be two occasions each year, one in the early spring before Easter and the other at the end of June, when we could have a visit with our families. The visits would take place between 2:00 p.m. and 4:00 p.m. If families arrived at 3:00 p.m., there only would be a one-hour visit. Each of us could write one letter home monthly, and we would receive letters once a month. All outgoing and incoming letters would be read by Sister Dolores. Newspapers would not be available. In fact, she emphasized that we would be forbidden to know what was going on in the world. We were ordered not to seek any information about affairs that pertained to anything that might distract us from our religious training. For the next year, we were to concentrate on prayer, study, and work. We would meet for recreation one hour every night and be supervised at all waking moments by Sister Dolores. With every rule that Sister Dolores listed and read, the doors of my world, one after another, shut tight. I felt that I would be living in a closed vault. I felt as if the color of my world would be reduced to mere black and white, the sounds of everything normal would be muted beyond the concrete and heavy gates, the sights of progress closed to our imaginations and creativity, and our tastes reduced to insipidness. Even at this young age, I had the acuity of spirit to remain undaunted. I was determined not to belong to the grip of iron that would leave me shackled. I would not bend to the will of Sister Dolores.

Sister Dolores continued her drone of other, not-so-important details. If we wanted to leave any space, we would have to kneel in front of Sister Dolores and ask her permission. We were forbidden to go to the dormitory during the day. We were not to complain if we felt sick. We were forbidden to complain about anything. We were to eat everything that was placed in front of us to eat. We were to work in silence. Being without books, newspapers, poetry, or music, which tickled my heart and made my soul soar, now felt like a fatal blow. I might have to leave the heart and family sitting at the hearth without me, but I was determined not to be without the hearth. I was determined to create my own place where my creative energy would continue to survive and perhaps even thrive. As Sister Dolores closed her rule book, something inside me unlocked, as she thumped the book on the desk in front of her.

CHAPTER FOURTEEN

THE GATE

September 12, 1966—1:00 p.m.

September 12, 1966, was a blustery day. We had been in the convent for four days now. We all were still shocked at the sound of the three knocks that echoed through the dormitory in the early morning dawn, calling us to leave our cold beds, perform our speedy, early morning wash and dress ourselves, which we had all by now perfected, and get to the chapel. We all slept well because of the exertion and monotony of the day.

I hurtled out of bed, careful to tuck my precious cardigan under my mattress. I habitually checked that it would not be discernible to the frequent inspections to which our little individual spaces were subjected. Every so often, Sister Dolores would appear in the dormitory just after we were dressed and perform random reviews of our bedside nightstand. Thankfully, she never looked under the mattresses.

Shortly after dinner, around 1:00 p.m., we assembled as a group in the back courtyard. The trees in the forest, beyond the reach of the convent, were much agitated by the hard breeze. We were ready to be initiated into our daily walk around the property. We walked two by two. As indicated in the morning instructions, we did not have to walk in rank. I looked forward to being able to talk with someone for an hour. Some of my companions had already begun to shut down and walk with their heads bowed, unable to cast off the yoke of submission they had to endure. I developed a different attitude. For me, this was a time to look around, to enjoy the sky, to see possibilities in the clouds, to take a deep breath, to break out of the captivity that grabbed me every time I walked over the threshold of any door that led into the convent. Those doors symbolized and personified the whole notion of being trapped and choked with rules and regulations and difficult expectations. The very act of walking beyond this was liberating and rejuvenating.

I began my first walk around the grounds in the company of Mary O'Brien. As we walked along, I realized that, like me, Mary seemed determined to find that rainbow in the sky no matter the storm that blew through the convent walls. The wind was sharp as a knife this afternoon, more so because we did not have our cardigans to wear. Sister Dolores sported a large black shawl and wrapped it around her tightly as she began to walk ahead of the group. We rambled around to the front of the convent. We had left the courtyard when everyone had gotten into lines of two and were led to the back of the house where the large garden was curtained off from the rest of the land by a thick, gray concrete wall, which had huge cracks running like spiderwebs on its entire surface. I saw some flowers growing in between the cracks. Parts of the wall had crumbled at the top.

At the far side of the garden, a big, glass house glinted when the clouds gave way to the dimmest of sunlight. A bank of manure was heaped in the left-hand corner of the garden, the smell making the air putrid and heavy when the wind turned course. Neat, furrowed rows of earth emptied of harvest filled the middle of the garden. Apple trees bearing crabbed fruit waited patiently to be picked. The blackbirds waited on the wall for a peck at some of the apples that were now fully ripened and looking large and juicy. The heavy garden gate, crusted in peeled green paint, creaked as Sister Dolores lifted the latch.

When the group was beyond the gate, Sister Dolores snapped the latch secure on the other side and ushered us onto the graveled path that led directly beyond the garden and took us to the front of the convent. Our little group huddled into the sweep of the property that lay before us. Lake Fennan ruffled in the breeze beyond the slope of meadow in front of the garden's green gate, its waters rippling furiously to take a bite out of its banks. This place was a different world. The grass was still a deep green. Racing clouds scrolled through the page of blue paint that wrapped itself around the sky. Birds dotted the horizon, gliding on the wind, sideways at times. They swooped and glided freely over Lake Fennan. I enjoyed their flight and freedom. They were liberated by their wings. This thought buoyed my spirits, and I immediately began to feel better. I needed a way to find flight for my spirit, and I would begin with this hour of walking.

The wind contained a ferocious bite. It snapped into the air and chilled us as we huddled together, waiting for the signal to begin walking. The bluster of the wind felt invigorating. The crunch of gravel winded its way along the edge of the fields. A few cows grouped around a copse of bushes to the right. A fence of barbed wire separated us from the animals. I felt they had more freedom than we had, despite the barbed spikes that kept them in their own space.

When we first appeared on the scene, a few of them rambled toward us a few steps, and then thought the better of their trundle. As we began our daily walk, Sister Dolores reminded us once again, as she swept her left arm towards the forest, "No one is permitted to go near the forest, unless we go there to gather winter kindling for the fireplace in the wing where the professed sisters are housed." The trees trembled as she pronounced those words. Mary O'Brien rolled her eyes to heaven. Winter seemed so very far away on this crisp September day in 1966. It felt as if time was standing still. I watched the clouds being sifted in the wind as I turned my attention to the sky. Sister Dolores walked stiffly as she began to lead us around the curved path to the main entrance road to the convent, which was well over half a mile long.

Sister Dolores increased her speed as she entered the main road. It took us almost twenty minutes, walking at a good pace, to reach the main gate. We trooped silently for a while, as if fearful of conversation.

"How's it going?" Mary whispered to me, as if she was afraid the wind would bring her words to Sister Dolores. Without letting me speak, she continued. "God, isn't this something?

I never thought I would be traipsing after one another like this. It is freezing. I need a coat." Mary was a little taller than I was and a little wider in girth. She breathed heavily as she plodded beside me. Her company was refreshing. The road had a few bends in it. As we walked, we were able to survey some of the almost seventy acres that was owned by this religious congregation. I was quite excited to be able to talk to Mary for an hour. One hour of talking during the day was pure luxury, especially if the companion of the day was a talker. Mary O'Brien was indeed a talker.

Sister Dolores was well ahead of the two of us since we were the last two in the line. Mary began to imitate how Sister Dolores walked. I really wanted to laugh out loud, but held back. I put my hand instinctively to my mouth to stifle any noise. I had to learn the art of laughing in silence. It was a hard thing to do. Mary had a great sense of humor. She screwed up her face the way Sister Dolores did and shook her head from side to side, mimicking Sister Dolores to perfection. This distraction certainly brightened my mood, and I soon forgot about how cold it really felt. Sister Dolores, of course, was completely oblivious to Mary's antics as she led the group around yet another curve in the path.

"I think there is a golf course on the other side of the road," Mary declared in her familiar northern tongue. I had to concentrate fully on what Mary was saying. Like myself, she pronounced with her northern accent, and while that was very familiar, Mary was inclined to talk fast. Mary and I walked at the back of the line very cheerfully, and I enjoyed her banter. I discovered that she was born and reared in Strabane in County Tyrone. She had a few brothers and sisters and complained that she missed playing the piano. She loved music and explained to me that she enjoyed classical music the most. I shared with her that I missed my family and hated getting into a cold bed at night. I stopped short of telling Mary about the cardigan my mother made, which kept my feet from freezing every night. I noticed that I was hesitant to trust Mary, but brushed that aside to concentrate on what she was saying.

Although wintertime seemed so far away on this crisp September day, it seemed to contain some of that season already. At the same time, it felt that time was actually standing still. I watched the clouds being sifted and tossed by the wind when I turned my attention to the sky. Something was moving at least. Sister Dolores remained ahead of the group, still walking stiffly as she led us around a curve in the pathway. The gravel path seemed to extend forever. I felt little pieces of that gravel in my shoes, but I was not going to stop for anything. This gravel path provided a grand view of the land. As we rounded yet another corner, I noticed that a large twig had snagged my black stockings on my right leg. I shook my leg to dislodge it, but was unsuccessful.

The little bramble walked along with me another couple of yards, before I stooped to free it before it did any additional damage to my stocking. I grasped onto its thickness and tugged it free. There was a hole in my stocking, but I would mend it at some point after I returned to the convent. I looked at the stick. As a child, I had played with such a thick stick in our back garden, pretending to be the school teacher. At quite a young age, I ensured that the bushes growing there were beaten into submission every day. I was merely imitating the teacher who ruled in my little elementary school by threatening every lapse of her students with her big stick, which she kept beside the fireplace in the classroom. I swept a few fallen leaves in the sway of my hand as they lifted in the breeze. Here and there, I scratched the gravel, enjoying my freedom to sweep wide into the air, as if conducting a great symphony. It felt magical. Mary laughed at my efforts.

Mary O'Brien raced her words together, and I enjoyed her mimicry of Sister Dolores, if only for the purpose of lifting the heaviness I felt on my chest. It dissipated as I listened to Mary, who was trying to synchronize the limp of the woman who charged ahead to the end of the property line owned by the nuns. It was amazing how fast she was able to walk with this hindrance. Ten minutes deeper into the walk, a big, black, wrought-iron gate loomed ahead, and Sister Dolores slowed down. The gate was open, tethered on either side with an iron clasp. I noticed the ironwork in the gate as I approached. The gate was a work of art. Black wrought-iron leaves straddled the sides of the gate. When the group of postulants clustered at the gate, Sister Dolores instructed us in her usual authoritative tone that, under no circumstances, should we ever go beyond the gate. If we did, we would be sent home immediately. There was no response from any of us. We all stood silently in the chill of the afternoon under the shadow of the wrought-iron gate, realizing that, little by little, we were in the process of being ensnared. I continued to hold the twig in my hand and, absentmindedly, started scratching at some of the rust that had taken hold of one of the handles of the gate. I examined the gate further, and as I was concluding that it could do with a good painting and imagining how that could be accomplished, given the height of the gate, I was hurtled out of my revelry when Sister Dolores suddenly exploded into my face.

"Now look what you have done, madam. You have deliberately scraped and destroyed the handle with that piece of wood you have in your hand. You will pay for this."

I was startled and dropped the twig instinctively. "But, Sister, the handle was rusted," I heard myself protest. It felt strange to hear the sound of my voice challenging this large, tyrannical figure. Sister Dolores wrapped her black shawl around her, as if depending on the tight wrap to hold her anger in check.

She managed the control for another second, and then the detonation of her disgust filled the chill. It appeared as if some volcanic eruption lived deep inside her, and it took very little prompting to make it brim over. I knew by now the lava of her words would follow with a flow that was engulfing and hot. Fire was contained in her every breath at this point. I steeled myself for the onslaught.

"Who do you think you are, madam from the north? Your mother and father will be responsible for sending money to paint the handle of the gate that you just intentionally destroyed. You will write that letter to your mother when you get back to the convent."

I felt the heat of her words strike my face. I felt humiliated at the characterization that I had destroyed something that was already corroded and peeling with the effects of rain and wind and time. Time was the corrosive instrument, not my little twig I had used to create a symphony of harmony as the clouds passed above us. Now there were thunderclouds on this pathway, and I had better absorb the blast. I felt my depth blush crimson and began to shake inside. The knot in my back twisted in pain. I was determined not to let this woman see how much effort it took for me to pull out of the verbal slaughter I had just endured. I was quite determined to retain a semblance of calm, as we stood gripped and assailed by yet another bombastic overflow of some diseased part of this woman that seemed triggered by the slightest effort.

The group turned to go back again along the gravel path. We all huddled a little closer, and silence held us in its hug, as if to help us get to the convent where we might find some distraction. I walked back, stunned by the harshness of Sister Dolores's words, which hit and penetrated me with the force of a stun gun. I already knew that I would be taking the evening meal standing in the middle of the refectory. My thought went to my mother and the letter I would have to write asking her for money to paint the gate. That thought made me profoundly sad.

On the side of the pathway, I noticed a trowel tossed on its side. Sister Kate O'Flaherty was bent over a bush in the driveway. She had a big shovel in her hands and was digging with some energy. I saw that Sister Kate had a splash of red and green paint on her sleeve. I wondered if she had heard the uncontrolled roar of Sister Dolores, if her harshness had been carried by the wind. I looked at the trowel and felt a strange sadness. My father had often put a trowel in all of our hands as he tended his plot of land not far from our house. I decided there and then that Sister Dolores would never pull softness out of me, no matter how hard she tried. I would not let her trowel that out of me. I wanted nothing to do with the hard core that was hers.

We returned to the convent, and I was quickly ushered to the classroom to write the letter to my mother. I quickly scratched that note to her and looked around me before I went to Sister Dolores, who would pour over it before it left for the postman to collect. I was impressed by the flatness of the place, the impeccable surfaces, and the clean lines of the tables and chairs all injected with a sterility that felt stifling. I steadied the bulk of emotion and exhaustion I felt on my shoulders and sighed at the coldness of the surroundings. I heard the shuffle of Sister Dolores behind me and felt her steel-cold eyes burning into the back of my head.

At that moment, I was very close to scratching a little dot on the top of my name as I finished the letter. I had arrived at this convent with high hopes and popping with energy just a few days ago, eager and earnest about the life I was hoping to live. In my dreams, I was to go to foreign lands and teach children who were poor and had little opportunities for education. My dreams had color and effervescence in them. Now I felt totally depleted as I sat in that room, holding that letter. I dug frantically for my inner reservoir to start flowing. I resolved that this woman would not take away my dreams. She would not take away my hopes and aspirations. She would not take my zest for life and passion for reaching beyond myself. In that moment, I wanted my spirit to stretch to a place where all this would be possible, yet the room pulled me into its sterility and lifelessness. It would take some work to get out of this depression that was a short distance away, waiting for me to enter its embrace. I would not. My spirit would take me to a place where all good things were possible.

I got up quickly, shaking the effects of the past hour, and handed the letter to Sister Dolores. She snatched the paper from me with trembling hands. Her anger had still not subsided. I thought she would ignite again, and I would continue to be burned by her flare. She breathed heavily into the paper. I believed if she had continued for too much more, that her breath would set the letter alight. She finally told me to get to the garden and start weeding with the rest of the group. I started on my way, noticing that my spirit felt less burdened.

Weeding never felt so good. All of a sudden, I realized that I was ferociously hungry. I snatched a handful of strawberries as soon as I got to the strawberry patch. They tasted like food from heaven. The next day, I was covered in hives from my salacious indulgence.

CHAPTER FIFTEEN

MARGARET FOLAN

I did not know anything about Margaret Folan (aka Sister Mary Dolores), other than that she loved Kerry and hated just about every other part of Ireland, and that she had a limp and a vocabulary that caused my heart to feel as if it were in a constant crucible. I did not know that she had a father who was an alcoholic, an abusive individual who was cruel to his wife and children. Tom Folan was born in County Limerick, and when he went to County Kerry to find work on a farm, he met and married Mona McCarthy. They had three girls. Catherine was the eldest, Fanny the middle child, and Margaret was the youngest. Every Friday night, as far as Margaret could remember, her father would come home drunk and beat his wife and children. In spite of the consistent, physical abuse that came their way, Mona never thought of leaving her husband.

According to church law, marriage was to last a lifetime. Mona would keep her vows. The four waited week after week for the violent onslaught that Tom Folan wrecked upon the household. One such Friday night near Christmas, when Margaret was barely thirteen years old, Tom Folan came home in his usual, inebriated rage. Margaret was sitting at the table in the kitchen, reading a book, when she heard the hard boots of her father thud on the floor inside the door. She instinctively realized that she should have gone upstairs, but she had been engrossed in the book she had been reading and forgotten that it was Friday night.

The thunder of her father's voice made Margaret feel like concrete, so much so that she could hardly move at the sound of those boots. They heralded trouble, dominance, and control.

When he got to the kitchen, Tom Folan roared at Margaret, “Stop reading that book and get me something to eat.” Margaret swallowed a whimper.

“Yes, Da,” she whispered as she closed the book and put it on the nearby dresser. She scurried to get the kettle to fill with water to make tea. She recalled that there was some ham in the cool shelf in the scullery and intended to go there to make a sandwich for her father. As soon as she passed him, he lifted his hand to slap Margaret, and it landed with such a force that she fell against the kitchen wall. She was able to avoid the main force of the slap, but lost her balance and slammed her foot against the wooden dresser. The dresser was made to endure the test of time. Margaret subdued the instant agony of the break. She did not utter a sound. She did not cry. The pain shot into every fiber of her body. She took short breaths to keep upright. Her eyes flooded with such a look of distain for her father that the flash of her enormous hatred would have brightly lit up a dark sky.

Margaret stumbled and hobbled her way from the scullery as she made the ham sandwiches in haste and set her father’s tea in front of him before her escape upstairs. She climbed the stairs on her knees all the while in excruciating pain. She grasped the wooden spindles of the bannister so tightly that she thought she would leave her fingerprints hollowed into the wood. She crept into bed as the pain engulfed her. She was not able to leave the house for days to go to school. Her father did not miss her. Her mother told her to offer up the pain for the souls in purgatory.

On the third day, her mother brought her a small cask containing whiskey and told her that it would help the pain. A few minutes after she drank the whiskey, Margaret’s body was enveloped in a great calm feeling and the pain subsided. She could at least sleep that night.

The cask was filled regularly, and the whiskey kept her in a state of relaxation that she had never known before. The whiskey continued to help the next few nights, until her mother finally decided to bring the doctor to examine Margaret’s foot.

It was badly swollen, and she screamed when the doctor touched it. He finally was able to wrap her foot in bandages and told her to stay in bed for a few weeks. He did not ask her how she broke her foot. Pain medication helped, but the whiskey helped more.

A few weeks later, her foot still had not healed properly. It was soon beyond repair unless she went to the hospital for an operation. Margaret decided against an operation, simply because the family could not afford it, and it would further enrage her father.

After a few months, a limp reminded Margaret every day that she hated her father more than anything else in the world. That hatred of him soon extended to include everything that came from Limerick. Over the next few years, Margaret Folan became more distant and solitary. She had few friends, and those who stuck with her were constantly disenchanted by Margaret's sullen ways and unpredictable verbal abuse. These outbursts became so frequent that no one wanted to be with her. Very soon, she had insulated herself from her school peers.

She began to be compulsive about cleaning. She would wash and scrub everything over and over again until her hands were red and often raw to the point of bleeding. She did not seem to mind. She just wanted everything to be clean. She always felt like she would explode if she did not keep scrubbing. She often took solace in the cask of whiskey her mother left beside her bed.

Margaret Folan held onto that cauldron of anger even when she entered the convent at the age of fifteen years. As Sister Dolores, she had thought nothing of the structure and discipline that was imposed upon her. She did not find it in the least difficult. She had been noticed pretty quickly by the superiors for being clean and neat and keeping things in perfect order. That was the type of person who would keep things moving and working in perfect, predictable order. Nothing was too hard for Sister Dolores, despite the limp that probably would have imposed restrictions on someone else.

She found mobility in her handicap and was faster and more determined than any of the other postulants who had entered with her. After some years in Fairview Convent, Sister Dolores was put in charge of the postulants' classes. Upon their arrival, they swiftly learned that they must keep busy—this place had to be kept *clean*—and, above all, order and subservience were marks of distinction.

Sister Dolores smoldered as she limped throughout the day. Anger seeped into everything. Her past kept her dark, seething, and white-orbed in a constant inferno of business and meticulous detail. Her anger yelped out of nowhere. Its edge was unstoppable. Sister Dolores sliced like a razor through every moment of every day, leaving her life and the lives of those around her in sharp shards of deep discontent and woundedness. The days and weeks and months in the convent were enveloped in that sharpness and imbued with constant negativity. She left everything jagged in her wake. Every day, her volcanic center distilled for the sole purpose of stripping those around her of any joy, no matter the day or season. The postulants very soon became hypervigilant around her every gesture. Her chill spilled over into every activity. They knew her fury over and over again, even without provocation. Their responses and reactions to her mining their deepest fears became robotic.

###

My mother received my letter and looked for any signs of distress, looking for a clue about how I was doing. I knew she would get the money for the painting of the gate's handle within days. She felt my urgency in the letter, no matter how I attempted to shield it from her. My cousin, Pat Geary, came to the house the day my mother received the demand. He heard about the rusty gate and the instructions for reimbursement. Pat slipped the money into my mother's cardigan pocket before he left the house and went home an angry man.

The years he had spent in Dublin with the St. John's Brothers had broken his spirit. He was determined to keep an eye on things when he visited the convent. He would drop a letter to me as often as possible. He already knew from his own experience that his letters would be read. He knew how things worked in religious orders, and he used that knowledge to try and make sure, as much as he could, that I would not be bullied there. He also knew that it was hard to penetrate those thick, high, institutional walls that kept those living inside stunted and withered, while those on the outside were totally clueless about the abuse taking place. As soon as any prospective member stepped over the threshold, it soon held them in darkness and muteness and led them to lose the power and influence of their voices. Some forgot how to speak. Some spoke in whispers, whispers that were never heard. Those institutional walls, he well knew, kept out the sun and rain and everything else that was needed for the proper development and growth of the young people who lived there.

Pat decided he would write a letter once a month, knowing well that Sister Dolores would read each carefully. He felt that the letters might save me from some serious abuse. He had become a wealthy man since he had left the Brothers in Dublin. After his departure from them, he kept to himself inside his mother's house, unable to go out and be normal. He received some help from a psychiatrist in Belfast. Once a month, Pat went to Belfast where he told Donal Moore, M.D., about the horrors he had suffered at the hands of the male religious community he had so hoped to serve as a young boy. Dr. Moore helped Pat recover, which took more than ten years, but he had to deal with nightmares for the rest of his life.

Pat had set his sights on hopes and dreams that had been dulled and destroyed, and eventually snatched away from him, in the years he spent with this religious congregation in Dublin. As a young entrant, he had been quickly cocooned in cruelty and suffered the heavy rod of physical and emotional abuse under the supervision of an abusive, novice master. This Brother Joseph thought nothing of awakening the young novices in the middle of the night by pouring hot water on their feet as they slept. The young men learned quickly to sleep without depth.

Pat felt his youth had been yanked from him. He had entered the religious institute when he was sixteen and left when he was twenty-one. Ten years after he left, Pat was able to start a construction company, building houses in Belfast.

He was determined to help me by smoothing my journey in the habit. Nuns and priests treated you differently when they knew you were connected to money. In the few following years, while I endured hardship, Pat gave monetary donations to the convent at Christmas and Easter. This was his sole method of trying to make my life more tolerable. When he saw that first letter I had written to my mother asking for money, Pat knew instinctively that the abuse was well under way, even though my first few weeks in Fairview Convent had barely begun.

CHAPTER SIXTEEN

FORMAL RECREATION

September 14, 1966—7:00 p.m.

Formal recreation was introduced to us at seven o'clock on the evening of September 14, 1966. Earlier in the day, Sister Dolores had told us that there would be such a gathering before nightly prayers in the chapel at nine o'clock. Not one in the group reacted. Not one of us asked a question about this nightly venture. At precisely seven o'clock, our postulant group trooped into the recreation parlor like we belonged in an army camp. Not one of us uttered a sound as we entered a cavernous space carved out of one of the sections of the convent. I could not tell which area of the convent we were brought to, but it seemed to be along some corridor under the dormitory.

Upon entry, I shivered. I found myself in another cold space. The room gave us the welcome of ice. It was hard. It was stiff. It felt uncomfortable. There was no vibrancy in that room. The cold was caused, no doubt, by the frosty air that seeped through the cracks in the two windows that were draped in heavy, green curtains. Threadbare flowers were suffocating in their folds. I heard the wind whistling outside the windows on both sides of the room, even pushing through the heavy curtains and leaving a chill there. The room was painted a pale-yellow color that caused me to shiver even more.

A picture of the Sacred Heart, pierced by three huge nails, hung on the right side of the room. A statue of Our Lady with her heart pierced with identical nails was positioned in a corner. I could feel their eyes follow me as I looked at them. In another corner stood a large statue of Saint Joseph carrying the infant Holy Child. The paint had peeled so profusely from the statue that numerous little grains and scraps of different colors lay around the bottom of the pedestal upon which the two from Nazareth stood. A long, dark-brown oak table, hugged by fourteen matching chairs, made up the contents of this recreation space. Large cupboards lined the far end of the room. They were painted with the same pale yellow, but here and there, brown stains clung onto the paint, giving it the impression that, indeed, not everything was in order.

The air felt heavy, despite the briskness of the room. The smell of polish seemed to be everywhere. The floor shone, and every step creaked as an echo in the room, bespeaking the hollowness that lived there. We took our places in rank almost without hesitation after Sister Dolores snapped her fingers. I sat near the bottom of the table. Annie Boyle was to my right and Jean O'Doherty flanked me on my left. Mary O'Brien was opposite me.

Sister Dolores shuffled to one of the cupboards and took from it a large cardboard box that she placed in front of her before she sat down at the head of the table. She opened the cardboard box and snapped a bundle of small, oval, transparent, plastic discs onto the wood table just in front of her. She leaned heavily into the table and took the transparent discs in her hand. She then got up clumsily from her chair and went around the table, throwing a few pieces of transparent, plastic discs in front of each of us. None of us stirred. Not one of us spoke a word. Sister Dolores then delved into the cardboard box again and withdrew another box from within. This box contained numerous, small, oval shapes of the Sacred Heart image that hung on the wall, replicating the heart with nails. Sister Dolores came around and threw the contents of this box in front of us. I turned over the discs that had fallen to my lot. The picture of the Sacred Heart was etched on every picture with those offensive nails. On the other side, I discovered the same heart pierced with a dagger. Written around the disc, both on the front and the back, were the words, "Sacred Heart of Jesus, I place all my trust in Thee."

The pictures were a fraction smaller than the plastic discs. I quickly concluded that, somehow, those pictures were to find their resting place between two plastic discs. Sure enough, Sister Dolores proceeded to show us all an example of the finished product. The sacred emblem was to be contained within the two plastic pieces that had exactly twelve tiny holes punched around the edge of the oval. The two discs on the front and back were held together by a variety of colored embroidery threads. It was easy to encase the picture within the plastic discs.

Sister Dolores instructed the group to pay attention. Some of the postulants at the bottom of the table strained and stretched to try and see how this project was to be accomplished. They did this out of concern for getting it right the first time. Sister Dolores inserted the picture oval in between the pieces of plastic. She made sure that the pieces of plastic matched perfectly and that the picture was securely in the center of the two plastic discs. With the discs between her thumb and finger of her left hand, she promptly took a small metal puncher and expertly snapped holes all around the rim. There were twelve holes, all at equidistance to one another. Sister Dolores then pulled out some red embroidery thread and a needle from another box in front of her. She cut the thread and tried to force it through a needle's eye. After several stabs, the thread went through the needle, and she grabbed it from the other side and pulled it through. She fashioned a knot at the end of the thread and tied it tightly. Sister Dolores stabbed the needle into the top hole of the disc.

She deftly drew the thread three times through the first hole, and then drew the thread into the top of the second hole. She held the disc so tightly that the tips of her fingers blanched. When she was halfway finished, she ordered all of us to start working on the discs. There were a few of us who were proficient at needlework. I noticed that Una Murphy, who was sitting next to Sister Dolores at the top of the table, did not seem to have any trouble starting the project. I slid the thread easily into my needle. Mary O'Brien could hardly hold the needle and thread together and struggled to get moving. When Sister Dolores got up to go to the cupboard, I snatched Mary's disc with the needle and thread and swiftly pulled it through. It was in Mary's grateful hands before Sister Dolores's eyes landed on them.

It appeared that we would have to be very productive and focused during every recreation hour. Mary was concentrating hard. While I was on my fourth disc, Mary was just finishing her first. As she started working on the second disc, she pulled the remaining thread from the first disc, rolled it in a little ball, and threw it in front of her. She was about to cut her scissors into a new string of thread for the second disc, when we heard a roar come from the top of the table that caused us all to stop with fright.

Within seconds, the atmosphere in the ice-cold room became threatening. Sister Dolores looked as if she was on fire as she expelled a tirade of ugly words at Mary O'Brien. She got up from her seat and hurtled towards Mary, her face inflamed with irritation. Her skin became splotched with angry blotches, signaling the menace that was about to be unleashed. She looked infectious. I felt frightened for Mary, because the manner in which Sister Dolores was approaching her, gave me concern that Mary might be at risk for bodily harm.

While Sister Dolores demanded that Mary kneel on the floor in front of her for having "disregarded the vow of poverty," Mary looked quite serene. She told me many months later, on one of our walks, that she was playing Mozart's *Concerto No. 5* in her head to deflect the harsh words that Sister Dolores hurtled at her. When Sister Dolores violently and verbally accosted her that night, her fingers were dancing over the keys of a piano that her imagination had conjured up to help her cope with the stress. She explained that she was so determined to learn this particular piece when it was first presented to her many years ago by her piano teacher because she was utterly amazed that Mozart had written this fully original piano concerto at the age of seventeen. She had devised a way to disassociate herself and escape the wrath of Sister Dolores by playing music in her head, a great mechanism to keep her sanity and self-control. She would have to use this unique method of disassociation many times in the next year.

Sister Dolores grabbed the small scrap of thread that Mary had just discarded from the table and unraveled it. She proceeded to rant about how the postulants would need to learn to save every scrap of thread they did not use. It could be used for other purposes. Nothing in the convent was ever to be thrown out or discarded if a second or third or fourth use could be found for it. Sister Dolores insisted that this was the essence of the vow of poverty, which we would all have to embrace. It just did not make any sense to me.

We sat riveted in our chairs, afraid to move. We were reminded that the sisters on the missions in America were working hard and sending money to Ireland for our upkeep and training. While Sister Dolores was continuing to spiral out of control, the chapel bell rang, summoning us to prayers. Mary was literally saved by the bell since, once that bell rang at eight o'clock, the convent was plunged into silence until after breakfast the next morning.

On my way to the chapel, I felt confused. How could we possibly concentrate on saying prayers downstairs after what had just occurred upstairs in that room? It was a paradox that presented itself on a weekly basis.

CHAPTER SEVENTEEN

THE LAY SISTERS

July 5, 1948

Sister Freda O'Donnell, fresh from the class of 1948, waited in eager anticipation for an assignment to teach abroad when her two years of training finally came to an end in Fairview Convent. During those years, she dreamed of going to Australia or South America. She had made a name for herself these past two years as a lover of poetry, and she liked to write. She also was able to draw anything when she had a pencil in her hand. She looked forward to teaching art one day. She also pondered the possibility of being assigned to Rome or Egypt. Chances to be assigned to North America or Canada were also distinct possibilities. Sister Freda O'Donnell had a sweet, singing voice and could play the violin. For the past two years, she had been forbidden to take up her instrument and play it. She looked forward to the day when she could.

With each new class of postulants, Sister Freda O'Donnell remembered the trauma of the punch she had been delivered at the beginning of July 1948. There had been fourteen members in her class. All fourteen looked forward to being released from Fairview Convent and sent to the mission lands this religious institution served. Sister Dolores and Sister Freda were both informed on July 5, 1948, that they would be staying in Fairview Convent as Lay sisters.

Sister Freda felt the cry in her throat, now long conditioned to silence, after two hard years in this place. She had spent her first year as a postulant and the second year as a novice. After the novitiate year, it was customary for each novice to receive a notice from the authorities in Rome to prepare to go to any part of the world that needed her services and talents. Most of the novices would teach in the multitude of schools run by the religious institution. Others would prepare to go to nursing school and become administrators of hospitals and clinics in the recesses of Africa or the outback in Australia. Sister Freda was assigned to help the cook, Sister Bridget Mary.

The blow of this notice regarding her assignment felled her immediately. Over the past two years, she had taken her turn helping Sister Bridget Mary prepare meals for the sisters, but she did this as part of a rotation system, ensuring that all postulants and novices took their turn helping with kitchen duties. Sister Bridget Mary was just three classes ahead of her, but in contrast to Sister Freda, she had always wanted to work in the kitchen. She had fully accepted the reality that she was destined to be a cook and serve in that capacity in Fairview Convent for the remainder of her life. Sister Freda, on the other hand, was totally unprepared for this moment known as Receiving the Obedience. Instead of navigating into missionary lands, Sister Freda would be confined to the shadows and work in the daily churn of feeding the community of sisters in Fairview Convent.

Sister Dolores was assigned to help the postulant mistress with the girls who first entered. She was content to do this. It gave her some power and control, and she would wield this power with all the negative energy that consumed her every day.

There were numerous applicants to the institution by young Irish girls from all over the country, anxious to give their lives for God's harvest. Sister Fintan, who was in charge of the convent at that time, was overjoyed that Sister Dolores was being given this job, because she would organize the work day, keep things running smoothly, and help the postulant mistress keep the annual classes of new postulants in their place.

Sister Dolores was perfect for that job. She calculated immediately that she would not let any postulant get away with anything, and she would help produce the groups of ecclesiastical robots that the congregation needed. She would eventually be assigned the job on a permanent basis.

After Sister Freda had time to process the devastating news, she became ill for the subsequent few weeks. She tossed in her fevered bed and festered with shame and disappointment. She wondered what her family would think about the seemingly menial task she was now burdened with fulfilling. She would be peeling vegetables and scrubbing pots and pans in obscurity for the rest of her life.

Her three sisters were nuns in other religious orders. Barbara was a principal in a school in Liverpool, England. Judith had graduated from nursing school and was now with her community in Glasgow, Scotland. She had helped found and set up a program for homeless mothers and children and already had received numerous accolades for her heroic efforts on behalf of the poor there. Gayle was in Boston teaching in a high school. Sister Freda agonized over how they would react. She felt like a failure. The doctor, who served the nuns when they were ill and who lived only a few miles away, told Sister Fintan that Sister Freda would not be ready for work for a couple of months.

Sister Freda had quickly descended into a severely depressed state, which encased her so that she could hardly move. After hearing her assignment, she felt like a block of concrete. On Dr. Murphy's orders, she was to receive no visitors. No one was allowed to talk to her. No one was permitted to go near her. Sister Freda was shaken, thinking about being trapped in the kitchen for the remainder of her days. She did not want to work in the kitchen. It was not what she had planned or hoped for after enduring the pain and challenge of the past two years. She wanted to experience liberation. She barely ate. She had nightmares when she closed her eyes. If she stayed, she would have the status of a Lay sister.

Lay sisters were novices who, after graduation from the novitiate, were appointed to conduct menial and mostly manual tasks in the convent. All who entered were quickly educated that such a status was considered a lowly one in the convent. Lay sister status essentially meant, for Sister Freda, that she would be cast aside, ignored, and become invisible as she labored to ensure that all meals were properly prepared from the cauldron of the kitchen. Lay sisters were easily identifiable because they had *Mary* at the end of their name. They did not change their names at the end of the novitiate and assume the name of a saint or a virtue. The others would choose the name of a saint and put *Mary* at the beginning of their name to honor Our Lady. Lay sisters always sat at the bottom of the table to take their meals.

Sister Freda was all too aware that she, like Sister Bridget Mary, would be separated from the rest of the body of sisters, even during prayers. Lay sisters sat at the back of the chapel. They did not have a prayer book. Instead of reciting morning lauds, evening vespers, and night compline, these nuns were to say multiple rosaries instead. At mass, the Lay sisters were not given a black muslin veil to cover their faces after they received Holy Communion, as was the practice for the remainder of the group. They could not recreate with the others. They had a lower rank than the youngest postulant who entered year after year.

Sister Freda O'Donnell would have to accept this assignment or decide to leave Fairview Convent. A part of Freda longed to return to her green fields and vibrant family. If she went home, she knew in her heart that her mother and father would receive her with open arms. So, she struggled with the decision that sent her into a pit of blackness for weeks. She struggled on her own in her room for many weeks before she came to her decision. Her spirit was broken. She eventually asked to speak to Sister Bridget Mary.

Every day for a week, Sister Bridget Mary was allowed to leave her kitchen duties and meet Sister Freda in a parlor near her bedroom. Sister Bridget Mary listened to Sister Freda's broken dreams. That was all she did. She was used to listening deeply and paying attention. She knew instinctively when a dish was cooked properly before she took it out of the oven. She knew without thinking how much salt or pepper a pot of potatoes needed before she poured milk into the pot and vigorously mashed the potatoes to a creamy consistency. When she knew there was something upsetting going on, she would deliberately keep aside some potatoes that held multiple lumps and orchestrated that this specific dish would go to a particular offender with some offensive spice mixed in.

Sister Bridget Mary was keenly aware of the need to keep her spirit alive, and when she needed a rest to refresh her spirit, she just went to the back scullery to sit down and write profusely. That exercise always provided therapeutic relief. Sister Bridget Mary was attuned to everything that was going on outside as well as in the recesses of convent life, even though she was confined to the kitchen for most of the day. She knew the time by looking out the kitchen window and reading the sky. She knew that a storm was brewing by the manner in which the birds were flying. She understood that it was going to rain when the leaves turned.

Sister Bridget Mary listened attentively until Sister Freda's face finally relayed to her that she had come to some peace. At that point, she uttered some quiet words. "Now, Freda dear, you know what to do." Those were the only words she uttered in the week she spent with Sister Freda. She knew the power of words and was keenly aware that the fewer that were uttered in this situation, the greater the clarity that would be heralded for Sister Freda. It was quite transparent to Sister Bridget Mary that the younger nun had moved through her pain. The wrestling was over. The fight was done. She had come to the end of her battle. After a few tortured weeks, Sister Freda emerged from her room. The combat she had engaged in was now over. She would now be known as Sister Freda Mary.

Sister Freda Mary wailed inside that day she heard about the slot to which she had been allotted. Her ground was taken from her. She was initially caught up in the stout winds of isolation and felt segregated, targeted to become invisible. Her hopes quickly evaporated. She had to surrender them. Her confidence had been trampled upon. Her mind and heart had to make a seismic shift. Finally, she accepted her new role and embraced it in the same way the sky embraces every storm that is flung at it. Things would settle in time. Having accepted this new reality, and having processed the hurt and feeling of humiliation and self-loathing that had engulfed her over the past few weeks, she emerged from her time with Sister Bridget Mary finally leaving behind the shock that had heretofore consumed her.

She decided to stay in Fairview Convent, knowing that she had a friend who would be with her in whatever was thrown at her in the road ahead. Now she knew she would have someone to help and support her, which gave Sister Freda Mary a stronger sense of assurance. Gradually, she felt her confidence return.

When Sister Freda Mary was finally able to get up and leave her room, the first person she encountered was Sister Mary Dolores. Margaret Folan had morphed into this new name, and nothing about her had changed. She sneered at Sister Freda Mary when she saw her. Sister Freda Mary absorbed the crush she felt, and in turn, made a mental note that Sister Mary Dolores would never be welcome in Sister Freda O'Donnell's kitchen. The line was drawn, and this alone gave Sister Freda Mary a feeling that she, at least, was getting a semblance of control back into her life.

Sister Bridget Mary and Sister Freda Mary became fast friends. They called each other "Freed" and "Breed." The two became a team instantaneously. They worked easily with each other, donned in their checked black-and-white aprons. Pots and pans and serving spoons never seemed to leave their hands.

By the time I arrived in Fairview Convent in 1966, Sister Freda Mary's face was a little more crinkled and her hands soaked in wrinkles. Her face held a perpetual smile of welcome. Almost twenty years in the kitchen had witnessed miles and miles of rosaries fingered and many a good conversation enjoyed with Sister Bridget Mary. She had become a proficient cook, but more than that, she was a wise and kindly woman who could pull only the positive part of life from the dreariest of situations. The postulants who had to perform kitchen duty confided in her on a regular basis. She could pull the arrow of her keen insight from her quiver when she detected the distress that was inflicted regularly on the young women who came in every day to wash the pots and clean the kitchen after each meal. She was careful in her approach to Sister Dolores's least favorite postulants.

Many wounds began to heal in that space. Every day, Sister Freda Mary worked to undo the damage that Sister Dolores dealt hourly. Sister Freda Mary's kitchen was a sanctuary in the wilderness, a place of comfort and healing. It was there that the most important lessons were learned, like the art of listening, of moving into the moment, of embracing the notion that true friendship has to be unconditional, and realizing that the gift of presence is the greatest gift of all. Sister Freda Mary and Sister Bridget Mary were the only two who were taken away in most hearts as the novices left Fairview Convent and ploughed their way into mission territories. The harshness they had experienced from Sister Dolores was eventually cast aside, and though the trauma she inflicted on their young lives was triggered now and again, it was the kindness of the two sisters in the kitchen that prevailed and became the fond memory of Fairview Convent. It was the sisters' tender ways, their friendly and caring dispositions that were recalled mostly by all who left Fairview Convent. Their way was etched in their thoughts. Their way stayed permanently with them and was mostly emulated as these young women forged their way to maturity.

The two nuns in the kitchen knew early on that Annie Boyle, of the postulant class of 1966, would eventually be assigned to the kitchen. Her initiation on the day she entered was abusive, and in their minds, was the beginning of Annie's trajectory to the kitchen. The violent episode with the mustard tore at their hearts, and they both took Annie under their wing in those early days. No one had the ability to raise her voice against this indignity. The episode would pass without anyone talking about it or processing it or addressing it. However, in the kitchen, it was a constant source of conversation as the two worked together and tried to figure out some resolution to this dastardly woman's evil ploys heaped upon these young, vulnerable women every day.

Sister Dolores had become the postulant mistress a decade ago and now had absolute authority over the postulants. No one had the power to intervene. Because of this, such abusive scenes had become so common that it became normal to these young women to be the object of scorn and derision. It had become so normal, in fact, and part of everyday life in Fairview Convent, that it was also accepted without complaint. Sister Bridget Mary and Sister Freda Mary would, at least, provide some place where the postulants would feel the warmth of welcome and care as the pots hopped and sizzled on the stoves and the breads baked in the huge ovens. It was all they could do, and it meant the world to the postulants.

CHAPTER EIGHTEEN

THE KITCHEN

Every Day—5:00 a.m. to 6:30 p.m.

The convent kitchen supplied the needs of more than sixty nuns who lived in Fairview Convent. The work in the kitchen was harried, tedious, and monotonous. Sister Bridget Mary and Sister Freda Mary had to arise at five o'clock in the morning to get the big pots on the boil for the huge casks of oatmeal that were required to provide a break from the fast that everyone was subjected to from six o'clock the previous evening. This was part of the rules of the convent that had to be rigorously adhered to. The kitchen cooks knew instinctively that the younger members were constantly ravenous with hunger. They always put extra oatmeal into the dishes that were served to the novices and postulants. Even the last one to take a dish, as it was passed to the end of the table, received a good dollop of oatmeal, which would keep her quite satisfied as she toiled with chores and classes until the noon meal. In rare moments, when they could absolutely ascertain which dishes would be put on the tables for the postulants, they would scoop a few spoons of honey into the hearty meal for a special treat. Phelim O'Connor, the farmer down the road, enjoyed caring for his bee hives, and every week he made a substantial donation of two pots of honey to the convent kitchen.

As well as taking care of the nuns who lived on the premises, Sister Freda Mary was responsible for preparing meals for Jimmy McGinty, who worked the convent land and milked the cows. On occasion, Phelim joined them in the scullery, and after Jimmy left to take care of his duties, stayed with the two cooks, chatting about every subject that the world and Ireland had to offer. While the members of the convent were not allowed access to newspapers, Phelim O'Connor bought a paper every day and saved them for the two nuns to read when they were able to take a break. Consequently, the two nuns in the kitchen were the most informed, outward looking, and visionary of anyone living within the thick walls there. In turn, the postulants they trusted got to hear how the rest of the world functioned while they lived in their bubble of isolation from it.

Jimmy McGinty was an important, additional link to their world. Jimmy was in his middle twenties by the time I got to the convent. He had a shock of black hair and the deepest blue eyes containing the essence of the sky. He was tall and strong. When I stole a glance at him here and there, when he passed through the garden, he reminded me of what I imagined Heathcliff looked like in Emily Bronte's *Wuthering Heights*.

From what I later learned during kitchen duty, Jimmy took over the convent farm when his father, Joe, retired and went to live with his sister in Dublin a few years ago. Jimmy had lived and worked with his father in the Gate Lodge after his mother died when he was four years old. He had been a bright young lad at school, but when he was fifteen years old, he decided to stay at Fairview Convent and help his father with the chores around the farm and care for the animals. He saw that his father was getting slower and finding it harder to complete all his duties and responsibilities.

Jimmy was officially hired by Sister Annunciation, the superior who had preceded Sister Fintan just before his father left. Sister Annunciation, who had been raised on her parent's farm, could see that Jimmy was more than able to handle the responsibilities of a farm. She was sorry to lose Joe, but she had noticed he was forgetting things and knew it was a good time for him to retire and go to Dublin to live with his sister. He had been a faithful worker and had trained his son well.

Hiring young Jimmy to replace him and secure the continuation of good service and oversight of the farm was the least Sister Annunciation could do to reward Joe's long, invested service to Fairview Convent. After his father left, Jimmy continued to supply the kitchen staff with daily banter as he took his meals at the table in the inner scullery.

When he went into town, he bought the nuns sweets and chocolates. That stash was hidden in a special spot on top of the highest shelf. The kitchen nuns had that treat on a daily basis. They enjoyed the news that Jimmy brought to them on a daily basis, as well. They knew what was happening in the town, and as time went on, learned about births and deaths and weddings and achievements of the local farmers and families. The nuns developed an interest in the local hurling teams and delighted in reading the scores and keeping up with the retirement of players and the hiring of the younger men who replaced them. While the rest of the nuns were in class, sewing in silence, cleaning all that was already clean without being able to interact with one another, or practicing in the choir, the kitchen spluttered and splattered with life.

Sister Bridget Mary and Sister Freda Mary worked hard as they scrubbed and rubbed and prepared meals throughout the day. No one ever interfered with the workings of the kitchen. No one lingered there. It was like a sovereign territory ruled equally by two people. You were welcome only if the two had vetted you, and together, had come to the conclusion that you could be trusted.

Once a week, the house superior came into the kitchen to get the long list of food the cooks would need to feed the hungry nuns. It was sufficient for her to appreciate that the kitchen help supplied the needs for the nuns in the convent to function. There was never any other exchange between the superior and Sister Bridget Mary other than the superior being handed a long list prepared by the chief cook. The superior kept a shrewd eye on the books and generally had a tight fist on the money. When it came to the demands of the kitchen's chief cook, she gave her what she wanted. In her kitchen, the usually mild-mannered Sister Bridget Mary was a force to be reckoned with if she was challenged in any way. She held the key to the well-being and health of the entire group. She was the most important person in Fairview Convent. She held the power. This was her space and very few were welcomed into it. Very soon, Sister Freda Mary began to realize the power she too possessed, and her heart soared when she saw the superior cower to Sister Bridget Mary's demands without question.

The food was delivered in bulk for the week, and even the truck driver, Cassidy Maloney, enjoyed his weekly visit to the nuns. After unloading the food, Cassidy enjoyed the fried eggs and bacon and homemade bread that waited on his plate. Cassidy Maloney owned the Food Market in town and was happy he had such good customers. The nuns paid their bills on time and made up a quarter of his weekly sales. The amount of their purchases rarely fluctuated, even for special occasions like Christmas and Easter. Cassidy often wondered about that, but brought an abundance of Christmas cakes and sweets for the nuns with his Christmas delivery. He also did that for customers who needed an extra hand at Christmas.

Cassidy Maloney was a kind and generous man. He was an avid reader when he found the time to indulge in this pastime. When he finished his books, he gave them to Sister Bridget Mary, who received them with great delight, and when she could find the time, proceeded to devour them with such a zeal he had never before witnessed. Occasionally, between meals, Sister Bridget Mary would recede to the inner scullery, take the book that was hidden in some old pot, and proceed to pour over each page. She seemed to savor and digest every word on every page, seldom taking time to come up for air. When she did so, her face was lit up, and she seemed to be transported to that place in the book, and she did not want to leave. She let the words absorb into her soul, such was the depth of her love for words. She seemed to hunger for them more than she hungered for food, and Cassidy Maloney provided for that in abundance.

Much of the food was supplied by the convent garden. The eggs and the milk came from the hens and the cows that were a part of the convent farm. Every day, Jimmy milked the cows in the morning and evening and gathered a multitude of eggs from the chicken coop. The farm kept Jimmy busy. He worked hard and he worked well and enjoyed the comfort of living next to the convent in his small house next to the lower convent gate. Once a month, he went to see his father in Dublin and stayed overnight with him and his aunt.

Jimmy enjoyed his work and his life. Saturday was his day off, so he made sure to get a local farm hand to fulfill the basic duties while he was absent. Every Friday night, Jimmy went to the local pub. He took his fiddle with him and enjoyed playing traditional Irish music with a few of his friends. The few free pints he received in payment for his musical efforts more than satisfied Jimmy. He received a few pounds a week from the nuns and saved most of it. His housing was free, he ate most of his meals in the convent kitchen, and his expenses were limited to ensuring that he had a good suit, shirts, and shoes for special occasions.

By the time Jimmy was in his late twenties, he had seen many classes of postulants and novices go through the rigor of Fairview Convent life. He saw them here and there, as he brought the cows through the pasture, and then more closely as he moved through the back garden on rare occasions. There was never a chance to have a conversation with any of them. He was instructed, when he got the job, that the only people he could communicate with were the house Superior and the two cooks in the kitchen.

He enjoyed the two cooks, and they all became fast friends. Their scullery was a refuge for Jimmy, and he looked forward to his mealtimes. There he shared stories with the two nuns around the big wooden table, often joined by Phelim O'Connor. They told jokes, discussed all manner of topics, predicted the weather together, and bantered in the scullery's hold. The state of the crops in the fields, the contents of the garden and its harvest, the condition of the barn, the ripeness of the greenhouse's contents, the firmness of the grapes on the vines, the state of the bushes that surrounded the property, and the health of the trees were all part of the musings between the friends. The kitchen withstood all political seasons and scandals.

The hue of the morning and evening skies compelled all of them to look up. There, in the gaze of the heavens, they heard the sounds of the larks, which ennobled their conversations. As they paused and became aware of the birdsong, they were often reminded that it was time to move to the next phase of the day. There was always a warm welcome in the kitchen for Jimmy, Phelim, and Cassidy. The tea kettle was always on the boil. In the heart of the convent kitchen, things seemed normal.

The work was hard in the kitchen and physically draining. It was constant. It was seven days a week. There was no break. The two Lay sisters never got a day off. On Christmas evening, the two sisters were not responsible for the evening meal; those were the only few hours they had off the whole year. If Sister Bridget Mary got sick, Sister Freda Mary worked all the more feverishly. She became very strong in the kitchen. She became fully engaged with all who came there. Her laugh resonated in the cavernous space at the same time the chapel was echoing chant. The kitchen glinted with life while the rest of the convent was muted in silence. Sister Freda Mary quickly began to savor life in the kitchen. Both she and Sister Bridget Mary had conversations that went to unfathomable depths. They embodied the reality that the most interior part of the convent, the part that no one saw or truly appreciated, flowed with imagination and energy. As the vegetable pots danced and bubbled on the flamed stoves, the spirit of the two in the kitchen was unencumbered. They brought together kindness, compassion, and concern. This is how life in its essence was supposed to be.

This space was a place of grace, lightness, and illumination. Having snapped alert, as dawn was still struggling out of the dark veil of morning, Sister Bridget Mary and Sister Freda Mary made dreams take wing. As they lugged and dragged the heavy pots and pans from the kitchen to the hot plates and made them sizzle with life, they developed a finely hewn sense of the humor contained in things. As the rest of the convent was buried in a sea of activity, straightjacketed in structure and order and predictability, the two in the kitchen sat atop the fray, secure in the ebb and flow of their lives.

In the kitchen, no days were ever the same. Outside the kitchen, the dull and uneventful was interrupted only by punishment for the slightest perceived infraction. Many scars and wounds were carried heavily into the kitchen. The bearers of such heaviness left the kitchen with wounds and scars bandaged by the aid of a listening ear and an understanding heart. There they received balm and respite and therapeutic recovery for their spirits. The healing flame of the kitchen was deeper than the classroom's burning core. That which Sister Dolores attempted to smother and erode, Sister Freda Mary and Sister Bridget Mary pulled back into life. The smudges that Sister Dolores rubbed into the hearts of the postulants were wiped away in the freshness of the kitchen, which became the place where strength was reinvigorated and spirits were uplifted for the postulants who were assigned kitchen duty every seven days.

I looked forward to my time in the kitchen. The nuns made sure I was fed extra fruit, and they had a slice of wheaten bread drowned with a surplus of butter and jam for me to eat before I left. The kitchen was a place of warmth and radiance and restoration. I was always rejuvenated when I left there. Sister Bridget Mary and Sister Freda Mary stirred oceanic curiosity in me. They talked about family and let me talk about mine. It felt good for me to hear my own voice. They never once made fun of or mimicked my northern accent. They told stories and jokes as they waited for the dishes to steep and the soup for the evening meal to cook to finish.

As September 1966 shrank into October 1966, I found solace one day a week in the kitchen. By that time, the three postulants from County Kerry were exempt from kitchen duty. In the kitchen one day, after the noon and evening meals, the creative rock inside me was cleaved. I drew deeply from the experience the kitchen provided me, which lasted for the remainder of the week. It became my forge. The kitchen was like the hearth at home, stoking the flames that pushed through the frigidity of the chapel and damp coldness seeping through every wall. It felt as though Fairview Convent was designed to create a permanent chill, and it fulfilled that function well.

The God of the chapel was a different God from the one who reigned in the kitchen. God was truly alive in the kitchen. I had found a new forge and fire there. The anvil I found in the kitchen taught me to keep looking forward in its flame.

CHAPTER NINETEEN

HAVE A LOVELY DAY

On October 30, 1966, before the recreation period began, Margaret Logue and I were summoned by Sister Dolores to the corner of the recreation room. Without hesitation, we both knelt down in front of the large brown frame of Sister Dolores. By now, we knew we had to kneel on the floor before her and look down until she summoned us to look up at the sound of her voice. This ritual was introduced to us a week after we entered the convent. I suspected the thinking behind this act of subservience was to remind us that we were less that she was. Even in my lowest bow to her, I never felt like that.

At last, her voice boomed into the air, signaling that we could look up at her. Her face looked distorted at that angle, and I always felt a giggle in my throat, which I forced myself to ignore. Margaret Logue was born in Dublin and had grown up there. Her family had been involved in the 1916 Easter Rising. Her great uncles had fought alongside the martyrs of the rebellion, and their subsequent generations held them in high esteem. Margaret had grown up speaking Gaelic in her home and was fluent in her native language. When she emitted that first Gaelic response within earshot of Sister Dolores one day on a walk to the gate, she was immediately verbally attacked and commanded to stop. All she had uttered spontaneously was, "*La brea ata ann*" ("The lovely day"). Margaret Logue saw the storm clouds gather on the face of Sister Dolores very quickly. For punishment, Margaret Logue was told to write out "*La brea ata ann*" ten thousand times during recreation. It took her weeks to accomplish. She spent recreation hour writing feverishly, and if her hand cramped during that time, Sister Dolores took a ruler from a drawer and slapped her hands until she resumed writing.

There had been a class lecture following the infraction, wherein Sister Dolores roared that we were being prepared to go to America, Canada, or Australia and would speak English only. The native tongue had no place in Fairview Convent. When Margaret had completed her punishment, we were all instructed to meet after the noon meal beside the incinerator, a fixture that was placed at the end of the garden wall. It was little more than a big, tin barrel. The wind seemed to pick up in that corner of the garden. Sister Dolores instructed Margaret Logue to bring the reams of paper that held the thousands of lines of the phrase she had spoken on her walk weeks before. Some of the paper was splattered in blood.

Sister Dolores snapped at Margaret Logue to put the bundle into the incinerator. Sister Dolores had a box of matches ready to strike to set the papers aflame. Margaret's face was drenched in tears as she stepped forward to throw the first batch of her precious cargo into the fire. Those pages were consumed by the fire quite readily. With the second batch, Margaret's reach was interrupted as she stumbled toward the incinerator. Some of the papers were caught in the flame, but a huge amount was snatched by the wind that was marching vigorously around the garden. The ignited papers quickly flew into the air, dancing in the delight of freedom. My first instinct was to clap, and I could see many smirks pointed in the direction of Sister Dolores, who, by now, was ordering us all to go out to the pasture beyond the garden and rescue the papers that had taken wing.

The three Kerry postulants were at the garden gate first, as the rest of us absorbed this wonderful lesson that the Irish language was teaching us. You can never get rid of the DNA of this great intrinsic gift of our culture. I wanted to sing as the Irish pages took flight into the air and showed us what true freedom really looked like. There was no way these pages would ever be retrieved. They were gone to the four regions of Ireland, unbound and unshackled. The wind took Margaret Logue's pain away, and she returned to the convent feeling that she was the victorious one.

CHAPTER TWENTY

THE SACRISTY

November 1, 1966

The very next day after the paper burning, Margaret and I were summoned to get on our knees before Sister Dolores. We were both aware that Sister Dolores had an extra razor edge to her. I wondered if this had anything to do with the flight of the Irish language. I smothered a smile as I thought of all those pieces of paper telling the Irish nation that it was a lovely day. Sister Dolores waited five minutes before speaking. We actually did not know whether to look at her or the floor at one point. I cast my eyes toward the floor and waited. I pondered the power of the wind and the fact that the language could never be harnessed.

Sister Dolores moved her right foot the way a bull pushes into the grass before he rushes. I dreaded what was to come. I did not look at her, but I am sure that Margaret Logue still wore a smile on her face from the great deliberations of the day before. Words suddenly splattered from Sister Dolores on top of us in a spray of venom.

"You two will be assigned to help Sister Mary Rose in the sacristy until the end of February. You will make sure that the holy vessels are never touched directly by your unworthy hands. You will wear white gloves to touch them. Only the blessed hands of the priest can touch these holy items. The holy linens used at Mass will be spotless, and the sacristy itself will gleam. Now, away with you two."

Her words spat into the air. A threat remained in her throat. I felt a new weight on my shoulders. It was as if the invisible mantle of misery was pushing me deeper into the ground. I was determined to ignore it. The job in the sacristy did indeed come with additional responsibilities. I came to realize very quickly, even after a short time in this convent, that pushing into the tread of chores willingly, releases a sense of control and freshness and newness, a feeling that brought a fragrance all its own. I could learn to fight or embrace the various challenges that were set before me. I learned quickly that if I embraced the obstacles constantly thrown at me, I could make them into stepping stones. If I did not embrace the challenges on a daily basis, life became a dreary drudge, and there was enough of that to face as day receded into night.

I remembered how Sister Freda Mary and Sister Bridget Mary were so welcoming, and that thought made me smile, a smile that took over my face as I got up off the floor. Sister Dolores was much too irritated to notice the smile, and Margaret and I went back to the recreation table to cut and paste and thread the Sacred Heart badges to be sold for the foreign missions.

The following morning after breakfast, Margaret and I went into the sacristy to meet with Sister Rose. We both stood at the entrance just inside the door and watched as Sister Rose, a tall, thin woman with dark eyes that looked like pools of black sadness, busied herself with work. When she turned, we saw that she wore a flush on her cheeks, and her breathing was heavy with concentration. She had furrowed brows that were set like concrete in the middle of her forehead.

She paced around the large room, opening drawers to count contents. Eventually, she lifted the Mass vestments and opened a wide door to a wardrobe at the other side of the sacristy There, with some effort and difficulty, Sister Rose heaved the sacred robes onto a steel, horizontal rod that held the entire array of vestments in assorted colors, which were worn at Masses for all the different liturgical seasons and cycles. I was struck by the color in that wardrobe, but the door slammed quickly, and the color was gone as swiftly as it appeared.

A quick glimpse around the sacristy showed that it was clean and polished and scrubbed. It was ordered to perfection.

The shelves were neatly laden with towels and altar cloths in various colors, representing the various liturgical seasons celebrated by the church. The glass above a set of utensils used for Mass gleamed and reflected cleanliness beyond anything I had ever experienced. Sister Rose eventually acknowledged the two of us standing at the door and gestured for us to come in further. I had the impression that she resembled my mother, but when she came closer, I realized she must be a good deal older. The long veil and headpiece ensured that Sister Rose's face was framed in a shroud of white material, like all the other sisters in the convent. She seemed to have some hesitation in her walk. Every step she took was done with deliberate caution.

Perhaps it came from the fact that the chapel was generally dim, and the flicker of the tabernacle candle in the sanctuary of the chapel was usually all Sister Rose had to rely on as she completed her duties there. Maybe the appearance of extreme care was just an extension of her work in that space as she had to make sure she negotiated the multiple steps to the altar in a half-light. She had to learn to walk and work in the dimness of the chapel. Her every move was slow and deliberate. She wore the weight of her responsibilities, and that mantle of heaviness made her even slower. She was responsible for all the sacred vessels used on the altar. They had to be handled with great care and stored under lock and key after every celebration of Mass. The vestments for Mass and benediction had to be folded in a certain way and hung in the wardrobe with the greatest of veneration.

Sister Rose smelled of incense. She had a nice smile for us when she came toward us. As we stepped further into the sacristy, we felt dwarfed by the high ceilings and expansive space. The floor was highly polished. Everything gleamed.

"Let me bring you into the sanctuary and show you what you have to do," she said after she smiled at us.

She did not even ask us our names. We trotted obediently after her, and she again assumed her cautionary approach into the sanctuary through the door to her left. The sanctuary of the chapel was a stark contrast to the lightsome sacristy we had just exited. The sanctuary contained the tabernacle where the Blessed Sacrament was kept. There, according to our Catholic faith, the presence of Jesus resided in the host that was located behind the curtain inside a square box decorated by a small symbol of the cross.

The sanctuary was a quiet space, a dark space. A red candle pulsed, tangibly expressing in its burst of flame the presence of Christ in this place of worship. The two windows in the sanctuary were made of colored glass. The one on the right of the tabernacle depicted the nativity scene and the other showed Jesus hanging on the cross at Calvary. There we were, in the dimness of the sanctuary, confronted by the basic tenets of our faith.

The divine child was born in a stable surrounded by animals, and his ending showed the excruciating agony of his death by torture and ultimate asphyxiation. All of a sudden, while I was feeling the grip of despair, the sun hit the windows, and a prism of color embraced the walls of the sanctuary and speckled us in a rainbow of bright colors, which changed with our every movement. I held my hands out to the light and played with the colors that glided over my hands. When the opportunity presented itself in the days ahead, I went into the sanctuary and played with the colors as often as I could.

Sister Rose was kindly disposed and easy to work for. As long as the floor and vestment closets were gleaming and in order, as long as the sacred vessels were glinting, and as long as the tabernacle candle was replaced every Saturday morning, she was content for the two of us to work together without much supervision. Sister Rose seemed to enjoy the fact that we were willing to learn everything there was to know about the sacristy, and we followed her instructions with energy. We both appreciated being out of the gaze of Sister Dolores. Every day, Sister Rose made sure that we took particularly good care of the sacred white linens used for the morning Mass. After the priest left the premises, Sister Rose made her way cautiously to the altar to retrieve the linens. It was our responsibility after breakfast to ritually wash the linens three times in the sink with a change of water each time, roll them in a white towel, and when almost dry in the early afternoon, take them to a special area in the laundry and iron them to perfection. If we left a crease in the linens, Sister Rose did not mind. She told us that the priests, who came to say Mass every morning, generally would not notice such a small detail. After all, she concluded, the priests rotated daily from St. Finian's, the local boy's boarding school, and seemed fatigued by the time they rolled into the sacristy just before the seven o'clock hour every morning.

The priests had to drive five miles to the convent and be back to teach the first classes at 8:30 a.m. Most of the priests who came to the convent taught the young men who went to the school, preparing them for the toughest university entrance examinations. The competition for places at university was very competitive, and the priests at St. Finian's were proud of their successes every year.

Not one priest spoke to Sister Rose in the morning. There was a silent nod when the priest entered the sacristy, and then she left the priest alone to vest. She entered the sanctuary every morning just before seven o'clock. She turned on the lights in the sanctuary, causing the altar's space to be illuminated, and then she climbed the six steps to light the two candles on the altar. She then checked that the tabernacle key was on the altar and descended the steps with care and took her assigned seat near the back of the chapel. After Mass, the priest placed the Mass vestments on the wooden rail in the sacristy and left as quietly as he had entered. There was something about the place that did not encourage lingering.

October and November passed, and December came as imperceptibly as day rolls into dusk. The regimented days tumbled into one another, and in the folds of each, we became further removed from the reality of the world just outside the convent walls. Since our entrance in September, none of us had put her feet outside convent property. Each hour had its familiar rhythm, and we all moved accordingly.

One day after lunch at the beginning of December, when the linens had been ironed and placed in the drawer, Sister Rose asked me to wait in the sacristy until the package of unleavened hosts used for Mass was delivered by Tom Gorman. I was further instructed that when Tom arrived with the hosts, I was to open the outside door that led to the sacristy, take the package from Tom Gorman, and then place the container in the top right-hand drawer just inside the sacristy. It was just after two o'clock, and Sister Rose told me that the package should be delivered within a half hour. I stood at attention beside the sacristy window, keeping vigil for Tom Gorman.

Sister Rose's request had surprised me, because the postulants were not supposed to open the door to anyone. This job was assigned to one of the Professed sisters, and she was known as the porter. This job had been assigned to the tall nun who could be seen now and again having to decide which door to open when different bells rang simultaneously. It was her responsibility to answer all the doors. By now, of course, three months into my time served as a postulant, I had learned not to ask questions. I obediently stood and waited by the sacristy window.

An hour passed, and I continued to keep vigil for Tom Gorman. The sacristy window had a view of the slope of the meadow that overlooked Lake Fennan. The outside looked expansive and fresh, and I felt renewed just looking outside that window. As I pondered the scene out there, I saw the landscape before me forever changing. At one time, clouds dimpled like curdled milk walking through the sky at a brisk pace. At other times, birds flew in the breeze. The window presented a living, changing canvas. The open space outside poured with an expansiveness that made the confinement of the sacristy all the dimmer and gripping.

In the distance, clumps of wool-bound bodies, head bent, nudged into the grass stubble. The sheep stood at every angle, full of concentration, no doubt oblivious to the presence of the other sheep in the field. They were isolated feeders. They munched vigorously, scattered in the same field, eating the same grass, and yet seemed to totally ignore one another. There was no interaction, no connection. Each was totally solitary. I stood entranced at the window. As I was gazing at the sheep grazing,

I realized that I was connected to very few of the nuns in this convent. I felt a bit like one of the sheep on that far hillside. I did admit, though, that I had a relationship of sorts with Mary, Nuala, Annie, and the two nuns in the kitchen. That was the extent of my trust and even that felt limited at times.

I wanted to inhale the view before me and not let it go. I became the view as I let it gradually soak into me. I tumbled into it as easily as I would into green dough in a bowl. The harshness and hardship of the past few months had dragged me to the bottom of myself, and I wanted to remain in this glassed moment for as long as possible. A mirror could not reflect the scene back to me. I immersed myself in it and let it sweep into me. I felt momentarily unfettered, unchained, and free. I felt I could touch the changing sky if I just reached beyond my fingertips. The minutes sped by.

I felt an ache in my back, but continued to stand, mesmerized by the pleasant peace that the window brought to me. There was no sign of Tom Gorman and the hosts as the sun slowly fell from the sky. The late afternoon's smudge was vanquished by wisps of spidery mist as it came off the lake. I felt a yawn come from deep inside. I was beginning to feel cold. Time continued its course. A faint, pink froth left by the waning sun poured like pink milk onto the horizon. I became part of the fading light. The brush of evening began to paint its stillness and penetrated the dim sacristy. Finally, I could see the hard, granite shelf of darkness use its lid to seal all light out. I stood still in the sacristy. I looked to the left. The only light pulsed red in the sanctuary.

At this late hour, there was still no sign of Tom Gorman. I learned much later that Tom was a retired postman and had decided he wanted to do some volunteer work for the church after his retirement. All Tom wanted in return was for the nuns and priests to pray for his soul when he died. He had been wild in his youth. While he was able to keep his job, he became a regular at the local pub in town after his wife died, shortly after they were married. He lost his faith. He did not go to Sunday Mass for years. In his later years, he suffered from depression and had visions of himself engulfed by eternal flames because of the excesses of his indulgences.

He wanted some tangible form of security and believed the prayers of these people secluded from the world would help him gain entrance through the pearly gates. He undertook keeping the local churches, monastery, and convents supplied with hosts for Masses. There was not a religious house, rectory, or any other premise where Mass could be said that went without its supply of hosts. Tom's devotion resulted in ensuring that every worthy woman, man, and child who was free from mortal sin would receive the Body of Christ every Sunday morning at Mass. This was Tom's gift to his local community.

The nuns and the priests received daily Holy Communion since they went to Mass every day; hence, Tom was kept busy with his volunteer work. He had made up his own schedule and was on the road three times a week. Three times a week, he went to the local cloistered nuns, who made the hosts, and picked them up in neat, little, cardboard boxes, each marked carefully for its assigned destination. On December 3, 1966, Tom Gorman had no intention of delivering hosts to Fairview Convent. He had delivered a week's supply the day before.

Just before evening prayers, Sister Rose snapped on the light switch and seemed startled by my presence at the window. She smothered her alarm immediately.

"What are you doing here?" she whispered anxiously.

"Sister Rose, I am waiting for Mr. Gorman to arrive with the hosts as you instructed me to do."

Sister Rose looked stricken with my explanation. "I think it is too late for Tom to come now," she muttered silently. "Go into the chapel. It is almost time for evening prayers."

Sister Rose was trembling and appeared confused as she uttered these words. I felt a knot in my back and a soreness creeping through me. I hastened to the chapel and took my place just before prayers began. I had stood in the sacristy for well over two hours. No one had noticed my absence around the convent because it was known that being assigned to the sacristy meant long hours of duty, and those hours changed from day to day.

I had been content enough to stand by the window at the edge of twilight. Just before Sister Rose had entered the sacristy, rain had begun to fall, and the window rattled as the wind picked up speed. I had felt the sweetness of peace within myself, a feeling that I had not had for months. It was as if I had stepped out of a suit of armor and felt the greening of life again. I became part of the freedom of the trees swaying in the wind, felt the ebb and flow of the lapping of water pushing against the bank of the lake. I took the greatest pleasure seeing the flight of birds as they whirled and twirled in the brisk breeze. I felt myself relax. I had the chance of exploring the crevices of longing in my heart. I felt the stirring of a great longing take hold of me and took great pleasure in the feelings I did not want to control. I breathed deeply again and again. I was able to carve out for myself a sense of movement within this rigid block of concrete to which I was now bound.

For a short period of time, I had discovered a part of myself. That inner core was a small portion of a trajectory that made me leap beyond the window and become connected to something alive and vibrant again. I had been enriched. Sister Rose's memory lapse had provided me an opportunity to defy the regimentation for only a few hours, but it was sufficient for me to be shaken into the embrace of something beyond myself, firing my imagination, and delighting my senses, though I was still completely confined in what felt like the bowels of this place. Despite my physical containment, my spirit could still span great distances. I could feel the sky again, even touch it, such was the sense of soaring that took hold.

The garment of darkness that had encompassed me had been turned inside out as I seamed, fibered, and bathed in a few hours of deep contentment. The stiffness of the vigil had enabled me to leap into another dimension, and I felt the strong vibrant feelings of youth. I felt human. I had moved through the ink of night and had grasped a glint of color and the glow of being able to feel good again.

I was quickly caught up in the routine again. After night prayers, I felt an urgency to get into bed as soon as possible.

My back was sore, but I ignored the ache. I felt some other sense settle and take hold of me, and I moved into it very easily, accepting the profound sense of joy it brought. I wrapped my cardigan around me as if to keep the joy from escaping into the silence that took hold of the dormitory. I settled into the quiet comfort, taking great pains not to make any noise. I stifled the deep moan that came from my throat. Very soon, I was asleep, soaked in the flush of pleasure.

CHAPTER TWENTY-ONE

The Power of a Whisper

The Scullery—December 5, 1966

I fell asleep in the stillness. When I awoke, I felt harnessed and trapped by the silence that enveloped me. My one great desire was to speak and have a conversation with someone. I missed the banter and bright, spontaneous humor of home. I missed the noisy hearth. I missed the spill of words around the fireplace. I missed the flame and the crackle and the spark of the fire when I felt a burning in the night, listening to stories being told about times long ago. Those stories were shared by neighbors, who recited tales from memory, probably embellishing some part of it in the telling. Some of them were gifted storytellers. Others were poets who listened and absorbed the lesson of the tales told and passed those lessons on in various other ways.

The day following the long sojourn in the sacristy, I was assigned to the kitchen to wash the dishes and help with cleaning duties after lunch. Sister Bridget Mary came to the sink to help me with the washing. I found myself lamenting to her that, in spite of my best efforts, things around me remained the same. Sister Dolores would never change. I felt the weight of monotony. I felt stuck. I felt lonely.

She must have sensed my total frustration. After the dishes were put away, with at least a half hour before I had to be in the sacristy, she invited me into the scullery at the back of the kitchen. There she produced a mug of tea loaded with sugar and milk and two slices of brown, wheaten bread slathered in butter and heaped with gooseberry jam that sat on the bread like a mountain peak. Sister Freda Mary joined us.

"I am going to tell you a little story. I want you to listen carefully. Sometimes we have to be like fermenting yeast. What we leave fermenting on the shelf for one hour, changes by the next hour. Change is often imperceptible. We sometimes cannot see it. It is in the smallest of things. If we listen carefully and respond appropriately, we can be like the yeast that changes the essence of things. The smallest things can be powerful and become agents of change. Sometimes all you have to do is wait."

Sister Bridget Mary had a smile on her face and in her eyes as she fiddled with the pen in her hand. It was relaxation time in the scullery. We embraced the space for a little while and listened to Sister Bridget Mary take flight. We gladly accompanied her, enjoying the wheaten bread and the sugary, milky tea all the while.

"It is a light movement at first, and then a slight rustle. The little sound is barely audible, but it makes those who are attentive stop and stop some more. It is a different sound. It certainly is not like anything anyone has ever heard before. It is not a mumble. It is not a voice; it is something that meanders through the cadences of voices. It enchants in the tangle of words. It delights in pauses and ponderings. It shudders its way into thoughts. It makes words tumble and roll and catapult great distances. It comes from the center of things. It lives in the center of things. It lives vibrantly in the heart of things. It is self-sustaining. It holds substance and depth. For those who notice and observe and linger, it slowly becomes quite clear that this rustle of sound is a barely discernible whisper. It leaps in the wind and dances in the contour of clouds.

"The whisper is free and unencumbered. It stretches its wings into the day and remains alive in the night. The night is when the whisper is best heard. In the night's hush, the whisper pays attention to darkness and finds light in blackness. In the night, it takes flight and cradles the moon in its softness. It stands on the chin of mountaintops and views a panorama that no one else can see. It can bend roads and still waters like mirrors. It is not shackled by anyone or anything. It spreads into every idea. It does not attach itself to any border.

"The whisper scrambles beyond words. It dances in the margins of pages. It tiptoes through fragments of thoughts yet unfinished and shifts and sifts them in a new and fresh direction. The whisper sits in the sunrise. It creeps to the edges of great boulders, obstacles for most things, and peers easily over the ledges of the edges. Sometimes the whisper sails in the creases of waves. It is always in its movement there. It is rarely heard. Sometimes in the middle of a storm, it hushes in hope and beacons to other harbors not yet mapped. The whisper nestles in the seam of life. It challenges new wings to strengthen to flight when they are held shackled to the ground.

"The whisper draws colored patterns in the air between the colors of the rainbow, piercing way behind the rainbow. Very few see behind the rainbow; just beholding the color is enough. The whisper seeps beyond what we can behold. When most are disinterested in the climb, the whisper sits on the tops of the highest trees, straining for sight of distant lands, yet sometimes finding those distant lands right inside its heart.

"The whisper knocks on closed doors when houses are locked in slumber. It probes the depth and hugs the width of all things. It sits at dinner tables, even when the shallow chatter and dish clatter seem to swallow it up. The whisper is best heard by people sitting around the fire like flames burning in the night. Sometimes the whisper sighs. Very few hear the long, deep sigh of the whisper. It is in this deep vastness of the sigh that she feels pain.

"Pain stirs her. Sometimes she wonders if she could actually become a voice with a unique sound, but always she reaches the same conclusion: is she meant to become a more intense whisper, like that of the gentle breeze that reveals God's embrace or the sliver of morning, furnaced by the sun's awakening, which never needs a word to capture it? She did know that, as a whisper she could, at a moment's notice, spread across her world on wings that are steady and supple. She can move more powerfully than any words that are etched in ink. She knows that, unlike words, she cannot be contained.

"The whisper knows that she can make her quiet way, sprawl and spiral onto pages in an effort to make words do something new. Her way is like no other, and very few have discovered it. Her way refuses to sit lifeless on pages. She refuses to be crumpled or creased or disposed of. You cannot throw a whisper into a bin like a piece of paper.

"The whisper takes hold and creates surprises and an openness to being awakened by those surprises. She shapes words to give them content that is more meaningful. The whisper delves into her own stillness and notices the drone, the chatter, the rumble of sameness all around her, and decides not to become part of it.

"She decides, in the cusp of her own astute keenness, that she is called to be fresh and to push the stale and stagnant words that are around her into new earth, to experience a new, appealing fragrance that she has never before encountered. She ensures that change will come as imperceptibly as night crawls into dawn. The whisper is not called to speak. The whisper may not be meant to be heard at all, but because she is there, words that are eventually articulated will be heard in a completely new way, in a different way, in a different time, and in a different place. The whisper is part of something that we cannot see or feel or taste or touch or even hear right now.

"The whisper is the splash in the wave, the bob of the ocean, the creak in the door, the crack in the pot, the fleetness of foot, the tick of the clock, the passing and dart of shadows, the plop in the puddle, the zing in the arrow, the space between words, the lilt in the song, the curl in the smoke, the heave of the breath, the fade in the bloom, the tightness of knots, the descent of a leaf, the print in the snow, the spring in the step, the breath of dawn, and the soft glow of twilight. These are places where very few abide for any length of time. Whispers do have vibrations that eventually can be understood. They take journeys and eventually arrive at their destinations. They live where words are not yet formed and where ideas have not yet taken breath.

"Whispers sometimes make their home in the dark for a long period of time. Every so often, if we are really seeking and searching and listening, they will come to us as gentle breezes, awakening us to something new and powerful, bringing us to the vast realization that change has, in fact, happened, and that a strong, vibrant river still flows under the deepest ice. Whispers often bring us to that place where homage lies. They make us bow low, notice, and bring us into their stillness where only God can be found."

Sister Bridget Mary stopped her thoughts. Both Sister Freda Mary and I were caught up in her words. Quite frankly, I did not want her to stop talking. I felt my energy return, and my zest become a little more tangible and secure. Instinctively, I knew exactly what Sister Bridget Mary wanted to convey to me. I had felt a little of that hope waiting in the sacristy the night before. Now, I did not feel so alone. I pinched into the plate with my right finger and thumb and enjoyed the last crumbs of the brown bread and the well-sugared, gooseberry jam.

CHAPTER TWENTY-TWO

THE REPLACEMENT

December 2, 1966

Sister Rose's forgetfulness began to be noticed that day in early December 1966. It became clear to both Margaret Logue and me that Sister Rose was not paying much attention to the detail that the work in the sacristy demanded. The day after asking me to wait for Tom Gorman in the sacristy, we were riveted with a new level of fear when we saw Sister Rose at the entrance of the chapel on her knees before evening prayers. She had to kiss the shoes of all of us who entered the chapel and ask for our forgiveness. I felt humiliated for her. We postulants had come to expect that we would be punished for the slightest perceived infraction, but Sister Rose had been professed and in the convent for numerous years. A different kind of concern unsettled us, and we did not have the opportunity to discuss it on any level.

I had not thought beyond the two years of training in Fairview Convent. I did not want to entertain the notion that this punishment could possibly travel with me and be part of my life in the future. It was definitely very troubling to have Sister Rose kiss my shoes when I went into the chapel for evening prayers.

It was now the season of advent in the church's liturgical calendar, and the crib was about to be assembled just inside the sanctuary. The dark-purple color of the advent season hung over the convent. The sanctuary was polished and scrubbed, and the gold-colored vestments used for the Christmas Midnight Mass were unearthed from the vestment vault. These gold vestments were used only for the Christmas Mass and re-vaulted as soon as Mass was over.

A few days after her punishment began, Sister Rose came out of the sacristy just before Mass. We expected her to mount the steps to light the candles on the altar. Instead, however, she came out of the sacristy and went straight to her place in the chapel after turning on the lights of the sanctuary. I sat frozen, wondering what was going to happen. Within a few seconds, Sister Annunciation, the nun in charge of the house, got up from her place in the chapel and went to poke Sister Rose in the back. A short conversation took place, and Sister Rose got up from her seat and crept with some difficulty up the six steps leading to the altar to light the candles.

The next day, just two weeks before Christmas, Sister Rose was no longer around. She simply had disappeared. It was as if she had never existed. No one mentioned her name. No one knew where she had been sent. Wherever she was, she went without saying any goodbyes to Margaret or me. By now, Margaret and I knew that questions were not welcome.

Sister Annunciation lit the candles at the beginning of Mass for the following two days. After that, Sister Tabor was introduced to us as we went about our morning duties in the sacristy after Mass.

Sister Tabor was a short, heavy nun who seemed to rumble as she walked. Huge spectacles sat on the edge of her large nose. Her breathing was labored and shallow, and she seemed to sweat all the time. She always carried a small, white towel with her to wipe her face regularly. After each swipe, the small, white towel was balled into the pocket of her long, brown habit. All her movements were slow.

On her first day in the sacristy, she told Margaret and me that she had a heart condition and required much rest. This seemed a lot of information to give to us postulants, but we soon discovered that our energy suited Sister Tabor greatly. Sister Tabor's only task was to putter around the sacristy before and after Mass, completing the bare essentials of making sure the vestments for the priest were laid out properly and put away after he left.

Sister Tabor created much drama with the simplest of tasks. She made the most of her stage in the morning as she approached the altar to light the candles before morning Mass. She definitely wanted to let everyone watching her appreciate that this task alone was more than sufficient for her for the day. She inched slowly up the steps of the altar, briefly held onto the altar to steady herself and get her bearings and balance, struck a match, and then struggled to make contact with the wick. Her hands shook before the match ignited the candles to flame. Often it took multiple strikes before the wick blazed to a flicker. I felt like clapping when I saw the candles come to life each morning. I was not quite sure if Sister Tabor was being theatrical or not.

For those who were dozing off in the chapel after an hour of morning prayers and meditation each morning, this little piece of early-morning drama became comical relief. There seemed to be a collective sigh of relief once this gargantuan task was completed, and Sister Tabor returned to her seat in the chapel. It was generally acknowledged that Sister Tabor would spend hours in bed after breakfast, recovering from this enormous expenditure of energy. The superior of the house just accepted that the morning drama would continue to unfold on a daily basis and said nothing about it. She was not going to assign Sister Tabor to other duties. In the sacristy, she was contained, and the young postulants would carry the load.

Sister Tabor had come from the African mission months ago for a break because of the challenges to her health. She had done very little in Fairview Convent during those months. As far as Sister Annunciation was concerned, however, it was time for Sister Tabor to come out of the cocoon of her self-appointed rest and retirement. It did not matter that Sister Tabor had spent forty-two years in Africa. It did not matter that she was approaching eighty years of age. She had to continue to be useful and work. Sister Annunciation concluded that, if Sister Tabor was going to reside in this convent, she would be expected to pull her weight.

Sister Annunciation had been instructed by Mother Benedicta in Rome not to let anyone know that Sister Rose had been placed involuntarily in a locked retirement facility in Dublin. I found out from Sister Mary Freda because every time I had to perform kitchen duty, I wondered out loud where my former, gentle supervisor had disappeared to. Sister Annunciation assumed it was the perfect time to get Sister Tabor moving and productive. The job as Sacristan was perfect for her.

By now, Margaret Logue and I had learned the demands of the work in the sacristy, and our efforts and enthusiasm suited Sister Tabor, who was kind and easy to work for when she was around. She left us to do the work. We organized the vestments. We polished the woodwork, swept the floor, and ensured that the holy utensils were fully washed and carefully stored. Sister Tabor was fussier than Sister Rose had been about washing and ironing the linens. Sometimes Sister Tabor would supervise the ritualistic washing of the linens. She watched us as we washed each batch three times in different water, rolled them in a bright white towel, and then, after a few hours after the bleach of the wrap, to make sure the linens were ironed to perfection. There could be absolutely no creases in the sacred linens. She examined them carefully every morning. As long as this rule was adhered to, Sister Tabor was satisfied. As long as Sister Tabor was perceived as working, Sister Annunciation was agreeable enough to her.

After all the long years spent in Africa, Sister Tabor found the limits of the strict convent regime stifling. Her heart attack in Africa found her at her limit's edge, and the medical care in the clinics there was not adequate to ensure proper care.

One day, unexpectedly, she received a letter from the superior in Rome. It was a simple notice and command: "Sister Tabor, your Obedience is that you return to Fairview Convent in Ireland immediately. Your new duties will be assigned to you in due course." It was signed by Mother Mary Benedicta. The notice came like a bolt out of the blue. There was no inquiry about her health or wellbeing, no sense of thanks for the forty-two years spent serving in an extremely hard environment in a village in Kenya. She had helped build a school a few years after she arrived. She had written to a multitude of friends and family, who sent her money to build that school. She was devastated. The people she had lived among for forty-two years were crushed as they said goodbye to her. Sister Tabor's greatest wish was that she died there among the people she loved and who loved her.

Quite soon after receiving her Obedience from Rome, Sister Tabor found herself back in Fairview Convent. She had spent her time in training all those years ago here, and now she found herself bound again in rules and regulations and meaningless regimentation. She noticed immediately that everyone was on guard. *When they have to be so vigilant*, she thought, *their spirits are not free*. As much as she could, she would give free reign to the postulants she was ordered to supervise. She saw immediately they were both focused and determined to do a good job. She was determined, in her own way, not to be subservient and docile. She had helped build a school in Africa. She had been involved with the people and their lives in Kenya. Her life had been full, energized, and occupied with challenges that enabled her to be vibrant and vivacious. She had made numerous good friends in the years she had been there. She had felt fully alive in Africa and lived a life that was consistently connected with others. She relished that effervescent connection.

Sister Tabor had deliberately ignored the pains she was experiencing in her shoulder and jaw. The attack on her heart came one morning during Mass. She could no longer ignore her condition. Sister Tabor was heartbroken when she was ordered to leave her beloved, adopted country. She wrote a letter to Mother Benedicta asking for some time to say her farewells and to adjust to her departure from Africa. She was sent a letter from Rome commanding her to depart immediately or she would be considered "rebellious," and that when she left, she was to have no further contact with the people there. She was told to make a "clean break."

The tone of that letter shattered her. She was determined that, as much as she could, she would continue to be connected to and correspond with her beloved friends in Africa. When she arrived at Fairview Convent, she quickly plotted and went about acquiring writing paper and envelopes. She would steal stamps if she had to. Keeping in contact with her friends was her lifeline. She soon found a good friend in Sister Bridget Mary, who always had a surplus of writing paper and was more than willing to share her resources with the retired missionary nun who sought her assistance.

Sister Bridget Mary asked Jimmy McGinty to purchase some extra stamps for her. There were always a few pennies in a jar in the kitchen. Phelim O'Connor and Cassidy Maloney had a habit of emptying their pockets and putting their spare change into that jar. They were more than happy to see that the change-jar was restocked on a regular basis. It was their way of showing appreciation to the two nuns who kept their spirits alive. The money in the jar did, in fact, come in very handy on occasion, and the purchase of a few extra stamps for Sister Tabor here and there was not a problem for Sister Bridget Mary.

The arrangement ran flawlessly and made the returning missionary from Africa more content with her adjustment in Fairview Convent. Not only did Jimmy get the stamps that Sister Tabor needed, he also forged an agreement with the sister allowing her friends to use his Gate Lodge address for correspondence. That way, she was able to skirt the Lent and Advent rule that forbade any of the nuns to receive or write letters during the liturgical calendar. Jimmy McGinty was soon receiving multiple letters from Kenya at his Gate Lodge address, and he slipped them to Sister Bridget Mary for Sister Tabor.

Sister Annunciation was pleased that Sister Tabor was also offering to assist in kitchen duty on a regular basis and wrote about this positive development to Mother Benedicta in her monthly report to Rome. Mother Benedicta was pleased that Sister Annunciation had been able to reign in Sister Tabor so readily and felt very pleased that Sister Tabor was adjusting so well upon her return to Ireland. Sister Tabor would be allowed to spend most of her afternoons resting in her room. Sister Tabor was, in fact, writing feverishly behind her bedroom door. Every nun moved quietly and quickly as they passed her bedroom, as they did not want to disturb her rest.

CHAPTER TWENTY-THREE

GATHERING WOOD

December 15, 1966—1:00 p.m.

The outside chill began to penetrate through the little cracks and crevices of the windows that attempted to pour light to the inside of Fairview Convent. While the sun sped through its early December sky, its warmth disappeared with it earlier each day. Since the middle of October 1966, we struggled to keep the chill from settling into our bones. It was a battle to keep warm. We hugged our tea mugs a little longer at breakfast and supper. We pushed hard into our chores, trying to generate our own body heat, only to have it snatched from us in the cold of the chapel. Prayer made us even colder. The chapel paradoxically became a place to which we resented going. Our long frocks helped a little, but once that cold chill snatched us in its grip, it was hard to shake.

We were delivered the good news that the little fireplace in the recreation room would be struck into life by the middle of December. We shivered in delight at the news, but I was not totally assured this would happen. I was losing trust by the bucketful as the days turned into weeks. But just the thought of a fire in that very small hearth kindled some good feeling. It was something to look forward to.

Sister Dolores had made the announcement one night with that threatening tone of hers lurking in every word she spoke. "We will light a small fire beginning eight days before Christmas in honor of the feast of the birth of the Christ Child. You each will take your turn after the midday meal, beginning with the youngest in rank, and take the wheelbarrow from the bottom of the garden, fill it with logs, and stack the logs against the wall next to the greenhouse. Mr. McGinty has been working this past month in the forest to ensure that we have logs. They are just beyond the tree line off the gravel path. You each will spend an hour and gather two wheelbarrows' worth of logs in that time."

There was no response from our little group. Not even a nod of acknowledgement was observable. We were getting to the point where we were keenly aware that even a response might incur fury from the woman who perched at the top end of the table each night.

December 16, 1966, came around, and it was my turn to gather logs for the fire. It was a mild enough day as I went to the garden in the back of the convent to retrieve the wheelbarrow from the side of the greenhouse. I put my hands on both handles and was surprised that it felt so heavy. I struggled to get it balanced and found the path to the garden gate. I was puffing heavily when I got there. I struggled to get the wheelbarrow out of the garden and push it toward the forest. For the first time in two months, I was alone. I was walking by myself. There was no one around me. It felt good to be alone. It felt good just being by myself. I found a song in my throat and began to hum. The wheelbarrow slid to the side when it heard my voice. I was suddenly aware that maybe I was not quite alone. I felt eyes scrutinizing my efforts as I journeyed with my bulky, tin companion to the gravel path. The song got stuck in my throat. As I became used to the weight of the wheelbarrow, I hastened my steps. I needed to get into the forest.

I found the trail signaling the spot that would herald the presence of the felled logs. I pushed the wheelbarrow through the tufted lawn and strained to get beyond the tree line. Once there, I had a feeling that I was safe. I took a deep breath and looked around for the pile of logs. A few steps further on, I saw an ax plunged into the center of a tree stump. Some logs near the stump were still too heavy to move. Another few strikes and the log would be split sufficiently for the fire. A few more strokes of Jimmy McGinty's arm, and they would be stripped of all their power. The blade of the ax was lodged deeply in the wood. I touched the handle and pulled at it. It did not budge. I thought of the strength it must have taken to bring it there. I realized that I was spending too much time looking around me, so I walked a little toward the tree line of the forest to try and find the logs that had been prepared for the fire.

I began to hum as I heaved the large pieces of wood into the gaping hulk of the wheelbarrow. I realized that I would have to make two trips and felt the pinprick of anxiety stabbing at me. I began to sing quietly to distract myself. My voice became stronger, and soon I was singing any song that entered my head as loudly as I could. I looked through the trees toward the cavernous building that held me captive daily. My singing became louder. My singing felt defiant. The forest held my defiance. It felt liberating. The whole experience of singing at the top of my voice felt really good. If it were not for the confines of the timetable I had to adhere to, I would actually relish doing this every day.

Soon the first installment of logs was in the wheelbarrow. I put my hands on the handles and picked up the bulk with some effort. I pushed the container forward and finally got some traction on the grassy lawn. Once on the pathway, I picked up speed and got to the greenhouse and unloaded the wood in a heap beside it. I picked up the empty wheelbarrow and ran with it as fast as I could to the clearing in the forest. Once there, I began to sing again, filled up the second load, and made it to the greenhouse again just within the hour I was given to get the job done.

Once every ten days, I went to collect wood for the small fire that would barely make its warmth felt in the recreation room during winter. Once every ten days, my singing exploded into the forest. I had found my voice. I could make noise again. My right to be acknowledged and heard, my right to become visible again, took deep roots there, far beyond the tree line, and those roots were as deep and long and wide as the tall trees that held my voice in its highest branches, maybe even making way for its resonance to reach the sky.

CHAPTER TWENTY-FOUR

THE SPIDER'S WEB

The Sacristy—2:30 p.m.

It was getting close to Christmas, and Margaret and I continued to attend to our duties in the sacristy. We worked particularly hard every Friday when we had to use thick cloths to polish the dark wooden cabinets. We also had to wash the two high windows, both inside and outside. I generally stood on a chair inside so that I could reach the top of the window. Of course, the chair had to be covered by a cloth so that my shoes would not scuff it. The windows were washed every Friday no matter the weather. During the month of December, it was incredibly cold outside. We had not yet been given black cloaks to cover us when we went outside, and our daily walk often left us all with our teeth chattering and our bones chilled. The black mantles would be given to us after we had spent a year in the convent and moved into the novitiate year, a year of exclusive study and preparation for vows. We had a significant wait before we could have this protection.

In the meantime, we could wear cardigans. When we went outside, that was all we had between us and the weather. Margaret Logue was taller than I was and liked the outdoors. She generally offered to go outside and stand on a stool, wiping at the windows, trying to ensure there were no streaks left for anyone to complain about. Margaret stood out there every Friday and did not seem to mind if it was raining, frosty, foggy, or misty. She got a small stepladder and stretched into the corners to erase the grit and grime the week had brought. Occasionally, we saw Jimmy McGinty going into the forest to cut logs. Often,

Margaret would give him a short wave when he passed by. He would respond with a smile. Every Friday, we had the sacristy shining by the time of evening prayer.

One Friday, in the early afternoon, Margaret and I were cleaning as usual. We were bathed in sweat, such was the effort we made to ensure everything gleamed. Sister Tabor had gone to rest after lunch and left us to get the cleaning finished. All of a sudden, we both froze at the same time. We spontaneously looked at each other. I thought I heard Sister Dolores's footsteps. Margaret obviously had thought the same. Sister Dolores had never prowled in the sacristy area before. We looked around. At least the place was perfectly clean, and if she came in, she would see that we were hard at work. The mirror sparkled; there was not a hint of dust anywhere. My heart began to beat fast. I could feel its pulse in my neck. I felt dizzy with fright.

Sister Dolores limped into the sacristy. She hesitated when she heard someone cough in the vicinity. She may have been concerned that Sister Tabor was out of her routine and in the area. Once satisfied that no one was around, she spewed a look of distain upon the two of us. We both felt confident, at least, in passing the inspection that we instinctively knew would take place. Indeed, that was only seconds away. Sister Dolores slid her fingers on the wooden vestment case and examined her fingers. She turned and reached to the top of the mirror and rubbed her thumb along the surface. She examined her thumb, snapping her fingers a few times as if expecting something to fall between them. There was not a speck of dust in sight. There was not a trace of dust on her fingers. She went to the windows and examined them. There were no streaks there that would lead to any admonition. She looked at us hawkeyed, filling the room with a sense of foreboding. I could feel the hands of dread grip me. We both sighed as Sister Dolores turned to leave, when her eyes quickly fixed on the corner just above the door. A small spider's web could barely be discerned above the lintel. Margaret's eyes and mine swept to the lintel just as quickly. We braced, knowing what was coming.

"You are lazy girls," she raged. "You will stand here until night prayers. Do not take your eyes away from that spider's web."

Suddenly, the small web took on the mass of a boulder in that tiny room adjacent to the chapel. I could even feel the weight of the web press heavily on my shoulders. Margaret and I stood just inside the door of the sacristy and hardly blinked as we stretched our necks to look to the top of the lintel. We did not move. Very soon, I could not budge or even flinch as I felt stiffness taking over my entire body. I felt like I was on an ironing board, being pressed, and the feeling of being trapped almost made me panic. I was petrified. The hours passed. I felt I was in a coffin. My back ached. I felt a knot there, and it was getting twisted to the point of pain. Yet. we continued to stand there like muted, heavy statues.

A few hours later, Sister Kate O'Flaherty came with a watering can to revive some plants at the statue of St. Brigid standing near the entrance of the sacristy door. Margaret and I must have looked like two concrete slabs as we continued with our punishment. I could feel Sister Kate stand right in front of us, but I was too frightened to take my eyes off the spider's web. We heard Sister Kate give a deep sigh as she left us. She was more than troubled. Sister Kate belonged to the part of the convent where the professed nuns lived. They generally lived, worked, and stayed in that separate part of the building. She had no authority to speak to the postulants. She moved away as silently as she approached us. Three hours later, Sister Dolores came into view and ordered us to go to the dormitory. We had not eaten supper. We had not spoken to each other. I was so weary I wanted to cry. There were no tears, however. They had dried up while trying to get through the ordeal of obeying this frivolous command.

When I eventually fell into bed and wrapped my cardigan around me, I was all too aware that the tension had taken hold of my body. I could hardly wait until the next day when it was my turn on kitchen duty. Sister Freda Mary and Sister Bridget Mary would help me look at this experience in a completely different way. I rubbed my neck. I was determined that this would not penetrate my spirit the way it took hold of my body. Margaret Logue was a little more brittle than I was. I could tell right away that she became a little more anxious after that experience.

Margaret had decided that she would somehow get news to her father about how she was being treated in Fairview Convent. Her father would not be pleased.

Sister Kate went to her room and documented what she had observed. Something had to be done about Sister Dolores, who was becoming more sinister, and her methods of dealing with the postulants bespoke an underlying, personal pathology that Sister Kate could not comprehend.

CHAPTER TWENTY-FIVE

THE FIRST CHRISTMAS

December 24, 1966—6:00 p.m.

It was the eve before Christmas 1966. The rain poured from the sky, sieved by a high wind and a deep fog. The water flooded down the windows in sheets, and the whole of Fairview Convent was saturated. The rain tumbled into the gutters and spouted in fountains where the leaves of autumn had gathered and stayed for the winter. The leaves were stuck there, despite the daily efforts of the wind to set them free. The gray stone of Fairview Convent stood mottled and caught in the panting snap of the icy wind. The fog snatched and saturated and choked everything in its grip.

Inside the convent, the damp filtered through every nook and cranny, crevice and crack. I never realized that fog could feel so heavy as I sat at supper looking to the skylight in the dining room. "Christmas Eve never felt so depressing," I uttered as I struggled to listen to a novice read from the Gospel of St. Luke, relating the story of the birth of Christ. The Bible the novice read from looked big and bulky. She looked awkward as she tried to raise it in her hands to catch the last light of day held in the fogged skylight. Her voice was full of hesitation. She moved nervously from one foot to another, jerking her words as she did so. She definitely was uncomfortable standing in full view of everyone.

I looked at her. Her face was flushed red, and she was concentrating on the text, blinking often in the semi-darkness. I wondered why she did not even have a candle to provide more light. I imagined she may have been undergoing some form of punishment. I realized, in that moment, that we postulants would probably move away from Sister Dolores when we completed our first year of training, only to be placed into someone else's charge to continue the religious formation that concentrated on stripping everything from us. I stopped that thought. It was Christmas Eve after all.

I continued to listen to the novice. I began to hope that her narrative would hurry along so Jesus would soon be born in the stable, the lambs hurried to the holy scene by the shepherds, and that this novice would end the reading and be put out of her misery. Here and there, the novice sounded as if she was in a panic. Her voice increased its high pitch to the point that it was making those of us who were really listening to her feel embarrassed and anxious for her wellbeing. She sounded as if she would stop reading permanently at any moment, and even if she stopped before Jesus was born, it would be a happy thing indeed.

She kept going. She coughed and hesitated, as if catching her breath. She spluttered out her words. She adjusted the book in her hand over and over again. Her hands trembled, shaking the pages as she turned them. The light continued to dim. When she finally announced that Jesus was born on a table instead of in a stable, I bowed my head as low as I could. That did sound funny, but I did not let a muscle in my face react. I did not flinch. At that point, I did not care where Jesus was born. I just wanted the meal to be finished so I did not have to continue to absorb this young woman's discomfort. I did not look at her anymore. Eventually, the bell rang and caused the automatic stir of dishes and clatter of chairs. I blew air through my mouth and began to indulge in some deep breathing, such was the relief I felt. The tremors in the novice's voice had distracted me on this Christmas Eve, 1966, to the point of discomfort.

The convent felt like a dark cave. I had entered three months ago, full of energy and effervescence. That was long gone. Loneliness huddled close to me, and I suspect, to most of my companions who had entered with me. At that moment, I felt that, even if we could have spoken at supper time on Christmas Eve, I am sure none of us would have mentioned home for fear of disintegrating. The silence we experienced was like a bulwark now, and it kept emotions from flowing freely. We were becoming more robotic in our responses and behavior. I noted that this was not normal and tried to keep that ever in mind.

Sister Annunciation rang the bell again in the dining room. Silence took hold of the group.

"Sisters, we will be retiring early tonight. You will make a brief visit to the chapel and then go to bed immediately after leaving the chapel. You will be awakened at 11:00 p.m. for Midnight Mass."

I looked around me and saw the haggard looks on the faces of most of the postulants. We were all exhausted. We had spent the past week scrubbing every part of the convent clean. We had scorched the floors and washed every window in the place. Every statue was scrubbed. The place was purged for the feast of Christmas. We had even emptied every closet, removed the contents, washed the shelves, washed or dusted the contents, and then replaced the items back on the shelves.

Our shoulders still carried the memory from a week of carrying a load to ensure that this homeless child sent from heaven would find a haven of cleanliness in every corner of Fairview Convent. We made a quick visit to the chapel before we went to the dormitory. The little nativity scene was placed in the sanctuary of the chapel. Sister Tabor had gladly sat in the chapel while the novices set up this Bethlehem scene. The figures of Mary and Joseph, the shepherds and their newly born lambs were secured nicely in between clumps of hay. A few angels sat beside the star on the top of the nativity scene, heralding the divine moment of a birth that changed the world. The baby Jesus was in the trough covered by a white cloth. The priest would remove the cover before he began Mass at the stroke of midnight.

I trudged heavily to the dormitory. Even though I had just eaten an hour ago, I felt the stab of hunger before wrapping my feet in my cardigan, and I quickly went to sleep. I did not remember my head hitting the pillow. An hour before midnight, a violin pierced into the night. We were slapped awake by the strains of "Silent Night." I felt I was in a stupor and struggled to get up. My stomach lurched. I was weary. For a second, I had forgotten that it was Christmas and needed to get myself out of bed. My heart ached. Outside the dormitory, the player impressed her bow firmly into the strings. The violin shifted and split into the cold night with a sweet melody and quickly left with the song's beguile settling on us in the clatter of silence as we got ready to go to the chapel for Midnight Mass.

The music gradually dissolved, and the sound projected into another part of the convent, quickly sliding into the quiet hush of that first Christmas Eve. Coughs and the rattling of beds made me bolt upright. I felt the sickness in my stomach return and wished I could just creep underneath the sheets. I still felt hungry. I had been in a very deep sleep and had enjoyed the gather of the warmth in my cardigan and was very loath to put it under my mattress. I knew that was what I had to do in order to keep it out of sight. I was reluctant to get dressed, but quickly accepted the reality that I had to get to the chapel quickly.

With that thought in mind, I sprang out of bed. I felt I was going to freeze. I struggled to grab my clothes. I felt the coldness of night stealth deeply into my bones. I began to shake and shivered loudly, but hurriedly got into my long black dress. I grabbed my cardigan and made sure it was hidden underneath the mattress before I left my shrouded cubicle. I thought of home and missed my family. I longed to be there, sitting by the fire and enjoying the crack and hiss and color of it. I remembered the candles that would be in our window and the glorious landscape of flickering lights in houses near and far. It was as if the whole world reflected that bright star that led the Magi to the Christ child.

I stepped into the dimness of the night that had invaded the dormitory. One bulb emanated the little light that enabled us to get into our rank. The ten postulants stood in the shudder of the damp dormitory awaiting the appearance of Sister Dolores. I could feel the rush of an ocean of tears and quickly stopped the surge with a few blinks. I stood there, thinking of the power of a blink, that almost imperceptible, momentary movement of the eye that can control the fullness of the ocean tide ready to spill from deep inside. I distracted myself while waiting in line just to pass the time in the dullness.

When Sister Dolores arrived to take us to the chapel, I felt I was in a dream. I wondered how my companions were feeling. We filed automatically behind Sister Dolores as she led us down the stairs to the chapel. Yawns sucked in the cold air. A red candle had been lit beside each statue standing heavy on each landing, retreating into the recesses of the darkness. The pulse of the candle gave the impression of the orb of life and moved like steady heartbeats, as Sister Dolores limped ahead of us, step by step, to the chapel several flights below. I, like my companions, wore the heavy mantle of night and sighed. Sister Dolores silenced the sigh with her pinched face and taut lips when she turned around to capture it.

We entered the chapel. It too was dimly lit. I had expected the splendor of light and color. The stained-glass window that usually produced some color was black as it stood against the night. The organ pedaled "Adeste Fidelis." When that hymn was finished, Sister Ella, like a lark, trilled "Oh Holy Night." Sister Ella's voice was strong and pure and filled the chapel like a welcome reprieve from the darkness and drabness of our wakening. It was midnight. It was cold. It was Christmas.

Sister Tabor was lighting candles around the crib when we entered. By the time Sister Ella had finished her magnificent piece of soprano work, the crib was totally surrounded by lit candles that radiated a warm glow, which I could not feel. Sister Tabor removed the white linen cloth that covered the Christ child. This was a task that ordinarily was accomplished by the priest before he began Mass. No one else had noticed this little touch of rebellion that, on occasion, Sister Tabor exhibited with deliberation. Jesus arrived in his trough. Everyone was still. The cold air crept into my bones. We waited for the priest to come from the sacristy.

My heart was back home. At this point in the night, I normally would have been helping my mother with the baking and putting presents out for Eileen, Rose, Christy, and Dan.

My older sister was good with decorations, so she undoubtedly would be putting the finishing touches to the Christmas tree. I had knit them all bright colored scarves before I left for the convent the previous September, which seemed a lifetime ago when color sifted, stitch by stitch, through my knitting needles.

The scarves would be placed on the table close to the fire. My mother loved bright colors. I wondered how she and my father were feeling right now. I wondered if the emptiness I felt would be felt all the way to Derry. Christmas was a bright time in our household, as it was for every family in my neighborhood. The anticipation was filled with childish wishes and dreams. The larder would be bursting with cakes and biscuits and sweets and meats of all kinds, filling the house with flavors that baited our senses and filled us with delight. There was always a Christmas tree in a corner of the living room, laden with decorations made by each of us. Some were crude cuttings from bright paper with Christmas stars drawn on them, and some were complicated snowflakes carefully cut out of white paper by my sister, who loved to create the most unusual crafts with her hands.

After Midnight Mass, I fought my exhaustion and trailed wearily out of the chapel for some tea and cake in the refectory. A blast of cold air hit me when I entered. The wind howled through the skylight, and dim lights ensured that we wrapped our cardigans around us more tightly as we took our places at the table. A bell rang, and the house superior gave us permission to speak on this cold Christmas morning. It was hard to talk when the words were encased in ice inside, sleeping deeply. I attempted a conversation with the two postulants sitting on either side of me, but did not garner much success with that effort. Everyone seemed to sense the collective melancholy that hung like a cloak over everything there. A dark light pervaded the conversations. In the middle of it all, I caught the twinkle in Sister Kate O'Flaherty's eyes as she nodded a smile in my direction.

Sister Kate O'Flaherty had long ago learned the art of observation and the power of gazing. She concluded, after her own introduction all those years ago upon entering the convent, that her eyes would become her way of communicating and connecting with others. Her eyes would become her voice. She quickly developed the art of good eye contact and the ability to hold onto the gaze of anyone she encountered. She assessed, from the very first days of her time in Fairview Convent, that if she was denied conversation to the point of muteness, she would have to devise another method of conversing. She developed the ability to read facial expressions, to capture the mood of another in the flash of an eye movement, the twitch in a facial muscle, the way a head turned, the distilling of a sigh, the taut edge of a frown, the poise of a smile, the eager posture of a look of expectation, the disappointing pursing of lips, and the shrug of shoulders, all too often showing things that would never move or change.

Sister Kate was drawn to the slightest changes and the minutest shifts in facial expressions that, to her, were written clearly and etched definitively in the now familiar faces of the postulants she had seen daily for the last three months. Their faces said it all. They were, on the holiest of nights, wrestling with the harshness of living on the edge of blackness in Fairview Convent. Sister Kate took note and heeded every sign of blankness and bleakness of this night that was, for the rest of the world beyond these walls, a night so full of light and promise. The promise she beheld in the refectory that night was fading right in front of her eyes. From her place in the dining room, she looked carefully at the bottom two tables where the postulants seemed cast like lifeless, concrete statues.

Una Murphy appeared to be in her usual aloof state of distain for her companions. She was the eldest of the postulants and seemed to carry this as a badge of honor, holding her apart from the rest. Nancy McCarthy was her usual serious self. While she wanted only to please others, her face, quite paradoxically, held the trait of shyness and resistance to any traces of engagement.

Mary Ita Ahern seemed sanitized of any emotion and seemed lost in thought. She was obviously lonely. Nuala O'Reilly yawned into her tea. She had a glint in her eye, which was a sign at least that she was feeling something that gave her some joy. Margaret Logue had the weighty air of privilege about her. Her father was a solicitor in Dublin, and there was no doubt that Margaret was used to something far grander in her comfortable house there. She looked as if she missed the blazing fire that must have been part of her midnight celebrations.

Julia Higgins looked as if the care of the world were heaped on her back as she bent over the table. Sister Kate secured the eyes of Mary O'Brien. Her eyes were full of puddles ready to brim over. Annie Boyle was creviced in the grip of apprehension, looking furtively as if she were dangling precipitously over her view of things. She receded into the dimness of the refectory wall behind her and seemed on the edge of disappearing. Jean O' Doherty shivered in the cold, as though feeling the damp husks of winter penetrating the walls.

I looked at Sister Kate at some point and found my own smile somewhere in the darkness, and I showered her with it. She nodded her kind nod. She had a twinkle in her eyes.

The bell rang. The tone triggered silence. I got up stiffly and, within a half hour, was asleep with my cardigan wrapped very tightly around my feet.

On Christmas morning, three somber knocks awoke us. I jumped onto the cold floor, and the reality of winter shattered through me. My blood felt like ice as it coursed through my body. The scurry and frenzy of trying to get ready before I heard the thud of Sister Dolores's limp pumped me into life. We went through the usual motions of morning prayer, breakfast, and the walk in the cold to keep us occupied. After Christmas dinner, we went to the recreation room and received our Christmas letters. We had not been allowed to have any mail during the Advent season.

I was eager to read my cards and letters and become lost in news from home. We all were left quite somber when we fully realized what we were missing. Here in this space, we had been fractured and broken these past few months. Instead of the balm I was expecting to feel after sorting through my mail, I felt bereft. I had lost something precious when I had entered those gates in September. I had lost the daily connection with my family, which had kept me vibrant and alive and feeling that I had a place where I belonged.

As the bell rang for night prayers and the ascent to the dormitory, I realized that the things that truly matter can be easily wiped from memory when numbness encases you. While the music of Midnight Mass had helped recapture the meaning of Christmas and pushed me into that time well beyond the convent walls when I was imbued by the explosion and expectation of that holy night that brought brightness and joy to my world, the contrast to that experience in Fairview Convent was startling and upsetting. As I went to bed that night, I felt encrusted in dashed hopes, and a sense of dread encased me. I was not able to capture the sense of joy that accompanied the season.

I lay in bed and stretched my mind to the northern skies miles and miles away. The happy memories of home on this special night only served to create an anxiety that lay with me for quite some time. I held my cardigan tightly to me and eventually wrapped it around my feet. It contained the heat from the hearth where my mother clanged at the brass needles, gathering the cream and green wool strands into her hands. "The print of my mother's fingers and hands are in this cardigan," I whispered silently as I hugged it close to me again. With that consoling thought on this dark Christmas night, I eventually fell asleep.

CHAPTER TWENTY-SIX

1967, THE NEW YEAR

12:00 a.m.

January 1, 1967, slipped into the convent so quietly that no one noticed. I had tried to imagine some way to get up at midnight to welcome in the new year and say goodbye to the old. That did not happen.

I lay in bed, thinking about home. In a few weeks, I could look forward to a visit from my mother and father and as many of my brothers and sisters as could fit into the car. I cheered at that thought and waited to hear the knocks at the door, giving us permission to get up for the early morning scramble to the chapel and the dull mining of another day.

There had been no celebration the night before, and no opening of the front door, as my father would do, to embrace and welcome the new year on our doorstep and ask for an abundance of blessings to ascend upon all who lived in the home. He would stand there, looking up into the night sky. He mentioned all our names, asking that each be blessed in the coming year. He asked for all good things for all of us and extended his arms to hug the twinkle contained in the stars. There was no revelry as the old year was ushered through the back door while my father again thanked God for the blessings of that year. He said goodbye to it with all the joys and challenges it had contained. Then he rejoiced by lilting some old Irish song from his reservoir of appreciation for the gift of nature he saw extended before him and the gifts of home for which he provided well.

I recalled all the brightness of that last night of 1965: the crackle of the fire, the cheer of family and neighbors, of welcome and expectation contained in the year that was to come. With that memory etched clearly, I resolved to say goodbye to the old year and welcome the new. I resolved to make the best of things. I would try to find a gateway through every barrier that I encountered and find life wherever I could. I would focus on the moment. I felt something new leap into my ears and a nudge to keep going forward. This was the beginning of a whole new year. Time, however, seemed to have a way of not moving in the convent. Every day was blearily the same. Everything was empty, devoid of real meaning, and very still. I would have to find ways to fill that void.

I knew there was a creative part of me that I was not using. I loved to read and write and draw. The captivity and strangulation of the whiteness around me had me feeling calcified. I fixed my eyes on the cracked, white ceiling above my bed. I smiled as I thought of what Michelangelo would do with those cracks. I remembered that Monet and Manet and other Impressionists had painted their canvases using one dot or one small stroke at a time to present unique, lightsome pictures to the world. That small dot and the most miniature of strokes changed the art world and the way in which people perceived light and color in the nineteenth century.

I was on the cusp of a new year, desiring color and vibrancy, but experiencing neither. I felt the stretch of a new canvas set before me. I would have to find my own way in the shadows of the black-and-white world that tried to hold me captive within its rules and regulations.

My mind wandered to my family on this new year's morning. I wondered about my brothers and sisters and thought about seeing them in six weeks. I felt some life surge through me as this thought took root. I listened to the sounds in the dormitory. The new year was barely seven hours old when the echo of the hard knock found its way through the door. The knock alerted our senses, and soon the postulants began the flurry of activity that would have us in the chapel in about a half hour. I placed my cardigan under the mattress, right after I sprang onto the cold floor that first morning in 1967, in a place that was so very far from feeling like home.

The first day of the new year began like every other, with prayers recited in the chapel in the usual monotone chant. This was followed by Mass, and when the candles on the altar were extinguished, everyone lined up in silence and proceeded to the refectory for breakfast. I snatched a look out a window as I filed in line. It seemed like a dense fog had been painted thickly into the trees, settling like a blanket over the lake, and the world I had come to know had disappeared totally.

CHAPTER TWENTY-SEVEN

THE IRISH DANCING CLASSES

January 7, 1967—10:30 a.m.

It was the first Saturday in January 1967. I was scheduled to be the last to take a bath that morning. It was getting close to 10:00 a.m. Sister Dolores had announced the night before at recreation that the weekly Irish dancing classes would begin the following day. She thumped the table before she began to talk so that we would pay attention. We did not know what to expect. It could very well be the beginning of a massive explosion coming to blast us as we sat there. She cleared her throat.

"Your dancing classes will begin here tomorrow morning with Fiona Feeney. She teaches Irish dance to the students at the local schools and has been coming here for the past seven years to teach the postulants. The lesson will begin at ten-thirty sharp, and all of you will assemble in this recreation room promptly at that time."

As she was speaking, Mary O'Brien rolled her eyes to the ceiling. Mary did this a lot. I suppressed a smile, but it must not have entirely faded from my face by the time Sister Dolores had finished her pronouncement because I noticed that she was looking at me and was not too happy.

"You, madam," she said to me, "will have your bath last tomorrow morning, and you had better be in this room at ten thirty."

Mary O'Brien rolled her eyes again.

Sister Dolores had been reminded by Sister Annunciation that the postulants were expected to perform for visiting missionaries when they visited Fairview Convent. Many nuns came to visit the convent upon returning to Ireland to see their families after years of working in America. It was a rule that once the young nuns were assigned to work in America, they had to wait fifteen years before they could return to Ireland and visit with their families. Each nun, upon her return, was expected to make this trip to the convent during part of her vacation. A list of those who realized this expectation was sent to Rome for perusal at the end of the summer. Mother Benedicta would send a reprimand to those who did not make the effort to visit Fairview Convent. I learned years later that many letters of reprimand had been sent to the offending nuns. Most of the missionaries only wanted to spend time with their families. They greeted sisters and brothers-in-law they had never met. They rejoiced in the birth and accomplishments of nieces and nephews they had not yet met.

They visited graves and grieved all over again for the parents and relatives that had died in their many years of absence. They met old neighbors and caught up with school friends. Most did not want to take the time to visit Fairview Convent, a place for which they harbored memories of abuse and victimization in the very fiber of their beings. They hated the thought of going to the convent and being reminded about their early years of formation in religious training in the convent overlooking Lake Fennan. The only nuns who went there willingly were those devoted to Sister Bridget Mary and Sister Freda Mary. The more docile came because they feared being admonished.

Most who visited during the summer came as a result of anxiety and fear or some kind of reprisal. Most had the expectation that there would be a group of young nuns ready, willing, and robotically able, at the snap of a finger, to sing and dance and exhibit their talents for the visiting nuns and their families. This is what was expected, so that every visitor could see how the people in authority made sure that every aspect of the person was enhanced and continued to flourish. The displays of dancing and singing helped perpetuate the myth that everyone in Fairview Convent was happy within its walls. The visiting nuns were wiser, but entered into the façade for a few hours, and then left to be distracted by their families before dreaded memories were dredged up to overflowing.

Now this crop of postulants was scheduled on a weekly basis, until summer, to be proficient and skilled in the art of Irish dances. They would learn the basic steps of the jig, the reel, and the hornpipe. There would be a singing component at each of the summer performances, but this was the sole territory of Sister Herald, the convent musician. Sister Herald let it be known to Sister Dolores that she would not be involved in any way with her or her postulants by preparing them to sign for the summer performances. The only involvement that Sister Herald would entertain was to agree that a postulant play the last hymn for Mass on some Sunday after Easter. It was the only time she would yield her organ stool, and it was her plan to use this opportunity to evaluate the one who had the honor of being chosen for such an occasion.

If the postulant showed some musical talent, Sister Herald had the authority to give her weekly lessons on the organ, and therefore, to prepare a future musician for missionary territory. So far, Sister Dolores had not been able to glean any talent in the years that she had become postulant mistress.

Sister Herald was responsible for the liturgical preparation of the novices who were herded into another section of Fairview Convent. There was no interaction with the novices and postulants. There was no communication among them whatsoever. The novices wore long, white veils and their movements, beyond what could be gleaned at seeing them in the chapel and refectory, were kept very quiet. They existed in a world of stealth.

At the end of January, four of the postulants would be scheduled for music lessons with Mrs. Moore and would be responsible for practicing one hour daily. Sister Dolores, of course, had the final word about who was going to be the chosen recipients for these treasured lessons. When I heard about this, I knew I would not be placed on a roster that ensured my getting a turn at providing for Mass and other services. I was not from County Kerry.

Mary O'Brien was adept at playing the piano. Her father, Joe O'Brien, was a music teacher at St. Patrick's Boys School in County Tyrone in the north of Ireland. After her entrance in September and after her family had left, while rules were not yet established, Mary had found a piano in one of the rooms in Fairview Convent and began playing Chopin effortlessly. Sister Dolores looked around her, realized that Mary was missing, and when she heard the music, she properly deduced that Mary was playing. Sister Dolores smarted and flinched. She clenched her fists to try and control a rising tide of fury. Sister Dolores had no appreciation of art or music or dance. Instead of bursting into the room where Mary was playing, Sister Dolores let Mary have her moment of pleasure, but it was one, she determined, that Mary O' Brien would never experience again.

On Saturday morning, as I enjoyed the fresh scent of cleanliness after my bath, the music I could hear in the dormitory seemed to dawdle from downstairs. I spontaneously began to move, hesitated, and then moved some more in the empty dormitory. I had washed my hair, and it felt good. As I toweled it dry, I thought I was listening to the click of a woodpecker outside the window, and then soon realized the quick hammer was from hard heels on the wooden floor in the recreation room beneath. My feet began to move in steady cracks timed perfectly to the music. I stopped suddenly as Arctic ice seemed to grip the fluidity of the dance, and I froze on the floor flooded in fear.

The great thing about ice is that the water still runs below its surface. The quiet murmur of that current travels through the freeze, reminding us that the water below is still alive and travels to the great, unfrozen seas. My short foray into normalcy and automatic response to the music had caused me to panic momentarily. I took a deep breath and listened again to the call of the dance, and the boom of that call crackled deep inside me.

For a few minutes, I danced in the middle of the dormitory to the sounds of the strains below, and in those moments, I felt free for the first time in months. After I stopped dancing, I bent low to hear the music again. While bending, I caught the rhythm of a new tune. I glanced at the tree outside the dormitory. Even bedeviled with rain and enveloped with fog this cold morning, it seemed to keep time with the music. I had the strong feeling that, though still encased in this winter moment, the tree was beginning to lean towards spring. I suddenly realized that I had better get downstairs. I flew to the recreation room. All the postulants were already there. I had been the last person to take a bath this morning, and I was anxious not to miss a moment of dancing.

As soon as I appeared in the recreation room, Fiona Feeney asked us for help moving the heavy table in the middle of the room over to the window to leave a space for the ten of us to move. The table was weighted with Sacred Heart badges and paper and plastic. Ms. Feeney did not realize the heaviness that the table possessed. All the while, the music continued on the record player in the background, and I felt that we were cradled in a space that was different and now transformed.

Miss Feeney was topped with a head of red curls, and her deep, green eyes held an ocean of mirth. Her face was thin, and she wore a broad smile. She seemed as light as a bubble as she moved to the center of the room, all the while keeping time to the music, which continued to stream out of the brown box she had brought with her. She finally gathered us into a circle in the middle of the room as she stood in its center.

"I have to warm up, ladies," she said in a sweet tone. She stretched a little, bent some more, leaned forward and touched her toes with both hands. Finally, she instructed us to move to a space on the floor and do the same stretches that she had just accomplished. Some of the postulants looked shy and reticent about the invitation. I was not one of them. I was just delighted to stretch and move to music that was not played by an organ. As we finished the stretches, Fiona Feeney told us that she would like to demonstrate how the reel was to be choreographed.

She put on a new record and stood in the middle of the floor. She stopped for a moment, poised, and then flung herself into the music. Each step she took hit the floor in a fleeting moment, like flint. She must have ignited its fire; it cracked her feet like sparks into the crucible of the dance. It looked as if the floor contained burning embers, and the agitation she created was bent on igniting the kiln that lay beneath. It appeared as if her energy emanated from the bottom of her feet as they wrenched in rhythmic, accelerated momentum. Feet flexed, toes pointed, she pushed vibrantly into the pulse of the music with crisp foot snaps and enormous, whipped leaps. Her arms looked like concrete pipes that she held close to her sides. Her upper body was stiff, yet her legs bounded expansively on the floor. She took in every inch that floor offered to her.

Even the air jostled for space as Miss Feeney redefined the total area of the room and forced the stale air into the walls. She continued her vaults on the floor, striking like a match that fueled the air in combustible relief. The room was harnessing a new power that had been built up during the long, tedious hours of making Sacred Heart badges, and it filtered that heaviness into a new distillation.

The music and the new energy in the room made everyone feel good. As I stood with the other postulants, I could detect something good stirring inside. The dancing teacher continued to be caught up in the music and was clearly oblivious of us standing around the edge of the walls. The searing intensity of the dance pulled me easily out of the swallow of darkness that had held me captive for such a long time.

I let the music move inside me until I was tapping my feet and enjoying the new flow of life coursing through my body. I was suddenly aware that I was very young. I was overcome by the deep realization that I was missing so much of that which could be found only on the other side of the convent walls. My feet continued to tap, timed perfectly to the music. I looked around me at the brightened faces and thought, if music could be pulled out of that room that held so much dread, then every one of the postulants was going to make it happen. It felt, at that moment, observing the joyous spectacle this woman had created, that these Irish dancing classes would pick up our spirits. I grasped this reality and took delight in something that would engender a sense of hope. Until then, we had had nothing to look forward to. I had the strong feeling that Fiona Feeney would be the light in the window holding darkness.

The last leap left Miss Feeney with a smile on her face. She was not even breathless. This woman was quick and fit and agile. I had a feeling that, with all the chores we had to do, we could match her agility and fitness. We were still huddled together in a thick pack, armored in our long, black frocks. Miss Feeney swooped her hands in a semicircle as if to bring each of us into her embrace.

"Gather around, young ladies. As you know, my name is Fiona Feeney. I run the Irish dancing school in the town here. I have been coming here to teach Irish dancing for many years. I need to know your names."

She had a list of our names in front of her and did a quick roll call. She learned all our names by the end of that first session and began calling us by our first names. It was a very simple thing, but new, and it felt refreshing and personal.

"I want you all to call me Fiona. I need eight of you who know how to do a reel," she declared with animation. Without hesitation, eight of us put up our hands. Fiona Feeney put on the music, and in a matter of moments, it felt like the eight of us were on fire, like human torches engaging in the heat and intensity of the eight-hand reel. It would not take too much longer for the other four postulants to be set alight and consumed by the flame of the dance.

CHAPTER TWENTY-EIGHT

POKING AT THE SUN

January 8, 1967—11:00 a.m.

In the late morning of the eighth day of January 1967, a long time after the silence and clatter of breakfast, I moved almost mechanically through the morning duties in the sacristy in the midst of pitched black silence. The late January chill was temporarily muted by the muscle of the morning chores. The tedium of the morning's regimentation was already stupefying, and at some point, I cast a quick glance out of the sacristy window. The place looked colorless today, but in spite of the overcast day, I was able to see some semblance of color in the great expanse beyond the lake. Various layers of gray and green and blue hovered together and sometimes side by side over the water of the lake. Dampness seemed to weight everything I looked at.

Everything was caught in the cool grasp of winter. Its cold breath stretched beyond Lake Fennan. The frozen lace framing the sacristy window was merely a short-lived work of art, melting somewhat as it met the sun whenever it shone between the fractures of the clouds. The brief glances of the sun gave me a sense of hope to face the tedium of the afternoon. Shadows fell heavily on the ground when the sun peeped through. Soon it would make all things green, and the trees in the forest would fully enjoy the canopy of its leaves. Life had stilled in the roots, but soon enough, everything would shudder into life and ooze out of the cold earth. At this point, all ached towards spring.

As I looked out the window, I noticed one of the older nuns shuffling toward the turn in the driveway with the help of a coarse, wooden stick. She was bent somewhat low, as if listening to things deep within the earth. She plodded through puddles that dotted the driveway, capturing the glint and sparkle of the sun now and then as the water held the embrace of its warmth for as long as it could. The old nun stopped at a particularly large pool of water, and as if on cue, the sun appeared in the sky. She looked at the sun in the water as if frozen in the moment. She lingered in the cold, catching the sun's reflection in the myriad of other puddles that pocked the driveway. From where I stood in the sacristy, it almost appeared as if she was surrounded by little pits of fire, and the scene drew me into it even more intensely.

Her bending low made her look as if she was listening intently, as though poised to hear the murmur of the earth's wintered moan. The old nun seemed stiff and hardened by the many seasons she had had to endure. She pulled her big, black mantle around her. I saw the trail of her rosary beads. They sputtered and sped through her fingers. They glinted in the sun, polished by her finger's time, as if sanded by the rhythm of constancy and the bite of monotony. They trolled through their laps, one by one, as the old woman ground each bead into a different shape and polished, like black jewels, keeping the old nun focused and mechanical. Here and there, she stopped and seemed to take time to burrow into the tunnel of the puddle, finding at least some solace in her bent look into the blue sky she had found in the puddle at her feet. She found it captivating that, in the catch of the driveway's hardness, she could fly.

When puddles contain the sky, the clouds, and the sun, they launch their own silent gasp of wonder as if knowing they will eventually evaporate back to their place of origin. The old nun's world was more colorful because she used these plops of water as keyholes into the filament. The shrouded lady roused the stick in her hand and poked at the sun in the water. She chortled at her effort and continued to pierce her stick into the water. Very quickly, strained by her efforts, she made her way to a tree at the edge of the forest.

The sun quickly disappeared in the sky. I was beginning to understand the ache for the sap. The trees stood tall out there, their branches spindled and taut in the cold of the morning. I longed to feel the depth and length of the sap, its stretch and its pull. As I continued to look out the window, I wondered if the sap from one tree ran into the next. I felt separate and disconnected from the others I lived and prayed with and yet, strangely, not really able to be in a relationship at all. We were all living parallel to one another. I would just have to trust in the rise and urge to fruit that I felt was deep inside me. I felt absorbed and swallowed by the darkness around me and was chilled as I stood and looked out the window.

The old mantled one, blanketed against the cold, picked up a twig from the cluster huddled in their winter's pile at the bottom of the tree where she was seeking refuge. She leaned against the bark, as if listening to the ghosts of leaves long gone from the tree. The sap had stopped flowing, but there would be plenty ready to rattle into life in the next few months.

She waved at the tree with the small twig of wood. Her gestural articulation orchestrated some great, iced symphony in the sky. Maybe she heard music in the chilled air and burned to flood it with its melody. There seemed to be more life in the old woman out there being nipped by the freeze than inside these convent walls. A shadow cut across the lone figure with the twig in her hand, and the vague glow of sunlight returned just as quickly as it had disappeared. The sunlight winked, and the little nun churned into life.

My attention to this vision beyond the frosted window helped me focus on the beyond. In some strange way, I felt that I had some control of my life, in much the same way the maestro under the tree had. Watching the old nun interact with the pulse of winter had helped me summon a sense of the life within myself. For this brief period, it felt good. From this small space, I was taught that the opportunity to see beyond the drab of the convent was in making an effort to escape from it just by glancing outside and reminding myself that it was solely up to me to bring the outside in. If the old nun could find the sky in the puddle and poke the sun there, I must seek to find instances every day that propelled me forward.

The old nun began her trudge toward the convent. She threw her baton on the ground and then changed her mind. Suddenly, in that moment, she seemed to carry the weighted baggage of winter's grim grasp. She bore the marks of darkness and the hard grain of loneliness well. The old nun, nameless and shrouded in brown and black, seemed to totter on the edge of balance as she turned around and faced the convent door. The gravitational pull of the convent door caused her to shudder as she moved toward it. Her thick plod gave the impression of reluctance, but I could sense it was the force of her daily schedule that was the imperceptible call to leave her secluded orchestra. Saturated with the strain of merely putting one foot in front of the other, the old one reached the big door. She placed her twig carefully against the convent wall, as if willing it to send its symphony into every isolated crack the convent contained.

For an instant, she appeared to resemble a fossilized remnant of a medieval past. I imagined her to be a peasant in heavy clothing, seeking a place to rest. She placed both hands on the door to steady herself and began to tug arthritically at its huge knob. She gave a glance toward the twig again. *She might pick it up and choreograph the wind yet another time*, I thought.

The old lady disappeared.

I did not know her name. I might not even recognize her when I sit in the refectory tonight. I might not even see her in the chapel, keeping vigil in the sleep and kneel of prayer. I wondered from where she sprang. I wondered what she did before she entered the convent. I wondered what her name might be. I wondered where she had been all her life. I wondered what her voice sounded like. The picture of the old nun poking at the sun in the puddle and playing her music in the trees touched the nectar of my heart. Some small wrinkle of connection was impressed in me, but crumpled as quickly as she disappeared.

I was struck with the distance I felt from my family. Back in Derry, my youngest sister continued to be sad. No amount of school or distraction kept the pools of emptiness she felt every day since I had left. She would come home from school, and something was never quite right. My mother tried to distract her, but she missed her big sister. She constantly asked when I would be coming home and could never quite understand how I could just disappear. She could never really absorb that. The explanation of this disappearance as being a "vocation from God" did not alleviate any anxiety and did not have the desired effect.

At night, when the house had settled into quiet breath, the floodgates opened, and for the youngest in the house, they never quite shut. There was always that lingering feeling of loss that persisted when a letter arrived from the convent. When I went home fifteen years later, there was still a discernible crack in her heart. Time dragged for her. She was told that she would see me in fewer than six months. Her life changed on September 8, 1966, when she was just seven years old.

I picked up the dust cloth and rustled myself back to life in the sacristy. This afternoon at two o'clock, we would be introduced to the sewing room.

CHAPTER TWENTY-NINE

THE SEWING ROOM

January 9, 1967—2:00 p.m.

The furious scold of percussive hisses steamed through the charcoal-colored radiators. Still, a heavy smell of musty cloth and the feel of rank dampness were in the air. We lined up in rank outside the sewing room on the third floor of the main section of the house, which was accessed by way of a spindly, spiral staircase made of wrought iron. Sister Dolores grabbed onto the iron railings and struggled to make her way to the top of the main section of the convent. We followed, making our way up, one by one.

The staircase reverberated with our weight, and its shudder echoed above and below us as we made the vertical tread to the top of the house. The air was heavy as we took a right into a small corridor. I felt the suck of air, as the drone and rattle of hard work cranked through a wooden arch leading to the sewing room. As we approached, we could see at least a dozen sewing machines whirring constantly under the consistent trundle leveraged by the novices as they hypnotically moved their feet robotically on the bottom lever of the sewing machines. Back and forth, the bottom frame stirred the needle into life. The nuns there all wore white veils in contrast to the lumbering, black sewing machines to which they seemed tethered. They were focused as if in a catatonic trance.

The rows of black machines were lined up like a military detail poised to destroy, eating up cloth in hungry snaps. A yellow mist filled the air. As I looked around me, I saw another wordless scene and was seized by the hard ache that penetrated the dull green walls. A putrid vapor emanated from the long, narrow room. The smell of acrid oil made me want to gasp for air. I concentrated on the women who poured themselves into the work in front of them. I looked toward the window bathed in a fog of fiber that the watery sun could not penetrate. A small can of oil, dripping with brown stains, sat underneath one of the radiators. The stains had brimmed over onto the floor. I thought it strange. It was different to see dust and disorder. Every other place in the convent was clean and sparkled with a lifeless gleam. I was glad to see a hint of messiness.

The novices operating the machines, obviously so used to the seal of the room, did not break away from their stupefied concentration. Sister Dolores motioned for us to stand beside a table laden with bolts of material at the left side of the room. No one noticed her. The workers droned on.

Sister Dolores clenched her fists and finally clapped her hands wildly. A sister in a black veil emerged from the roar of a machine in the corner of the room. Her eyes darted like swift arrows toward Sister Dolores, whose face was as dark and unyielding as the stealth of an upcoming storm. The two women glowered at each other.

The other nun stood tall and thin. She wore her brown habit like a suit of chain metal and seemed to be dried up by life. Every now and again, she coughed, as if the fibers and the smell in the room were causing this distress. As we moved closer to the heavily laden table, I thought I heard the rumble of another machine and the faint hum of a song coming from a room adjoining the sewing room beyond the table. *It cannot be the hum of a song*, I thought. There was no such thing as the spontaneity of bursting into song or verse, so, I concluded, the hum must definitely be coming from another source trying to absorb the chaotic scene into which I was suddenly tossed. I could not wait to get into the kitchen on the morrow and share all this with Sister Freda Mary and Sister Bridget Mary.

Sister Dolores, with more disdain than usual in her voice, declared, “Sister Flores, these are the postulants. They have come to learn how to make their under-tunics.”

Sister Flores took little notice of Sister Dolores, who immediately left. I imagined her making her way down the spiral staircase with fire in her eyes. Sister Flores began to snip at a bolt of black material she had snatched when she first noticed Sister Dolores. It seemed as if she was attached to the cloth, the dark, heavy bolt merely an extension of her.

She cut and snapped into the cloth with the concentration and steady hand of a diamond cutter. When she finally bolted upright, startling out of a trance, she began to speak to us. Her words came like stitches, were measured like stitches, stapled like stitches, and penetrated like stitches. They also hurt like stitches.

"You all had better be attentive or you will find yourselves in the middle of the refectory floor doing some penance."

The nuns in the white veils continued to sit entranced with the sewing machines in front of them. Their frantic feet kept pace in a constant tempo, shifting the air in the room and enabling the rancid air to circulate. The sound of the steel needles echoed, leaving rips in the emptiness. The sputter and roll of the machines fueled the air with the heavy smell of petrol.

The machines needed to be oiled on a regular basis, and the smell was hard to get used to. I was more familiar with the fragrance of polish and soap, so being in that room was a challenge. I felt a sickening in my core, because I realized that this is where I would be next year as a novice. I forced myself not to think about it and was drawn into the drone and moan of the machinery that was so hard at work.

The machinists were totally encased within the hypnotic groan of the room. The pierce of the needle's point in each machine ruptured into the cavernous echo. The whir in the misted room cascaded like the gathering might of a storm and then ebbed before the stir of yet another momentum. Here and there, intensity poured out of the gnarls of thread that pushed into the machines, energizing the room and changing the cloth forever.

Every person in that room seemed so ardent in her task. There was no interaction. There was no spontaneous connection. There was no looking up for distraction. There was no hint of curiosity as the mantle of boredom spread throughout the room. The room was saturated with the dredged tedium sitting on the shoulders of all who worked assiduously. It left the air filled, as if plastered with caked, yellow muck. The picture here was one of fierce regimentation, while beyond the window, the open and unpredictable space of sky was filled with fluffy blobs of clouds in one instant, and in another, with white wisp-strips racing and charging in the weft of the wind. I wondered how often this picture I beheld in this room would be repeated.

The convent had existed for at least fifty years. Staleness lived in this room. The connection between then and now was at once seamless. The long stretch into the past was dark, and the thought of becoming part of that continuum buffeted and momentarily smothered my spirit. I forced myself back into the heaviness of the sewing room. The force and fury of the machines continued to be relentless. The shelves around the room heaved heavily from the weight of cloth. I felt their load on my shoulders, but quickly summoned something inside of me that refused to let me remain in the concrete of despondency. This distasteful current would create its own dark movement and churn the life out of me if I stayed in it. My mother used to tell us that nature had no boundaries, and life could be found in crevices. I decided there and then that I would make whatever I found into my reality, even if it was the bleakest, and go beyond that imperceptible boundary to find life, even if I had to endure the chokehold of authority and power. I would find a path through the inevitable crevices of this convent life. The material and thread that stretched knotty and snarled in that room would provide me with at least a new distraction from the monotony and tedium that stretched a little into the future.

As we stood there, we became aware that we would have to endure another tart cocktail of verbal abuse from the sarcastic Sister Flores. I glanced around me. Annie Boyle was already eaten by anguish. Mary O'Brien was fingering material and seemed to want to explode with a smile. "It is hard to create an appetite for something I hate to do," she whispered to me at some point. Mary seemed mesmerized with the surge and splutter of the machines, as they continued to snag and cough, while swallowing mounds of cloth. They stopped and started and stopped again, as the novices adjusted their weight to balance the load that they carefully conveyed into the eye of the needle.

"We had better pay attention here," I relayed quickly to Mary, as I noticed the stiffness Sister Flores was sporting.

"She looks like she just got up from that table," Mary declared. She smiled at me as quietly as she could. We each knew by now that even smiles could be heard. I looked around and wondered about this place where the whir of the machines was more important than the lilt and cadence of Irish voices.

The County Kerry girls stood together. They were ready to obey any orders that were thrown at them. Mary lumbered a little further into the room and knocked over a chair. She lifted it just before Sister Flores looked up from a black sheath of cloth.

"When I call you, which I will do by rank, come to me so that I can cut your tunic. After I cut it, you will wait in the quilting room so I can instruct each of you how to sew it." The words slid out of her like puffs of venom.

We lined up in rank. As we approached her, each in turn, Sister Flores looked at us, measured our size by sight, and then expertly cut a pattern in either a dark blue or dark green material. She slid the scissors expertly into the bolts of cloth and produced a shape that would approximate the wearer. When it came to my turn, she snapped into the blue material. I was delighted, but tried not to show it. I grasped the piece of material tightly. I would have to sew this myself. I was just glad to have a piece of color in my hands again.

When this task was accomplished, a stern Sister Flores ushered us roughly into the room adjoining the sewing room and instructed us to stand quietly around the room until she returned to show us, in turns, how to use the two machines that she put at our disposal. It took about ten minutes for each of us to be instructed, so I had time to stand around the room for quite a while, because I was the lowest in rank. As I held onto the material and entered the quilting room, I saw a wave of color that I had not experienced in a long time. I wanted to hold the texture and feeling of the moment.

The creativity I felt stirred a sense of well-being and an awakening to the reality that maybe any new experience would leave me feeling newly charged and changed, if I could stay open to that possibility. Like the bolts of cloth I saw before me, I knew instinctively that I would continue to be pierced through and through. Like the material, I would be ripped and torn and cut. I had been feeling disheartened and dispirited in the dark days since Christmas. This room had the magical quality of raising my spirits, exactly as the time spent in the kitchen did.

The machine stopped suddenly, just as I stepped into the archway, ready to be called to the sewing room to get started on my tunic. Sister Flores stood in front of Mary, who was beside her, ready to be called to the sewing room.

"Sister Mary Alma, you had better start getting this place tidied up."

The sister at the machine nodded in acquiescence. Sister Flores looked at me.

"You there with the blue material, help Sister Mary Alma tidy up quickly and put the bolts of material up on the shelves."

I tucked my tunic under my arm and went around the sewing machine and the rest of the alcove, happily doing as I had been instructed. When Sister Flores returned to get Mary and me to take our seats at the sewing machines in the other room, she looked at me and told me that I was to make time every Friday to come and help Sister Mary Alma tidy up. She added that she would tell Sister Dolores of her expectation. This was an order that sent thrills through me. I could not understand the authority this nun wielded over Sister Dolores, allowing her to interfere with my schedule like this. There were things I still did not know about how the scald of authority worked in this place. At this point, all I knew was that I would be holding colorful fabric in my hands on a regular basis. My spirit soared.

As the weeks and months sped by, I learned a great deal from Sister Alma. Every Friday when I went to that room in the late afternoon, I was constantly surprised and charmed by the specter of color that lay haphazardly in a heap at Sister Alma's feet. I was attracted to the color-filled spill in this room as iron filings to a magnet. Sister Alma treasured every scrap of material. She stitched the smallest shards of material into the corners and ends of the fabric to make the material stronger. The tiniest pieces were, by far, the most indispensable because they bore the brunt of the wear and tear of the material.

The quilt maker showed me, for the moment at least, that I would have to take charge of the swath of cloth that was my own life. I would have to learn to develop skills to become adept at making sure that my needle's point was kept at just the right tension in order to avoid breaking. I would have to be tuned into the warp and weft of every thread, even the flawed thread I was given to work with, and see the possibilities in those places and spaces that lacked vigor and brightness.

Every Friday afternoon when I entered the alcove where the quilt maker worked, I was quite aware of my own threading. Like the needle in the sewing machine, I felt myself stitched to the place where I was living, cognizant that I was sinking into its depth with every step I took. I became steady and deliberate, even if the forces around me cut into my stride. In my time with the quilt maker in the convent of Fairview, I developed an interior perspective in my steps, as they mingled on top of so many other steps that already had, for decades, trod in that hard slap of a place.

CHAPTER THIRTY

THE QUILT MAKER

January 9, 1967—3:00 p.m.

A mound of material lay around the only sewing machine in this little alcove room that abutted the main sewing room. A small window was etched in the right-hand corner, its light subservient to the color it smiled upon. A heap of quilt maker's black-covered, bent back was stiff with concentration, stuck and poised and ready to lurch forward. I caught my breath. For a long time now, I had felt stripped. My whole world had been reduced to brown and black and white. I felt at home in this room.

I glanced at the sewing machine. The needle had stilled for a moment and stood like a sentry, pointing sharply toward its target. Yellow, orange, green, purple, blue, and bright-red strips of color bulged from the quilt maker's hand. I waited breathlessly for the slightest foot movement to break into the color. All of a sudden, the needle began its controlled jerk. The still center began to stir, and the material began to pitch steadily into the needle's eye. The point of the needle pierced and pitted and set the colors on a collision course. Suddenly, there was combustion in the cloth; it was on fire with life. A brilliant storm roared and whirred and thundered through the small steel needle, giving it power to change the pieces of cloth with which it came into contact. The sewing machine spewed, stitched into the bright bolts, and transformed cloth into a new life on the other side of the needle. In an instant, the material was expertly gathered and quickly caught in the vortex of the spin and spurt.

The intensity and focus of the quilt maker grew. The nun kept her foot moving frantically on the lever of the sewing machine. Her foot seemed to be separated from the rest of her body, which was in her full control. The sewing machine sprang into a symphony of sound and movement, heralding the birth of color in that room. The quilt maker's cheeks were full. She blew into them so they appeared as if about to explode.

The needle continued its sharp, constant descent and rise. It drew the pieces of fabric into its unsuppressed motion. The march of cloth was constant. It moved in and out of the needle and fell beyond, forever changed into an invigorating cascade of color-filled spread. The center became convulsive and volcanic, distilling slices of colored strips into bands of boldness that changed my black-and-white world into pleasure before my eyes. The voluminous bolts of cloth spat and charged, and suddenly, in a quick sigh of a crescendo, spluttered slowly to a stop. I held my breath.

The quilt maker looked around as she stopped to pick up a few more remnants from the floor. She momentarily glanced at me. Her sky-blue eyes smiled and twinkled with a million shimmers of light. This woman appeared to be lit from the inside. The color she was working with instantly made her appear vibrant. She turned as she calculated the match of material she would use and again pushed into her own vibrancy with every stitch. Very quickly and expertly, the quilt maker pierced and fit together the various strands so that the whole work, not merely the individual parts, became a fascinating sight.

I felt a passion in that room. The colors flowed. The colors spilled. The colors circulated. There was a generous outpouring of vibrancy assembled there. I felt a flow of life rise inside me. I felt immersed with something creative and beautiful. I knew in that instant that, while the violent storm of coldness and lack of humanity mantled around me and sat heavily on my shoulders, my eyes could behold the goodness to be found in alcoves and cracks and crevices.

I was determined to hear the center's silence and keep my eyes on color. I was going to set a new course for myself. I felt that I could keep the texture and feeling of that moment with me, no matter the cruelty that abounded around me. The creativity of this quilt maker created a sense of well-being and an awareness that any experience could leave me newly charged and changed, if only I kept myself positive. Like the material I saw before me, I realized that I may have to be pierced through over and over to retain my own creative spirit. I would take any opportunity I could to come to this room; any time there felt luxurious. I was always charmed by the specter of color that lay seemingly haphazardly in a heap on the floor.

As the weeks and months wore on, I learned a great deal from this woman, and every Friday afternoon found me attracted to the color-filled spill in this room. The quilt maker showed me, over the course of many months, that I would have to take charge of the swath of cloth that was my own life. I would have to be tuned into every thread, especially every strand that had a flaw, and see in them the possibilities in the places and spaces that lacked the vigor of brightness and the boldness of vision. I became conscious of my own threading every time I was in the room with Sister Mary Alma. Like the needle in the sewing room, I felt my own stitching to the earth, aware that I was sinking into the depth of my own bolt of material there. I became steady and deliberate, even if the forces around me cut into my stride.

During my time with the quilt maker in Fairview Convent, I came to an understanding and appreciation that I was fused with the past there. I had to chisel out of the concrete and harshness of daily life to find a softness in that colorful room at the top of the spiral staircase. How ironic that it was so out of the way and so inaccessible. In that room, I heard the echo of older companions and trumped my own sense of well-being into a freshness and newness that I did not experience anywhere else, other than with Sister Freda Mary and Sister Bridget Mary. I learned very early on that my deepest cloth, held together with my own thread, could spill color into every space I entered, if I claimed it and owned every part of that process.

In the two years that I spent on the edge of Lake Fennan, in the grip of oppression, cruelty, and abuse, the quilt maker taught me to walk with bright threads coiled around my heart. I felt the call to life there and eagerly looked forward to Friday afternoons.

CHAPTER THIRTY-ONE

THE BLUE TUNIC

January 9, 1967—4:00 p.m.

Mary O'Brien and I were finally called from the color-filled alcove by Sister Flores and quickly found ourselves sitting adjacent to each other in the sewing room. Mary also got a piece of blue material for her tunic, but dreaded the task that lay before her—she could not sew. Her fingers enjoyed the touch of keys on a piano, but never before had she held a needle and thread. She just hated to sew, and where she found herself at that moment caused the usually tranquil Mary O'Brien to be more than uncomfortable as she sat beside me.

Sister Flores had given us some preliminary instructions on how to sew the tunics, and then disappeared to some other space in the room, leaving us to our own devices. Mary placed the material between her fingers and finally shoved it, with great awkwardness, under the needle of the sewing machine. She had never used a sewing machine before. Sweat poured from her hands with the strain of effort, staining the material. I instinctively grabbed her piece of material and slipped mine into her hands. Within ten minutes, I had Mary's tunic stitched to perfection. Looking around me furtively and seeing no sign of Sister Flores, I grabbed my tunic from Mary, and then worked quickly on my own. For me, there was nothing complicated about putting the front and back pieces of a simple garment together and thrusting it through the machine. Within the hour, we all had our tunics sewn.

With a sigh of relief, the group assembled in rank and made its way to the bottom of the iron stairs and waited for Sister

Dolores. She must have heard the rattle of our descent because she appeared within seconds. Mary O'Brien, at some point, glanced at me, and I could see the gratitude exude from her smile. We returned to our own quarters and automatically lined up so Sister Dolores could inspect our tunics. She was silent as she snapped a tunic from each of us for examination. I was confident in my own sewing skills and handed my blue tunic over to her when it was time to do so. When I looked at her face, I felt a strange dread inside myself just as Sister Dolores exploded in fury.

"You think you are so great, madam? Now you can spend the night ripping this out. You will stay up as long as it takes, and you are forbidden to use scissors."

Sister Dolores's face turned purple. She threw the blue cloth into my face, and at the shock of her eruption, I felt myself shaking inside. I could not understand or grasp what the problem was. I looked at the blue tunic. Nothing registered. It appeared to have been sewn perfectly. A tear jettisoned onto the cloth, and I rubbed the dark, salty stain into it with my thumb as quickly as I could so that Sister Dolores could not see it. She had stepped away from me, trying to contain herself, her fists clenched. She finally put her hands into her pockets.

I tried to examine the tunic again and realized what had happened. In my hurry to finish Mary O'Brien's tunic and begin my own, I had not checked that the lighter blue of the material signaled what was to be the inside of the garment. I had sewn my tunic inside out. I felt panic. I would have to rip the tunic without the aid of scissors, which would be useful to make that all important start, because, once that first stitch was cut, it would only be the first of thousands that would have to be undone.

After the recreation period was over, Sister Dolores stood in front of me. She stood straight and starched. She looked as if she had just catapulted from a sharp pin. She cast a shadow over me, with night in her face. She instructed me to begin ripping my blue tunic. She turned out the light and lit a small candle in front of me as I took my place at the table. The darkness shrouded her as the flicker of the wick shuddered. The troupe of postulants made its way to the chapel to say night prayer. I wondered if anyone would miss me. I felt that familiar ache in my back.

The candle was small, and I calculated that it would take me a long time to get through this chore. I was already fatigued by the work I had accomplished during the day. The task in front of me already felt enormous, even before I began. The light of the candle was inadequate and shed a meager glow. I realized that the dye had been cast, and I would have to use a needle to wrest the stitches from the cloth. I felt myself already in the firing process. All I needed was a kiln to sit in. The crucible of the furnace I felt pulled me into the prickle of the night.

I pushed into the hot core of feeling and fright. I became aware of my every breath. I felt the pulse in my neck and the beat of my heart racing. It throbbed under the weight of the night loaded upon my shoulders. I tried to take deep breaths to calm myself, and the candle quivered at my effort. The thin, yellow candle cast a glow in a very small circle around me. I pushed the small, thin needle into the stitches, straining to extrapolate the thread from the material. The dark blanket of night continued to weigh on me. My shoulders were stiff now, as I tried to focus. I strained in vain at the piece of material that was now wrinkled in my tight grasp. My knuckles were white. I looked around me. The large pictures of the Sacred Heart and Our Lady that provided a source of solace in the daylight suddenly began to take on a more sinister form, and I felt scared. I swallowed the bile that had begun rising in my throat. I turned my attention to the blue tunic and tried to forge a plan to get the work started quickly, so I could get to bed as soon as possible. I began to focus totally on the cloth I had in my hands.

I had better concentrate. I pushed into the stitches as expertly as I could in these conditions, trying to pry even the smallest fray from its tight connection to the cloth. That first stitch was important, and it refused to budge. The air chilled. The door creaked in the crease of the cold. I felt the bead of fear rise in my hands, and they became rigid. The needle of anxiety poked into the tips of my fingers. My hands felt prickled by a thousand points. I put the needle on the table and wiped the cold sweat from my face with the back of my hand. I tasted the salt in my mouth.

I shook the perspiration from my hand and shivered in the cold. I felt enfolded in the cramp of darkness that was encasing me. I took the rough, textured material and tried to focus on the job ahead. I used both hands and began rubbing stitches into each other as one would rub pieces of wood together to try and start a fire. I had observed my brothers trying to set dry grass on fire with this method. I realized finally that this method would not work.

I decided to hum in my head and let the rhythm of an Irish reel move in my hands. I heard a banjo and began tapping my feet on the floor. I stabbed at the stitches and material as music careened into the darkness at the end of the table where the candle flickered. I grabbed at the tunic and concentrated on getting that first stitch ripped. I tried to weaken the thread by rubbing it with the tips of my fingers and then by pulling it with my fingers and thumb together. I felt the thin needle numbing my fingers. I rubbed my fingers together and blew into my hands to try and get some life back into them. The needle was not strong enough to even create a fray in the thread.

I snatched the cloth and poked one stitch over and over again with the needle. I snipped and penetrated one particular stitch feverishly, struggling to loosen the stubbornness in the fiber. I would have to be even more stubborn. One stitch would give me a start, and I would be well on my way. There were thousands of stitches in the garment, but I needed just that one to snap. I was suddenly aware of the clock ticking its way through the dread of this room.

The candle cried wax tears, and the flame tried to stretch into the darkness. I heard my breath becoming shallow and fast. I realized, in my urgency, that I was pulling closer to the flame and the power of that very shallow breath almost cost me the candle's sallow light. I pulled away just in time for the candle to burst back into life again. I pulled into the compass of the flame and directed my breathing into my chest. I began to massage the texture of the material again, hoping in some way that one stitch would burst and give me the opening I needed.

I suddenly remembered that I had a ruler in my drawer and exhaled deeply. I found the ruler and placed it over the stitches and, using it like a saw, pushed with all my strength into the material, hoping for a break in the stitchery. I eventually detected a fray and mentally felt a surge of relief release itself in my whole body. I exhaled deeply, almost causing a blackout. I had a long way to go, but the fortress was now breached. I heard a crack on the wooden floor somewhere in the distance and shuddered. I felt as if a hail of ice had moved through me. I hesitated for a moment, and then returned to the invisible mold of movement I had created there, as I hunched over the blue tunic that now shrouded my lap in blackness. The garment had carved out a spot there, barely visible now that the candle's glow was in decline. All color loses its uniqueness in the dark. I hoped that would not happen here.

I was aware that the statue of the Virgin Mary stood vigil over me in the corner to my left. I had the impression that I heard breath coming from that direction, and it was distracting. I felt the hand of fear snatch at my neck, as I gave a furtive glance at the statue. I viewed the mound of stitchery I had yet to plow through. The ripping seemed interminable. My breath sighed, and I felt a million tears begin to tunnel their way wearily behind my eyes. I could taste their salt already. I swallowed hard to get rid of the lump that had settled in my throat like a stone slab. I gasped the air in giant gulps. The fear was beginning to take over my body, and I could feel myself tremble. The fear was discernible. It sliced into the air and surrounded me. I could not escape from it. My heart beat faster. I had found my outer limit. I was on the ledge of the edge of panic, and I knew I needed to get back to the grip of reality. I even began to feel buffeted by the small glow of the waning candle. In order to survive here, I knew that I needed to go deeper and grasp inner resources. The cloth began to feel heavy. My shoulders ached. My hands began to tremble in the cold.

I cupped both hands to my mouth and blew hot breath into them. My hands continued to shake. I put my hands to my mouth again and blew deep warm breath into them. In spite of the cold, I felt I was burning inside. In spite of the darkness, I felt an inner light keeping me there. In spite of the shaking, I became more determined to get this done. I could bend that flicker of light, I felt, into the harshest of places. I could be a fiery inferno orbed into that frozen space. I refocused again. I rubbed my hands together and looked at the small swell and fall of the candle's flame on the wall.

I became aware of hard cracks of wood in the distance. I heard creaks and bumps. The wind picked up and whistled and howled now and again through the windows. At one point, the crunch of the trees made me bolt upright. I struggled with the hard, unyielding stitches in the cloth. I got the better of another, and then another, and suddenly began to experience triumph in the rip. I got an inch of thread that I was able to release with the needle and pulled it tightly around my right finger so that the material puckered and wrinkled. I continued to be successful, and the thread succumbed under the pluck of the needle. I was on my way. With this rhythm, I pulled as much thread as I could around my stiff fingers, over and over and over again, as the thread snapped and released many stitches in its wake.

The sharpness and strangle of the thread bore a groove into my skin. A drop of blood blotched the material, and my heart blushed crimson. I could not stop now. The candle's shadow flickered and floundered vaguely on the green wall. More time passed. Exhaustion pulled me deeply into the hours beyond midnight. The minutes lurched forward, one interminable second at a time. The candle still held tenaciously to the smallest flame. I continued my long rip. Now I was really tearing in a rhythm, and I felt I was accomplishing something. The wind picked up its intensity and, with that, I picked up speed. I heard the clock strike again in the distance, and it resounded in the space where I was sitting.

I suddenly was aware of footsteps near the room. I felt a whimper in my throat. As the tread of the steps got closer, I was seized with fear and soon felt drenched in a cold sweat. A whimper unfurled. I felt I was in a crucible. I was stupefied by exhaustion and encased in panic. As I glanced at the wick that barely held a flame, I was deep in the firing process and felt the prickled barb of night on the back of my neck. I imagined that an invisible hand would snatch at me. I tried as best as I could to forge ahead with the work, and I pushed hard into the core feeling of fright. I was aware of my every breath, the pulse in my fingers, the beat of my heart, and the pain in my fingers. My heart sank. In that bereft moment, I realized that I did not enter the convent to experience this insanity. Questions propelled me to confront this reality that felt like acid.

A wisp of surprised acknowledgement took hold of me and percolated to the surface. I was a mere number here. I was not a person. I was not to have a personality. I was nobody here. I was being sanitized of my humanity. I felt that the plan for me was to become passive, subservient, docile, pliable, and dried up. But I knew that I was not supposed to fit into the night and blight of cruelty like this.

Outside, the rain reached deeply into the soil, splashing the windows on its way down. It brought me back to life. I had better stay strong, be flexible, and try to maintain some effort to stay spontaneous. Behind me, I detected a hint of breath. Out of the corner of my eye, I discerned a jagged shadow creep through the door behind me. I was iced in dread.

I flew to the statue of Our Lady, standing in her pale-blue plaster in the corner, as if she could somehow come down from her pedestal and save me. I felt the explosion of a scream, as the encroaching creature moved closer to me. I flung myself into the cold marble of the statue. The room filled with sound. I clutched my blue tunic to my face.

"Get to bed, you witless idiot," Sister Dolores' voice spat at me.

Very soon, the chime of full-blown vulgarity was flung at me. I let everything drop and turned around, feeling the slap of an angry hand on my back. I was stunned momentarily. I left the room with the sting of the nun's hand imprinted on my back.

Sobs came from my depth, which I could not stop. I made my way up the stairs, distraught and incredulous at what had just happened. I was almost convulsive as I reached the dormitory and knelt at the door to try and control myself. I was still convulsive when I slid into bed. Annie Boyle, who was in the bed next to me, tried to calm me.

"Try and go to sleep," she whispered. "Put it away for yourself, otherwise you will get sick. Find a way to get beyond this."

With those words, Annie had just risked being sent home for breaking the great silence and whispering in the night. Mary O'Brien coughed a familiar cough to let me know she was waiting for me. I calmed and settled myself a little bit. I struggled to go to sleep, but even the whisper and cough of companionship did not soothe me. The dormitory was dark, and the cold grasp of blackness hung heavily over my bed. The darkness was so intense that I had no choice other than to breathe it in. I felt raw and mutilated with loneliness. I wrapped my cardigan around my legs. My bed creaked over and over. I did not fall asleep. Mary O'Brien and Annie Boyle stayed awake for the rest of the night, too.

CHAPTER THIRTY-TWO

THE LAUNDRY

January 10, 1967—10:00 a.m.

The first days of January 1967 dawned damp and cold. There was a constant shiver in the air, which shuddered even through the sturdy walls of Fairview Convent. Rain streaked constantly down the windows in a driven persistence, whipping and sliding sideways. Here and there, the rain flashed in sheets of iced water in a whirl of winded fury that exploded, faded, and blasted again. Lake Fennan was angry and spewed up its fury onto its banks. The gray grit of its water lapped with great propulsion and violence that would no doubt leave erosion as it headed north. The cold on this frigid morning made icicle lace, which fused with the dirt on the windows. Ice framed the tops of the windows in various lengths and held their tight grip almost as soon as they were formed. Laced water appeared inside some of the windows, such was the blanket of cold experienced within these rock-hard walls.

Mary O'Brien was assigned to the laundry for the month of January. That first morning, she bent over the gaping sinks and pulled a wad of clothes into her hands. She grasped onto the wet load, and with both hands, circled the clothes into a wet snake and began the tedious task of squeezing out as much water as she could. She struggled until she could lift the load onto the wicker basket at her feet. When the basket was full to overflowing, she stopped to try and come up with a plan to use the sturdy mangle that was standing in its bulk in the middle of the laundry floor. A handle crank protruded from the right upper side, and when any leverage was exerted, the rollers of the machine sped into life, moving, touching, and squeezing each other, as their heavy rubber rollers met.

Mary pulled the wicker basket of clothes to the mangle and made sure that a bucket was securely placed underneath the rollers to catch the water that was squeezed out when the clothes were pressed through the rollers. She pulled some wet clothes from the wicker basket, and with her left hand, tried to bait the mangle with the clothes. It generally took the bait, but this was Mary's first effort at this venture, so she took her time to try and figure out a strategy. The actual accomplishment of getting the clothes through the mangle in a constant flow was yet another challenge.

Mary untethered some of the clothes from the pile in the basket. In spite of her best efforts at the sink, the clothes were still laden with water. Her apron was soaked through, and she could feel the water seeping heavily through her dress. She pulled to untangle the heap sitting at her feet. She took one garment at a time and snapped it between the rollers while jerking at the handle, which galvanized the roller blades into life. Piece by piece, she packed another wicker basket with the clothes that crawled slowly out of the rubbery squeeze, a little lighter for their time spent there. She slowly got to the bottom of the basket of sodden garments and wiped her sweat-covered brow. She felt quite exhausted. The load of clothes was heavy, but she would rather have it heavy than have to go into the freezing laundry courtyard one extra time.

Mary dragged the basket to the door leading to the courtyard and the multiple clotheslines that soon would be full of these wet items. She waited impatiently for a break in the iced rain so she could get to the clotheslines that swayed wildly in the inner courtyard adjacent to the laundry room. In her mind, it was futile to go through this fatiguing effort to get clothes as dry as possible and then struggle to force them onto clotheslines that would continue to saturate them with rain. If she did that, the clothes she had struggled and wrestled with to get through the mangle would be wet again within minutes. Every piece of clothing was numbered, and everything was washed together.

Mary had pushed and levered every item through the mangle, forcing a great amount of water out of them, and now wondered why she had made the effort.

The handle of the mangle had stuck here and there, and she had had to push feverishly and with great effort to make sure the grinding rolls snapped each morsel of heavy, wet cloth it was fed, swallowing it in the process, and squeezing excess water into the tin bucket underneath it. Mary had had to empty the tin bucket multiple times. The mangle certainly worked. Mary returned to the sink and leaned over it to try and garner some energy. Her neck was sore, and her arms and shoulders ached. She also was soaking wet, as the water continued to run down her legs. She made no attempt to dry herself. She just wanted to get the clothes on the lines and return to the laundry to tidy up. She braced herself for her time in the courtyard.

She could not wait for her assigned laundry month to end. January was among the coldest of months. And laundry was a heavy chore, a solitary chore. There was a constant shiver in the air, even in the laundry room, where the hot water ran in abundance and filled the air with a warm mist. The shiver penetrated through the fortress walls that were Fairview Convent, and nothing seemed to be able to stop it.

Today, the rain streaked constantly in a driven persistence. Here and there, it came in sheets of iced water. Lightning lit up the darkened day, and when the lightning eventually made its way into the sky, it faded and exploded, often sending ice pellets with its brightness. When the bands of lightning came, Lake Fennan twinkled in spite of the grit of fog that speckled throughout the landscape. The sun was somewhere in the sky, no matter what was thrown at it, and it had the power to penetrate through the worst of weather. There was no sign of the sun today.

The convent stood strong, in spite of being whipped and crafted constantly by the elements. At this point, it was steeped in the grip of a long, hard winter. Mary stood by the window to the courtyard. Blobs of brown muck decorated the panes of glass. A glaze of frosted ice formed inside the windows in the laundry when the steam of hot water hit them. Mary O'Brien was only too aware now of the blanket of cold experienced within the rock-hard walls. She stood before the wicker basket of clothes and stiffened herself to face the brace of winter outside in the courtyard where she was to hang them. Sister Dolores had forbidden her to cover herself against the winter's blast with the heavy mantle that was hanging on a wooden hook just inside the laundry door.

Mary bent low as she dragged the weighted load the short distance from the warm laundry to the courtyard door. She was tired. She had not slept the night before as she was worried about me. She halted at the thought of spending the next twenty or thirty minutes hanging up clothes that would freeze on contact with the arctic-like air. She put her hand to the hard, heavy latch, and with great effort, she finally pried it up so that she could open the sturdy door. The wind caught her off guard as she dragged the clothes into the courtyard. The cold hit her like frozen sod. Her hands numbed immediately, and she shook them on contact with each garment she was to hang.

Mary pulled hard at the material, which was quickly freezing in her hands and becoming as stiff as a board. She managed to fight the swinging clotheslines and pegged the laundry as quickly as she could, fighting to catch her breath at every attempt. Her eyes watered, and the tears hardened on her face. Her apron had frozen to her body and felt heavy, like a piece of armor, and began quickly to weigh her down. She had to fight for each piece to grip the line.

Twenty minutes later, she grasped the latch of the door, but did not feel it. She had to fumble to get inside. She gasped for breath just inside the laundry door. She went to the sink and turned on the hot water, leaned over the sink, and coughed hot breath into her cupped hands, which were purple and pained with the penetrating harshness of the morning's weather.

Cold is hard to work with, especially when there is nothing to keep one protected. Mary felt like an ice cube. The cold did not budge once she was inside. She would have to move and shake it off, otherwise she would continue to be frozen from the inside. She had brought in the freeze with her, and the only way to get rid of it was to force it out. She stamped her feet over and over on the floor, trying to awaken any heat her shoes may have held, but they were soaked, and they squished as she padded her way inside. She shook her hands frantically over and over again, as she tried to free herself from the shackle of ice that had crawled under her skin and invaded the creases of her long frock. No matter what she did, the cold draped over her like a blanket and penetrated her very bones.

The cold was incessant. It pierced through every piece of clothing she wore. She stooped over and folded her clenched hands into her chest in an effort to gather some warmth to herself. Then she punched the air to get the feeling back into her arms. I came into the laundry just at that moment to place the holy linens on the table to iron them. I stood behind Mary, imitating her boxing the air. When Mary was satisfied with the final punch, she turned around and yelped when she saw me. We could not speak to each other, but the two of us collapsed over the sinks, shaking with laughter.

The laughter put some life into Mary. Tears ran down her cheeks, and this time they did not turn to ice. We finally looked at each other, and I gave her a reassuring look that I had recovered from the turmoil of the night before. I pointed to the iron, which I was going to use shortly for the sacred linens, so I plugged it in and tried to dry her dress as best I could on one of the ironing boards. The steam rose in the air. We both knew, in the silence of the laundry room, that if I was caught doing this, there would be an enormous mountain of abuse hurled my way. After a short while, she pulled away, and I completed my work there and left to go to the sacristy. I hoped she would find some heat left in the iron if she wanted it.

When I left the laundry room, Mary returned to the sink and poured some hot water into a basin. She put her hands in the basin and soaked them, trying to move the heat into other parts of her body. Mary looked out the window to see the filament of a slice of sunlight glaze the icicles on the pane of glass. She felt soothed by even a glint of the sun. The pane of glass represented a beguiling work of splendor, and as quickly as it formed, it disappeared and then reappeared in the glass of the wind-swept window. Like the happy quality of a well-savored piece of chocolate, the moment did not last too long, but it was enough to bolster her spirits.

Mary stood stiffly at the window and put her warm hands on her neck to rub the soreness out of her bones. Sister Dolores crept past the laundry door and frowned when she saw Mary bending into the sink for a moment to catch a few seconds of relief before she took the new load of clothes to the clothesline. Mary had another few hours to go before she finished her work. She pushed up her sleeves and plunged both hands into the water to catch another mound of clothes and prepare them for the mangle.

Back in the sacristy, I thought of what had happened the night before. I was thankful to have Mary as a stalwart companion in this gaping, hostile house. Mary stood out from the shadows. Her joyous personality resounded, even in the depth of the silences in which we found ourselves encased. She had a quality about her that did not fade. I gazed out the window. Moments ago, I detected bright diamonds on the cold windows. They had disappeared or simply faded, readying themselves to come into view when the searchlight of the sun's rays sought them out. There was very little sun today, and in the distance, I heard a roll of thunder, which did not bode well for Mary.

In the laundry, Mary glanced at the wicker basket. It was brimming over. She braced herself for the drag of another heavy load.

CHAPTER THIRTY-THREE

THE SHOES

January 11, 1967—6:00 a.m.

It was extremely cold these mornings. I still hated the slap of chill that enveloped me when I got out of bed. By now, everyone had achieved a certain quality of adeptness at getting washed and dressed in minutes. The dormitory was like an ice box, and the postulants wanted to get out of it as quickly as possible once the nightly cocoons of their beds were no longer available. If nothing else, the chapel was at least a little warmer.

The light beside the tabernacle pulsated. Simply looking at the constant throb of light the candle produced gave the illusion of warmth. It was enough for me to get rid of the chill that had settled in my core when I hit the floor this morning. When I had put on my shoes that morning, I noticed holes in the soles of both of them. As I sat in the chapel, I thought of what I was going to do about those holes. My shoes were worn, and my stockings were almost threadbare. I could feel the marble floor beneath my feet.

Mass started, and I forgot about my shoes. The morning chores brought some heat into my body. All the while, though, I knew my shoes were going to give me trouble. My feet were quickly soaked from hanging the sacristy towels in the laundry courtyard. When I came inside the laundry room to put my basket down, I looked for something to insert into my shoe to give me a bit of relief. I could not find anything suitable.

I took off my right shoe. The hole in the sole was large. I had never encountered this problem before. My father took pride in our sturdy shoes. He knew they would have to withstand tree climbing, running up and down the lanes as we chased one another at play, and walking miles back and forth to school every day. He polished all of our shoes every Saturday night, and they kept their shine at least for a few days afterward. I realized I had a lot of work to accomplish before the day was through. I would be racing from one chore to another. Already, I must have put thousands of miles on the shoes I was wearing since my arrival in this place. I took off the other shoe, which was not any better. I looked in the corner of the laundry and saw a few cardboard boxes stacked there.

Each box was sealed and marked with the names of the various liquids, soaps, powders, and detergents they contained. It was at once evident that, though there was an ample supply of cardboard in the corner, I could not break any seal to open a box. Such behavior was looked upon as the manifestation and needless exercise of personal control over something, which was frowned upon.

I would have to ask Sister Dolores for permission to open a box. If we needed supplies of any kind, even a bar of soap, we had to go to her at the beginning of recreation, kneel at her feet, and, while on our knees before her, ask for the desired object. Sister Dolores would always ask us to show her the remains of the almost depleted item before she gave us permission to go to the supply cupboard and retrieve the new item. It was her way of shackling the postulants.

Very often, permission was not given for a bar of soap or toothpaste or the replacement of a broken toothbrush. We often had to resort to brushing our teeth with our fingers, which was becoming the rule rather than the exception. The thought of asking for a pair of shoes was something I did not want to consider any time soon. I was determined to look around to see if I could find something to put inside my shoes to cover the holes there. If I could not do that, I would have to prostrate myself before Sister Dolores one of these days, and grovel and beg and receive the humiliation that was hurled at me. I wanted to retain some sense of dignity at this point.

I had brought four pairs of shoes with me when I entered the convent in September. It did not take me very long to realize that these shoes had been sent to the other side of the house to be used by the older nuns. I had recognized at least one pair in the chapel the week before.

The bell rang for the midday meal and brought me out of my reverie. I made my way to the refectory, now very much aware that the chafing of my shoes was getting worse with each step I took. After the meal was over, I went into the kitchen to help wash the dishes. Sister Freda Mary winked at me and nodded for me to go to the inner pantry. I knew there would be something special waiting there for me before I left for the afternoon. I looked forward to that treat. I felt the roughness of the tiles underneath my feet as I moved forward. I wiped my hands on the apron I had just donned and took off my shoe to show it to Sister Freda Mary.

"You will have to get another pair of shoes right away," she said to me very earnestly.

"I am afraid to ask," I responded in a dejected voice, now very aware of the strain that the request would put on me. "Do you have something I could put inside them for a few weeks?" I asked hopefully. "I want to delay this request as long as possible."

"Then let me see what I can do to help the situation," Sister Freda Mary offered. She went into the scullery and brought out a wad of newspaper. "This will not keep for too long," she said with a sigh, "but let us see how much time you can get out of it. This paper might hold you for a day or two. You just cannot go around with those shoes for much longer."

She put my shoes on the ledge beside the sink, snapped a pair of scissors from a drawer, and cut around my shoes with the scissors. She put the cut-out wad of newspaper inside each shoe and gave them to me. I continued washing the dishes, and before I left, I hurriedly ate the last piece of homemade, wheaten bread that was lathered in thick, creamy butter and dolloped with strawberry jam. *It is a dessert fit for royalty*, I thought as I relished every piece I put into my mouth.

I made my way to the recreation room to find that some of the postulants were already on their knees with their humble requests. The thought of asking for a pair of shoes felt overwhelming. I would have to ask for a pair of shoes soon, but not tonight. The thought left me feeling fretful. I took my seat at the bottom of the table and grabbed a needle and some thread as I started to stitch the Sacred Heart badges.

The next day, I was on stair duty. I was assigned to wash all the stairs outside the dormitory, down as far as the chapel floor, and the ten extra steps leading to the lower basement. It was a heavy task. There were fifty-six steps that took in every flight. I was expected to scrub each step on the stairway with water and a scrubbing brush from one bucket with detergent in it, and then using a cloth, rinse that step from a second bucket that contained only hot water. Then a dry cloth was used to feverishly wipe that step until it was as dry as possible, before I progressed to the next one.

The first time I had this chore assigned to me, I kept looking down each flight. As I bent over the bannister and looked at the territory I was to cover, many different, creative ideas sped through my head about how to get the job done quickly. No matter how creative I became, the reality of the specific orders from Sister Dolores to rub, rinse, and wipe dry one step at a time, left me without the ability to realize any creative solutions. I thought about scrubbing two steps at a time, and then rinsing and drying them. I figured out a way to extend that plan to include three steps at a time.

Sister Dolores was forever adamant that her orders be carried out to the letter. With her voice ringing in my ear, I felt the imagination and creativity creep out of me, and I knew I had to deal with reality. I would have to do the job one step at a time. I held the large scrubbing brush and plunged it into the bucket of soapy water held in my left hand and began the tedious work. On the right was the bucket I used for rinsing. The water in that bucket would get dirty as quickly as the other.

At the end of each flight of stairs, I had to change the water in both buckets and begin each new section with clean water. Those orders were ringing in my memory. At times I had the urge to just tip over the bucket with the suds and pour it down the stairs. I chuckled at the thought. As I tried to hurry, some water spilled onto the lower steps as I robotically went through the three-step regimen.

By the time I had finished the first flight of stairs, the errant water had soaked into the soles of my shoes. I sat on the top of the next flight of stairs before disposing of the two buckets of dirty water in the nearby bathrooms and refilling them with clean water for the next part of my journey. I took off my shoes and looked at the sodden wads of black-inked paper I held in my hands. I wanted to cry. The realization that I would have to ask for a new pair of shoes filled me with dread. I would have to ask soon.

I dragged the buckets to the bathroom and emptied the contents. The water was thick with dirt. I filled both buckets again, put detergent in one, and struggled to carry them to the second flight of stairs. With clean water in both buckets, I became aware of my exhaustion. I thought of the two remaining flights to scrub and garnered some energy. I was seized by the thought of getting the job done quicker by doing three stairs at a time.

I looked up and down the stairs furtively, and with my heart throbbing and my arms aching, I pushed myself into a frenzy. I went down to the fourth step and stretched the scrubbing brush to the top step. I descended quickly to the next step and then the one just in front of me. I took the cloth from the second bucket and frantically rinsed the three steps and then proceeded to dry them with the towel. I enjoyed the thought of finishing this task ahead of the schedule I had set for myself. I hauled the two buckets down another four steps and stretched the scrubbing brush once again, pushing it to get the next three stairs washed, rinsed, and dried with a fury and an energy I did not know was within me at that point. Deciding that my plan was successful, I dragged the buckets to the next set of three steps. Out of nowhere, I felt a hard slap hit my back so sharply that I flinched and almost fell backwards. I turned around to find a dark glower in the face of Sister Dolores, who had a broom in her hand.

I dreaded the bellow that was in store and expected a torrent of abuse to hail from her throat. The bellow did not come, and the torrent was held at bay. I stood with my soaked apron and heard the squelch of wet paper in my shoes when I moved from one foot to another.

Sister Dolores quietly hissed out her words. "Madam from County Derry, when you have finished the remainder of these steps, *one at a time*, you may go up the stairs by starting from the bottom stair and climbing to the top stair on your knees. That might teach you to listen and obey my orders."

I almost dropped the scrubbing brush that was in my hand. I had worked on these stairs for almost two hours already. Sister Dolores smirked as she left me to finish my work. When I was finished, I made my way agonizingly up the flights of stairs I had just scrubbed clean. Little did I know that Sister Dolores returned to make sure that I was obeying her. She noticed the holes on the bottoms of my shoes. She would contain the rumbles of thunder that were already rolling through her for another time.

It took me well over an hour to climb the three flights of stairs on my knees. When I got to the top stair, there was no sense of accomplishment. My knees hurt so much that I wanted to cry. I would keep my tears for greater challenges, which I knew were tucked somewhere within that cruel quiver, which only Sister Dolores could access.

CHAPTER THIRTY-FOUR

THE LEAK

January, 14 1967—8:00 a.m.

I took my place at the bottom table of the refectory after Mass. I felt tired, and my knees still pained me when I knelt in the chapel. I heard dishes being passed in silence. Some novice was reading a chapter from the life of Saint John of the Cross. Absentmindedly, I took some porridge from the hot, steaming bowl and began to eat, surrounded mostly by silence, except I heard the sounds of spoons scraping the contents out of the steaming bowls. I heard the jangle of cutlery being placed on the enamel plates and the distant thud of some work being accomplished by one of the nuns in the kitchen. I wondered where Mary O'Brien had disappeared to a few moments after we left the chapel.

Shortly into our morning meal, Mary appeared with a bucket, obviously filled with water. The water splashed and brimmed over the edge of the bucket as she made her way into the middle of the refectory floor. Once there, all eyes were on Mary. She was having some difficulty kneeling beside the bucket and put her hand on the bucket to ensure her balance. I wept inside for my friend.

"Forgive me, sisters, for causing the sink to overflow in the laundry room!"

Mary shouted the words from her epicenter, and they sounded as if they went through the skylight, such was her bugle call. I suspected that Mary was not in the least affected by the theatre she had just created. For some reason, Mary O'Brien was able to sustain her composure, no matter the challenge placed before her. She took an enamel cup from the bucket, scooped water into it, and then proceeded to drink it very slowly. We all realized that Mary was going to have a stomach full of water for breakfast this morning.

I heard the Kerry postulants snigger. They never received any type of punishment and reveled in that fact so much that they had a confident swagger in their walk. Other postulants were assigned to bring in the clothes from the courtyard. While the rest of us pulled up vegetables in the garden and peeled and sliced them in the shed, weeded, raked leaves, collected firewood, and did the heavy work in the house, the Kerry postulants folded the dry clothes when they came in from the clotheslines in the comfort of the laundry and were responsible for making the butterballs in the creamery attached to the barn after Jimmy McGinty had churned the milk. There was no kitchen duty, no time in the sacristy, no stairs they had to clean or windows to wash. They had it glaringly easy.

As breakfast continued, Mary drank a few more cups of water, and then decided to sip it instead. It was clear to me that she had had enough after about ten minutes, so she was spending the remainder of the breakfast triggering the pathology that sat just beneath one layer of Sister Dolores's skin. Every so often, Mary would chug and gurgle as she dramatically got through this ritual. It did not seem torturous at all. In fact, I really felt that Mary was using the time in the middle of the floor as a stage. If she was not allowed to play the piano, then she would act.

Some of the older nuns sitting at other tables had smiles on their faces. That was rarely seen, and when Sister Dolores noticed it, she became uneasy and squirmed in her place at the table. When the bell rang to end breakfast, she stomped toward Mary O'Brien and stood over her.

"You can kneel there for as many meals as it takes you to finish the entire bucket. Go and leave it in the corner of the pantry, and you can get it before the next meal, and I do not care if you have to kneel in this refectory for another week."

Mary got up awkwardly and did as she was told. Sister Freda Mary would find time to go to the pantry during the morning, and with the enamel cup, throw a little of the water down the sink.

These theatrics were a result of Mary's bright idea while in the laundry the day before. She thought that, to save time, she would put some of the clothes she had just washed into the rinsing sink while she rushed to hang the items on the clotheslines that she had just put through the mangle. She estimated that while she was at the clothesline, the clothes in the rinsing sink would be ready for the mangle when she returned to the laundry. She had managed three loads of washing this way. While she was hanging up the clothes, the water in the sink was filling up, which would save her at least five minutes on each load.

The sinks were gigantic, and it took a lot of water to rinse the clothes. Instead of standing there, waiting for the water to cover the clothes, Mary had developed a more efficient method of coping with the mountain of clothes she had to sort through each day. She was quite delighted and felt a certain enjoyment when she saw that this new method she designed was working so well.

She encountered Sister Dolores in the laundry room as she raced to take care of the fourth load in the rinsing sink. Mary's blood froze in her veins. She was not afraid of Sister Dolores or the venom she was capable of producing. She was annoyed at being caught.

"Get down on your knees immediately after you have turned off that water!" Sister Dolores screamed.

Mary did not pay any attention to the screaming. It was as if she just automatically tuned it out. Mary turned off the water, which had just begun to overflow, and then knelt down. "I am a right idiot," Mary heard herself utter under her breath, but Sister Dolores was so enraged that she did not hear her. Mary felt defiant. She had seen Sister Dolores slap a postulant on the face recently and kick another, and she was quite determined that this would never happen to her. Sister Dolores detected the defiance in Mary's face, and her eyes shifted uncomfortably. Mary imagined herself wrestling Sister Dolores to the ground and pummeling her. She felt very smug and satisfied in that thought, and some semblance of confidence must have appeared on Mary's face. Whatever it was, it was enough for Sister Dolores to step back and take stock of the situation. She seemed to back off as she reflected on Mary's large frame kneeling in front of her.

"You, madam, will bring a bucket full of water into the refectory tomorrow morning, and you will kneel in the middle of the floor for every meal until the contents of that bucket is emptied. I do not care if it takes you days to finish it all. Now, get up and get the rest of this work done."

Mary felt like sniggering, but stopped herself from doing so, thinking of the nonsense she would have to endure. She would take the punishment and put it behind her. It was a ridiculous thing she was ordered to do, but at this point, the days were rolling by so quickly, she could already envision herself away from the snares and the guile of this woman.

Mary struggled to her feet. She often told me she was jealous of the way I could get on my knees so readily and get up with the greatest of ease without any help.

Now, after breakfast, Mary O'Brien looked into the bucket. She realized that she could be there another two days on her knees. Part of the punishment, of course, Mary determined, was that Sister Dolores could forbid her to go to the bathroom and just have her stay in the refectory for hours. Sister Dolores had not thought of that, and it was sufficient for Mary to drink from the bucket at successive meals.

The saga of Mary's bucket lasted only one more day, as the contents of the bucket were being gradually diminished when Sister Freda Mary got up in the morning and went to bed last thing at night. After dinner the following day, Mary was finished with the water. Her real struggle was getting onto the floor and enduring the cold flagstones under her knees for the duration of the meals and then struggling to get to her feet. Mary wanted to be finished with the physical discomfort because that was the greatest ordeal. She was not concerned about being in the middle of the floor with everyone looking at her. When she finally put the cup on the floor to signal that she had finished her punishment, Sister Dolores approached to view the bucket.

Before she was able to do that, Mary turned to the bucket and vomited into it. This development was more than Sister Dolores could tolerate.

She screamed at the top of her voice, "You bitch! Get back to your work in the laundry and make sure you clean that bucket!"

Mary was quite surprised to find that she was feeling sick, as she took the bucket to the laundry to clean up. "This one will never break me," Mary said to herself as she made her way to the laundry room. She turned on the water in the rinsing sink and spent the next twenty minutes letting gallons of water flow freely down the drain. She knew that Sister Dolores would not follow her there. Mary returned to her duties in the laundry and used every opportunity to use more water than she needed for her chores.

CHAPTER THIRTY-FIVE

THE MUSIC LESSON

Mary Ita Ahern tended to be on the quiet side. Convent life suited her personality. She was not too easily affected by the grand silence, and the rules and regulations that strangled me seemed to be easily tolerated by her. Initially, she was alarmed by the absence of any kind of humanity from Sister Dolores, but she accommodated herself readily and quickly to the climate that the postulants found themselves in. She generally found that Sister Dolores ignored her. Mary Ita Ahern had learned to stay within the margins of the rules and did not stand out in any way. The only gift that she brought to the convent was her general mediocrity in everything she did. She did not stand out as being great or adept at anything. In fact, Mary Ita just blended into life in Fairview Convent. Her strengths were minimal. She did not get enthused about anything. She kept quiet. She was always involved in things, but she got lost in the crowd. She never expressed any level of emotion. She stretched neither to the right nor to the left.

Mary Ita completed her assigned chores without expending too much energy. She listened in class, but she never ventured an answer to a question unless called upon to do so. When giving an answer, she always gave a satisfactory one. There was no intellectual brilliance housed in her brain. She gave the shortest version to any biblical question she was asked to relate. She never expressed any emotion. In her months so far with the group of postulants, her affect was proven flat.

Mary Ita Ahern created no waves, put her head down when she was working in the garden or scraping vegetables and did not get in anyone's way. She never made any false moves and stayed beyond the sight and grasp of Sister Dolores. Mary Ita was vigilant about never breaking any rules. She just seemed to fade into the woodwork.

Mary Ita had been raised by her grandfather, Finn O'Sullivan, when her mother died shortly after she was born. Finn O'Sullivan had been the local blacksmith in the countryside near Ballyeden, County Mayo, where Mary Ita had lived a quiet life with him. When he was younger, Finn O'Sullivan had a good, healthy business that was tucked far from the forest bordering his land, near the edge of the river that flowed through the village. The farmers all around the hinterland came to him and had to wait, sometimes for hours, as Finn bellowed the flames and punched the iron to perfection to ensure that every horse in the vicinity was properly shod. Mary Ita often came to watch him, which he allowed, as long as she kept a safe distance. She was fascinated by the constant punch of the heavy hammer on the anvil and mesmerized by the white heat required for the iron to respond to the punch.

Fire crackled and sputtered and streamed from each blow that fell in bright sparks all around her grandfather. Each punch contained the next punch. Each clear cling and clang of the metal instruments inspired another, as the hammer forcefully hit into the air in splitting, pounding regularity. The banging resonated one bang at a time. Mary Ita remembered seeing her grandfather wipe his brow with a cloth, as water hissed and sizzled, covered by a constant flush of water pellets that ran down his face. Finn worked well into the evening, and the sparks from the anvil blows often lit up the night. The punch of the hammer was steady and focused and resounded deeply.

When he was older, Finn shut down the forge. Shortly after that, Mary Ita told him that she wanted to enter the convent. He felt he was too old to object. He had not been to Mass since his daughter died. Mary Ita entered Fairview Convent the next year.

In the middle of January 1967, Sister Dolores let the postulant group know in class one morning that she was going to pick four postulants to take music lessons. Sister Dolores already had her mind settled on the four individuals. We knew that the three

County Kerry girls were on her list, but she surprised us all by choosing Mary Ita Ahern for the fourth person to receive this honor. All had very little or no understanding of music. Mary O'Brien, who played the piano brilliantly, had been forbidden to go near the piano. This command, uttered by Sister Dolores, who had heard her play a few days after she arrived at Fairview Convent last September, tore at Mary's heart for months.

"What was that you just played, madam?" Sister Dolores had asked Mary, her eyes brimming over with envy.

Mary had found a piano the second day after her arrival, and not yet schooled in the rules and regulations of what to touch and what not to touch, had sat at the piano in one of the parlors and put her hands on the keys. She was in a state of sheer delight as she began to play one of her favorite pieces. She was totally enthralled by the music when she heard Sister Dolores breathing heavily beside her. She was fidgeting with the large rosary beads that were knotted tightly around her waist. They looked like a weapon in her hands.

"Sister, that was part of Liszt's *Liebestraum No. 3 in A Flat Minor*," Mary relayed in a disappointed tone, already sensing that she would not be permitted to finish the piece. Sister Dolores snapped her fingers, signaling Mary to stop and leave the room. She felt a sense of incompleteness. She had been enraptured by the music, and everyone, who had heard the piano played so vibrantly in those few minutes, was struck with awe. Mary O'Brien had a gift, which could never be taken away. In the weeks following her removal from engaging in one of her passionate connections, she found herself composing symphonies in her head. Such was the extent of her talent. She found her own way to play her cherished instrument. Often in the chapel, Mary's fingers were rarely still. She would practice, no matter what. Just by moving her fingers to the music in her head, Mary was intent on keeping it alive in her depths. It would be so deep that even Sister Dolores could not reach it or disturb it.

Mary Ita Ahern had never played the piano before and was glad for the opportunity that came her way. It would take her out of circulation for one hour a week with music lessons, and then she was to practice every day for one hour. The music teacher, Mrs. Moore, came from the local town. She was a small bundle of energy, a widow in her sixties, and her only son had gone to England to work as an apprentice carpenter when he had finished high school. Mrs. Moore had taught in the local school and took students into her home on Saturdays to tutor them in the art of playing the piano. Mrs. Moore was active in the affairs of the town and generally known to be a hale and hearty soul. She was a welcome respite from the drudgery of the daily tasks that had to be done around this big house. The chosen four could be heard by all of us as we performed our chores in proximity to the lessons. One sounded as bad as the other, but Mary Ita Ahern proved to be the greatest challenge of all for Mrs. Moore.

At the first lesson, Mrs. Moore sang the scale and asked Mary Ita to sing the scale after her. She noted immediately that Mary Ita was off key as she tried to intone the octave. Mrs. Moore, therefore, was not surprised that the lack of musicality transferred to the keys of the piano. Mary Ita had no sense of rhythm or beat. Though she practiced the simplest of tunes over and over, first with her right hand and then with her left, Mary Ita had trouble playing with both hands at the same time. Mrs. Moore had never had such a student. She wondered, more often than not, why Sister Dolores had put this young woman in her hands for music lessons. It was obvious from the very first lesson that it would be a serious chore to extract any music from her. Mary Ita would never bond with the instrument, even though she spent an hour every day at practice.

Every day, the strangled strains of "Amazing Grace" resounded on the second floor of the convent. Every day, the effort echoed in a cacophony of sounds that jarred once Mary Ita used both hands. The notes played by the right hand were never in synchronicity with the notes played by the left hand. There was no harmony, even with her most earnest efforts. Mary Ita was quite determined to succeed, though and focused on the hope that, at some point, Mrs. Moore would recognize the tune she was playing. Mary Ita had begun to enjoy the hour she spent in the music room by herself every day. It was her only chance to be alone. Inside the music room, she slowly began to realize that this felt much better than being around Sister Dolores.

A month later, the tune that emerged from the walls of the music room while Mary Ita played was indiscernible. She showed meager progress in spite of spending her allotted time to practice. Sister Dolores heard her play every day and smirked every time she passed the door. Mrs. Moore kept coming to give lessons, and Mary Ita kept playing. Mrs. Moore knew that there was very little hope for Mary Ita. Sister Dolores met Mrs. Moore one Tuesday afternoon as she was coming in the main door of the convent to deliver the music lessons to her four students.

"May I have a word with you, Mrs. Moore, before you start your teaching?"

She brought Mrs. Moore into the main parlor to the left of the front entrance. The room was dark, but Sister Dolores showed no interest in turning on the light. She did not close the door and stood in the room, filtered by a semblance of light from the window panels of the front door.

"Mrs. Moore, I would like you to prepare Mary Ita Ahern to play for Sunday Mass at the end of the month."

Mrs. Moore was astounded and found herself trying to mumble her way to articulation.

"Sister Dolores, Mary Ita struggles with the simplest of pieces I assign her to practice. She definitely puts the time and effort into the work, but she really has no ability. I do not think she would be able to accomplish such a task. Besides, piano work does not easily transfer to the organ, especially in that you have to learn how to hold the keys down with your fingers."

Sister Dolores ignored the plea that was so evident in Mrs. Moore's voice.

"Surely you can teach her the simplest of hymns, Mrs. Moore. The hymn 'Now Thank We All Our God' seems such a simple melody. Have her ready to play at the end of March. That is what you are being paid for. You can begin to practice on the organ in the chapel today. Thank you, Mrs. Moore." Sister

Dolores waved her hand dismissively at Mrs. Moore and exited the door.

Mrs. Moore sensed a foreboding in the exchange. She made her way to the music room on the second floor where Mary Ita was sitting erect on the piano stool, waiting her arrival.

"Sister Dolores wants me to teach you a very simple hymn for the end of February. We had better get to the chapel and get started."

Mary Ita looked somewhat surprised at this news, but she made her way to the chapel and began to feel good about herself. She thought she had impressed Sister Dolores in some way. It was generally considered an honor to play the organ for Sunday Mass. Mrs. Moore went to the back of the chapel and unlocked the organ. She felt totally dejected. The task ahead felt monumental. She decided that there was no way Mary Ita could learn to play the pedals with her feet. She would keep this as simple as possible. She would pull out the stops that were simple. She took a deep breath as she spread out the sheet of music for "Now Thank We All Our God" above the keys. She asked Mary Ita to play the first line.

I was cleaning the sacristy with Margaret Logue when we heard a plaintive wail come from the organ at the back of the chapel. We peered out to see what was causing the disturbance in this sacred space. We looked at each other, wondering what was happening. The noise continued for an hour. Neither Margaret nor I recognized the hymn Mary Ita was attempting to have emerge from the black-and-white organ keys. Mrs. Moore was pressing Mary Ita hard, having her repeat one line of the sheet of music at a time. More than once, Mrs. Moore looked to the tabernacle in the sanctuary and asked God for patience.

CHAPTER THIRTY-SIX

ASKING FOR NEW SHOES

Recreation Room—7:00 p.m.

It was a cold January in 1967 on the banks of Lake Fennan. The winds howled most days, and the rains poured from the heavens. Every day when I got out of bed, I tested the thick wad of paper in my shoes. At one point the week before, when I went into the kitchen, Sister Freda Mary had cut up some old linoleum she had found on a shelf and put a piece in each of my shoes, which lasted for two days. When the linoleum cracked, it tore into the soles of my feet and made them bleed. My feet were beginning to be really sore, and I felt I could not even endure the wad of paper that had to be replaced every other day. My chores required that I often go outside, and I found myself limping around, suffering in cold, wet shoes. I finally decided to ask for a pair of new shoes.

On a Sunday night in the middle of February, just before recreation began, I went and knelt before Sister Dolores.

"What do you want, madam?" Sister Dolores snarled.

I spoke quickly so that my request did not take too long.

"Sister, both my shoes have holes in them, and I need a new pair. May I please have a new pair of shoes? I know that I brought four pairs of shoes with me when I came in September when I arrived here."

The last remark created blackness in the eyes of Sister Dolores. A fury was already brewing there, and it was my simple, last remark that had unleashed it. Sister Dolores began to breathe heavily and tap her foot. She bent over so that the blackness of her eyes stared into my blue eyes. I held my gaze, but I could feel what was going to come. Sister Dolores stood erect and spluttered and spewed and ranted for the next ten minutes.

"Who do you think you are asking for new shoes? Do you realize that the nuns in our mission territories are working night and day, not only to run schools and clinics, but also to maintain our convent and keep everyone in it fed and clothed and properly sheltered from the elements? They are killing themselves, working for the likes of you. If you ask me, they are wasting their time. They toil night and day, and you have the audacity to ask me for a pair of shoes. Do you think that they get new shoes every six months? You are a miserable weakling, taking advantage of every opportunity offered to you here."

She droned on and on, and I was determined not to respond. I continued to kneel and focused on trying not to hear the words she was saying. I imagined the words bouncing off me, as I knelt in my coat of armor. Eventually, I felt a knot in my stomach and the muscles in my back seize. I did not flinch. Sister Dolores continued to spit her words into the air. I did not know it then, but much later, I learned that mission territories in the United States, Australia, and England were being administered by many of the nuns who had gone through the rough handling of Sister Dolores while they were in Fairview Convent. The majority of these nuns, who worked in these places, were glad to leave Sister Dolores's abuses behind them. Nothing they had to endure in their work even slightly compared to the abuse and cruelty that had been leveled on them daily on the banks of Lake Fennan.

For those who did not come from County Kerry, time spent in Fairview Convent was a period of deep pain and unease as they crept quietly into each day, fearful of the eruptions Sister Dolores so frequently produced and the terror she regularly engendered. It was a place of serious cruelty, and the abuse was etched into them in ways they could never forget and that was often discernible. The young women sent to missions to work in schools and hospitals and clinics were glad to have the experience of Fairview Convent behind them. They considered the convent a place of torture, heavy burden, and despair.

There was very little humanity served there. Cruelty was on the cusp of every new day, and going to bed at night, getting in between those cold, white sheets, covered by a threadbare blanket, was the only relief they had until the knife of morning pierced them into the reality of another hard day. The anxiety started all over again as soon as their bare feet hit the cold, dormitory floor.

Many of the nuns who went to America and Australia and other parts of the world developed serious mental health disorders after settling in the new territories. Some became hypervigilant and chilled at any unusual loud noises. Others had to be sent to psychiatrists to be treated with therapy and medication. Every day, a number of them exhibited conditions that emanated from the trauma, stress, and bullying they had had to endure at the behest of Sister Dolores.

Mary O'Brien and I were among the few who endured the abuse of Fairview Convent and went on to lead relatively normal lives that were fruitful and creative. Our lives were full of good friendships and were meaningful and purposeful.

###

"Give me those shoes, you utterly despicable and good-for-nothing lout!" Sister Dolores shouted into my face. She had bent low again to try to gain some semblance of control.

I became aware of a shooting pain in my back when I tried to lean backward to avoid the spit that was dripping from her mouth. I reached back and took off both shoes. My feet were feeling very numb at that point and taking the shoes off created some warmth. My feet were like blocks of ice. Sister Dolores took the shoes and threw them into my face.

"Go sit down, you ungrateful wretch. How dare you come looking for shoes. These will do you just fine."

When I stood up, I felt six feet tall, for some reason that I could not understand. Maybe it was just the relief of getting this challenge over. No one paid much attention to this exchange. I thought how very sad it was that this abuse had become so normal that no one was shocked by it anymore. I went to my place at the table and threaded my needle to start sewing the Sacred Heart badges before me. Mary O'Brien rolled her eyes to the ceiling. Annie Boyle looked at me and tried to smile a welcome. Nuala O'Reilly tapped her fingers on her Sacred Heart badges. I knew I had their support. That was enough for me.

The next morning when I got up, I found a pair of shoes outside the curtain of my bed. My heart skipped a beat. Just as I was thinking that Sister Dolores might have a bit of a heart after all, I picked up the shoes to examine them, and realized that, not only were they different sizes, but also both were for the left foot. They would have to do. Something churned inside me. I put on the shoes. One crushed the toes of my right foot and the other slipped off my left foot. I would just have to adapt to them. I would have to adjust to a new way of coping and walk in a completely different way to hide my agony.

By the end of February, my right foot was chaffing and sore. I got some cotton wool from Sister Freda Mary to help me with the wounds on my toes from the too-tight shoe into which I had to squeeze my foot. There was no balm for the distress that was creeping very slowly into me as I coped with the pain the shoes inflicted with each step. Soon after, when I had to do kitchen duty, the two nuns in the kitchen let me take off my shoes as I worked. That alone gave me tremendous relief. Sister Bridget Mary found a pair of thick socks and gave them to me while I was in the kitchen.

One day, Sister Freda Mary came up with a concoction that helped sooth the discomfort I was experiencing. About ten days later, I found a new pair of shoes at the bottom of my bed in the morning. I put them on, and while they fit me, they hurt my feet. I delighted in the shoes. Hopefully, the discomfort in my feet would disappear. I had forgotten what it was like to live without pain. As I was leaving the chapel that morning, I thought that maybe the only reason I got the shoes from Sister Dolores was because I was to have a visit from my family in early February. I wondered a little uneasily if the shoes would be taken away from me after I had spent time with my family.

CHAPTER THIRTY-SEVEN

THE FIRST VISIT

February 2, 1967 was the Sunday before Ash Wednesday and the beginning of Lent. It was the first visit we ten postulants were allowed to have with our families. It had been five months since we had crossed the threshold from life as we knew it to a life that continually astonished us with its stringent rules and regulations. Care and connection and communication were all rationed in this place. Most days they did not exist, and we went about our duties on automatic pilot. We gave little thought about what we did.

There were more than sixty nuns living in various wings of Fairview Convent. We were not knit together by any sense of community. We gathered for prayers and meals and performed our chores. There was no effort at forging friendships. We barely acknowledged one another as the weeks became months. We hurtled through the day with the sole purpose of cleaning the house, pruning the trees, and weeding the gardens to ensure that we were fed. We were united in silence. The Grand Silence was imposed on us beginning with night prayers and ending after breakfast the following morning. But talking during any part of the day was discouraged, and we lived lives that ran parallel to one another. There was little intersection of those parallel lines. If we met another postulant on the stairs or in the corridor, the younger in rank had to stand back and bow to the older postulant. Camaraderie did not exist. Within weeks after entering the convent, we learned that we were totally subservient to authority. We could not question or discuss anything that was proposed for us.

Authority controlled and authority imposed its weight on us by being demanding and vigilant in laying down the rules and regulations that commanded the way we talked and worked and spoke. Little by little, our confidence eroded. Little by little, most of the energetic personalities who had been bright and vibrant and effervescent last September slowly wilted to robotic-like living. Very few friendships were formed. Mary, Nuala, Annie, and I seemed to be the healthiest because we had found a way to bond. We quickly realized that we were all from the northern part of Ireland, spoke with the same accent, and definitely felt there was no great welcome for us in Fairview Convent. We found a way to communicate with one another, despite the imposition of strict decrees and useless and meaningless edicts uttered by the harsh tongue of Sister Dolores, who was the embodiment of all who lacked any semblance of humanity. Our lives were becoming more dull and grim by the day, but we somehow managed to smile at some point. Chores became rote. They had to be done. We had to be kept occupied every moment of the day. There was just no fun in anything we did.

By the time the first visit for the postulants came around, five months after our entry into Fairview Covent, we were walking a little slower and were less energetic. We were bent under the load of dreariness and only now and again caught brief glimpses of the sun's rays. We walked on thin ice all day, and we needed to be constantly aware that we could crash through at any moment. The thing I realized about ice was that the quiet murmur of the current underneath can often be heard. We were frozen in the ice of time. There was no life or liveliness around us. We had not been exposed to any glimmer of happiness since coming through that big, dark door on that September day the previous year.

We four friends had been beaten low enough to hear the depths of breath we had to reach in order to survive. We learned to feel the touch of the other's voice because the intonation of our words had to be cast in a special mold to let one another know that we felt the stresses and challenges we were draped in every day. We four shared a special loaf, having been kneaded together on the coldest of stone slabs.

On February 2, 1967, I awoke to a dawn steeped in the sound of stillness, punctuated here and there by the echo of a sigh or a cough. Today, I would finally get to see my family. It had been five long months.

I unwrapped myself from my cardigan and pulled it around my arms. The cardigan was full of heat, so I pulled it closer to me before the arrival of the knock that would inevitably thrust itself upon the dormitory door. When I opened my eyes, I saw my breath sputter out of me like little bursts of smoke. The dormitory was freezing this morning. Every little puff of breath looked like bursts of steam. Under the icy feeling in this dormitory, I could still sense a strong current of life beneath its surface. In this cold place, which at this moment felt like a freezer, I would have to chisel this ice back to life. I would have to strike boldly into the thickest part to find movement. I would have to develop an indomitable spirit to melt through the most encrusted regulations in this religious congregation. I would have to break the most embedded rules in order to bring a freshness to the glow that was still in my heart, a glow that had been forged long ago, as I sat around the hearth in my home in Derry. I should bring that fire from the kitchen hearth wherever I went. The thought of my family stirred excitement in my heart.

All was suddenly warm that cold morning in that dormitory iced within the pod of oppression. I felt I could set fire to that dormitory that morning. I glowed in delight and enjoyed the anticipation of seeing my family that day. I felt my tunic and stockings underneath me. Weeks ago, I had learned to put my tunic and stockings in bed with me at night, so they would retain some of my body heat, giving me a bit of comfort as I froze each new winter morning. Today, I would see my mother and father and many of my siblings. This morning I could not wait for the intonation of the words, "Let us bless the Lord," and the accompanying loud thud on the door of the dormitory that would send me into the tumble of the day.

It would take my family almost three hours to get to Fairview Convent. My youngest sister was extremely excited. Her eyes blazed with nausea as my cousin's car rumbled over the cattle roads at the entrance of Fairview Convent. My cousin noticed that the gate had been freshly painted.

I waited for them outside the main entrance, opposite the lake, as today we were allowed to stand outside the front door and talk to one another. Nuala, Mary, Annie, and I stood together. The cars from Northern Ireland were the first to arrive. Mary and Nuala had just taken their family members into the front parlors, when I saw the Derry car pull up in front of the convent. I could barely contain my excitement.

When my mother and father got out of the car, I ran over to them and hugged them as tightly as I could. My mother looked at me and told me the color had gone out of my cheeks. My father just smiled and seemed glad he was there. My mother asked me if everything was all right. I gave her the best smile that I could muster. She did not seem reassured, but quickly became distracted by herding my brothers and sisters into the dark gape of the door in the convent.

Dan, Rose, Christy, and my youngest sister, Theresa, were awestruck by the immensity of the place once inside. Theresa was not happy when she saw the black dress I was wearing—I had always worn the brightest colors. When she examined my black, polished shoes and black stockings, the color drained from her face. I reached out to give her a hug, but she suddenly bolted across the lawn, her heels kicked high behind her, giving her more and more propulsion.

She was a powerful symbol of a spirited and free life. She looked as if she could actually take flight. As I watched her sprint into the distance towards the lake, I felt as if my black, polished shoes were stuck in the concrete of Fairview Convent. Theresa's buoyancy in the wind made me realize that her journey was just beginning, and I no longer would be a big part of it. I sighed to myself.

As Theresa hurtled at full speed, her tears fell on the grass below. They splattered down her face. They fell into the reeds covering the lawn. She kept running. She spread her arms further into the wind. She gave the impression of being in the air. She needed to fly before she could feel the long, cold drink of the visit. When she finally stopped at the fence, she blew fully through her cheeks and felt sick. She gulped deeply from the trough of raw air. It hurt her to breathe, and she had a pain in her side. She was breathless, as she came through the convent door. I grasped her hand, and, when we went into the parlor for tea, she quickly nestled quietly beside me.

Sister Dolores visited every parlor. She had warned us the night before that we were not to utter a word of complaint when we met our families. Before the visits took place, we had been commanded to write to our parents and ask for various items. Our families presumed we would enjoy their gifts, so it was with great delight that they had engaged in this extra shopping.

At the end of our visits, we went to the recreation room with the gifts from our families—biscuits, cakes, baskets of fruit, boxes of candy, various sweets, combs, toothbrushes, hairbrushes, and other items—and placed them on the table at the end of the room. When recreation was over, a group of nuns from the other side of the house came and scooped up the items, taking them to their own quarters. They looked forward to the visits we postulants had with our families because it was an opportunity for them to restock their depleted items.

Sister Dolores had told us that, if she detected any member of any family looking at her with distain, or if she suspected that we had used the opportunity of the visit to complain to our families in any way, we would not get another visit, or we possibly would be sent home. This last threat left some of the postulants afraid and distressed.

Mary, Nuala, and I felt secure within ourselves and our friendship with each other. When we had the opportunity to talk on our daily walks, we agreed that, if we were ever sent home, there would be very little work accomplished. We would have worked enough. At night, now, just before we fell asleep, we connected with each other merely by sneezing or coughing. We loved to break into the Grand Silence by coughing into it or sneezing into it. The Grand Silence held our sighs and often our tears.

###

During this first visit, my mother was anxious to find out all she could about how I was doing. Immediately after Sister Dolores left the parlor and we were passing the sandwiches to the younger ones, my mother commented about how cold it was in the room.

"It is freezing in this place," my mother commented when Sister Dolores finally closed the door. "How are you doing?" she asked.

I knew I had to be careful enough with my answer because I did not want her to leave this place worried about me.

"Mum I am doing well. It is hard enough, but I am managing."

My mother did not look at all convinced. My father poured another cup of tea for everyone and made sure the younger ones were eating.

"I have been looking for that little sign in your letters. You have to know that if you want to leave, we will be here in a matter of hours to pick you up. You do not look warm enough." She poured me a cup of tea and proceeded to open her bag and bring out a huge piece of Christmas cake. "This is for you. Now eat it up. We kept it for you. It will do you good to eat it."

I knew my face brightened, and I savored every piece of the heavy, fruited cake. As I ate it, I was conscious of being anxious about Sister Dolores coming into the room. My mother sensed my discomfort and poured some more tea. I think I made it worse for her by spending too much time trying to reassure her that all was well.

Whenever I moved to pour tea or got up to fill the pitcher of milk, I would wince because my back was sore. I knew I had become a little thinner, and when they kept telling me that the color had gone from my face, I realized I had not been aware of this—we had no mirrors in the convent. My sisters asked me what I did all day. I gave them a vague sketch of what a typical day looked like, embellishing every fact so that it sounded better than reality. They asked me what I learned in the classes and wondered if it was like a real school. When I told them that Sister Dolores was the only teacher, they turned up their noses.

They asked me if I prayed all day, sang hymns all the time, if I was allowed to sing any Beatles songs, or to look at the television. I think I lied with every answer I gave. I had not seen a television anywhere in the convent, though I did not go to the living quarters of the older sisters. I had not seen a newspaper. My only source of information about what was happening in the world came through my time spent in the kitchen.

Theresa asked me when I was coming home. I lied to her and told her I would be coming home soon, which was good enough for her. She drew in her breath as she took in the news and seemed never to want to take a deeper breath, in case my promise disappeared.

All too soon on that Sunday before Lent began, it was time for my family to leave. I wanted time to freeze in that moment. We reluctantly left the parlor and made our way to the front entrance of the convent. My cousin knew instinctively that something was not right. He was aware that Sister Dolores was somewhere in the shadows nearby, and when giving me a hug, he declared loudly, "Now remember, if things are too hard for you here or you just want to come home, you only have to let us know. We will be glad to have you back in Derry. You know that, don't you?"

I nodded my head. I swallowed the tears as I let each family member go after a tight embrace. As they walked through the dark and into the light of that late afternoon in February, I strongly wanted to jump into the car with them and go home to the comfort and welcome of my family. The wind's slap unfurled and whipped and flapped into the air.

"It is warmer out here than in that convent of yours," Pat declared as he said goodbye to me. All the little groups of families were packed into their cars for their destinations all over Ireland. We postulants clustered in a black heap and stood outside in the cold to wave every group a goodbye. The group seemed quite constricted except for Mary, Nuala, and me, as we waved furiously to our families, more to keep from crying than anything else. I smacked a kiss into my hand and blew it at Theresa as their car passed by. She caught it, and her eyes lit up. Theresa was determined that the kiss would stay in her hand. She held tight to it all the way home. I had whispered to her that I thought about her every single day and that I would see her again soon. The calendar had stretched much too long for Theresa, and she hoped that the time would be shorter before the next visit.

As soon as she was beyond the cattle roads, she settled between Dan and Rose in the back seat. They left with the fiery inferno of a sunset hanging like a work of art over Lake Fennan.

Very soon, on the way home, Theresa fell asleep as the sky darkened. She dreamed she was flying in the wind, holding something precious in her hand that she would never let go.

CHAPTER THIRTY-EIGHT

THE DEATH OF A DAD

The day after the visit, another cold day dawned in Fairview Convent. Two more days until Ash Wednesday, the beginning of Lent. Lake Fennan churned endlessly under an inch of thick fog. Nuala O'Reilly looked out the window of the dormitory that morning and wondered at the frost spreading its mantle over the trees. Hopefully, it would evaporate before noon.

Today, the priest had announced that we would be celebrating the feast of the Presentation of Jesus in the Temple. The gospel this morning heralded, for most of the postulants, the reality of those like Simeon, the old man who had waited all of his life in the temple to see the Messiah, and who had told Mary that a sword would pierce her heart. The message that a heart could be pierced seemed to stay with many of us during the day. We realized that the pain of evaporating dreams was taking place every day. We were aware that the experience of being part of something good and holy was subsiding every moment. The notion that our entrance into the convent was fleeing from what was good and wholesome in the world was taking hold.

"It should not be like this," Nuala said out loud, as she turned from the window.

This place made her look inward all the time. The feeling of being caged in and having to master the art of surviving on a daily basis was beginning to sap her energy.

By now, six months after her entrance into the convent, Nuala was aware that her every move was becoming more and more robotic. Every interaction was monitored. There was constant supervision. Much time and energy were given to the form and the appearance of things. It was so important that everything gleamed, that everything was clean and starched, glinted and polished. Every speck of dust was disposed of everywhere every day. The fact that the postulants were strained under such a load of expectations, that we were kept busy with the smallest details, made these limitations diminish our boundaries. As time went on, our world became smaller and smaller. It became like mere pixels on a picture with no appreciation of the whole, mere dots on a canvas with little understanding that the color was being drained out of our very core. Some postulants felt isolated from one another. More and more their connections were contrived. Connections were easily fractured when there was no depth.

Nuala was feeling hollow from the blow of emptiness that chimed in every hour of her day. Gone was the banter, the laughter with friends, the glee of simply being together with others. Her voice was practically silenced. Her Northern Ireland accent was frowned upon. But at least she had that in common with a few others. She was only allowed to nod, to bow her head, to blanket her emotions, to smile through her tears, to swallow the hurts, and to breathe in shallow breaths.

There was barely any exchange when the opportunity presented itself. If it were not for her northern friends, she would have been lost. Winter brought the fog and frost and the dull sky. Fairview Convent brought the fog and frost and its dullness inside its doors and there it thrived. Most of the postulants were able to continue to endure the harshness there. Today, on the Feast of the Presentation, the numerous candles displayed at morning Mass attempted to illustrate that Christ illuminated the world by his very presence. That the Light of God had come today just did not resonate with many of the postulants, and Nuala O'Reilly was one of them. Instead, there was the usual heaviness in the air that day. It hung low and steady, and it hung there all the time.

At breakfast that morning, the bell rang, signaling the benevolence of the house, allowing us to engage in conversation. Talking at breakfast yielded very little from Nuala's companions on either side of her. Their interactions were stilted.

They were cocooned from the reality of the world, and their conversations mirrored this reality. Nuala found great delight when she could talk to Mary O'Brien and me on our daily walks, but it was so cold on those walks that we could barely wait to get inside.

The nuns at the top tables were like sentries, and we felt that our every movement was being watched and our every expression tallied. In response to their vigilance, I felt that we were becoming a reflection of what was in front of us at the top tables. We were gradually shifting into the frigid, self-encased mirror of what was ahead of us.

Nuala felt a sifting inside. On one hand, she could appreciate the idea of the selflessness of the missionaries who had been in her position when they started their training, but she froze at the idea that she might, indeed, be looking in a mirror, and that she too would become fruitless, hollow, mechanical, and withered. She was horrified at the possibility, as she looked at the pale, lifeless, listless faces staring into space on this Feast of the Presentation, the Feast of Light. She felt stricken, as if lost in some foreign place, a place segmented and separated, a place that hurt her heart and pierced into the brightness of things, preferring to be stealth in the shadows rather than light to the world. The darkness even seemed to be creviced in the forced smiles sitting flat on faces and robotic gestures that pulled them away from enjoying the slightest exchanges with one another and restricted the last frontier of communication. Smiles that meant anything and expressed the joy of living did not come readily now. Nuala was not a willing participant in this way of doing things. She was used to the happy exchange in the community from which she hailed. Her sister, Fiona, was funny. Her father was funny. Toole O'Reilly found humor in everything. His friends called him "Toolo."

Mrs. O'Reilly was a jolly woman who shook physically when she laughed. Both of Nuala's parents pulled glee from every occasion and passed this art onto Fiona and Nuala. When Nuala had announced her application and acceptance to Fairview Convent, Toolo greeted the news with good humor.

"Ah, my dear Nuala, you'll not last a month, but your old da will pick you up. No worries." Then he went off to his tool shed, whistling all the way to the back of the garden.

Almost six months later, she found that she was not a willing inhabitant in this house where laughter was frowned upon, imagination trampled, and creativity stifled. On this Feast of Light, Nuala O'Reilly was groping in the dark, hoping to make sense out of her situation. Every day she expected some break in the cracks. She held on to some hope that the feeling of being trapped would evaporate. She wanted her hopes to take flight, but now she could not find the energy to make that trajectory. She found herself wasting and withering.

Nuala O'Reilly had been born in Omagh in County Tyrone. Toole O'Reilly was a carpenter by trade. Her mother taught in the local elementary school. Nuala grew up always wanting to be a teacher. She was gregarious, funny, and fired with a bright imagination. In her world, at a very early age, a stick in her hand became a magic wand or a baton or the source of a lightning strike. That stick propelled an old wheel into motion. It scolded the rain, it orchestrated the choirs of birds that sat in the trees in their garden, and it chided the boldness out of the fiercest of dogs. Cardboard boxes became her castles and citadels and steps and stairs, leading to a platform, where she would strut and pose and speech her way through happy days of childhood. Her friends joined her most days, but she was just as fearless and energetic when she played with Fiona. She had changed her world in her back garden with a mere stick and a box of cardboard.

Nuala O'Reilly had learned the importance of being inspired by anything she had at hand. She came to Fairview Convent with an imagination that was unfettered. These walls would just have to fall. She would have to find a way through the tightrope of containment that was restricting her. This structure with armored walls would have to be used to step into another world. She was contemplating this when the meal ended, and they were told to go to the chapel and meditate for an extra half hour.

Twenty minutes later, Nuala heard the peck of shoes in the distance. The dark wood of the chapel seemed to amplify every sound and sent it echoing through every portal of this place. Sister Dolores stepped into the chapel.

Nuala felt a tap on her shoulder, and Sister Dolores summoned her to the door. Once outside the chapel, Sister Dolores stood upright to give Nuala the news.

"Your father died last night when he returned from visiting you, so go and get your good frock. You are very lucky that you are not a novice because you would not be able to go to the funeral if you were. You will travel tomorrow with Sister Kate O' Flaherty. Mr. McGinty will drive you. Your father will be buried on Thursday. It is a disgrace that you will be missing Ash Wednesday here. Now go and finish your meditation. You are not to discuss this with anyone."

Sister Dolores left Nuala O'Reilly standing outside the chapel. The clock in the hall struck two chimes.

Nuala could not find her breath. A thick fog engulfed her. She stumbled into the chapel and sat in her place. No one stirred around her. They seemed oblivious that she had even been missing for the past five minutes.

She was numb and dizzy with shock. She wanted to cry out and tell everyone that her great father was gone. She could not even imagine the world without him. Tears ran down her face and darkened her black dress. She sat alone in the chapel. There were sixty nuns in the chapel, but she felt totally isolated from every one of them. The stark reality of emptiness filled her. A thick fog engulfed her. The air became heavy, and she found herself unable to breathe. She stumbled through her chores for the next few hours, unable to talk to anyone. Everyone was deeply involved with chores themselves and barely noticed Nuala stumble into the vegetable shed to make sure the peelers and knives were sharpened for the daily vegetable preparation the next day.

When the evening prayers were finished, Sister Dolores approached Nuala and told her that she was to take her meal in one of the parlors. When she sat to eat, she saw a note sitting on her tray. *Be ready at six in the morning and come to the front door of the convent. Your overnight bag will be ready for you.*

I looked at the empty space at the table in the refectory and wondered where Nuala was. When she did not appear for recreation, I became a bit anxious. When we went to the dormitory, Nuala's curtain was already drawn shut. We did not have the courage to find out what the problem was until well after dark.

Mary O'Brien slipped out of bed and counted her way to Nuala's cubicle in the darkness.

"Da died," Nuala whispered.

I heard her. My heart sank as I tossed and coughed, letting her know I was thinking of her.

CHAPTER THIRTY-NINE

THE WAKE IN THE NORTH OF IRELAND

Rain scrambled down the car window, aching to leap into the whip of the wind. On the morning of February 3, 1967, Nuala O'Reilly found herself in the back seat of a car going to her father's funeral. Sister Kate O'Flaherty sat beside her in the back seat. Jimmy McGinty had borrowed his friend's car for the journey to the north of Ireland. The car chugged along in the cold of the early morning and soon was consuming the bumpy road that lay ahead.

Nula felt frozen in a block of ice. The hot, black tea that she had taken earlier still left her shaking inside. She was bundled in a thick, woolen mantle that had been hanging just inside the side door on the coat rack. Sister Bridget Mary had grabbed it and wrapped her tightly in it. No one owned these mantles. They were there for general use. The postulants were not supposed to use them, but Sister Bridget Mary was not going to have Nuala O'Reilly go home without something to keep her warm in the car.

She had made thick ham and cheese sandwiches and delivered a small brown box to Sister Kate O'Flaherty containing a thermos of tea and cups if they wanted to stop and have something to eat by the side of the road. Sister Bridget Mary only learned about Toole O'Reilly's death and the pending journey because Jimmy had told her the night before that he had been instructed to make arrangements for the journey.

Nuala felt suffocated in the enormity of the mantle. She just wanted to get home. Sister Dolores had met her outside the kitchen before she went to the front door to get into the car.

"You are lucky that you are not a novice. You consider yourself very lucky that you can go to your father's funeral. If you were further along in your religious training, you would not be allowed to go."

She turned around abruptly as Sister Kate O'Flaherty appeared in the hallway. Once they got outside the gates to Fairview Convent, the car sped along the road at about forty miles an hour. The welcome of the road seemed to keep the car going on its way. Here and there, the potholes forced the car to slow down, but Jimmy was adept in navigating these roads. The urgency to get home surged in Nuala's throat. She churned with anxiety. After about an hour, the flat landscape began to disappear, morphing into hills that signaled the approach of the north. Cows, staunch and rain soaked, watched from the slopes on either side of the road. The fields were waterlogged, reflecting the gray sky.

Eventually, in the distance, the Sperrin Mountains were visible in the embrace of thick mist. The mist dulled the horizon. Nuala could only imagine what was ahead. Tears tumbled down her cheeks, and she sat in the back seat, wiping them with the back of her hand. She felt a sob take hold of her and tried to distract herself. Sister Kate O'Flaherty reached into her bag and handed her the bright white handkerchief that she found there.

"Nuala, you will be fine. I am right here with you, dear. Let me know how I can help you get through these days."

The road curved ahead and propelled through a tunnel of browns and faded-green colors as it razored and edged its way toward the border towns. Nuala was aware of her every breath. She pulled deeply in and let her breath seep out slowly. Suddenly, they were at a black hut that had a Union Jack flag flying high from a pole on the roof. They were stopped by a uniformed man who greeted McGinty. The man asked him where he was going. Jimmy explained that they were going to a wake and funeral and the uniformed man waved the car onward. The car started and heaved its way through a few more towns beyond the border. Union Jack flags slapped a welcome on poles on both sides of the road. Nuala breathed a deep sigh of relief. The British flag signaled to Nuala O'Reilly that she was indeed home.

The car stopped at a crossroads and stalled. Jimmy McGinty got out of the car, stretched, and proceeded to unhook the hood of the car and examine what was in front of him. On his way to the back of the car, he opened the door and declared, "Nothing to worry about, Sisters," and hurried to the trunk of the car and retrieved a plastic container. While he was doing this, Nuala opened the back door of the car and stepped outside. She took in a deep gulp of northern air and felt its strength. She let her breath drink deeply of the power of the wind. She shuddered in the cold. She shook in the loss that she would have to embrace. She glanced at Jimmy McGinty, as he carefully poured some kind of liquid into one of the cylinders in the engine. A lone bird flew in the sky, gliding on the power of the wind, and then flapped its wings against the resistance.

She could imagine the wing prints this bird had left in the sky, as it was scooped by the steady sweep of the staunch early breeze. Jimmy slammed the hood of the car and wiped his hands with a cloth that he pulled from his pocket. Nuala took one last look at the bird, now in full flight. The solitary avian was now high in the sky, in full control. She realized she would have to be as strong as that bird and find her wings in the storm of grief.

Nuala climbed back inside the car. At the turn of the key, the car sputtered, gave way to the thrust and throttle, and then began its roll along the heath. The mountains now looked blue in the distance, barely readable beyond the clouds smudged in various hues of gray. The side of the road was spiked with shrubs made sturdy by the endurance required on this windswept wilderness.

The car settled again into the fluid of the rough tarmac. The speed became steady and sustained. There was a seamlessness in the flow from one field to another. The cows became blobs of black and white and brown as the car sped past them. The cows mostly grouped in the copse of trees, huddled together on the brink of morning. Nuala felt anchored at the sight of them. Jimmy came to the fringe of the hinterland that was Omagh. He stopped at the edge of town. There were multiple roads ahead of him that he could take. He turned off the radio station he was listening to.

"Which road do I take, Sister?" he asked hoarsely.

Nuala sat up and guided him through the narrow streets. There was no prescribed route home. All streets led there. Eventually, she would be sitting outside her house.

Jimmy stood at the side of the car and let Nuala and Sister Kate go into the house. Neighbors barely stopped to looked at the three as they got out of the car. Nuala's mother and sister sat beside the fire in the small living room. It was warm there. Nuala threw off the weighted mantle and gave her mother and sister a hug. There was complete vocal failure as the three sat in the jaws of loss. The convent of Fairview seemed a million miles away.

On the Thursday after Ash Wednesday, Toole O'Reilly was buried. There, in the cemetery that sloped on the crest of the hill, overlooking the town, the damp earth, sodden and heavy, mounded around a gaping grave. A piercing wind whistled through the mute crown. The slim pine coffin slid skillfully into the muck. The chill snapped through Nuala's body and left her numb. A sob lay frantic in her depths and stayed there, trapped. She wished the coffin would burst open and her father would emerge, like Lazarus, and rise from the dead. She could not imagine her bright, funny father lying under clay. God felt very far away.

Sister Kate had been well instructed that she and Nuala would be housed in the local Convent of the Incarnation and that Jimmy McGinty would be lodged in a local rooming house. They had been ordered to return immediately after the funeral had taken place. Sister Kate told Nuala about the arrangements, which she promptly forgot once she saw Nuala with her mother and sister. She let Nuala sleep in her family home the nights of the wake and funeral. After the funeral, Sister Kate told Nuala that the car had to be serviced for its return journey, and they would have to stay an extra night.

Jimmy McGinty was happy to play along with these new developments. He enjoyed an extra night in Omagh at O'Hara's Pub in the center of town, where the patrons made him feel welcome. When Sister Kate called Sister Dolores, she was not pleased that the car had broken down and needed service. She could have accompanied Nuala O' Reilly, but then again, she did not want to go over the border to Northern Ireland.

On the first Friday of Lent, Nuala said goodbye to her mother and sister. She climbed into the back seat of the car beside Sister Kate. Mrs. O'Reilly had pulled Sister Kate aside and asked her to try and look out for Nuala when they returned to the convent. Mrs. O' Reilly had not had a good feeling when she had met Sister Dolores only a few short days before, though she did not share her concerns with Sister Kate.

As the car pulled away from the street, pellets of rain dotted the windows. The drops seemed immobile, even as the car started rolling down the street. Nuala fully expected the rain on the car windows to trail to gravity, but they did not. They held their course, seemingly stuck, glistening in the sun's creep into the noon of the sky. The drops stretched through the windows like speckled glints of silver. There was a hint of movement in them when the car stopped, but they remained stuck on the outside of the glass, like suction cups. Each drop of water was a world unto itself, and the whole pane of glass looked like a galaxy of stars in the sunshine.

Nuala put her hand on the car window. She could almost feel the water on the tips of her fingers. She could touch them, but they were removed from her. She thought about the distance these little drops of water had traveled to end up on a pane of glass to distract her after her father's funeral.

The outpouring of love and concern for the family had been most evident. At the wake, many people came to share funny stories about her father. Many had slipped money into Mrs. O'Reilly's hands because they owed her husband a debt for some work he had completed months before. There were stories told about his childhood that Nuala had never heard before. When she was at home, she had been shrouded by love and care and concern. Now that was gone, and the separation that Nuala felt was as clear and as hard as the pane of glass she was looking through. The pellets of rain did not budge, even when the car lurched forward. They looked as if they could catch fire when they caught the rays of the sun. In those moments that they were imbued with light, they did not move. Maybe they would ride with her from their northern flight all the way to Fairview Convent.

She thought about her father. He used to have some very funny sayings. He could crack the thickest of cement with his great sense of humor. His spirit and zest for life stretched to his own horizons and well beyond. "If the world was my oyster, I'd rather be a crab with a map," he pronounced one night as he sat with his family around the dinner table. "I'd rather be an oyster than a crab." Nuala had responded. That conversation went from discussing oysters and crabs to wondering about the state of the whale in the oceans.

Toole O'Reilly had many interests, and the plight of the whales was one of them. He sent money to the Save the Whales Foundation on a regular basis, and if he could find a T-shirt with a whale on it, he wore it until it was washed threadbare. Toole snatched at every piece of sunlight. He sought gaps in the undergrowth to cushion his children's falls and bumps and bruises as they grew older. He held his family in the heat of his heart during their storms. When dark days unfurled, when the neighbors got sick, when friends lost their jobs, Toole was always there in the background with a lending hand. He was rarely repaid, but he did not care.

Within the four walls of his home, he had everything that mattered to him. Toole O'Reilly's inner compass burst into every direction. His home life was his north star. He had great devotion to saying the rosary. He recited the rosary by himself every evening in the kitchen. After dinner, when his family went to the living room to watch television or do homework, Toole knelt before the picture of the Sacred Heart in the kitchen, bowed his head low, took out his rosary beads, and said his prayers. It was the only time in the day that he was alone, and he relished that quiet time every evening.

Toole O'Reilly forced all who met him to look outwards to places and spaces well beyond the borders that contained the six counties of Northern Ireland. While he had been mostly confined to this territorial plot all of his life, never having had the opportunity to travel far, he wanted his girls to see everything and experience more than he had been able to do. He brought them fishing on Sunday afternoons. He hiked with them up Mourne Mountains. He developed an interest in beekeeping and eventually procured a few beehives that he placed in his back garden. This opened a whole new world for his girls as they learned about keeping the bee colonies safe and the influence of pesticides on the health of the bees. He wondered in awe with them about the earth's dependence on the well-being of his little creatures.

He taught his girls to be attentive and mindful and to listen carefully to what other people had to say. He taught them to laugh and see the brightness in the bleakest of days. He encouraged them to get involved in school activities and to live life to the fullest every day. *Tooleisms* developed around town. When he met someone, who complained about the bad weather and the chills and aches and pains that accompanied it, he would laugh and say, "Don't miss out on your summers by dreading the oncoming winters." When someone was undecided about how she could get someone to do something, he would say, "The power of suggestion has the ability of flicking on the switch." The person would get that message quickly and be on her way to accomplish her goal. When someone felt guilty about taking time off after working hard for weeks, he would simply tell him, "You have to pamper yourself a little while when your boat docks, and the fish are unloaded." Toole O' Reilly was a happy man. He was a man who was very content with his life.

Toole O'Reilly's voice sat in Nuala's head all the way over the northern border. She fell asleep and woke up a few times on her journey and felt saturated with loss. It was dusk when the car pulled into the gravel drive overlooking Lake Fennan. There was light here and there in some of the windows glinting out of the bulky, dark building. Those windows looked like bright eyes, looking out on the lake, while darkness seeped into every room.

Nuala heard the door of Fairview Convent vault shut behind her. She put her hand into the pocket of her long, black dress and found her father's rosary beads. These would help her get through some very hard nights. She felt every muscle tighten at the slam of the large, oak door behind her. Jimmy McGinty whispered goodnight to her, and Sister Kate O'Flaherty helped her unbundle the large mantle that held her warmth. Sister Kate told Nuala that if she experienced any distress, to put a small stone into the plant outside the sacristy, and Sister Kate would find a way to connect with her.

Nuala trailed to the refectory behind Sister Kate for tea after the journey. Nuala sat opposite her at the bottom of the refectory. Tea and toast were consumed in silence. There was no sign of Sister Dolores. There was no welcome back.

After washing her dishes, Nuala made her way to bed. I heard her come into the dormitory and waited until I heard her heave into bed before I coughed in welcome. Mary O'Brien and Annie Boyle followed in quick succession. Nuala slipped into bed, frigid and frozen, feeling the barb of exile take hold. She held her father's rosary beads in her hands and fell into a fitful sleep.

In the morning, Nuala lifted herself into the raw rush of morning. The hush of numbness lay on her face. I watched her struggle as she walked down the stairs to the chapel in the morning. Today, it was sufficient for her just to get through the morning prayer exercise and breakfast. I knew Nuala was trying hard to be strong and steady. Nuala felt completely alone. After breakfast, Sister Dolores called her into one of the parlors and spoke stiffly to her.

"You are not allowed to speak about your father's death at any time. You are expected to be a pillar of strength here. If you pray hard enough, you will get over him very quickly."

Nuala felt the sting in Sister Dolores's words. The sister also instructed Nuala that she would be helping Margaret Logue and me in the sacristy, and that the three Kerry girls would take over her duties of getting the vegetables ready for the next day.

It would take the two of them to accomplish what Nuala had accomplished alone all these months.

"Being near the chapel will help you to focus on prayer and why you are here in the first place. You will forget your family and get on with your religious training."

Sister Dolores slapped both of her hands together and told Nuala to get to the sacristy immediately. When Nuala arrived in the sacristy, Margaret and I welcomed her. Later, I gave her a furtive hug. She told me she felt like she was in a wilderness. It was obvious that the loss of her father beat inside her like a throbbing sore, resonating like the thud of a large drum in her ears and shuttering her to a lonely journey at the edge of her heart. She had no map for this journey that had been thrust upon her out of the blue. Her father had not prepared her for this hike.

There were no mountains laid out here, no valleys were in sight, no clear paths that she could forge, and no rivers to point her in the flow of the right direction. She felt lost. She thought of her father's words that he would rather be a crab with a map, and all she could do was stumble around in a fog. Wherever this map was, she could only see the scroll of fog.

Her feet felt heavy, like they were full of wet muck, as she walked. For now, she would have to plod through each day and navigate this new landscape alone. She felt the ice cold of a metal sword through her heart. She would forever remember the Feast of the Presentation. She certainly knew the strike of the sword and its deep piercing this day after returning from Northern Ireland. She told me that she felt the pull of deep sadness when she saw the last Union Jack snagged on its flagpole as she crossed the border. It whipped and cracked strongly in the wind, bidding her farewell.

CHAPTER FORTY

LENT 1967

Lent had begun while Nuala O'Reilly was at her father's funeral in the north of Ireland. Ash Wednesday, the beginning of the season of Lent, crept quietly into Fairview Convent in early February 1967. The night before, Sister Dolores had announced that we would have to get up one hour earlier each day during Lent for extra prayer in the chapel before Mass. I balked at the idea of getting up in the shiver that greeted us each morning. The windows in the dormitory leaked cold through every crack. As usual, I could see my breath as I tumbled out of bed that first day of Lent. The extra prayers were monotonous and took every effort to respond to multiple litanies of the saints. An extra rosary was thrown in to keep us awake. Marked with the ashes of the season during Mass, we made our way wearily to the dining room for breakfast. Lent was to prove a harried time in Fairview Convent.

The six weeks before Easter in the Christian calendar were set aside as a time of penance. Usually in Derry, the public houses suffered great monetary losses, as many patrons gave up drinking for six weeks. In every household, the children gave up sweets and biscuits while the adults followed the rules of the church regarding daily fasting and abstaining from eating meat every Friday.

It was part of growing up in a Catholic home. Lent and the coming of spring went hand in hand. Spring was a time when the buds on the trees began to sprout, and the warming of the earth was evident by the sight of daffodils and tulips. Lent was also seen as a time of spiritual greening and reawakening, of a time when people concentrated on prayer and fasting. It was a period of penance that the church imposed on everyone under its tutelage. Inside these convent walls, the iron fist of rules and structure veined through every moment and monitored every step the postulants took. For the postulant class of 1966, our experience in the convent for our first Lent was less than life giving.

As a postulant at that first Lent, I found it to be a time of sacrifice and testing. It was Sister Bridget Mary who prepared most of the postulants for the harsh reality we had to face during the six weeks. She told the postulants what would be expected of us during the days ahead, as we helped to wash the kitchen dinner dishes.

According to Sister Bridget Mary, Lent would be a hungry, penitential time in Fairview Convent. She informed us that, on the first day of Lent, we would go into the refectory after Mass and find that our chairs had been removed from our tables. The postulant and novices would be required to kneel for each meal during the six weeks of Lent. All the other sisters, except the infirm, would have to kneel on Ash Wednesday and Good Friday.

This did not feel to me to be problematic, but on one of our walks, Mary O'Brien said she felt some recalcitrance about doing this. She was very conscious that she was bigger, and since her bulk was quite difficult to manipulate, she said the prospect of kneeling for every meal was weighing heavily upon her.

"I will never be able to get back up after each meal without some serious help," she laughed to Sister Bridget Mary, who broke the news to her.

"Then we will have to get you a hoist, Mary," replied Sister Bridget Mary, pretending to be serious. "Tell your friends that there will be an extra piece of cake behind the cups in the back cabinet when they finish up here, just in case I forget to let them know."

Sister Bridget Mary wanted to make a treat available now and again to the postulants during the harsh, prolonged season of Lent. She also put a few spoonfuls of honey into the cereal dishes for the postulants and delivered them personally to their tables just after morning Mass. No one dared question the fact that she had left the kitchen to do so. She knew the extra ingredient would help them get an added bit of nourishment for the long, arduous days they had to face.

The food portions the postulants received during this season were meager. The work was heavier during Lent, and the gnaw of hunger became more burdensome, as we postulants tackled our chores. It was evident as we went through our daily routine in that first week and began putting more sugar into our tea to try and retrieve our waning energy levels.

By the second week of Lent, the sugar disappeared from the table. The sugar bowls would return to the tables on Easter Sunday. I felt pounded from the constancy of the stout winds of fasting. The extra hour of prayer that was inserted into the regular schedule was, in itself, a big change for me. I felt myself in the steady lashings of the penitential whip. The first Lent in Fairview Convent was long and hard and stretched me much too thin.

This was a harried time in Fairview Convent. Every day, we were whirled into a frenzy of cleaning that would culminate with the Easter Feast. Every inch of the place was dusted, washed, wiped, and polished. Every light fixture was removed and cleaned thoroughly. We had to get a ladder, climb to the top, and strain to remove the light bulb and fixture, then wash it, dry it, and then return it, gleaming, to its perch in the ceiling.

There were hundreds of light fixtures. Every window in our section of the building had to be washed, both inside and outside. We climbed on ladders to reach the top windows. We stood on the window ledges and pulled down the windows, leaning out with wet cloths, and stretching our arms down to remove the grit and grime. Then we had to wipe them clean with newspaper. Any detected streaks meant that they had to be redone.

When the dozens of windows on each of the three floors were clean, we had to clean the inside of those windows. Arms flailed in the morning and failed by early evening. I ached through the six weeks of Lent. I fought fatigue. The work was never-ending. For six weeks before Easter, we were fastened to mops and buckets of water. The brooms and brushes we used swept and scratched at every scrap and morsel of dust they encountered. The morsels probed and pinched into the crevices of the heavy wooden floors. By the last week of Lent, the entire building boarded order and perpetuated a feeling of sterility. Its polished cleanliness embodied an arrogance, a smell of threat, a hankering of the past. It spoke of conformity and the assurance of permanence and predictability that nothing would ever be transformed into something new. There was no room for change in that polished air. The polish sealed the cloister. The convent had no sense of the clutter of normalcy. After all the effort to clean and dust and wash every part of the place, there was still no welcome in its throat.

There was a strict fast on Good Friday. At that point, I did not even notice. Every day during Lent in Fairview Convent had been seamless, and we felt the yoke of exhaustion in our every breath. By the time Easter Sunday arrived, I was wilted, withered, and exhausted. A big Easter meal was prepared by the two nuns in the kitchen. I was full after a few bites and struggled to finish what was left on my plate. Annie Boyle whispered to me that she felt sick and struggled with her food, trying to pretend she was eating it in case Sister Dolores came flying at her. We were given permission to talk, but even Mary O'Brien could not find the energy for more than a few words.

The letters we received during Lent had been kept from us. We were handed a little bundle of letters at the end of dinner and were allowed to spend time reading them. According to the rules and regulations, they had all been opened and read. As I was enjoying being transported home by my mother's letter, one novice yelped in distress after opening her letter from home. Later, we learned that her mother had died three weeks before Easter. The novice was excused from the buzz of the refectory. The nameless novice was not seen again.

CHAPTER FORTY-ONE

NOW THANK WE ALL OUR GOD

April 2, 1967—7:30 a.m.

More than a month had passed since Sister Dolores had instructed Mrs. Moore to get Mary Ita Ahern ready to play a hymn at the end of Mass on a Sunday in March. It was now the middle of March, and Mrs. Moore kept putting it off, coming up with every excuse she could think of to delay the performance. Mary Ita had been introduced to music lessons in January, and two months later, she had displayed no musical talent. Every week since the beginning of March, Sister Dolores had insisted that Mary Ita Ahern be prepared to play at the Sunday Mass. Finally, a date was set. She would play the final hymn at Mass on the last Sunday of March.

Most beginners would have been able to accomplish this reality within this time frame—a weekly one-hour lesson and a daily practice schedule of one hour for the past three months. By the time the end of March arrived, Mary Ita's practice time on this simple hymn totaled over eighty hours. It was only by the middle of March that the two working in the sacristy began to recognize the hymn that Mary Ita was attempting to crank out of the organ in the back of the chapel. Mary Ita had confided to Mrs. Moore during one of the performances that she had taken piano lessons for over a year just before she entered the convent, thinking that the skill would help her in some way.

With that revelation, Mrs. Moore became more concerned; however, by the middle of March, the hymn was slowly emerging, and Mrs. Moore began to experience a little hope that Mary Ita might be able to pull this off on the last Sunday of March.

After discussing the schedule, Sister Dolores realized that the last Sunday of March was Easter Sunday, and there would be no way that Sister Herald, the convent's musician, would let a postulant play the last hymn on such a feast. Sister Dolores fully realized the folly of that thought and told Mrs. Moore that she would arrange with Sister Herald for Mary Ita to play the Sunday after Easter. When Sister Dolores approached Sister Herald about this proposal, Sister Herald readily agreed, only because she did not want to spend any time in discussion with Sister Dolores.

With the date set in stone, Mrs. Moore began to encourage Mary Ita's performance, and before and after each of Mary Ita's lessons, she prayed fervently in the chapel for a miracle. She was realizing more and more that her little part-time job might actually be in jeopardy if Mary Ita Ahern failed. After all this time, it would be a reflection on her own ability.

Mrs. Moore pushed Mary Ita harder. This young woman, with absolutely no predisposition for the most elementary musical notes and whose hands had great difficulty with coordination to fashion a melody, might actually be able to do this. Mary Ita, too, was beginning to feel more confident as she detected a change in Mrs. Moore's attitude toward her. The only outstanding problem was that Mrs. Moore had transcribed the hymn to its simplest form. She had rewritten the piece by hand, and the hymn was now contained on several pages, so that Ita would need someone who could read music to stand beside her and turn the pages. When Mrs. Moore had approached Sister Dolores about this development, Sister Dolores was annoyed with this complication and momentarily thought about asking Sister Herald to do it.

Sister Herald assembled everyone together at various times during the year for choir practice. She was the one who was responsible for providing concerts for visiting nuns and priests who came to Fairview Convent during the summer. She also ensured that the Christmas and Easter feasts were outstanding, liturgical performances. She only used the novices and nuns who had taken vows for these accomplishments. She did not want to deal with Sister Dolores for any reason, so she did not ask for the postulants to be part of any of her choirs. The postulants would put on their own little show for entertaining the summer schedule of visitors.

Sister Dolores realized that there was no way Sister Herald would be involved with this dilemma. She would deal with it within the confines of her own responsibilities. She could not accept any input from any of her peers. She would remain independent and find a remedy for this situation by herself. She quickly realized that there was only one person who was capable of reading music. It would have to be Mary O'Brien.

At recreation the night before Mary Ita was to play, Sister Dolores instructed Mary O'Brien about her duties for the next morning.

"Madam from the black north, you will assist Mary Ita Ahern as she plays the last hymn for Mass in the morning. I will hold you personally responsible if Mary Ita Ahern is not able to play this hymn in the morning. You will be sorry if anything happens."

"Yes, Sister," Mary said with a grin. She was glad to be near a musical instrument.

The next morning came. Before Mass, Mary practiced turning the pages of the hymn several times with Mary Ita. This was a simple hymn to play, and the hymn had been made really easy to play by Mrs. Moore. Mary recognized that Ita had practiced very hard and really hoped that she would get through the performance successfully. Even after all the practice, Mary noticed that many of the notes were being skipped over, while some others were being played incorrectly.

Mass began, and the priest droned through the Latin Mass with his usual monotony. After communion, Mary and Ita made their way to the back of the chapel to the organ that had just been vacated by Sister Herald, who had chosen the most majestic of hymns for that morning's celebration of Mass. Mary Ita slipped onto the long stool and put her hands on the organ, ready to start with a signal from Mary O'Brien. As Mary O'Brien stood beside Mary Ita, she could see Sister Dolores sitting in front of the postulants.

The priest gave the final blessing. In unison, the nuns uttered the words *Deo Gratias*, and Mary O'Brien nodded to Mary Ita to start playing. Mary Ita attempted to put her hands on the keys of the organ and froze. Realizing that Mary Ita was in a panic, Mary O'Brien, in an instant, was sitting beside Mary Ita and began the refrains of the hymn. Mary O'Brien did not need music. She was finally reunited with her beloved keys. The music sprang from her fingers. The intonation and splendor of the hymn emanated from her heart. The hymn never sounded so good. Even Sister Herald was shocked.

With so much energy and emotion that came from the organ, the nuns filled the chapel with the hymn, their own voices infused by a new and different energy. Mary O'Brien literally pulled out all the stops of the organ. The priest in the sacristy stopped when he heard the impressive organ playing and the inordinately beautiful voices that invaded even the sacristy.

Mary O'Brien realized, as she took Mary Ita's place, that Sister Dolores did not look to see who was playing. Sister Dolores would not give Sister Herald any hint that this performance was any different than expected. She stood up in the front and knew that Mary Ita was not playing the organ. Her plan to humiliate Mary Ita Ahern had been turned on its head. Those of us who knew of Mary O'Brien's talent smiled, and those who did not, were quite surprised that Mary Ita Ahern had come such a long way with her music in such a short time. After Mass, Sister Dolores made no comment about the hymn to either Mary Ita or Mary O'Brien.

The next time that Mrs. Moore came to give her weekly lessons, she was apprehensive. She was stopped at the door, fully expecting Sister Dolores to tell her that her services were no longer needed.

"I hope Mary Ita Ahern did well at Mass on Sunday," declared Mrs. Moore hesitantly.

"She will not be playing again, and I am replacing her with Margaret Logue," Sister Dolores replied with distain in her throat. With that, Sister Dolores took away the only pleasure that Mary Ita Ahern had known since coming to Fairview Convent. Sister Dolores took untold pleasure in that.

CHAPTER FORTY-TWO

THE STAIN IN THE BOTTLE

The April winds skipped and played on the ripples of Lake Fennan. I was assigned to duties in the sacristy again. It had, at this point, been my third tour of duty there since I arrived. Margaret Logue had been replaced this month by Nuala O'Reilly. Margaret had been assigned to oversee vegetable duty in the garden, and then she went twice a day to the creamery to help Julia Higgins churn milk into butter. Jimmy McGinty left the buckets of milk in the morning and afternoon, and on occasion, he was able to nod and say hello to the two postulants waiting for the milk delivery.

At this point, I knew where every linen cloth for the celebration of Mass and benediction was folded and stored. I was cognizant of the contents of every shelf and drawer. I knew the protocol for storing and safely depositing every sacred chalice and monstrance used for every liturgical feast and religious ritual. Everything was kept spotless. It was now the middle of April, and the sun was beginning to appear a little more regularly, and the trees were budding to display their leaves. Gradually, some color was reappearing outside the window. New growth was appearing on the shrubs, and the birds were frantic in their flight to get the recently hatched throng in their nests. Life was moving outside the walls of Fairview Convent. After Mass that morning, Nuala and I clattered around the sacristy. The cavernous room echoed as we robotically cleaned the sacred vessels, wiped the floor, and dusted the shelves. We made sure that every container was gleaming. Everything was in its place. I was now intent on securing a sacristy as clean and as well organized as I was capable of producing.

Nuala was a good worker. She enjoyed going outside, climbing on a ladder, and making sure the windows sparkled. While Margaret Logue and I had washed the windows once a week, Nuala decided they should be cleaned daily. It was her way of being involved. It was her way of being distracted for a while as she felt the sun's rays on her back. I was, by now, pulled into the day's structure and its attenuating duties after Mass each day. My final task was always to soak the linens used for Mass in the wide glass bowl in the sink. I would return later and wrap them in a special white towel for them to dry. Later, I would go to the laundry to iron them to perfection. I had just placed the sacred linens in the glass bowl and turned the cold water on when I was aware of a slight rustle behind me. I was peripherally sure that it was Sister Dolores who had entered the space in her usual manner, by stealth. Since she did not say anything to me, I continued to soak the linens in the water all the while Sister Dolores was hovering behind me.

After soaking the linens, I turned around to find Sister Dolores wiping her thumb on the edge of the dark wooden ledge where the vestments were usually laid out for the priest in the morning before Mass. Even with all the flurry of the morning's momentum, she was not able to skim one speck of dust onto her veined fingers. She made her way to the small table near the window, which contained the altar wine. With a shadow on her face, she picked up a wine bottle to examine it. By now, Nuala O'Reilly had returned indoors, and when she put her head into the sacristy and saw Sister Dolores with the bottle of wine in her hand, I motioned her to leave. She could return later and help me finish up. Sister Dolores walked to the window and held the bottle up. In the glassed light, she thought she perceived some kind of spot in the bottle. As she further strained to scrutinize the bottle in the grasp of the morning light, she eventually noticed a small stain that had the appearance of a clump of black threads fused together in a spindled weave just below the label. Everything felt heavier with Sister Dolores there.

With one eye on her, I continued working at the sink. I gushed the cold water at full force into the glass bowl and placed the sacred linens there to soak. Just to distract myself, I placed my hands into the cold water and gently squeezed the white cloths that had been on the altar barely thirty minutes before. I was very conscious as I moved my fingers through these precious cloths, considering that they had touched the consecrated hosts and wiped the sacred chalice on the huge altar a few feet away. Without a hint of warning, I felt a crack on the right side of my head and fell forward toward the sink.

Sister Dolores had slammed me on the side of my ear with the wine bottle. I held onto the sink, stunned and nauseated by the blow. I felt my legs buckle and could not focus. I fought to stay upright and grabbed the sides of the sink, determined to stay steady, fighting to stay upright. I stayed in the shake of what seemed a very long time. I was jostled at another level when the screaming began. I pulled with a deep breath to grip my inner control. I had never been struck physically in my life. I had never been physically disciplined growing up.

All my senses were engaged and heightened in alarm. I felt threatened that another assault was imminent. The shock of the thud of the sharp crack stayed on the side of my face. Sister Bridget Mary was in the chapel, enjoying a few minutes of reprieve from the kitchen, finishing one of the rosaries she was obliged to say as a lay sister. When she heard the thunder in the sacristy, she stiffened and put her rosary beads on her knees. Then she decided to move forward in the chapel to hear everything that was going on.

I tasted the acid of shock in my throat. I closed my eyes after the initial stars in them dimmed and floated for a while in front of me and then finally disappeared only to return. I felt the trickle of blood run down my right ear and splatter into the sink. Some red drops fell into the water and mixed with the sacred linens. I plunged into an inner calm. I stayed there in full control in spite of the rants and the screech into the back of my head.

Finally, when I felt my strength course through my body, I turned around to face my bully. I was in the hug of sheer control. I looked up to face Sister Dolores, who was shaking in the throes of her own fury. The bottle still shook in the air above me with the contents reverberating like a small wave in the bottom of the bottle. She gripped the bottle so tightly that I thought it would break. Her fingers were white. I stood strong in the hold of my own authority and continued to slam a steady gaze into her direction. Her face was barely inches from mine as she leaned in towards me. I could smell the acrid breath, but I would not recoil.

"You intolerable, stupid thing!" she yelled. The bellow aired all around me and boomed in my ears. I stood in the resistance of my own steel. I did not step out of it. I braved into the moment, stretching into a poise, a composure, and an intuitive intensity where I winged myself into perfect balance. By now, in the seventh month of my religious training, I had endured and secreted so much hurt and vicious assailments that were heaped on me on a daily basis that this outburst did not have the same impact on me as it had last September. I knew, as I stood there in that moment, that I could never normalize this egregious behavior and stood steadfast to its wake. This conduct would have to continue to shock me. I stepped somewhere inside myself where I found safety in some wrinkled barrier where I could barricade myself from this furor. My brain was now sharpened by the edged razor that could automatically meet the constant charges of assault. Sister Dolores backed away from me.

"You have committed a mortal sin. You will have to go to confession. You have invalidated all the Masses that this bottle of altar wine was used for. But what can I expect form anyone who comes from the north of Ireland?"

Her words poisoned the air. I refused to breathe the air around the woman and held it until she moved further into the sacristy. I felt unflappable. I shifted seismically into my own, inner, quiet space. The white orb of control surrounded me.

Sister Dolores breathed in shallow breaths. Her face was purpled, shadowed in the freeze of her own darkness. She glowered at me. I clasped my hands together and gripped hard, staying solid in the thump of harshness and the hard rub of this encrypted morning.

"Get that blood off your pinched, ugly face."

At this command, I knew that my eyes beamed like search-lights in the blackness. She felt that I was standing on rock. I felt its assuredness underneath me. I would move in my own time. I refused to budge. I finally saw Sister Dolores slump and back away. I held her gaze. She would be the first to blink. Sister Dolores began to falter. She turned and walked away. She stopped at the door and leaned against it to steady herself. She clenched the bottle with her right hand, her white knuckles wrapping the glass. She summoned a final spurt of energy and smacked the wooden bench with the bottle.

"You will take your breakfast tomorrow on the refectory floor with this bottle beside you."

I did not blink. She threw the bottle at me, but not before I let her see that I refused to hold out my hands and catch it. I let the bottle fall. It hit the floor and rolled away from my feet. In a moment, she was gone.

I stood still for a while, trying to let what had happened seep away from me. I slowly turned to the sink and cupped some water in my hands and splashed it on my face. The water felt like ice. It felt good. I took my handkerchief from my pocket and wiped the blood from the side of my face. My ear felt sore, but I felt good.

I had faced my bully. I had stared steadfastly into the dark eyes of a woman that reflected deep pools of spite. After months of being flogged into submission, I realized my inner strength and had tapped into my reservoir of resources. I had maintained and sustained myself as the air in the sacristy was soaked and pummeled with profanity. I felt the need to open the windows and let in fresh air. As I did so, I realized that I was alive and well. I felt my assuredness return. I returned to the sink and rinsed my blood from the linens and soaked them in clean water. The stream of red water ran into the drain. At the sight, I felt new life surge through me.

Sister Bridget Mary told me later that she had heard every-thing that had gone on in the sacristy. She could not interfere with the storm that was brewing there, but she was determined that Sister Dolores would suffer in some fashion for the abuse she had inflicted.

CHAPTER FORTY-THREE

FURY IN THE REFECTORY

The next day dawned bright and breezy. The sun hinted in the blue sky and left the lake speckled with silver dust. After Mass, I brought the wine bottle to the refectory, took my dish of cereal, and knelt in the middle of the floor with the bottle of altar wine beside me. There was silence all around me, except for the clatter of spoons and dishes being rattled. I was used to this drill by now. Performing the so-called penance in the middle of the refectory floor was so common that it was barely noticed by any of the nuns who quietly ate their morning meal in silence. By the look on the face of Sister Dolores, she was still frothing in the memory of what had happened in the sacristy the day before. She wanted public humiliation. She approached me in the middle of the floor, and while I knew it was she, I simply continued to eat my cereal.

I heard a hint of an eruption hit the back of her throat, which lurched out of her tortured mouth, spitting steel words meant to burst through the tightest armor.

"You have disgraced us. You have insulted us in front of the priests who saw that bottle of wine in the sacristy. You have made us the joke of every priest and religious house in the area. I should think of a penance worthy of that, madam from Northern Ireland."

The violence of her words shook her into a frenzy. No doubt she could not take the sight of my composure because I had put an imaginary shield around me to block out the fury of her words. I continued to eat my cereal from my chipped enamel bowl. I continued to kneel undisturbed in front of everyone with the offending, brown bottle of wine beside me. The ferocity of her words shook her into her own frenzy. While there was barely a glance in her direction at first, when I now looked around me, I saw that the women in the refectory were now listening. They were experts in the art of insulating their awareness of such matters, but this display warranted observation.

Sister Kate O'Flaherty kept her inner radar keen and alert on this occasion. She was ready to get up and intervene if Sister Dolores stepped over the line into a physical assault. She had heard from Sister Bridget Mary about what had happened in the sacristy and had been alarmed at the tale. Sister Kate wrapped her hop-tea in her hands and gave her full attention to the scene unfolding before her. She looked around. The others seemed to be fidgeting and getting a bit uncomfortable.

I felt strangely safe in this place at that moment. I knew that all eyes and ears were on Sister Dolores. Every gesture of this tortured woman, every word of hers, flew into the hard core of their feelings and penetrated even those who lived with the heaviest of steel encased around their hearts. Every inflection of Sister Dolores's voice tolled and tinged with rage. All who sat in the refectory were being gradually brought into the fearful glow of unrestrained temper.

Sister Dolores was unraveling and losing control in front of everyone. I felt cushioned in the group and realized that it was Sister Dolores who was the object of scorn here. Yet, no one moved. They sat as a group in the concrete rules and regulations that commanded there be a separation of powers in the hierarchy of established order that existed in Fairview Convent. I was a postulant. Sister Dolores ruled completely over me, and no one could interfere in her absolute rule. Her wretched words caused her to convulse in fitful starts and twitches.

"You think you can just kneel there after committing a fearsome sin, after you deliberately violated all the rules of canon law? You deliberately put the wine in this compromised bottle on the sacred altar at Mass! You should be whipped! You should be flogged!"

She cleaved the air with the hatchet of her voice. The sharpness could slice milk into chunks. She was high pitched, deeply agitated, and seemed to totter off the precipice of striking me in public. She continued to yell about the stain in the bottle, about my ineptitude, my laziness, my lack of proper care, the violation of trust that had been put in me. I felt insulated. I felt the stretch of the pendulum propelling right and left as the minutes sped by in front of me. I felt galvanized in that balance, that center, where the pendulum passed before its journey to the other side.

Some of the women were petrified with fright. The old, the thick, the wrinkled, and the veined sagged in their seats. Sister Kate sat poised, ready to intervene, but I suspected that she sensed my nascent, inner balance. I felt in that moment that I had acquired unyielding strength, and that made me robust as I knelt on that floor. That part of me would set me apart from the cold inflexibility of this Fairview Convent.

I continued to feel the pulse of life inside me as Sister Dolores fumed and stamped in the refectory while those around her were reduced to listen to the drone of a painful blast of profanity. And still she continued, unabated.

Sister Kate shivered inwardly. She continued to hold the cup of tea in both of her hands, trying to let the lingering warmth soak into them. She noticed that some of the nuns were alarmed at the abuse being perpetrated right in front of them. Sister Dolores was coming apart in front of everyone. Some of them finally finished their morning meal, their eyes downcast, and were glad that they were not the object of such scorn. Their voices were muted, silenced, and they bowed in acceptance of this onslaught. By failing to habitually redress the abuse and question the actions of this woman, who was often seen to be out of control, they, too, remained constantly subdued and shriveled in the face of her poisonous spillage.

Sister Dolores seemed to be in the throes of a serious, fevered contagion. The disturbance gradually subsided. I ate my toast unscathed. I would not yield to this battering ram. I pressed into the cold air of that refectory. I glowed in the ice there.

Sister Bridget Mary again heard about the fit of temper displayed at breakfast. She put an extra measure of molasses in a dessert dish at lunch time, which found itself at Sister Dolores's seat in the refectory. For the next few days, Sister Dolores was not able to function and had to stay in her own quarters. Sister Annunciation called Mother Benedicta in Rome to get permission to replace Sister Dolores for the week so that the postulants would continue to have guidance. Sister Annunciation suggested Sister Kate O'Flaherty and Mother Benedicta agreed.

Sister Annunciation often wondered where Sister Kate O'Flaherty was at any given hour. She saw her in the garden. She saw her as she came out of the greenhouse. She saw her in the forest with cutting shears. She saw her up the driveway with a shovel. She saw her in the convent with a watering can, making sure the plants were properly cared for. She seemed to be all over the place, but at least she kept herself busy, and that was all that mattered to Sister Annunciation.

Nuala, Mary, and Annie let me know over the course of the next few days that they were very impressed by my composure in that scorch of a cold morning when Sister Dolores had poured her lava of words upon me.

When Sister Kate O'Flaherty was with us for that week, there was a greater sense of fun. It was a welcome break from the weight that normally hovered around us, holding us encased in concrete since last September. With my friends, I seemed to have found some cracks in that cement and had found a way to function under its mighty load. I felt we had sowed some seeds in those cracks, and, who knew, maybe someday flowers would grow there.

CHAPTER FORTY- FOUR

THE NODDERS

I had been sent to the kitchen after lunch to help with the dishes. After the dishes were completed, Sister Bridget Mary stood at the sink beside me.

"Ann, I am intrigued by that bright smile you have on your face after what you had to endure this morning. That twinkle has not disappeared from the heart of your eyes, either. You have a great, strong spirit. It is made of such resolve that no one can put even a dent in it. It is palpable. I can almost taste it. Now sit down and have a wee treat."

I enjoyed the soft slice of wheat bread that had just come from the oven. Sister Bridget Mary slathered a ton of butter on it and spread strawberry jam in a heap above the thick, yellowy shelf of butter. The taste was delicious, and I savored every crumb before I left the kitchen, full of its sugary sweetness.

Since Sister Bridget Mary had a few hours to herself, because supper was well under way, she was alone for a few hours, as Sister Freda Mary was in bed for a few days with a flu. To pass the time, Sister Bridget Mary decided to indulge in her favorite hobby. She went to her inner scullery, sat at the table, and took out a thick sheath of paper to collect her thoughts and write them down. She took her pen and dipped it into the jar of ink and thought more about the incident in the refectory that morning. She was upset by the reality that not one nun who had witnessed the onslaught there had had the courage to intervene and address the egregious abuse that had taken place in front of them. In their silence, they displayed their acceptance of the abuse and were all essentially nodding assent, enabling the behavior to continue. This incident needed to be talked about.

She had to capture the situation in some way. She had to write it in the only way she knew how.

In her mind, she blessed Jimmy McGinty for supplying her with the paper and the ink. She would have to ask him to get her some extra nibs for her pen. She made sure her supply of blank paper was without wrinkles. She smoothed the bulk of the paper with both hands. Once satisfied that the paper was flawless, she was ready to write. She leaned lightly on the nib and plunged it into the ink jar. She always enjoyed the smell of the ink and the scratch of the pen. Sometimes she would lean too heavily on the nib, and the ink would splash on the page, making its own mark. Sister Bridget Mary smiled when that happened. *Ink has a life of its own*, she often thought. She had a feeling of total contentment when ink splashed over the paper. No matter how many splotches of ink painted its own canvas on the page, Sister Bridget Mary never discarded one piece of it. To her, they were works of art in their own right. After a short time, Sister Bridget Mary began to write.

> Once upon a time in the village of EFAS, there was a patch of ground that had been vacant for a long time. The villagers passed by the vacant piece of land and paid no attention to the fact that it was, indeed, vacant. They were happy that the birds found their homes in the trees that stood sturdy there, and that the rabbits and other little animals roamed freely among the gorse and the purple heather that grew there in abundance.
>
> One day, the chief administrator of the village decided that it would be most impressive for all who visited the village to have an official garden they could enjoy. She called a meeting for all the villagers, and during that gathering, announced her plans to cultivate an official garden where the vacant land was situated. She told them that she wanted a garden full of flowers. She felt that it would be lovely for tourists and other strangers to visit the official garden. She wanted them to be dazzled there and to be able to gaze at the abundance of color that the garden would provide.

The chief administrator was very busy and wanted the decision about the official garden to be made quickly so she could arrange for the garden to be ready by spring. Mack and Lily were two friends who went to every meeting in the village. While everyone else in the village hall nodded in agreement and were ready to vote readily for the agenda regarding the official garden to be passed, Mack and Lily were not in agreement.

While everyone in there nodded in agreement to the plans for the official garden, Mack and Lily spoke boldly to the group, listing all the reasons they thought that the vacant patch of ground should be kept intact.

Lily, who took care of some of the children in the village after school, insisted that the patch should be kept as an open space for the children to enjoy their play. It was a place for them to use their imagination and pretend that they were on a pirate ship or in a castle or in a tree house. It was a place for them to make believe, a place for them to skip and hop and run and hide and enjoy the twitter of the birds and the dart of the rabbits.

Lily pointed out, too, that the children needed an opportunity to climb trees so that they could grow strong in their own limbs. Mack just enjoyed the open space that the vacant patch of ground provided. She lived a very busy life and needed a place to breathe and enjoy nature. Every day, Mack took the time to walk through the trees that this patch of ground on the outskirts of the village of EFAS provided. She glowed there as she listened to the rustle of the leaves in the trees and was left in a state of animation after enjoying the colors of the heather and gorse.

The chief administrator asked the group if any agreed with lily and Mack. No one said anything. Not one word was uttered. The chief administrator told the villagers that the official garden would be good for the village. It would draw many people to the village, and everyone would benefit. The only two who objected again were Lily and Mack.

Finally, the architect stood up. Afraid to go against the wishes of the chief administrator, she declared that she would draw up the blueprints. No one knew anything about drawing up blueprints. Everyone nodded at the architect except Lily and Mack. The architect declared that she would design an official garden that would encompass great order.

Each variety of flower would be assigned its place within a predetermined shape. Their borders would be clearly delineated, and the paths of the garden would be straight and narrow and well defined. Everyone nodded. Lily said the flowers that grew there presently spilled into the grass and around the hedges, the shrubs, and the bushes. Since no one objected, the chief administrator stated that the official garden would be built and the architect would create the design for it.

The local teacher, trying to please the chief administrator, timidly stated that the official garden could create an opportunity for the children in the village school to learn about pollination and photosynthesis and other scientific concepts. The teacher felt important after she said this. Everyone nodded. The chief administrator cheered the educational value of having an official garden. Lily responded that the children already enjoyed dancing through the daisies and buttercups and often took a bunch of these flowers home to surprise someone they lived with. Flowers were abundant and free.

The local stonemason, who was a large man, stood up and spoke of the need to build a wall around the official garden in order to keep order and ensure that animals would not prowl among the flowers. The villagers nodded. Lily and Mack urged the villagers to vote against the wall. They argued that it was unnecessary. Both of them loved their own gardens and knew that a wall would cast a shadow and shut out the sun. They wanted the flowers to experience the light of day and every second of the sun's mighty rays. Since no one else spoke, the chief administrator declared that a wall would be built, and the local stonemason would be in charge of building it. Everyone nodded.

The stonemason too felt very important and stated that he would immediately arrange for the stone for the wall to be quarried from far away and brought to the village. He warned the villagers to be prepared for the rumble of trucks, as they carried their large loads of stone, because the wall would be high and wide and thick. Everyone nodded, except the two friends.

The blacksmith was the next to speak. He convinced the villagers that the official garden would need a gate to ensure that the people would adhere to a schedule, making the official garden available only at assigned times. The villagers nodded. Lily and Mack said that the whole purpose of a garden was to make it available for everybody at any time anyone wanted to be there. The blacksmith went to his forge to stoke his fire into white heat to prepare for the delivery of iron for the creation of the gate.

Over time, the patch of ground at the edge of the village disappeared. The trees were toppled and the birds left to find other trees in the distance where they could build their nests. The rabbits found other gorse and purple heather to run through many miles away. The color and music and chatter of the lot at the edge of the village very quickly disappeared. Lily and Mack felt lonely when they did not hear the birds or see the animals. They also missed the color and fragrance of the purple heather and the tangle of the gorse. The children could no longer tumble and climb and dance among the daisies.

The official garden was soon designed, seeded, planted, and bordered. Within a few months, the daffodils shone bright yellow in the sun, and the roses blushed crimson in the rise and set of the day. The villagers and anyone who visited the village walked straight along the new garden paths within assigned times of the day. They nodded to one another as they walked along. The village children had to keep strictly to the pathways. They were not allowed to explore beyond the borders containing the bright new flowers. The gate was opened every morning and closed every evening. The blacksmith lived near the village and told the villagers that he would be responsible for opening and closing the bright shiny gate. The villagers nodded in agreement. Sometimes when business was brisk at the forge, the blacksmith forgot to open the gate in the morning. On those days, no one was able to walk in the garden or dared climb over the high, thick, wide wall.

Time passed. One day in early summer, the chief administrator decided to go and check the official garden. After the official opening of the official garden, the chief administrator went back to work in the official offices of the village of EFAS. Since that time, she had been very busy organizing the affairs of the village in her office, making sure that things were run and working like clockwork or a well-oiled machine. She never had time to go to the official garden. She never thought about it. She did not visit it. She had negotiated all the contracts with the horticultural society and left the culture of the official garden in its hands. The contract stated that the horticultural society would inspect the garden once a month, and that is what they did.

Finally, in the middle of summer one late afternoon, the chief administrator decided to go to the official garden. She nodded to the few people she met there. She looked around her and was aghast to see that weeds were spreading in abundance in the garden. The chief administrator thought she would be criticized for all the weeds that were growing there among the flowers, so she called a meeting to discuss the current condition of the official garden. She really did not know anything about gardening, certainly not enough to save the official garden now being overtaken by weeds.

The chief administrator told the villagers that the task of weeding the official garden had to be accomplished immediately. The villagers nodded their heads. The architect was silent. The teacher looked out the window. The stonemason examined the condition of his hands. The blacksmith appeared to be asleep. Finally, Lily and Mack stood up and volunteered to take care of the official garden, and everyone nodded.

Lily and Mack had their own agenda for the official garden. Their agenda could not be put into words. It poured out of their hearts and was the result of the stillness and silence they had previously enjoyed in the vacant patch before the official garden had been developed there. Their stillness had scratched into the silence, and they had been distilled and nourished by the peace they had found there. Lily and Mack knew all about gardens. They knew they could save the official garden. Lily and Mack would work together on it in their spare time.

The two friends arranged to meet in the official garden every evening. Once there, they chatted for a while and began to push into the familiar silence of their work. Lily was good at weeding, so she concentrated on that. She bent low to the earth and tugged at the weeds until she was able to pull the roots out of the ground. Mack agreed to do the watering. She attached the hose to the watering tap and felt the fullness of the hose expel into the dry earth, night after night, when the sun went down.

In a few weeks, the official garden began to experience new life again. It began to look more beautiful than it had ever been under the auspices of the horticultural society. The villagers and tourists began to flock to the garden again.

One Friday afternoon toward the end of summer, Lily reached behind the shrubs to weed against the wall of the garden. To her surprise, she found a few little pansies in the crack of the wall. She was thrilled. She looked at Mack, who was enjoying the low evening clouds, as she held the watering hose absentmindedly at a high, wide angle so that most of the water was flying way beyond the wall. Water was god in any direction. No matter where it landed, it always brought life. It was good for things we do not see and things that are beyond our reach.

The pansies in the cement wall built by the burly stonemason were being well-watered, too. The pansies thrived there in the darkness that sometimes overshadowed them. A few weeks later, the two friends were delighted to observe that flowers were sprouting in abundance beyond the wall of the official garden, and they seemed strong and wild and free.

By the end of the summer, the flowers in the garden had become quite withered and wilted, but the wildflowers beyond the wall took hold of the hillside near the village of EFAS. They became so plentiful that the little children danced in the daisies and buttercups once again. These flowers were hardy. Their color grasped the hillside, filling it in splendor. The people of the village began to bring their picnics to the hillside and enjoy the life that had been reclaimed. The flowers struggled through the autumn's fall and the winter's bite.

In the springtime, the wildflowers enveloped the whole countryside again, while in a dark corner of the official garden, the chief administrator of the village of EFAS agonized as she calculated the amount she would have to budget for a new season of bulbs and seeds there. The chief administrator shuddered to think of the amount of money the village would have to expend to cement the wall and paint the rusty gate.

Sister Bridget Mary looked at her little script and blew on the paper to dry the ink. She gathered the papers and placed them carefully in her little leather satchel and put them carefully in the kitchen drawer. Sister Mary Joan, who was appointed for a few days to help her while Sister Freda Mary recovered from the flu, nodded to her when she entered the kitchen.

CHAPTER FORTY-FIVE

THE DOG COLLAR

Nancy McCarthy, number 1993, was born in Tullamore, County Offaly. Her father was the headmaster in the local national school, and her mother taught piano to some children in her home after school in the afternoon. There was music and brightness and fun in this home tucked in the center of the village.

Lars and Nora McCarthy were involved with events in the village and were interested in all that impacted their lives there. Nancy was their only child, and most of their attention and devotion was lavished on her from the moment she came into the world. Nancy was taught piano by her mother at an early age and had a proclivity to be engaged in music in various other ways. She loved to sing and had a flare for composing songs. She seemed to always have a tune in her head and a song in her throat. It was something she always did. It was part of her. She looked upon it as a kind of hobby, something to entertain others in her school concerts, something to do when she had finished her homework, and when the long nights of winter settled in the village. She loved to garden as well. When she was young, her love of the soil and plants and flowers made her think she should be a botanist when she grew up. Her father had assigned her a large patch of land in the back of his property. Nancy was there for hours in the autumn, spring, and summer, coaching the earthen patch to life and color.

Lars McCarthy was not happy when he learned about Nancy wanting to go to the convent. He would not interfere with her decision, but, up to the last minute, he harbored the hope that she would change her mind. He felt that she was too young to enter the convent at seventeen and suggested that she finish her schooling and see a bit of the world before she made such an enormous decision.

Nora McCarthy was silently brokenhearted when Nancy came from school that day and announced she wanted to join a group of missionary nuns in September. Lars had been alerted by the parish priest, Father Flynn, that he would allow the recruiters from the missionary religious order to visit all the classrooms before the school year had ended. Nancy was smitten by the tales these nuns had imparted to the students during the few hours they spent at Holy Family School in the village.

Nancy entered Fairview Convent on September 8, 1966, leaving her parents with a deep sense of loss.

Nancy had endured the bitter blast of abuse with most of her postulant companions since entering the convent. On June 1, 1967, Nancy was in the garden at the back of the convent. She heard the whisper of nature, which felt like a song to Nancy. Despite what was going on in the house, there was a song to be heard and composed there, and Nancy was deeply attentive to it.

She took the rusted handle of the trowel lying on the narrow pathway between the thickets that protruded from the garden wall next to the tool shed. She knelt on the moist flower bed and pushed the trowel into the dark earth, unsettling the weeds that had accumulated there. Weeds spoke to her of the choking of life, and she was determined to get rid of them as soon as possible. Shortly, she had a flush on her face. She clumped the small instrument rhythmically and expertly into the dark soil until she glowed with sweat. She wiped her face with the back of her hand, continuing all the while to push into the roots. She pulled the weeds, shook off the excess clay, and when she had enough heaped beside her, she put them in a tin bin at the side of the garden gate. She repeated this throughout the afternoon until it was time for her to go back into the convent.

Nancy relished her time in the garden. It was good to feel the warm air of June on her face. It felt good to be immersed in the abundance of color. Recently, the color of the garden had taken her by surprise. It whetted her appetite for the embrace of the brightness of the summer months ahead. She looked forward to the long delight of days stretching more and more into the bite of night.

By now, Nancy had lived through the first winter in Fairview Convent as if the sun had been totally blocked out. The world, as she had known it barely ten months ago, had faded quickly into the distance. Her dig into the earth, in the early dance of the summer days, made her realize how fossilized she felt, a mere remnant of the energy that had been hers last September. She had endured the cloistered freeze in the drab, harsh rules and cruel regulations. Her initial feeling, when she had first entered Fairview Convent, was that she had taken flight and landed in another reality. She had been quick and light right before her entrance, and now her steps had become hesitant, halting, and heavy. She used to skip through the day. Now that skip had detoured somewhere else, and she felt the constancy of stumbling into this strange territory she was barely able to navigate. She had lost the great confidence that was hers. Her self-esteem was trodden down, and her assuredness had become brittle.

Here, in the convent garden, on the first day of June, however, she felt the flowers nudge her into a new awareness and another opportunity for freshness and reawakening. She thought she might find here a rekindling of energy for the dreams that were now withering inside her. She was assigned to work in the garden for the month of June. As soon as she entered, the garden's embrace began to open, and she accepted the garden's welcome. When she shifted into a new area of the flower bed, she automatically looked toward the convent. She wondered at the many lives that were locked in stone inside those walls. A song came to mind, and she felt herself humming now and again.

The postulants were not allowed to hum in the convent, and gradually the melodies and the music she had held in her head had been squeezed out. She became conscious of the happy sound she was making and enjoying. She stopped and looked furtively around her. She *needed* to be in the garden, and a hum might jeopardize her month here. She stopped abruptly.

Around her, Nancy McCarthy saw the flowers open fully in their own brightness and bathe in the richest of hues. Some opened towards her as she gently extracted the weeds around them. Nancy had a definite mission in mind, and she was determined that the blooms have plenty of space to breathe and spread. Some flowers stood straight, exploring a stretch into a hope for something they could not quite attain. Brilliant bouquets exploded, spewing their colors amid the dazzle of petals. It all created a sense that she was in harmony with the season's passing.

The blooms provided an emotional connection for her and cut through the chokehold that the stalwart convent walls had on her. For a while, she felt free from the concrete cave she had been living in, which was stifled with heaviness and shackled in containment. The garden was awakening her to freshness and new possibilities again. She drank fully of the feeling of freedom, appreciating the prod and prickle of a new breath inside her. When she paused now and again, Nancy realized that she was inwardly exhausted after wintering in Fairview Convent. She was glad that the slow crawl of spring was well behind her. She looked around. It was an extraordinary thing that such vibrancy was born in this garden under the crust of frost.

Nancy listened carefully while she was in the garden. Once inside the convent doors, she would become woven into the stifling entanglement once again. She recoiled at the thought of being stuck within the loom of the convent's limitations. Here, for this moment, she felt free, yet rooted in a sense of being connected to something that moved. She could feel the current of new life flowing through her. The ice water that had dammed inside was cracking, and she could almost hear the boom of its cracks. She felt the rise of the sap and the urge to fruit. In the garden in the month of June, Nancy was yearning to find the pulse of new life again. She could almost hear the new life flowing in the thicket beside the tool shed. Nancy shook the clay from the last weed and speared the trowel into the earth to await its work for tomorrow. She hoped that it would not rain tomorrow. She got up from the flower bed, aware that her neck was sore.

She had not used these muscles for a long time. She shook the specks of dirt from her apron and arose from her deep contentment to organize herself before returning to the convent for prayers. She bundled the weeds into a bag and flung them into the tin bin. She was careful to make sure that the lid was on good and tight. As she walked near the door, she took off the old boots she was wearing and scraped the clay from their worn tread. These were among three sets of boots that were shared by everyone for gardening. This pair was a little too big for her, but she had tied them well and had not noticed their extra bulk.

Nancy put on her shoes and automatically tied them tightly. She turned to look at the brightness of the garden. She had the sense that she would portal into that place just beyond the threshold where this strange mixture of women—old and young, big and small—were all dying together. She shook off the feeling and gulped at the fresh air before she entered the convent. In that instant, she turned and took a second look at the garden. A crushing loneliness pulled at her, sabotaging her efforts to keep the surprise and joy of her time spent in the garden intact. In the next few days, Nancy was thrilled with her days in the garden. After a few more days there, hunkered and hunched over flower beds, the mold of her bent shoulders seemed to stay with her.

At evening prayers on Friday evening, Nancy felt her neck stiffen and put her hand at the back of her neck to rub at the stiffness, trying to alleviate it. If she was home, she could cover her neck with a warm towel and get some relief and ease the ache. Here, all she could do was try and forget about it.

Sister Dolores noticed every move that Nancy made and was not pleased that she was not sitting or standing straight. She noticed her bending over her food in the refectory. In the recreation room, she was bending a little too much over the Sacred Heart badges. Sister Dolores frowned every time Nancy did this.

Nancy sat at the large table in the recreation room, completely unaware of the displeasure she was causing Sister Dolores. Nancy still held the brightness and cheer of her time spent in the garden on her face, but the ache embedded in her shoulders was making her shift here and there with the throb. Her muscles would certainly get used to the work, she convinced herself. It was just a matter of time.

Nancy was intent on finishing the allotted portion of her weekly quota of Sacred Heart badges tonight. Most of them were already completed. If she got two done tonight, she would only have one more to complete tomorrow night. She drooped into the task at hand. Sister Dolores noticed the slump in Nancy's shoulders.

"Your head and shoulders are very bent, madam," Sister Dolores curdled.

Nancy was tired, and it took a second for her to respond to the thickening of the air. "My neck is not yet used to working in the garden, Sister," Nancy replied, carefully trying to sound lighthearted. She bent lower into the embroidery and concentrated on her work.

Sister Dolores yelled at her and broke the concentration.

"Well, madam, you will not be seen walking around here as if you were carrying the weight of the world on your shoulders!"

She glowered at Nancy. Nancy sat very still. The pain had disappeared from her shoulders, and she straightened in her chair.

"Go to the closet at the back of the room and get me a cardboard box, madam," Sister Dolores ordered.

Nancy put her work in a heap on the table and stood up in obedience to this command. Most of us did not look up, though I noticed Mary O'Brien's eyes met Nancy's bright blue ones and held them for a second in support. Nancy went to the closet at the bottom of the recreation room, glancing at the statue of Our Lady for some kind of intervention. It did not happen.

Nancy creaked open one of the doors, quickly exhumed a cardboard box, and brought it hesitantly to Sister Dolores, who grabbed the box. With hands shaking, she took a pair of scissors from her drawer and cut a deep, oblong shape out of the thick, brown cardboard. She got up from her seat and went to Nancy. She put the oblong shape around Nancy's neck to measure it. It fit perfectly. She picked up a bolt of black material from a table at the side. She placed the oblong shape on top of the bolt of material and cut liberally around it so that the material took its shape. She did this a second time. She came back to the table, gave the two pieces of black cloth to Nancy, and instructed her to put the cardboard between the two pieces of material and sew around the shape so that the cardboard was encased in the black material.

When that was finished, Sister Dolores whispered to Nancy, "Now sew two pieces of string at each end to tie behind your neck. That will keep your head straight. Dogs wear collars for a reason," she gloated.

We were aghast at what we saw happen in front of us. Nancy could feel the tears well in her eyes and stopped them before the gravity could pull them onto her face. She swallowed them. She was told to put on the dog collar. It was bulky and cut into her neck, even while sitting at the table.

"See how you work in the garden tomorrow with that on," Sister Dolores snapped as the bell rang for night prayers.

Nancy McCarthy's spirit took a beating that night. Within a week, all but three of us had to make dog collars for ourselves. The three Kerry postulants were again exempt. The dog collars were bulky, and with any movement at all, gnawed at our necks. The brand of cruelty that uniquely belonged to Sister Dolores was well hidden under our dresses with high collars. It was worn in a fashion that no one else could detect. The cardboard dug into the skin of the seven of us who wore them, and soon we were dealing with our necks bleeding. No one noticed the blood on the black material. A week after wearing the stiff bulk around my neck, I was on kitchen duty. Sister Freda Mary came to me at the sink.

"Have you got a stiff neck or something? You look very awkward today washing those pots," she laughed.

I took my hands out of the water and told her the story of the dog collars. Sister Freda Mary called to Sister Bridget Mary. She needed to consult with her. My neck was particularly sore as I tried to wash the heavy pots that day. Sister Bridget Mary found the strings at the back of my neck. She saw that my neck was red and raw. At her direction, Sister Freda Mary made a concoction of relief and rubbed it into my neck and gently massaged the raw skin. I could tell that both of them were startled. Sister Bridget Mary brought me into her inner scullery and gave me a glass of milk and a piece of cake. Once there, the balm around my neck penetrated into my skin, and it felt a little better. I knew the two nuns in the kitchen were angry. I heard Sister Bridget Mary tell Sister Freda Mary that in a few days my neck would have been infected, but believed that I received help to prevent that just in time. She said she was going to tell Sister Dolores that she needed my help in the kitchen for the foreseeable future, keenly aware that Sister Dolores would agree to any request by Sister Bridget Mary. I felt the welts around my neck and tried to forget about them.

After a short while, I came out of the inner scullery. It was not yet time to go back to the sacristy, so I waited at the sink when Sister Freda Mary announced that she had to make some bread. She told me that she made extra bread when she was upset. It soothed her. She soon became engrossed in her bread making. She scooped a few handfuls of flour from the vat sitting opposite the huge table in the middle of the kitchen, dusted a wooden board with an initial spray of it, and then spread it so that the board was fully covered with the flour. She then mixed water, flour, and a touch of yeast in a large bowl. She put her right hand into the bowl and began to massage the ingredients together. Gradually, I noticed that the flour mix was being pummeled by Sister Freda Mary's large hands as she moved her body in total concentration at the task that had stolen her attention and focus. It appeared that something was being constantly torn apart and tossed around in that bowl, and at the same time, being made into something new.

Sometimes the mixture was swallowed in Sister Freda Mary's hands. She pushed her hands vigorously into and around the contents of the bowl, kneading the dough until it became pale and pliable. After a while, I could see satisfaction settle on the baker's brow. She plopped the dough on the lightly floured surface of the board and patted the top gently with the back of her fisted left hand. She flattened the clump that came out of the bowl. Using her right hand, she pulled the far edge of the dough towards her. With the bottom part of her left hand, she pushed firmly into the flour mixture and pushed the dough away from her. The dough stretched in the pull and push.

Sister Freda Mary rotated the dough, stretching it, folding it, and pushing it into the wooden board. She kept the movement constant and firm. The board moved a little here and there, but held the strength of the sister's hands that were working expertly above it. She worked the mixture until it was soft and smooth. Finally, she smacked the dough, handling it now roughly at times. Putting the lump of dough on the newly floured board, she flattened it at the top with the touch of her fingers, leaving soft wrinkles on top. She slapped the dough and padded it into an oblong shape, indenting the top lightly into the form of a cross with her thumb so that the indentation became part of the rising. She went to the back of the kitchen to test the cold shelf that would hold the bread to await fermentation. Sister Freda Mary explained to me that it was important to keep the shelf at an even temperature. She said that was why the shelf for fermentation was put in the back, far from the heat of the kitchen.

"It is very important for this mixture to be given its time," she told me when she returned. "Good bread takes time, but not our time. Only the one who bakes the bread knows the exactness of the yeasting. Longer is better. With speed, the flavor of the ingredients is lost or compromised or seriously diminished."

She put a white cloth loosely over the plump dough and placed it on the yeasting shelf. Sister Freda Mary took another loaf she had placed on the shelf earlier. This loaf was now twice the size of the one she had just produced. Sister Freda Mary lightly floured a baking tin and placed this dough into the tin, pressing it carefully into its seams. She told me that the bread would take the shape of the tin it was put into, since it is in the nature of the ingredients she had used to be soft and malleable. This particular tin was circular. Another part of the same mixture went into a square container. The shape of the bread would be different, but the taste would be the same.

I paid attention to Sister Freda Mary's explanations and was glad of the relief I was experiencing with my neck. Instead of piercing the top of one of the loaves with the two lines of a cross, Sister Freda Mary indented the initials BM with her thumb. I thought it was for the Blessed Mother, but she smiled.

"It is for Sister Bridget Mary. Today is her fiftieth birthday. The people who eat some of this bread will think the same as you, but they will be eating her birthday bread. She will have a big slice of both ends. That is her favorite part."

Sister Freda Mary laughed heartily. No one was allowed to celebrate her birthday in the convent.

When Sister Bridget Mary returned to the kitchen, we both sang a hearty "Happy Birthday" to her. There was a tear in the baker's eye when we finished singing. Sister Freda Mary put the bread in the oven and entrusted the loaves to bake in the intense heat there. As I watched from my little stool at the edge of the table, I saw that great things happen in intense heat. Here the flour rises, becomes a golden brown, and a crust is formed. I became hungry for the taste.

I still had plenty of time before I started my next series of responsibilities in the sacristy. By this point, Sister Tabor was happy that I did most of the work there. I looked around me. Wooden spoons and bowls of various sizes and shapes sat in order on the shelves in front of me. The aroma of the loaf baking spilled beyond the oven. I wondered how the use of these simple bowls and the power of one's hands could produce a loaf that so stirred the memory of my own kitchen at home and evoke such a good feeling of comfort. The aroma of the bread could not be contained. It permeated my clothes and seeped everywhere.

After a short time, Sister Freda Mary announced that the bread was ready. I got off my stool. Sister Freda Mary hovered over the oven, as if intuitively knowing the very second the bread would be ready. She donned an oven glove, opened the oven door, and took the loaves deftly from the crucible. The loaves were golden brown.

Sister Freda Mary placed the loaves on a rack on the table and carefully placed a white muslin cloth over them. She stood over the loaves for a little while and seemed to drink in some deep memory as she hovered there.

Sister Bridget Mary returned to the kitchen and checked my neck. She gave me a soft cloth to wrap around my neck. She grabbed the dog collar and threw the cardboard covered in black material into the garbage bin. I was startled, but she gave me a look of reassurance, which told me clearly that I would have nothing to worry about. I breathed a sigh of relief. Sister Freda Mary cut the birthday bread, and I enjoyed the hot treat slathered in butter with a heap of jam plopped carefully in the middle. In the warmth of friendship in that kitchen, I forgot how sore my neck was.

Years later, I learned that Sister Bridget Mary and Sister Kate O'Flaherty met in the afternoon to discuss the outrage. The two older women wondered why they had not noticed the postulants as they did their daily chores, suffocated and restricted by the stiff cardboard collars they had to endure. Both of them sent terse letters to the headquarters in Rome, demanding that something be done about the treatment of these young women. When the other postulants had kitchen duty, the first thing Sister Bridget Mary did was untether them from their collars. Very soon, none of the postulants was wearing a collar.

Mother Benedicta took note, especially the letter from Sister Bridget Mary. Her words pierced through the paper they were written on and finally moved Mother Benedicta to write a letter of reprimand to Sister Dolores, who was unabashed that she had been so reprimanded. She jeered at the letter in her room when she received it. Rome was far away. She would have no compunction about continuing her harsh ways. She was in charge of the postulants. She would find more subtle ways to test these young women. She herself had suffered. She had been treated badly all her life. Most of these young women would get great opportunities for travel and education when they went to serve in the mission territories as teachers and nurses, some even as social workers.

"They should be toughened up," she choked with rage as she sat at her desk, grasping both sides of the wooden frame. "Why should they get away with anything? I will put a crack in each of their halos that is for sure."

As she said this, she emptied the last dregs of the glass of whisky she had poured for herself. She had a hiding place behind her bed that no one ever saw. Tom Gorman would make his delivery to her at the garden gate tomorrow morning after he delivered the hosts to the sacristy. One bottle used to last her a week. Now she needed two bottles to take care of her responsibilities. She would assure Tom Gorman of her continuous prayers.

CHAPTER FORTY-SIX

FAREWELL

Sister Kate O'Flaherty died on July 5, 1967. She was sixty years old. We got news of her death as we sat in the chapel that morning. A simple announcement was made after Mass by Sister Annunciata.

"Sister Kate died in her sleep. Her wake will be held tomorrow night. She will be buried the day after."

I gasped at the words. I could hear the moan of Mary O'Brien and Nuala O'Reilly. Nuala put her hands to her head. Annie Boyle gasped and bent over as if she had been struck. Nancy McCarthy started to cry, and soon after, tears were rolling down my own face, and I could not stop the sob coming from deep inside. I felt bereft. I felt something collapse within. I cried softly at first, and then I felt my body shake. I could not control the depth of feeling that exploded inside me and came to the surface. I felt totally stricken.

The other nuns in the chapel were in a mode of self-control. There were only a few of us who reacted to the reality of Sister Kate's death that morning when the announcement of her passing was so unemotionally declared. Besides a few of the postulants who had developed some kind of connection to Sister Kate, there was barely a stir in the chapel.

Sister Kate had always been there to give encouragement: a wink of an eye when she knew that someone was discouraged, a tap on the shoulder when we did a good job. She was the face of humanity in an otherwise disinterested crowd. Her smile lit up her face, and anyone who was gifted that smile was pulled into her heart and soul. The postulants who bathed in that refuge of kindness got the courage to go on, were reinvigorated in their efforts, and mobilized to do their very best. The example of her care in the desolation that hugged this convent, which tried to smother anything that was creative, imaginative, fresh, or new, gave us some hope. In spite of being belittled, humiliated, burdened, and bothered by all the rules and regulations, Sister Kate modeled the joy of living beyond the margins. A chill devoured me, and I shuddered. I realized that I had lost one of my best friends. She was gone, and she had barely spoken a word to me in all the months I had been in Fairview Convent. Such was the gift of Sister Kate O'Flaherty.

Sister Kate was waked in silence, buried in silence, and spoken of no more. Every day, I slipped through the convent garden after my chores, picked whatever flower was in season, and put it on Sister Kate's grave. Sister Bridget Mary and Sister Freda Mary provided a haven for the feelings and stripping that sudden loss brings. The four of us who had been particularly attached to her experienced deep gullies of wounded feelings. The sadness of her loss was constant. It moved with me all the time. It blasted its assault unceasingly. It was with me during the day; it probed and prodded my deepest sleep. The pain of loss burned low. It burned in the daylight hours. It burned even brighter in the night. I felt I was in exile, in a wilderness of struggle. The wall of grief got higher and higher by the day. I performed my duties in the sacristy robotically. I attended daily classes with Sister Dolores, who had instructed us not to talk about Sister Kate. I went on the daily walk and worked in the garden, feeling all the time that part of me was missing. My world was suspended, and each footstep was mired in fog.

The jolt of Sister Kate's loss was fine-tuned into every breath I took. Everything was lived in slow motion. The light was dimmed, and I went through days dulled. The fire had gone out. I felt as if my heart was scorched constantly with boiling water. My head hurt, and stretching my neck to see beyond the next step often felt like too much to accomplish. The loss pushed me into white hot night. Sparks from the anvil of grief just kept coming. They jumped into life as soon as I opened my eyes. My heart was beating in some other sphere the weeks and months after Sister Kate died. I felt my pulse had gone somewhere else. Some sharp instrument kept hollowing me in my center.

The kitchen was the only place I experienced relief. I could cry there, and two people who actually absorbed my sadness were also there. It was a long time before I could smile. I eventually did. Sister Bridget Mary told me stories. She let me talk, and she was forever writing on those patches and scraps of paper every chance she got.

Sister Kate O'Flaherty had been the fresh, life-giving force to me and the other postulants who opened up to her. She had helped redefine the harsh landscape for us early on when we had first entered Fairview Convent. Her very presence was an anchor for me. Just knowing that Sister Kate was around was enough to help me get through some difficult times. For a long time, darkness blanketed me. Sister Kate taught me many things, particularly that not one of the dark moments I was experiencing, could be wasted in its own time. Darkness births the light, and the deepest night contains the day.

CHAPTER FORTY-SEVEN

NOVICES

On the morning of August 1, 1967, the class of novices took their vows and moved their sparse belongings to the section of the convent reserved for them. They had recited the vows of the religious order and received the black veil. They went home after the ceremony for a few days before receiving their first assignments, or what was officially termed their *obediences*. These assignments would send them to different parts of the world. Some went to Africa, others to Scotland, some to Australia, and others to America. They had left their quarters in Fairview Convent emptied for the new class of novices that would take their places. On August 5, 1967, just a month after Sister Kate died, the postulant class of 1966 now moved into the novice section of the convent. On August 5, 1967, we took our first vows as novices.

One person was missing from the new group. Margaret Logue, number 1997, had left the convent the night before. Her father, who had become a judge in the high courts in Dublin, had persuaded Margaret that she would never progress in this religious congregation. He had noticed on the few times he had visited her that she was becoming more and more anxious, and her spirit had been depleted. He spoke to her in their native language, and she became hesitant, searching now and again for the correct words to finish a sentence. She would never be head of the institute.

Judge Logue wanted his daughter to aim for other things in life. Margaret did not take long to decide to leave. In the kitchen, it seemed rather too much of a coincidence that young Jimmy McGinty, that very same day, announced that he was leaving his job and going to Dublin to spend some time with his father. He thought he might find work there and stay. The two nuns had realized early on that when Margaret Logue was scheduled for kitchen duty after meals, Jimmy inevitable found some excuse to come into the main kitchen. His furtive looks toward Margaret did not go unnoticed by the two nuns. They were very happy for him.

We spent the next year in Fairview Convent learning theology and engaging in the study of the Bible and the history of the institute. We read the lives of all the saints who had ever been canonized in the Catholic church. We studied the documents that had been published since the Second Vatican Council. We read all the encyclicals that the popes from the late nineteenth century imposed on the faithful of the church. Above all else, we rarely saw Sister Dolores and that, in itself, was one of the biggest realities we embraced on that fifth day of August. This year we were given our assignments before we took our vows. The assignments were dispersed at the beginning of July. I was the only one who was assigned to the United States mission territory. The three Kerry novices were sent to a nursing college in England. Mary O'Brien, Nuala O'Reilly, and Mary Ita Ahern were sent to Australia. Annie Boyle was assigned to the kitchen in Fairview Convent. Nancy McCarthy was sent to Galway to attend college. After we took our vows on August 5, 1968, my group of friends promised we would stay in touch for the rest of our lives.

CHAPTER FORTY-EIGHT

COMING TO AMERICA

August 26, 1968—8:00 a.m.

On August 30, 1968, Sister Floret accompanied me to the early bus at the South Station bus terminal in Boston. I had been in the convent at Cambridge for just four days after arriving from Ireland on August 26, 1968. I arrived in Boston after taking the longest trip of my life. I was not used to travelling and had some difficulty with the many signs posted throughout the terminal.

The heat was a shock to my system when I finally exited the terminal. It was unbearable. I had arrived in my long habit and veil. Seventy degrees was considered a heat wave in Ireland, and I had never experienced such heavy humidity and sweltering temperatures as when I stepped outside Logan International Airport that late afternoon upon my arrival to the United States. It was an intolerable ninety-four degrees. I thought I would lose my breath. I struggled outside to get fresh air to the point that I nearly panicked. I noticed a nun in a similar brown habit wave at me, which is when I met Sister Floret. She gave me a swift hug and welcomed me to the United States. She was a welcome sight and made every effort to assist me with my suitcase as we made our way to the taxi stand. Evidently, the Convent of Saint Paul, where I was supposed to stay for four days, did not possess a car.

Sister Floret explained that the sisters depended on the friendship of neighbors for rides; otherwise, they took the bus or the subway. I climbed into the taxi as exhaustion settled on my shoulders. Boston looked very different from Derry. The mass of concrete buildings leaned heavily into the sky. Sometimes it was even hard to see the sky from my vantage point in the taxi.

By the time we arrived at the convent, I was finding it hard to move quickly. The push to get myself to the United States had been urgent and tedious. While I was the only one who received an obedience to go to the United States, I also was the only one who was told that I would have to apply for a visa myself. The immigration process was lengthy, and since no resident in the convent had actually applied for a visa, I was left to my own devices to wade through the myriad of forms that constantly arrived from the American Embassy in Dublin before my visa to travel was issued. It was a relief to see the finality of my work that would set me on a path to the United States, but it also deepened the loneliness that, in all the years of living and working in Fairview Convent, had become a daily companion. Maybe it was the reality that the troubles in Northern Ireland were still in full swing. More likely, it was the simple fact that it would be a long time before I would see my family again.

CHAPTER FORTY-NINE

LEAVING BOSTON

August 30, 1968—7:30 a.m.

August 30, 1968, was a very hot summer's day when I left Boston to travel to Syracuse, New York, to settle into my first assignment in the United States. Without too much fanfare, I was brought to the bus terminal by Tim O'Connell, a kindly man who lived around the corner from the convent after having said goodbye to the superior of the convent. Tim took my suitcase out of the trunk of the car and helped me up the steps at South Station bus terminal. He told me where I should get on the bus and told me to have a good trip.

The bus rolled out of South Station, lurching now and again, as it lumbered heavily onto the crowded, concrete streets. The bus was almost full to capacity that day, but I managed to secure a seat alone. There were many nationalities represented on the bus. An Asian family—man, woman, and two small children—sat behind the driver. The woman sat in front with one child, and the man sat behind them with the other child. The man and woman talked at a high-pitched, frenetic pace, and it was obvious that the driver found their exchanges annoying.

A few teenagers teased one another at the back of the bus. The surrounding seats held a mixture of various cultures of people with various accents. One man sounded as if he had come from Ireland. I wanted to talk to him. There might be an opportunity ahead. The sound of his voice made me feel at home, although it was really three thousand miles away.

The reality of my departure from Ireland was dawning slowly. I tried not to think about it. I was tired from the heat and the new environment. In the few days I had been at the convent in Cambridge, I discovered that no one was particularly interested in listening to me or connecting with me in any way. The nuns living there taught at the convent school a few hundred yards around the corner from the church. Every morning, the bell rang in the hallway at 5:30 a.m., summoning us to get out of bed and prepare for morning prayers in the convent chapel on the first floor.

Most of the nuns spent long days in their classrooms. They began preparing for the start of school after Labor Day. Someone explained to me that Labor Day marked the end of the summer. It did not feel like the end of the summer to me as I struggled every night with the hot, hostile air in my room at the top of the stairs. A fan blew noisily, and its whirr kept me awake. I finally turned it off, and with difficulty, I drifted into sleep the few nights I was there.

We rolled onto the Massachusetts Turnpike and left the bustle of Boston. Within a half hour, we had definitely left the concrete and cemented high-rise buildings far behind. The bus swayed around a few bends, spilling us onto a fairly straight trajectory of a roadway that spanned four lanes of traffic. I was truly fascinated by the speed and the vastness of the highway.

I was used to winding roads with hedges draped on each side of the road in Ireland. Driving in Ireland always felt like we were confined or hemmed in in some way. Here, in this huge bus, the world unfolded in a wide expanse beyond the window. It was definitely a different experience, and I snuggled in my seat to enjoy it. I was glad to be in the front of the bus.

Rather quickly, we slurped and gulped into the sheath of miles rushing forward. The clouds sat like white wads of cotton wool in the sky. We bumped and hurtled along the Massachusetts Turnpike. Soon the blue-hued Berkshires sat in the distance, engulfed by a sea of trees. The bus slithered through the deep grip of the mountain path at a good clip. The bus driver was a fixture of pure, refined concentration. He looked as though he had sifted every mile multiple times, and even in this rain, the road left an indelible imprint on this man as he controlled the wheel in his firm hands.

The roads in the distance scrawled lines up and down through the hills. The road swallowed us and sucked us into its own long drink. The trees on either side were a flush green, waiting patiently for water to come tumbling from the sky. The leaves exposed to the scorching heat had enough green on them. They would survive the scorch. After all, they had been hardened by the winter for the approach of summer's high noon. The other passengers and I were drawn to the side of the road and beyond, to whatever was over the horizon, atop trees, way over yonder, miles and miles away.

The bus snapped and jousted with the speared path, jostling along, fumbling along purposefully. The air surged around the bus, dispossessing it of memory. I looked to the left, as we pushed into the climb of another hill, and wondered if someone was watching us in the hills, some wistful onlooker keeping vigil over us.

We slurped along, shaking now and again, in rhythm with the bus. The long snap of time rolled along as smoothly and as lightly as any cloud in the sky. The clouds resembled white marble after a while. I wanted a scalpel to fold and slice through them. They left their prints in the air. At some point, I closed my eyes and woke up as we pulled into the bus terminal in Albany, New York.

The bus spluttered and spat a little before we came to a complete stop. When the driver turned off the engine, the bus lurched and shook a little as it positioned itself in front of number twenty-four, its allotted spot. The bus driver blared that we would be stopped here for forty-five minutes. I unraveled myself from the comfort of the bus, exited it, and entered the bus station. It was quite cool in the terminal, which felt good. I went to the bathroom and drank greedily from a water fountain outside the facilities. There was a small cafeteria in the terminal. I saw some of the passengers in there. I had no money. For the first time that day, I felt hungry. I had eaten a slice of toast at six in the morning. I had been hungry when I boarded the bus in Boston.

###

Corn crops swayed in the height of harvest. We sped along at a steady, sustained pace, passing the fields in one seamless blur. The sides of the road were spiked with hedges here and there, as we flowed along the fluid, deep-gray tarmac. The dotted, white lines hemmed the route like stitches, and it became mesmerizing. I fell into a trance as I looked ahead.

Tiredness clawed at my shoulders, and I tried to fall back into the hug of the seat. I was becoming a little anxious now that the first green-and-white sign heralded the name of the city that was to be my first home in America. *Syracuse, New York*, the sign declared on that hot boiling day. I shuddered.

CHAPTER FIFTY

ALMOST THERE

August 30, 1968—4:15 p.m.

The bus coughed and hissed as we started to make our way out of the Albany bus station. A new landscape developed ever so slowly as the bus rumbled along. Within a half hour after the bus had tumbled out of the huge concrete jungle of the large city, little bits of farmland crept into view.

Here and there, as we sped into the bend in the road, cows lumbered in fields as far as my eye could see. For quite a while, cows and the occasional horse dotted the landscape, totally ignoring the speed and hurtle of traffic. I noticed that the fields, which must be so full of promise in the springtime, were, at this point in the height of summer, almost totally scorched. The farm animals stayed mostly in the shade of hedges or trees on the farmland and looked as if they could not move. They looked as though they were posing for a painting. The thought amused me, but it must not have been any fun sitting out in the sun all day.

Huge barns dotted the landscape here and there. The scenery was hypnotic, and I found myself dozing off as I tried to hold onto the little bag that contained my passport and the phone number to the convent in case of an emergency. I had no money to make a phone call and just trusted that someone would meet me at the bus depot.

About two hours into the journey, a sign appeared on the side of the road and slipped past me quickly, but I had already glimpsed at what it heralded: *Syracuse 28 Miles*. I estimated that I should be at my destination within the hour. My stomach lurched with a feeling of panic.

The air was oppressive when I finally got off the bus. It was even hard to breathe. It did not help that I was cloaked in a frock of heavy, brown material. It was much better suited to another climate, three thousand, lonely miles away.

The sun found me soon enough and heated me up like a furnace, as soon as I stood beyond the shade of the bus that was still spitting life from its engine. I bent into the cavernous hold where my case was waiting for me. I finally figured out that I would just have to wait until all the passengers had pulled their cases from the hold. I was happy enough to wait.

A man grunted as he inched out a huge duffle bag, sighing as he threw it heavily onto the ground. He wiped his sweated face with the palm of his right hand and then wiped the sweat onto his shirt. He dragged the bag away, leaving room for a woman who had been waiting patiently to secure her small suitcase and stroller. Her little girl was stuck to her side, and as soon as the woman expertly lurched the stroller into life, the little girl sprang into it, nestled in, and began sucking her thumb. I waited until the remaining passengers snagged their suitcases expertly, pulling heavily, most grunting under various degrees of weight, from the hold of the bus. Finally, it was my turn. The cargo hold was empty except for my case. I thought it strange that I was first on the bus in Boston and last to secure my luggage in Syracuse.

The first shall be last, I mused, recalling somewhere in the recesses of my brain that biblical verse. Now, it really made sense. I leaned forward into the back of the hold and edged the suitcase around so that the handle was facing me. I poured every ounce of strength I had in an effort to free it from the clutch that had held it on its journey from Boston. I strained at the awkward angle trying to reach it.

When I eventually got my hands on top of it, I felt a sharp slice in the palm of my hand, and a trickle of blood appeared just as quickly. The handle was broken and looked like a knife sticking out at the top of the case. Indeed, it had felt like a knife as it pierced my hand, certainly accomplishing the work of a knife. I pulled feverishly at the case, and it fell to the ground.

There was no way I could lift this suitcase, now smeared with my blood. I stood beside it for a few minutes, struck by the absurdity of having no handle to work with. The case was not going to move without one. I finally pushed it with my legs over to a wooden bench just outside the bus terminal. I was hot. I felt molten in the heat of the early afternoon. I finally sat on the bench and waited. I was finally at my destination. I was in Syracuse, and I was tired and alone.

My hand was bleeding profusely, and there was no one to meet me. I pulled a white handkerchief from my pocket and used it as a bandage. Both hands were stained with blood, but at least the cloth had stopped the flow. It felt sore enough, but did not seem too important to be concerned about it at that point.

A bearded man in a gray uniform came through the terminal doors. He had several plastic bags tucked into the black belt around his waist. He quickly looked to his left and nodded to me. Then with one vast swoop, he gathered the contents of a trash container. As he did so, some of the contents tumbled onto the concrete as he attempted to tie the bag at the top. He did not react to the spill. It was as if he expected this to happen. The man in the uniform turned, and I read his name scripted in red embroidery on his uniform just above his heart. *Shawn*, it read.

Shawn gathered the errant items and stuffed them expertly into a bag that was already overflowing. He steadied the contents, and then put his foot on the bag and stomped on it until he was satisfied that he had crushed and fractured and pulverized the items. Then he tied the bag in a knot at the top. Once this was done, he pulled a green bottle from the other side of his belt and sprayed the empty receptacle. The bottle's fumes lifted into the air. Some of the spray missed its target and quickly disappeared in a sizzle that lasted a mere second as it found its way to the sidewalk.

At that point, Shawn got out a new bag. He bent into the trash receptacle to ensure that the new bag was tucked into the bottom to await another load of disposable trash. Looking at him made me perspire. Half of his body had disappeared into the trash can. I wondered at his meticulousness and dedication to his work. He seemed determined that this bag would hold just as much as the one he was about to drag away. He seemed to pour himself into this very menial, dirty task, ensuring that his every effort would make a difference in the way this plastic bag was placed. It was obviously important to this man.

Something about that held my attention. He had brought great dignity and purpose to the task of emptying a trash bin. As he turned around with his load, he nodded in my direction again. I was charmed by the connection he had made with me. He simply could have ignored me and gone on his way. He had made me part of his day, and for some strange reason, it made me feel good, even though I felt as heavy as the bag he dragged behind him as he made his way to the back of the terminal.

I contented myself to sit in this strange part of the world that seemed to hold no oxygen. There was no discernible air, no breeze, nothing moved. A few trees that dotted a nearby driveway stood heavy and dry. Nothing moved except for the buses that droned into the terminal and sputtered to a stop, only to drone away again after a passenger or two boarded. There was nowhere for me to go. I could not go inside the terminal because my suitcase would not budge. It sat on the sidewalk, and I imagined all its contents, everything I possessed, baking inside it. Surely, someone from Saint Gertrude's Convent would pick me up soon.

I waited almost an hour in the burning heat. I started getting a headache and felt the need for some water. I became more aware that my hand was throbbing. While I examined the bandage, I became alerted to a maroon-colored station wagon that had rumbled in front of me and stopped. A woman who appeared to be around fifty got out of the car. She came toward me and apologized for being late. She held out her hand to shake mine, and I automatically offered her my bandaged hand.

"Hi, I am Pat," she said with a bright, white smile. "I see you hurt yourself." She did not ask about how it happened and seemed more interested in getting the suitcase into the car. Her face was flushed and her graying hair was fashioned in a bun at the top of her head.

"I am sorry I am a late, but I was stuck behind some school buses. Some schools have already started, and the buses create havoc at this time of the day. We have some nice iced tea waiting for you when we get to the convent."

At this point, I was just glad she had showed up. It suddenly struck me that she was not wearing a veil. In fact, she was wearing a pink T-shirt with some obscure writing on it and a pair of pants that came just below her knees. She wore no stockings. A pair of stylish sandals covered her feet. The image that Sister Pat portrayed was a bit of a surprise to me, as I stood before her drenched in sweat, and clad in a long, brown, heavy dress, with a huge crucifix on my chest and a small, black veil covering my head. Without having time to process this reality, because of my need to use the bathroom, I left her to keep watch over my bag while I made my way inside the bus terminal to use the facilities there. Once I entered the building, I was immediately hit with a blast of cold air. I had not realized that the building was so cool. I wondered at my resolve to stay outside in the burning heat to wait for my ride. I could have stood inside and looked out one of the many windows that overlooked the parking area. I welcomed the contrast of air.

The toilets were self-flushing, and I was taken by surprise. I freshened up a little bit after sitting outside for so long. There was a water fountain outside the bathroom, and I drank from it as if I had never tasted water in my life. The water was warm, but it refreshed me. It was all I needed to feel some life spring back into me, which propelled me to hurry.

I went back outside and found Pat sitting inside the car. She had safely stowed my suitcase in the heart of this huge vehicle. I slipped into the car and sat in the front seat next to Pat. I delighted in the fact that the car, too, was cool. I had never been in a car with air conditioning. I soon became comfortable, and a wave of exhaustion pulsed through me.

Pat pointed out some significant sights on our way to the convent. Mostly it was a blur, since my head throbbed, and I felt sick after the long journey. I tried to act interested in what she said. She spoke rapidly, and, every so often, her speech was punctuated with a burst of laughter. She seemed easy and free from any constraints as we tumbled along the streets that gradually became narrower and lined with trees. Soon, we were bumping around in the suburbs.

Pat explained that the convent was home to ten nuns. She said there were two elderly sisters who stayed at home and kept each other company. Sister Agnes and Sister Carmel had spent a lot of time together and had been cooks in many different convents throughout the United States. Since both had family in Syracuse, they had opted to return to St. Gertrude's to be near family and to cook for the remainder of the nuns, who taught at the parochial school across the street.

I tried to pay attention to Pat as she talked while driving. She was light and jovial. That, at least, was refreshing and so much different from anything I had experienced with the other sisters. The nuns in Cambridge had found it hard to conjure up a smile when I made an effort to engage with them. I had not been successful. In that short car ride in my first day in Syracuse, Pat gave me a feeling of hope after the long, lonely journey from Ireland, and the overwhelming hurt and humiliation I had been subjected to there.

CHAPTER FIFTY-ONE

MEETING IN CHICAGO

October 12, 1968—Noon

It was a wet October day in 1968 when we made our way to the Convention Center in Chicago. It was the Catholic Schools National Convention. Four of us from St. Gertrude's had flown to O'Hare Airport the night before. We went to our convent in the city to be accommodated for the time we would be at the convention.

I was excited to get away from Syracuse for the weekend. I wasn't trained as a teacher yet, so teaching the fourth grade was a challenge. I was enrolled in Syracuse University for Saturday classes to prepare to become a teacher but it would take me years of weekends and summer school to get my degree. Since credits were transferable, I could be sent to any state where the religious institutes had a school and enroll in a university in that state. This was all new to me. I was glad of the break.

There were hundreds of nuns, priests, and brothers attending the annual conference for Catholic teachers. At that point, a few years after the Second Vatican Council, when Pope John was determined to open the doors and windows of the Catholic Church and modernize it in the early 1960s, most of the nuns had stopped wearing the traditional long habit, so there was a mixture of nuns in full veil and habit, while others wore suits of gray, brown, or beige. There was very little color sported there. Some nuns, like us, wore skirts and blouses with sweaters and jackets.

We lined up behind tables of volunteers who gave us our name tags and told us to head toward the main auditorium where the key speaker, Sister Sadler, was to speak about the relevance of religious vows in the world of the 1960s. The day was to be filled with workshops about curriculum and the newest religious books that were available for our classrooms.

Outside the main auditorium were dozens of religious displays selling new books for purchase. There were displays for all grades, including examples of religious crests that could be purchased for the variety of different Catholic uniforms, including all colors of tartans. They could fill any parochial school in any diocese in the country. There were bags of free pens and calendars and candy bars of every variety. Numerous displays offered ideas for fundraising events for the schools. There were gift-wrapping displays, cookie sale ideas and samples, and subscriptions to magazines. Free items were eagerly received by nuns grabbing the opportunity to fill up their convention bags.

I went to the registration table, and someone snapped a name tag on my jacket. Then I went into the main auditorium and was met with the drone of conversation before the introduction of the keynote speaker. I found an empty seat close to the door and looked around me. The nun beside me was quite elderly. She was sound asleep in the midst of all the activity. I settled in beside her and flipped through the day's agenda. Nothing stood out.

While fascinated by the new surroundings, the air in the room was heavy, and I quickly realized that I, too, could soon be asleep beside my companion on my left. Shortly after the seats filled, the speaker was introduced. She was from a religious order unfamiliar to me. The priest who gave the introduction informed the audience that Sister Miller had just received her doctorate in mathematics from Harvard University in Cambridge. I was quite pleased that I had been to Cambridge, even if only for a short time. Maybe that was why I fought through the heavy, stale air in the auditorium and attempted to make sense of what she was saying.

Sister Miller encouraged the people in charge of managing the money and properties of their respective congregations to think about investing in social justice stocks. She decried the existence of multi-national corporations, gave an overview of why religious orders should separately incorporate their schools, and boasted that two nuns from her congregation were pursuing law degrees. She presented her particular religious institute as being extremely progressive, which caused much conversation and criticism from many nuns at the conference. Everyone clapped, however, after she had finished talking.

I looked at the clock, which registered noon. I could not believe I had spent two hours trying to listen to and absorb every word this woman had said. I was exhausted. I slipped out of my seat and walked to the entrance of the convention center. I needed to take a brisk walk to wake up. I stood by a huge window and watched the people pass by. A tall young man approached the window and stood beside me. I turned to him. He had a broad smile and eyes that held a piece of the bright, blue sky.

"I need a break," he said deliberately. "I have been sitting in that hall for the past two hours and am falling asleep."

"Me too," I replied. "I am attending the conference for Catholic teachers. I feel as if I have been in a trance," I replied, delighted at this man's friendly manner.

"There is a coffee shop over there across the street. If you like, we could go get a cup of coffee and wake up."

That was my first introduction to Jim Dunne. Without hesitation, I went with him across the street, and we talked for two hours over three cups of coffee each. He told me he was an only child, and that both of his parents had died while he was young. He had been raised by his grandmother in Syracuse. He had stayed in Syracuse and gone to the local university. He wanted to work in some aspect of medicine and was attending a conference here that explored careers in pharmaceuticals. His whole life was centered in Syracuse, and he had no firm plans to travel far from his roots.

The story of his life was encapsulated in ten minutes. The sharing of my own story took much longer. When we finally decided to return to the conference center, he asked me for my phone number and promised to call in a few weeks. I gave him the convent number and returned to the conference just as another speaker was being introduced.

When the conference ended, I returned to Syracuse and the hum-drum reality of teaching the fourth grade. The children were bright-eyed and eager to learn. The twenty-eight children, who appeared before me daily, were a delight to have in my classroom. It took them a while to get used to my accent. And it took me a while to navigate the art of teaching these children without any professional training. By October, I had learned to fit into the convent regime and worked hard nightly to ensure that I was challenging my students.

One evening toward the end of October, I received a phone call. When I picked up the phone and heard Jim Dunne's voice, I was quite surprised, because I had not given him a second thought since meeting him in Chicago. He asked me if I would like to meet him in town for a cup of coffee. We decided on Saturday, since it was free day for the nuns. I could wear civilian clothes, and in fact, had secured a nice, brightly colored blouse and green pants since coming to Syracuse. We were allotted a monthly allowance of ten dollars. It all felt quite new and liberating to be able to go into town by myself and meet someone for coffee. We met in downtown Syracuse and immediately picked right up where we had left off in Chicago.

For months, we met weekly for coffee and soon had told each other all about our lives, our hopes, and our dreams. I even ventured to tell him, bit by bit, about the time I had spent in Ireland in Fairview Convent. His ice-blue eyes laughed at some of the stories, but they turned dark with shock at most of them.

CHAPTER FIFTY-TWO

THE FIRST TIME: MARCH 29, 1969

Jim picked me up at the edge of the park on Elm Road about a mile from the convent. While full of apprehension at the unknown, I only knew that, for this afternoon at least, I wanted to be with him at his apartment. We had talked about this for weeks. We felt that we were more than friends now, but I was still conditioned in the solidity of my religion. I had taken my vows and was in a state of confusion about the depth of feelings I had for Jim.

When he saw me, he got out of the car and opened it for me. Once he was back in the driver's seat, he kissed me lightly on the lips.

"What am I doing, Jim?" I asked when the reality of what I was about to do seized me.

"Ann, we are going to be together for a few hours. You know how I feel about you." He put his left hand on my thigh, and I could feel desire rising.

"I have never gone the whole way," I somewhat pleaded to him.

Jim turned off the main street and found a discreet spot there. "Honey, we can go into town and go to a movie instead. We can go and have a cup of coffee. We do not have to go to my apartment today. I want you to be totally comfortable."

We kissed intently. I looked out at the cold winter that was beginning to grip Syracuse. My desire for him increased.

"To your place," I said, convinced it was where I wanted to be.

His penis was enormous, and I could not wait until he was inside me. I was hardly able to breathe. He rubbed my back hard as his tongue pressed into mine, and we pushed against each other. I was on fire, just as he was. I opened my eyes for a second, awash with desire. His eyes were closed, and I enjoyed the lingering pleasure that had swollen his groin. I felt the great desperation and wet that only wanted him to satisfy my deepest desire. He was hard against me and moaned.

We stripped quickly. He brought me to the bed and kissed me urgently. He gently climbed on top of me. He pushed himself, full and erect, between my legs and straddled me. He found his way inside the tide of wetness that had gushed unabashedly from me. I felt his fullness, and he easily slipped in with deep, delightful thrusts. Over and over, he filled me. He pushed so urgently and moaned and groaned in great bursts. He came slowly, building somewhere inside my core and catching me in moments of utter bliss that poured through every sense. He savored every thrust.

The vortex of pleasure became more profound until an explosion of the greatest feeling took over my depth. I craved every moment of it. He moved quickly, becoming faster, with urgent bursts. I moved with him, synchronized with every breath he took. I moved under him, and we both moved towards a place that could never be described. It was a new world for me, a world that made me feel complete and whole and totally connected. I savored the depth of pleasure I had never before experienced. All was bright.

I got up eventually and looked out of the window, watching the shades of evening night begin in the distant sky. I got dressed quickly and told Jim that I had to go.

He let me off close to the convent. When I entered the back door of the convent, I knew instinctively that no one was home. I took a quick shower and went to my room. I did not sleep that night. I was surprised at what had happened that afternoon, but I went to bed fully aware that things had radically changed in my life, and I felt more alive than I ever had. Jim and I continued to meet regularly at his apartment on Saturday afternoons.

One night at the beginning of May, I had to answer a phone call. I could not imagine who could be calling me. It was Sister

Olive, the administrator of the congregation in the United States. The content of the conversation was simple. She instructed me that, at the end of June when school was finished in Syracuse, I was to pack my bags and teach in St. Joseph's High School in Boston. They needed someone to teach English literature and history. I asked her to reconsider her request, and she did in an instant. She told me that I would be assigned to teach the eighth grade in Rockford, Illinois. It was clear that I could not enter into a conversation about my future. I tasted Sister Dolores in that conversation.

When the end of the school year came, I put away my feelings for Jim and shelved them in a place that I could never access. I obediently packed my bags and went to Rockford, Illinois. Jim was upset at my departure. I did not see him after that. He called me often. He wrote to me frequently. He begged me to leave the convent. After a while, our correspondence gradually faded, but it did not stop completely. He remained in the background of my life, like a shadow seeking an opportunity to come to life.

CHAPTER FIFTY-THREE

PEACE AT LAST

August 17, 2011

It was August 17, 2011. I had spent the last three days visiting two of the nuns who had been sent to a retirement home in Dublin. Sister Bridget Mary was about ninety-six. She was almost bed-ridden, but the staff got her up to sit in a chair a few hours each day. Sister Bridget Mary was still mentally sharp and as astute and as keen as I recalled her having been in Fairview Convent. In spite of the great distance that had separated us for so long, we had kept in touch for over forty-five years.

She had spent the better portion of her life in the kitchen at Fairview Convent in Kilfennan, County Meath. She had made her kitchen the welcoming embrace, the balm in the midst of the scald of those early years that I, along with some very fine companions, had spent in the convent as a teenager. It had been a trying time. It had been harsh within those convent walls. There had been little comfort there. It had been a hard experience living there. It had been a place that was barren and devoid of any sense of humanity. It had been an environment that was smeared and seared with the breath of stale, old ways that would never be exposed to the sun. There, the air had been oppressive, cruelty abounded, and abuse in every form readily found a home and thrived within those walls.

On this brisk summer day, just before I said goodbye to her, Sister Bridget Mary asked me to pull a large, brown envelope from her clothes trunk at the back of the closet in her room. I opened the closet door and was struck by the sparseness of her possessions. Her entire earthly possessions now consisted of a few brown dresses and cardigans that hung on plastic hangers. That was all she had. There were no shoes or coats to be seen. Her residence was adjacent to a hospital, and it was easy to accept the reality that Sister Bridget Mary would not need a significant wardrobe. She would transition to the hospital facility if that became necessary.

I bent into the closet. Her old, stained trunk was the only item in the back. I pulled it into the room and snapped open the clasps, now encased in rust. A faded, black, leather satchel was the only item in there. I picked up the satchel, expecting it to be light, but found that I needed both hands to grasp it and pull it from the trunk. I placed the satchel on the bed beside Sister Bridget Mary's chair and pushed the trunk back into the closet. She asked me to open the satchel and remove its contents. The satchel contained a heavy, thick, brown envelope that felt full. I opened the faded and torn envelope and pulled a vast chunk of paper from it. There were hundreds of pages bulked inside the envelope that, at my handling, I thought were going to spill onto the floor. I managed to keep the papers intact and quickly carried them to the table on the other side of Sister Bridget Mary's chair. Her eyes brightened as she looked eagerly at the spread of paper before her. I picked up some of the pages and flipped through them.

The pages were all numbered and handwritten, with various consistencies and variations of ink colors. Some of the ink was black, some blue, and others in various hues of purples and greens and reds. Every inch of each page was covered with writing. Each page was scripted in neat lines. On some pages, words even found themselves running along the sides of the paper. They were packed and bulging with words that invaded every spot the page had to offer. Some of the words were blotched with the overflow of ink. Some of the ink splattered over the words, giving them tentacles that connected them forever to other words. Some words were difficult to decipher.

The package definitely emitted a smell of a time gone by. In this age of computers, I had almost forgotten what ink smelled like. For a moment, I had a mental image of myself sitting with a scratchy nib at my desk in elementary school, dabbing the pen into the inkwell over and over again, as I completed some writing exercise for the teacher.

"Ann, I want you to keep this. I want you to read it. I actually could have written a thousand more stories. The groups of postulants that came through our hands in the kitchen numbered so many in the years I spent in Fairview Convent. Each one had a story and burden to share with Sister Freda Mary and me. There were so many broken spirits that needed mending. I decided to write their struggles and stories early on, and after Freda Mary came to help me in the kitchen, I had a little more time to write. I miss Freda Mary. She struggled so much with that old disease for so many years. May she rest in peace."

Sister Bridget Mary picked up some of the pages and looked at them, as if looking into a mirror. She saw things there that I could never see. She continued after a brief reflection.

"Most of the postulants had to push into the hard pain of life in that convent. Some of you blossomed in spite of the dirt and hurt piled upon you there. You were all challenged just by being teenagers within those walls and coming to terms with growing into young adulthood. It was a hard place for you to live.

"That postulant mistress was a vile and reprehensible woman. She sent out ripples of cruelty in every direction, and because of that, she left a shocking legacy of abuse."

Sister Bridget Mary sighed and leaned back in her chair. She took a deep breath.

"Before I go to the pearly gates, I want you to have this. I trust you with this. I know you like to do a bit of writing yourself. I recall writing a journal of the things that happened on a daily basis. That is there somewhere. I wrote little fanciful pieces and a good bit of poetry. It is all in there. There are many things written in the margins and beyond the margins. Sure, isn't that where most of life is lived? Yes, outside the margins is a very special place to be, and writing takes you there in an instant."

I nodded. She gave a sigh of relief, letting her lifetime of writing, scribblings, and musings leave her possession and entrusting them to me.

I put the sheathes of paper carefully into the faded envelope, put the envelope in the satchel, and placed them in my bag. We said goodbye. I told her I would keep in touch. I gave her a hug and she let me go easily. I told her that I would now go and see Annie Boyle, my old classmate.

"Give her my love," Sister Bridget called after me. Then she called me back into her room. "I forgot to tell you that Margaret and Jimmy brought their first grandchild to see me not so long ago. Those two have done well together."

I had some memory that Margaret and Jimmy had gotten married. I had forgotten that.

"A little boy. They called him Joseph."

I smiled with Sister Bridget Mary and left her to the silence of her room, and then I went to find Annie Boyle. Annie was on the third floor of the retirement home. I took the elevator to the third floor, and once there, I asked a young woman with black curly hair and the widest of smiles where I might find my old friend.

She pointed in front of her and lilted lightly. "Sister is just around the corner there at the nurse's station, the first door to the right. I think she will probably be sleeping."

I thanked the young woman, and within seconds, I found myself at Annie's room. I pushed the door, which was ajar, and looked into the room. Annie was indeed asleep and looked pale and thin. She was breathing in short, shallow breaths. I stepped into the room and closed the dark, wood-finished door, which was a striking contrast to the deep yellow tinge that soaked into Annie's face and hands.

She was in a deep sleep in her armchair in room 128 of the Alzheimer's unit. I did not know whether I should wake her up. I had traveled a long way to see her, and Sister Bridget Mary imagined this might be the last opportunity for me to see Annie. I sighed heavily as I sat on her bed. The armchair seemed to consume her. A thin woolen blanket covered her legs. She had become so diminished since the last time I had seen her.

As I sat on her bed, I became flooded by the memories of when we were young and fresh and full of energy together. Time was erased in that room. I remembered the Annie with a twinkle in her eye and crimson cheeks the day we entered the convent together.

I was catapulted out of my reverie when Annie began to stir. I coughed, and that woke her up. She looked at me with a vacant stare. I spoke her name, but she did not respond. I took her hand into mine, and the memories of my early years in the convent saturated me, leaving me with a feeling that I was drowning in quicksand. I pulled myself out of that memory as I had done a thousand times before this day. I patted Annie's hand.

"Hello, Annie. It's me, Ann. We were postulants together in Fairview Convent. Do you remember me, Annie?"

Annie stared at me blankly. There was no life in her eyes. A sense of being connected with the world, her room, her chair, or me did not exist. There was no inkling of a response from her. She barely blinked.

I stayed a little while, until she closed her eyes again. I eventually got up from the bed and turned to leave her in the grip of that colorless, dim room. A big crucifix hung above her bed. Annie had gone through her own crucifixion as a young nun. God only knows she had earned this quiet respite. I decided to leave Annie alone with her thoughts.

As I pulled the door behind me, I felt something tug at my heart. It was a deep ache that clutched at me and would not let go. No time seemed to have passed since I last saw Annie in the kitchen in Fairview Convent over forty years ago. The curtain of time was drawn aside, and I saw myself hug my old friend in that kitchen just before I left to go to Dublin airport and leave for America on that late day in August, 1968.

On impulse, I turned and went back into her room. Annie's eyes were still closed. I put my hand on her arm.

"I know you remember me, Annie. I just want you to know I have never forgotten you."

She opened her eyes and closed them again, as if she had no memory of the place or even of me. I whispered goodbye in her ear and left the retirement home.

I made my way to the bus depot in the heart of Dublin, satisfied that I had met the struggle of the past face-to-face in the company of Sister Bridget Mary and Annie Boyle, and I had been able to endure it a little.

Sister Bridget Mary died on September 8, 2011. She had given me one of the greatest treasures I could ever possess with her writings and scribbles and stories contained in that heavy satchel. In reading it all, I was helped to leave the scalding memory of Fairview Convent behind me. The memory has continued to sear into my life at times, when I least expect it, to always leave me feeling vulnerable and abused and victimized all over again.

CHAPTER FIFTY-FOUR

THE ROAD FROM DUBLIN TO DERRY

I left on the bus in Dublin, Ireland, at 13:45 p.m. It was a fair enough day by Irish standards on this August 17, 2011. It was enough for me just to sit on the bus and look out the window after visiting two nuns I had been friends with for over forty years. With the load of words Sister Bridget Mary had left me and the smell of the ink emanating from the pages in their tattered envelope, I felt suddenly anxious to be on my way. In spite of my delight in seeing Sister Bridget Mary, my interaction with Annie Boyle had left me disconcerted. I settled into my seat on the bus, happy there was no one sitting beside me. It gave me permission to shift and move without worrying about invading anyone's space.

The bus throttled into life and quickly left the bus depot behind. We eventually left the Dublin traffic and soon leaned into the beginning of the journey northward. Just outside the city, we crossed the Boyne Bridge above the cold, gray push of the Boyne River. The memory of the Battle of the Boyne is scripted still in the flow of that cascade. The water was dark, even on this bright day in August, and flowed steadily at full brim. It surely contained within its memory the thunder and boom of that day so long ago, which is forever etched along its banks. The clouds were gray above the green fields, hedged with still greener thickets. The roll of the hills unfolded as we were swallowed by the turn of the road. Fields emptied of their full harvest awaited another tilling and were taking a breath in between.

The bus churned at a fair speed and opened up to the blue splash of sky as we left Dublin behind. The blue-hued mountains cut into the distance, their majestic, magnificent granite dotted by chunks of boulder and skirted by the caress of the bold sea. Above them, puffy clouds emboldened by the wind raced in the sky. It was as if an artist had pushed sheathes of gray and white paint on top of a canvas and constantly blew at the work because it was moving and pulsating with life. A streak of blue peeped out of the sky here and there. The mountains, capped in thick blobs of the same clouds, stood ready and firm, no matter what the weather threw at them.

The journey is all in the call of the distance. It is in the pull of the road. Birds dotted the sky and glided on the wind, sideways at times, looking to free fall, and then, sensing the gravitational embrace of the earth, rebounded, as if newly awakened to flight in their instinctive urge to height and expanse. It looked cool enough out there. Inside the bus, I was comfortable.

The Doire-Derry road took a sharp turn to the left, and in a glance, the Dublin mountains quickly fell back into the distance, and the stab of blue was gone from the sky. We were well on our way to caress the Northern Ireland skyline, which sits its welcome over the thick, green landscape in the distance.

To the side, I noticed bales of hay tossed around the fields, like cork bottle tops scattered by a strong northwest breeze. The script thudded to the floor, and I lifted the heaviness back onto my lap. I did not want to put it on the empty seat beside me. I just wanted to hold onto it, fearing its contents and dark secrets would be spilled prematurely.

I had to get used to the idea of peering into the past again. I had to convince myself that it was time to unseal and deal with all the hurt that had happened in Fairview Convent. I would need to be in a safe place to do that. This was going to be a dredging experience.

My mind wandered back to Sister Bridget Mary and Annie Boyle. I was glad I made the effort to go and see them every time I returned to Ireland to be with my family for a few weeks. The two nuns were once a very important part of my life. Mary O'Brien had done well in Australia. She was head of the music department in a high school in Brisbane, and she excelled after she left Fairview. She attended university in Brisbane and graduated with a master's in music. She emphasized to me that she graduated with distinction.

Nancy McCarty left the convent after her father died and returned to Ireland to take care of her mother. Nancy, Mary, and I stayed in touch, though we never met again, since we had gone our separate ways. I pulled the worn satchel close to me and wondered what tales Sister Bridget Mary had entrusted to me.

The roundabout arrows pointed toward the N2 and County Monaghan. It was littered with many colorful posters and advertisements. Just beyond the northern turn to the bend, a red farm stand, with potatoes and vegetables stacked all around it, was framed by a broad oak at the side of the road. It needed the shelter of the oak right now to protect it from the lash of rain that had just started. There were signs along the road pointing to places that I had never heard of. These little villages, acknowledged in black-and-white signs at the edge of the grass, were clustered on the outer perimeter of the outskirts of Dublin.

Rain began to plop heavily on the windows. The windshield wipers plodded and screamed their way loudly across the front window of the bus. Back and forth and back again they went, streaking and staining the glass in a regular, hypnotic swing. The glass wept and was constantly wiped as the rain was cast away in rapid, definite, timed response. There was no time for tears to soak on the front window of this bus.

The next sign, *Monaghan 54 kms*, declared itself as we rolled northward. Outside on the tarmac, the white, oblong markers ran together, sometimes forming into a long, white, continuous streak in the middle of the road, and then it slipped back to separation. The white markers pointed the way home as sure as arrows hit their targets after time spent in the quiver.

There was an old fellow in the front of the bus leaning into his seat. His heaviness spread and was just about contained in a purple shirt. His glasses shifted up and down as the cadence of the wheels adjusted to the surface of the road. His sleep appeared to be sound enough.

We sped up a little for a short time, but, because of road work, we found ourselves slowing down as we entered Castle-blayney. Orange cones abounded around a cluster of men with spades in their hands. They seemed to be digging diligently around a huge crater in the middle of the road, totally oblivious to the traffic around them. The bus slowed down, as we passed the crater, and the men working there. The driver accelerated. Soon, we passed the Patrick Kavanagh Center, which looked like some kind of sports complex. Dundalk was posted as *N53*. St. Patrick's sports stadium sat littered in emptiness. It looked cold out there. Tubs of red and yellow flowers lined the streets, pouring color into an otherwise drab day.

We passed a graveyard at the side of the road on the right-hand side. I thought to myself that it was amazing how anyone could rest in peace over there with the constant drum of the traffic speeding past all day. A bronze sculpture of Jesus and the Woman at the Well looked chilled near the cemetery on the grounds of a large church that had been painted blue. Jesus would never have experienced such a chill in rain like this. The name of the church was blurred in the window's soak and splash. It looked like a strong little church. I did notice the front door flung open in a hug of welcome. The rain continued.

We slowed down into the neck of traffic ahead. We passed the Old Coach Inn, Hair Creations, The Corner Pharmacy, Tavey Brothers, Coyles, Sherry Fitzgerald, and the Tackle Box. A young, freckle-faced boy with carrot-red hair looked into the bus, and I caught his glance. He was hurriedly crossing the street, and the bus had cut into his stride. He looked at me momentarily, and then he was gone in the fleet of an instant. The memory of that blue-eyed boy with the scarlet-red hair is still branded in my memory. We darted off again.

Cows brown, black, white, brown and black, and black and white stood stubbornly in the rain. In one field, they were scattered, and in the next, they were huddled together around a copse of trees. The bus pushed forward. Some homes newly built seemed to hang off the hillside, others, dirty and gray, sat not too far from the side of the road. The fields here were empty of harvest.

A group of travelers and their tin homes came into view. Red, blue, green, and white clothes, already fully saturated, lined the hedge rows. A tumbledown brick home slept on the edge of the next roundabout. We were off again and at full throttle along the road that leads to Derry.

I took a short doze and jolted awake to see a large tree toppled in a field to the left, its roots exposed after much time of keeping vigil, standing proud and erect in this place, which was its home. It still looked proud lying in its spread. A round tower, fifteenth century, stood tall and straight and not too far away. I bade goodbye to both of them, proud symbols, one roundly refusing to fall and the other seemingly cut down in its prime.

I shifted my weight and sat up a little, refreshed by my short period of slumber. I looked out the window to my left. Two men were slating a roof. Another trimmed a hedge. Yet another was power walking. I realize that I could see much on my way to Derry sitting on an Ulster bus. Not too far away, Monaghan Cathedral sentinels in its rain-soaked granite shelf. The granite was so drenched that it looked black and ominous in the gray sky.

The sign at the side of the road read *N2 Doire*. Next, we ambled through the Armagh to *Doire/Derry* signs. Several rows of red, brick houses pointed us toward the center of town and the bus depot there. There was no doubt that we would pick up some passengers and leave some behind. The spire of the cathedral spiked into the air. Car parks, schools, slaps of walls, and newly cast malls loomed in the distance. The driver braked and started and braked some more.

We passed the Garda Station. There were a few police cars parked there, but no signs of life. Finally, we got onto the North Road and rumbled slowly into the bus station. I wondered if I would ever see this place again. The plans I had discussed with my family had been so clear and final. I had no intention of returning to America.

Young girls gaggled together outside the bus. Most of us just wanted to use the bathroom facilities inside the depot. A sign read: *This yard will close at 9:00 p.m. SHARP*. The fresh air bolstered the conversations that were taking place outside the bus. The laze of the bus ride had temporarily been injected with activity. Ten minutes later, with some passengers obviously barely satisfied with the stop, we heard the blare that the bus to Derry would leave in one minute. Some passengers ran to the bus in panic. I dawdled to the door and ascended the steps awkwardly and with some effort as I held onto the bag containing Sister Bridget Mary's writings. I secured my seat and relished the fact that I had no one beside me still. There was a commotion at the front of the bus. The bus had just started, and some young people were running along the side of the bus, gesturing wildly. The bus driver stopped reluctantly. Some passengers tittered and snickered when the latecomers were permitted to get on the bus. We rounded the corner of the North Road and snaked our way out of Monaghan to Derry. The digital clock on the bus was emblazoned by the time: 16:13. The sign ahead heralded, *Derry 111 kms*.

St. Macartan's College slipped away to my right. The bus shivered and groaned around some challenging corners. I looked at the emergency exit. I felt the driver was going much too fast. I leaned to the right and then to the left in the thrust and turn of the bus. We had gone off the main highway. All of a sudden, I was keenly aware of the speed of the bus. It seemed to be flying low. We definitely tumbled at a great rate toward the border. A traffic calming road appeared, and there was no lull in the speed of the bus. *Drive Carefully* we were warned by the Monaghan County Council, as we left there.

To the left and right, pools of water resembling large ice blocks puddled the fields. It definitely had rained there. We passed over Mountain Valley River. The bus stopped for traffic lights. I was glad the lights were red. All felt well again in the crawl of the traffic. We crept through the little village, and then a swift goodbye found us on the road again. More puddles, more fields full of sheep, their white coats looking like balls of cotton appeared, and we sped quickly by them. The bus lumbered a while and then picked up speed again. This was a better maintained road we were on, so the speed did not feel so urgent It was 16:25, and all felt better. The driver hit his stride, and the miles began to fly by.

The man in the purple shirt came to life and produced a newspaper, in which he became engrossed in reading. The bus chugged up a steep slope. I wondered what the down slope would feel like. A woman near me tore open a bar of Twix and crunched into it. The aroma of the milk-chocolate bar poured out, and I was aware that I was hungry. The bus continued to struggle up the hill. The rain splashed off the pavement. The bus lurched to a stop at Sally's Restaurant, and one man got off the bus. New signs declared the road to Enniskillen. We took the road to Ballygawley and Omagh.

The road suddenly felt like a rise through a tunnel of green. My senses were fully awakened to the lush of the green and its movement. The bus was encased in a forest of green trees for a few minutes. It felt cozy. Mobile phones began to ring in the band and flow of the road north. We had obviously reached the border that separated our two Irelands.

The bus hugged and gripped the side of the narrower road and slashed the hedges here and there. It bumped heavily along. Then the bus stopped and two young men stepped on the bus. The road then widened. There were signs for the M1 and Belfast. I began to feel at home and in a jolly mood. They bantered with the bus driver as they paid for their tickets. Across the street was a shop that advertised the National Lottery. I was definitely in Northern Ireland now. The time registered 16:58, and we were four miles from Omagh.

We glided along the scenic route. A little, brown-mucked lane laced itself through the fields to my left. A mud-caked road stood stark as it snaked and wafted its way to the top of the green mound of hills. The road looked laden and well-traveled. It wound its way, and I lost the wisp of it as it headed to a roundabout and made a turn that put us in the direction of Omagh. It was now 17:04. We heaved into the bend of the road again. The dark, wet sod rolled miles in front of me. The brush of the landscape flecked and bristled, as if some dark green paint was squished on its canvas. It was a splendid experience to glide along this road, speckled with a narrow brook that reflected the changing sky. White fleeced dollops, sheep that have found their height, planted themselves aloft the highest spectrum. I felt that I could reach out and touch them for they stood there immersed, no doubt, by the long drink of the view.

We soon rumbled into Omagh. The First Presbyterian Church was on the left before we entered the bus station. There was a sign outside which read, *It Is Time to See the Lord.* We stopped at stand number eleven, and numerous people exited the bus. The fresh air smacked them in the face as they went through the door.

"Happy days," someone uttered. The bus took off again quite quickly. The next stop was Strabane. The clock declared 17:09. Omagh City Hall whisked by us on the right, and after, the war memorial that commemorates the Second World War. This space was a colorful contrast to the dark in the late afternoon sky. The flowers that surrounded the memorial had taken on a life of their own, giving great testament to the dead they helped commemorate.

Immediately on the outskirts of Omagh, hills appeared from nowhere, topped with an icing of clouds. A river cut into the bottom of a hill nearby. The river ran fast and furious, intent on getting to its destination as soon as possible. I could identify with the river's urge. I was getting very tired. It was now 17:24, and it had been a long, emotional day.

We lurched over Derg River at 17:30. Now we were headed towards Sion Mills. Strabane welcomed us beyond. The Ulster bus station was located near the Lidel warehouse where we chugged to a stop. It was 17:49. There were very few of us left on the bus at that point.

By 17:58, the River Foyle was rushing to my left and the cathedral spire claimed the Derry skyline first as we sloped ahead. We slid over the Craigavon Bridge. The Foyle looked like a bucket of muck. The two sculptured men at the end of the roundabout cast in bronze, both a symbol of the Protestant and Catholic communities that are still separated there, have still not grasped hands. It will take a seismic shift for that to happen.

At 18:09, we pulled into the bus station. I climbed out of the bus and felt stiff in the blustery air. I went to get my suitcase, but someone got there before me. In seconds, I was looking into the gaze of sky-blue eyes.

Review Requested:

If you loved this book, would you please provide a review at Amazon.com?

Lightning Source UK Ltd.
Milton Keynes UK
UKHW01f2001140918
328919UK00002B/278/P

9 781948 260619